Marcel K Andrews

THE BROADLAND TREE

Limited Special Edition. No. 16 of 25 Paperbacks

The author, Marcel K Andrews, comes from Norwich and works in the construction industry as a bricklayer. He is married and has a teenage son. His first steps into writing began back in 2007 when he learned to use a computer by tracing his ancestry and turning his research into a book-type document, copied and shared among his family. After this, he was inspired to write *The Broadland Tree* by a feature on a breakfast television programme. Since then, he has written a sequel that is yet to be published.

Best Wishes !

To Catherine and Logan

Marcel K Andrews

THE BROADLAND TREE

AUSTIN MACAULEY PUBLISHERS™

LONDON • CAMBRIDGE • NEW YORK • SHARJAH

A CIP catalogue record for this title is available from the British Library.

ISBN 9781788789967 (Paperback)
ISBN 9781528956567 (ePub e-book)

www.austinmacauley.com

First Published (2019)
Austin Macauley Publishers Ltd
25 Canada Square
Canary Wharf
London
E14 5LQ

Many thanks for the help and support of Cheryl Reynolds, Keith Watts, Anne Thompson and Catherine Andrews.

Introduction

In 2007, my wife, Catherine, convinced me, with very little effort, to buy a desktop personal computer for our new home, of which we had moved into just a year earlier. Now, being a manual worker, a bricklayer by trade, I had never found any real use for one in my past and had no knowledge of how to use one. However, I did think her idea was a good one, because at that time I was starting to feel that I was becoming one of the last of my generation to allow the computer age into my life. I had a feeling that if I didn't succumb to the inevitable, I would be left behind and be perceived by future generations in much the same way I would see an illiterate adult today. So the day came when our new computer was installed, but there was a problem, only Catherine knew how to use it. I suggested to her that maybe I needed to go to an evening class at the city college and learn how to use it. I had heard they held courses on teaching computer illiterates such as myself how to get to grips with these new machines, but she didn't agree. "Why waste your money going there when I could teach you?" she said. "Once you get started, you could play around with it and teach yourself." She was half right, I did get to learn some of the basics but made loads of mistakes on the way (and am still making them).

Then one day, it came to me, the one thing that I had always wanted to know was my family history. I had never known my family's past any further back than my grandparents and that was only a few tales my father had told me. My paternal grandfather had died fifteen years before I was born and my grandmother a week after my birth. This was the way to both learn the use of the computer and discover my family's roots. Little was I to know, however, that the task to teach me computer skills was to become one of the most fascinating projects I had ever undertaken. I found that researching my family tree most rewarding, especially when presenting my finds to my father, who also knew nothing of our past. Over the course of time, I gathered more information and arranged my findings in a chronological order. I wrote a section on each ancestor of all the facts that I had learned of the lives they had lived and put it all together with copied church documents and any photographs relating to each subject. Put together in a file, the whole project formed what could be perceived by some almost as a book document.

My father was still in contact with many of the surrounding family, mostly cousins that I hadn't seen in years. He told them of my project and soon I was printing copies for them too. To me, this almost felt like I had written a book. It gave me a great sense of pride, in having those people read my material and to be told that they enjoyed what I had written. This had never happened to me before. Then one day, there was nothing left to do. I had found as much family information as I was able to find and one by one, my searches came to an end and there was nothing left to print. This was about three years after I had begun the project in the first place, and it had indeed achieved its objective in teaching me how to use the computer. But what was I to do now that the project was over?

One morning, I was watching breakfast TV on the BBC before leaving for work. The girl announcer began a feature with the words, "They say that everyone has a book in them," and preceded with an interview with a lady author whose name I didn't catch. She asked her for tips on book writing for beginners and she replied, "To structure the book, write a little at a time and to keep a notebook with you at all times to write ideas that may come." I wrote down all her tips and decided that my next project would be to try and make a story from the findings of my family tree, as the structure had already been made. Maybe it was time to see if I had a book in me. So, nearly three years after this book writing idea and six years after the computer was installed, this is that story that I have tried to form from the findings of my family tree. This story follows the line of where I inherited my surname. For reasons of not wanting to appear too self-centred, I have changed the surname of Andrews to Allen in this story, as Allen is another surname to appear in my family tree on my father's maternal line. All of the characters did exist, the only name changes made, aside of the surname, were that of Jacob who was in reality called John after his father, John; this was obviously done to avoid confusion. The maternal characters did exist too, and with their factual maiden names included too. Sarah Fox, Anne Fox, Amelia, Beth Metcalf and their mother, Elizabeth, all existed in name. Their birth, marriage and death years were all accurate, only Edward and Elizabeth's story was non-fact based, other than the birth of their son John, who I have called Jacob. Unfortunately, this was where my family search ended and I had no information on their lives before their son's birth, so their story was made up and set in the close-by village of Crostwick. The genealogist Martin Allen was a fictional character too. I thought it better to invent that character to maybe develop another story from him in the future. Overall, this book is a fictional story loosely based on historical facts.

This story is set in the county and the city I am privileged to call my home, Norwich in Norfolk. On my search for my roots, I developed a fond interest of our local history and have added some tales and facts of the area into this story, of which I came to learn during my research. I have many local authors to thank, as their books on local history proved to be invaluable reference points for my research. Pamela Brooks, Frank Meeres, Neil Storey and Keith Skipper. If it hadn't have been for these great local historians, I would never have known where to look in the records office in Norwich, and I thank them for that.

It cannot be said that this is a story full of unpredictable twists and turns and clever plots like a Tom Clancy novel. This is just a tale of the lives of ordinary people living within their time, who suffered hardships and pain, as well as enjoying the simple joys that life gives, falling in love, young passion and having children. As the seasons passed, they lived their lives in accordance with it and enjoyed the beauty of their surroundings while the years slowly passed.

I hope that someone out there enjoys this tale even if it was written by a bricklayer with basic computer skills, but don't worry if not, I can always stick to the day job, because I can at the very least build a nice wall. Lastly, I would like to thank my family for their patience while I wrote this novel, namely my wife, Catherine; and my son, Logan.

Marcel K Andrews

Chapter One

A silent feeling of euphoria suddenly comes over him. *This is it!* He thinks in quiet managed excitement, silently reading out his discovery. "Jacob, son of Edward and Elizabeth Allen, baptised 24th August 1777." This is what he had been hunting for, after relentless checking of records of endless parishes in and around the Norwich area.

His name is Martin Allen. He is sitting in the records office of the central library in Norwich, or 'The Forum' as it is better known, and he has been tracing his ancestry. He had taken up genealogy some six months ago, finding it to be one of the most fascinating and rewarding projects he had ever undertaken. But two and a half hours of relentless checking through old records, in old handwriting, has now taken its toll. His eyes are feeling sore, maybe it's time has to take a break.

Quickly printing out his newly discovered information, he puts the micro film back in its file and puts on his jacket, from there he leaves the records office and heads downstairs towards the coffee shop. With a medium latte sat on the table in front of him, he sits close to the main entrance of the Forum and watches people entering and exiting through the revolving doors. He is deep in thought as to what to do next to continue his search. The next step is to look for any siblings of Jacob and to find his parents, Edward and Elizabeth's marriage, possibly in the same parish, he thinks.

After ten minutes of pondering, he drinks his coffee and makes his way back up the stairs towards the records office to resume his search. He finds the correct micro film and continues searching.

The Norwich parish of St George's Tombland was where he had left his search, so he checks the baptism records up to ten years before and ten years after the 1777 baptism of his discovered ancestor to find any siblings of the baptised child… He finds nothing. Then he tries to find any record of a marriage between Edward Allen and Elizabeth, maiden name unknown, at around the same time period… he still finds nothing. He relentlessly checks the records of surrounding parishes… still nothing.

It becomes clear to Martin that he has reached the end of the line of his search today, maybe it's time to go home. He gathers up his notebook, pencils and printed documents and again proceeds downstairs towards the revolving doors of the main entrance, from there he exits the building.

He always catches a bus on Saturdays rather than driving his car. Not for any particular reason other than making a change of routine, and he often likes to stop at the Norwich market at one of the tea stalls to have a cup of tea and a bacon roll whilst on his way to the bus stop at Castle Meadow.

Martin is what many people may call, though maybe unfairly, a middle-aged, middle-class suburbanite, possibly rather dull to those who don't really know him. He is thirty-eight years old and is a quantity surveyor for a construction company. He is married with two children and his family have a pet dog, a golden retriever called Charlie. They all live in a 1970s' built three-bedroom semi, in the heart of a Norwich suburb, and he has a forty grand mortgage.

On his bus journey home, he wonders who his latest-discovered ancestors were. All he knew about them were their names. There was no other documentation about them whereas all of the other discoveries he had made seemed to tell a story of their own. These two, Edward and Elizabeth Allen, were a mystery. A thought came to him, that maybe the internet may solve the problem, he would try on his computer later upon his return home.

After a thirty-minute journey, his bus arrives at his stop, just a short walk from his house. He lives at Sprowston, a suburb about three miles from the city's centre. Sprowston had once been a village in old times, situated on one of the main link roads into the city, but in the passage of time, it had grown into a full-grown suburban district, bordering the city from the countryside, and it housed mostly upper working and lower middle class people just like him.

He arrives home, calls "Hi ya!" to his family as he enters the house.

"Did you have any luck this time?" asked Helen.

Helen was his wife of ten years. They had met on a night out in the city with a crowd of mutual friends and very soon they became lovers. Eighteen months later they were married, and soon after, Helen became pregnant with their first child.

"Yes I did, I managed to go back another generation to a baptism that was held in 1777, a direct ancestor," Martin replied. "Unfortunately, I hit a brick wall, and after that I couldn't find anything else. I tried all the surrounding parishes but found nothing. They could have come from anywhere. My only chance left is the internet."

Helen smiled and nodded. She pretended to be interested, though in truth she wasn't, but she couldn't hurt Martin's feelings, that wouldn't do. Her interests lay with her family life, especially her children, Luke, age nine and Jasmine, age six, this was what took up her time.

Later that evening, Martin tried again, he checked out the new names he had just found on the various genealogy sites that he had logged into on his computer. Trying out the names Edward and Elizabeth Allen within the county of Norfolk at approximately the correct time period, and still nothing was found. *There's just no trace of them,* he thought. It's looking like the end of the line. He reasoned out that with nearly seven hundred parishes in Norfolk and only a few of which were on the internet. He would have to look for them manually at the Forum and that would be like looking for a needle in a haystack. His decision finally came. He had gone as far as he could with the search and it was time to call it a day, but there was always going to be that troubling feeling. Where did Edward and Elizabeth Allen come from, and what was their story?

Chapter Two
The Story Begins

Back in time, over two hundred and thirty years, lay the answers to Martin's questions, answers he was never to know. To be exact, it was the springtime of 1775, and the place he was searching for was the small rural village of Crostwick in the county of Norfolk. This was where Edward and Elizabeth Allen's unknown story had begun, leaving only a record of the baptism of a child to be one day discovered by a descendant two hundred and thirty years later.

***

At this time in history, King George III is the reigning monarch of Britain in the early years of its growing empire. The first shots have just been fired on what would become the colonial war in the distant Americas, on the fields of Lexington, Massachusetts. Lord Frederick North is the prime minister of Great Britain.

It was a typical rural scene of the time of which farm life dominated. Most of the community lived or worked on or around the farms and each village lived within its own independent community. The farm was the place of work, it was the village shop of provisions and outside trades, blacksmiths, farriers, millers etc., all relied heavily upon it. Without the farms, there were no communities and no supplies to feed the nearby cities. Rural life at this time was the main employer of the working population, only a minority worked in the manufacturing trades of the towns and cities. This story begins in the setting of one of these farms.

Some six miles north of the centre of the city of Norwich is the village of Crostwick, a village much like many others, consisting of a village green and cottages housing the families of tradesmen and farm workers. There is a village pub and a church situated just off a main road which runs alongside the village. Aside from the road, the village borders fields, woods, meadows and a nearby stream. Almost adjoined at its north-westerly side is the small neighbouring village of Spixworth, again with just a small population of mostly farm workers and landowners with its own church, it is a separate parish with a joined community. The setting of this story is Spring Farm, one of three main farms situated around the fringes of Crostwick village. The other two are Greys Farm, owned by the Grey family and Church Farm which is just a smallholding belonging to the church rectory. Spring Farm and Greys Farm were the two largest of the three, and George Lutkin was Spring Farm's proprietor. He had inherited the farm after his father's death, as he, being the eldest son, was bequeathed the full estate as was the traditional way. His wife, Anne, had given him two sons and three daughters, and it is George and Anne Lutkin's second child and eldest daughter, 'Elizabeth', of whom this writing tells a story.

With her dark hair, piercing blue eyes and young fresh complexion, Elizabeth was considered a looker. Her slim petite form made her desirable but out of bounds among the young men of Crostwick, her father's influence had made it that way. He was to have higher sights for his daughters in the coming years and no local tradesmen or farm worker was ever likely to have been considered as a matrimonial match.

Her siblings with her were her elder brother, George, who was twenty-one and named after his father. He had recently married Sarah Grey from the neighbouring Greys farm. The couple had just moved into a farm cottage within Greys farm estate and hoped to start a family of their own as quickly as possible. Next, there was Martha Lutkin, closest to Elizabeth's age, she had just turned sixteen and was Elizabeth's closest friend as well as sister. She was a clever girl just like her mother, Anne, not a beauty but she carried warmth of character within her that people liked and responded to. Then there was her sister, Jane, she was thirteen and was in the transition to womanhood, though aspects of her childhood were still present within her nature. Richard Lutkin was just eleven years old, though the youngest, he was now at the dawning of his working life. Both of the younger two siblings had just started to be given menial tasks around the farm but it was Richard who was expected to do full a day's work for wages working on the land with the rest of the farm hands.

Elizabeth Lutkin's story begins on a fine sunny morning in early April. She had been working in the garden with her mother and her sister, Martha, busily sowing seeds of carrots, beans and cabbages, and planting seed potatoes. Every available parcel of land was used for growing food at the farm even the garden and Elizabeth, though being the daughter of the landowner farmer, was still expected to help with the housework and with garden chores. These were times of strict hierarchy, and the landowners and the peasant workers beneath them all knew their place. George Lutkin believed in leading by example and expected his children to show a willingness to work as an example to his workers, including his daughters. Elizabeth didn't disappoint her parents either, she was a hard working girl who seldom complained and would just get on with the task at hand. On this fine morning, however, Elizabeth toiled in the soil of the garden when a gang of five farm hands happened to be walking past the garden on their way to the fields. In amongst the group of farm hands was her younger brother, Richard, who passed by without comment, almost as if embarrassed to be seen near them among his group of working colleagues. That was, however, till a voice called out from in amongst the group.

"You can say hello to your mother and sisters if you like, Master Richard!"

Mother and daughters looked up, and at a glance spied Richard in amongst the group of workers. "Hello Richard!" his mother called out, causing smiles and chuckles from all around. Elizabeth returned a smile back at the group, but it was the farm worker who had called out the cheeky comment who her eyes fixed upon, Edward Allen. She had seen him many times before, he had worked on the farm since he was a boy. The children of the farm hands were often used to clear large stones off the fields and Edward as a boy was no exception. His father, Nathaniel Allen, was a long serving experienced farm worker at the farm, and his two sons, Edward and James, had both followed their father's lead to work there too. Edward smiled politely to her as he walked by. She returned a quick smile back but said nothing and continued with her work.

Edward Allen was nineteen years old and had by now become a fairly experienced farm hand who had worked full time at Spring Farm since the age of ten. He had an Anglo Saxon look about him so commonly seen in eastern England, of light brown to fair hair and with blue eyes. He stood up at about five feet and ten inches, quite tall for the times, and was of slim build but strong and solid; hard work had shaped him that way.

George Lutkin's farm, Spring Farm, was not one of the huge farms owned by the gentry of the time but it was a fair estate none the less, especially for a village like Crostwick. But George was no gentry, he had inherited his farm from his father, William Lutkin, who began his rise in status by renting a smallholding within the neighbouring village of Horsted from one of the rich landowners and country squire of the area Alfred Watts. In time, the pair had become friends, despite the difference in social standing, and soon a mortgage agreement was made between the two enabling William Lutkin to purchase Spring Farm, and so begin his slow rise in both wealth and social standing. George, however, had not only inherited the farm, he had inherited his father's knowledge for farming and business affairs, he was more farmer than gentleman. A strong character, often intimidating, but he knew where he had come from, working in the fields with the rest of the farm hands. He had also inherited his father's ambition, both for his farm and his family. He was in stature, a thickset man of middle age years, his dark hair was beginning to grey on the sides just above his ears. He stood about five feet nine inches and was more commonly than not, seen wearing a green jacket, grey shirt and breeches, and a dark green three cornered hat, sometimes sat on top of his best silver wig which he wore on special occasions. His face was slightly wrinkled and red blotches were starting to appear. Hard work in all weathers, and smoking and drinking had all taken its toll upon him as he aged.

Later that day, as it was Saturday afternoon, the farm hands began to return back in small groups to the farmhouse to report to George Lutkin to collect their wages. Edward arrived at the house with Jim Yallop and young Richard Lutkin. They were all allowed to come in to the farmhouse on this occasion for this purpose as George and his wife both sorted out the workers' pay. Elizabeth was in the front room, seated and working on embroidery. She could hear the voices of Jim Yallop and Edward talking to her parents, so being curious, she put down her embroidery and rose from her chair, she left the room and entered the main entrance hall where the men were being paid. Edward looked up towards her and she returned a glance with a slight smile, which in turn caused Edward to return a smile back.

"That's three shillings for you, Jim, and two and six for you Edward," said George, as he handed the money over.

They both thanked their employer and turned to leave the main hall where outside other workers were gathering to collect their wages. Edward's eyes once again were drawn towards Elizabeth though he tried not to stare. He had known her only slightly, more just by sight than socially, from a time when they were both children. No untoward thought had been given to her in their past other than she was the governor's daughter, but now she had become a young woman, she was pleasing to his eye. She was small and petite compared to his tall frame, with shoulder length dark hair, the same colour as her father's before the grey had come, and she had a face that bloomed with her smile. Edward had seen many pretty girls before, both in the village and in Norwich, but Elizabeth seemed to strike an awareness of her charm within him at that very moment. Maybe it was her smile to him that had triggered the awareness, he didn't know, but she was fixed within his thoughts as he left the farmhouse.

"You wanna be careful there, boy," said Jim.

"Why, whus the matter?"

"You know, I saw you looking at the governor's daughter."

"What are you talking about you, old fool, I just smiled that's all."

"If he caught you smiling at her, you'd be for it."

"Better not let 'im catch me then," said Edward, causing chuckles from both men.

The following morning arrived with the same fine spring weather that had been the previous day. Edward and Elizabeth both woke knowing that they were to spend their Sunday morning in the usual way, that of attending church Sunday service with their families. This was always a good day when the people could get together and enjoy company of others, away from the monotony or harshness of their working lives. This was a time of social gatherings, enjoyed almost as an entertainment, though not so much the disciplined service within the church itself.

The Reverend Jonathan Nash stood standing at the church entrance to welcome the parishioners in wearing his clean pressed cassock and his freshly dusted wig. The turnout of parishioners was high as was usual, those of higher social standing had their usual seats at the front of the church. There was a pecking order of seating arrangements and everyone knew their place, the lower the social standing, namely the farm labourers and their families, the further to the back of the church they sat. George Lutkin and his family sat next row from front behind William Fry's family, he was a local magistrate and lived in a large country manor on the edge of Crostwick. Close to the rear of the church sat Edward and his family, his father, Nathaniel, his mother, Mary and younger brother, James. From his usual vantage point Edward could see the Lutkin family in their usual place up front in the distance. Occasionally, his view would be blocked by the movement of worshippers up front.

Then the service began. Prayers were said, sermons were said of how the righteous would be saved, and a baby boy named Benjamin Briggs was publicly baptised. No hymns were sung, singing in church was to become popular practice within the next century to come. An hour or so later, the congregation left the church. Sunday service was over and the Reverend Nash once again stood at the church entrance to bid his parishioners farewell.

Elizabeth broke away from her family, they were standing in the churchyard exchanging pleasantries with Reverend Nash and some of the other higher standing local gentry. These routines of social standing Elizabeth found tedious, so she made her way towards the gateway of the churchyard in a slow stroll, allowing for her family to finish their pleasantries and catch her up at the gate.

"Good morning, Miss Elizabeth," came a voice from behind. She turned, it was Edward.

"Good morning. How are you?" she replied politely.

"Always well on a Sunday," he replied. "No work for the rest of the day."

She smiled again and continued her slow stroll to the gate to wait for her family. Momentarily, she looked again in the direction of the bold charmer of a farm hand who was Edward Allen. He was by now out of the gate and heading in the direction of his family home in the company of his mother, father and brother James. Soon after, she was joined by her own family whereupon returned back to their farmhouse home. Together, they prepared and enjoyed Sunday lunch as was usual, then to settle down to rest for the afternoon.

After an hour or so, Elizabeth became restless and bored, and announced that she was going out for a stroll. This was not uncommon for her, she would often go for walks on Sunday afternoons, sometimes with her sisters and sometimes alone, but always taking the family dog with her, a dark grey lurcher named Nell. The family paid little attention on this occasion, some were asleep and didn't notice, while others were reading or playing cards.

She would always take the same route, heading right at the gate and up the road towards a meadow. From there, she would cross the meadow to a small river or stream known locally as 'Dobb's Beck', and walk along its banks for a while, then to return back home along the same route. As she walked through the meadow, a mild breeze gently blew the tall grass and spring wild flowers while the sun shone, its warmth stirring up the first insects of the year, honey bees and bumble bees gathering the first nectar of the year from early blooming spring flowers. She neared the stream, taking in, and enjoying the sights of the new blooms and wildlife that would inhabit the domain of a riverbank. The dog who accompanied her would now and then run off to explore but always kept within an earshot's distance of Elizabeth, and return close to her. George Lutkin had made the dog that way, she dares not run off too far or she would feel the wrath of one of George's rages. Elizabeth continued along the bank of the river which was in reality just a small tributary stream that was to eventually lead into the larger river Bure. In the distance, she caught sight of a person walking along the bank in the opposite direction towards her, she could just make out at first that it was a man, and he was alone, but could not make out his identity. As he approached, her dog, Nell, also curious, ran towards the stranger to investigate, prompting Elizabeth to call her back.

"Nell! Come back here!" she shouted.

Nell, however, was oblivious to Elizabeth's calls and made straight for her quarry who, when confronted by the dog, just knelt down, and patted and stoked the animal, showing no fear or apprehension, whereas Nell just wagged her tail and greeted the stranger as an old friend. Elizabeth neared the man and dog to the realisation that the stranger was in fact Edward, who Nell did indeed know well as a friend from the farm. In truth, Nell was never an aggressive dog unless you were a rabbit or a hare.

"It's alright, Miss Elizabeth, she knows me. She's chased many a stick I've thrown for her on the farm."

Elizabeth smiled. "Hello again, what are you doing wandering alone up here?"

"I was bored at home, everyone was sleeping so I thought I'd come out for a stroll. Haven't been up here for a while and forgot how nice it is. How about you, Miss, where are all your family?"

"Same as yours, mostly sleeping," she replied.

"Don't they mind you wandering out here all on your own?"

"They never mind. I often come here if it's fine on Sundays, besides, I'm not alone I've got Nell with me."

Edward chuckled to himself knowing how little protection Nell was likely to ever give should trouble ever arise.

"Why aren't you out with your friends from the village?" she asked.

"No reason, just bored and fancied a stroll. I expect they're all at home resting too, they'll be up early for work tomorrow."

The pair began to stroll along the riverbank back towards the village.

"Do they all work on farms like you?" she asked.

"Most of 'em do, some work on Spring Farm and others on Greys, one or two of 'em do other things. Sam Davey's a carpenter and Herbert Bygraves is a bricklayer, but most are farm hands like me."

"Do you always want to work on a farm?"

"I suppose so. I've not really thought hard about it, I've always worked on a farm, and so have all my family. Wouldn't know what else I would do."

"You've never thought of wanting to see the world? Like a sailor or soldier, or maybe learn a trade?"

Edward thought for a minute... "Wouldn't mind seeing a bit of the world, but I wouldn't want to join the army, or go to sea for that matter."

"What about a trade?"

"Often fancied Blacksmithing, but it's too late for that now."

"Can you read or write?"

"Me? No, not at all, never been taught. Can't even write me name."

"You can't write your name?"

Edward shook his head, slightly embarrassed. "I suppose you must know how to, a young lady like you is bound to be educated."

"Yes, I do, my mother taught me."

"None of my family has ever learned to read, they've never needed to."

Elizabeth didn't reply, she just continued her stroll along the chalk stream, momentarily stopping to pick something up from the banks edge. Edward didn't see what she had picked up and didn't ask her, feeling it too impertinent.

"How about you, Miss? Do you ever feel that you would want to leave, maybe see the world?"

"Oh, I don't think things like that ever apply to a girl such as me," Elizabeth replied. "It's the expected thing that I marry a man and bear his children. Us girls can't dream of things like that."

Edward chuckled. He could sense the subtle point that Elizabeth was making but thought it best not to reply. Secretly, he agreed with her.

The couple strolled along the stream for another hundred yards. Nell ran ahead reaching a group of three beech trees all evenly spaced about ten yards apart and roughly the same distance off the riverbank. She sniffed at the trees, other dogs had been there before. A few moments after Edward and Elizabeth reached the trees, then Elizabeth stopped, which confused Edward. "Follow me," she said and led him over to the first tree.

"Right," she said. "Let's see if we can teach you to write your name."

Again, Edward was confused, that was until Elizabeth produced a small chalkstone from her apron pocket. One she had picked up earlier along the chalk stream bank. Now she had found just what she had been looking for, a smooth surface to write upon with a piece of chalk, and the smooth surface on the bark of a beech tree was ideal.

"Write my name?" said Edward. "Oh, I dunno about that."

A huge apprehension had overwhelmed him. He didn't want to make himself look a fool in front of this pretty young lady, and his employer's pretty daughter at that.

"It's easy," said Elizabeth. "All you have to do is copy what I do. Look, this is how your name begins." She wrote a capital E onto the bark of the first beech tree. "That's an E for Edward and it's also an E for Elizabeth too. Just copy that E."

Hesitantly, Edward copied the E, and the end result was good.

"Well done, that's good. Now, this is a D."

She wrote a small d beside. "E-d. As you can hear, the letter sounds much as you say it."

Edward again copied his teacher, and step by step, Elizabeth wrote out Edward's name onto the bark of the tree. He in turn copied her writing.

"Well done, you've written your name for the first time. Now let's see if you can copy the whole thing together."

Edward slowly copied out his name without guidance from his teacher, and he copied a perfectly readable *Edward* onto the tree.

"There you see, it's not all that hard, is it?"

Then Elizabeth wrote a capital A onto the bark and then repeated the process to form the word *Allen*. Again, Edward followed her instructions until his surname was complete. He smiled at the result.

"Thank you for that, Miss Elizabeth. You just couldn't know just how dead chuffed I am for doing that for the first time. I'll try and remember it so as I can do it again."

"If I can find something to write on, I'll write it down so you can practise. All you have to do is copy and remember."

They continued their stroll along Dobb's Beck then cut across the meadow back to the village. On entering the village, Elizabeth spotted an old piece of wood laying on the side of the road, obviously shed from an old cart at some time. "This will do nicely," she said, and promptly wrote Edward's name on it. "Now all you have to do is copy and practise, and you'll be able to write your name on your own."

Edward thanked his teacher again before they departed in opposite directions towards their own homes. Edward left feeling very pleased with his new-found skill, while Elizabeth left with warm a feeling that she had achieved something good.

That week, Edward practised writing his name just as Elizabeth had told him and very soon, had it mastered, this in turn stimulated a wanting to understand more of these letters and the sounds they made. Elizabeth had inadvertently triggered a desire within Edward to learn more. All his life, he had seen writing all around him but had never known just what it all meant. He had never felt a need to learn any of it until now, reading and writing had never been a skill needed in his life. Elizabeth had changed all that in just one chance meeting on a Sunday afternoon stroll. Maybe, he thought, there could be more she could teach him, and maybe help him begin a process of learning more words. He decided that he would make a point of being beside Dobb's Beck the next Sunday in the hope that Elizabeth may be there again. She did after all seem to enjoy showing him how to write his own name.

The following Sunday arrived, and after yet another lazy lunchtime routine, Edward set off towards Dobb's Beck at much the same time as he had left the previous week. Elizabeth's family did indeed follow much the same ritual as the week before. Her parents were both enjoying an afternoon nap while her brother had left to climb trees in the woods at neighbouring Spixworth. Her sisters, Jane and Martha, were playing cards on a small table brought out into the rear garden. Not wanting to play cards, she called Nell who immediately jumped up knowing she was to go out for a walk. As they left, Elizabeth picked something up that she knew to be laying on the ground at side of the driveway just before the gate entrance, and put it in her apron pocket. Then both left Spring Farm and headed towards the meadow that would lead to Dobb's Beck.

Crossing the meadow, Elizabeth and Nell soon reached the steam to stroll along its bank. They neared the three beech trees where she had taught Edward just a week earlier, and she looked to see if maybe he would be there again. He was, he was sitting on the ground, his back up against the trunk of the second tree, staring at the stream and seeming to be waiting.

"Hello again," said Elizabeth. "Family asleep again?"

"As always, Miss, thas why I'm here," Edward replied. "I was hoping to see you again to thank you for showing me how to write my name."

"There's nothing to thank me for, it joyed me that it meant so much to you. I was glad to be of a help."

"Well, the thing is, Miss Elizabeth, I was wondering if you could write all those other letters down for me to copy, so as I could know what they are. I might be able to work out what other words are too."

"You mean, you want to learn the alphabet?"

Edward looked confused.

Elizabeth smiled. "The alphabet is all those letters, all of them. You would need to know all what they are all called. There's twenty-six of them and you'll have to remember all their names in order. Once you can do that, it should help you to understand the sound of words and how they are written."

"Twenty-six of 'em? Sounds difficult."

"It's not really. If you keep reading and memorising them, you'll soon do it without thinking."

"Could you show me? I've brought a piece of slate I found lying around at the farm, and I've got a piece of chalk too."

Elizabeth smiled, and then she too pulled out a piece of slate from the large pocket of her apron, the one she had found lying on the driveway near the front gate. "That's funny, I thought that if I may happen to cross your path again, you may want to learn some more," causing a chuckle from both.

Elizabeth crouched down and wrote down the full alphabet onto her piece of slate. "This is what I want you to copy. I want you to copy it over and over again, and in this order too, till you can do it without thinking. I'll tell you the names of the first seven and I want you to memorise those names."

Elizabeth told Edward the names of the first letters from A to G over and over again until he was able to say them all unaided.

"Well done," she said. "If you practise this, I'll go over the next seven with you next week."

"Thank you, Miss Elizabeth," said Edward. "When I know all the letters and what they sound like, I might be able to work out words for myself."

"You might, but you really need to be taught... I could show you, step by step."

"Are you sure about that, Miss? Would you mind? It's a big thing to do."

Elizabeth thought for a moment... "I've quite enjoyed teaching you so far."

The reality was that Elizabeth had found herself somewhat drawn to Edward, in much the same way he had for her. Like many young people, she had acted before thinking of any possible obstacles or consequences.

"Would your mother and father stand for it? Meeting a boy from the farm every Sunday. How would they feel about that?"

Elizabeth hadn't thought of that. He was right, her father would never stand for her meeting Edward, and wouldn't tolerate a farm hand who could read either, they were supposed to know their place in life. She thought for a moment...

"They wouldn't have to know, I could meet you here every Sunday afternoon and teach you just like today and last week."

"Here?" said Edward. "We'd be seen sooner or later."

"Well, somewhere quieter then, where we won't be seen."

Edward looked around... "How about over there?" he said, pointing towards a small wooded area in the distance across the meadow, and known locally as Primrose Hole. "No one should see us in there, it's away from the river and off any paths."

Elizabeth looked towards the woodland. "You're right, we could meet there if you like, but it would have to be discrete."

Edward nodded. "People could think the worst."

Elizabeth nodded. "Each lesson shouldn't take long, less time to get caught. Most of the work would have to be done by you at home once I have set tasks for you to do... And by the way, you can call me Elizabeth, my friends do."

"It'll have to be Miss Elizabeth in front of your mother and father."

Elizabeth smiled.

The couple strolled on across the meadow and then headed back towards the village, both talking and planning of future reading lessons to come, both looking forward to their future project.

***

As agreed, the couple met the following Sunday, and every Sunday after when the weather was clear. Elizabeth brought Nell with her on every visit. Edward brought his slate and chalk. He was taught the alphabet and then simple words. He learned quickly as adults do when their interests have been stimulated, and soon sentences were written for the first time. But the pair kept a disciplined behaviour towards the other and just worked tirelessly at the task at hand. These were times of peasants and gentry, and everyone knew their place in society. A young farm hand had no place in secret company with the daughter of a landowner. Just suitors of the same class or higher would do for George Lutkin, and chaperoned at that. The utmost secrecy was kept, albeit laughed off by the couple in question at the time. Of course, their rendezvous were not always unseen; you can rarely remain unnoticed in a small country village, and they were sometimes noticed as they walked towards the wooded dell. No suspicions of anything untoward were thought at first, there were always meetings between young people, both innocent and not so innocent. But in the passage of time, one or two people who had happened to see the couple together over the months passed, started to look and started to wonder. Then, after more time, began to suspect a fondness between them, and after even more time, began to quietly gossip.

Anne Lutkin was hanging out the washing on a cold, breezy but unusually bright December morning. Elizabeth had been to the well and was returning with two buckets of water suspended from a wooden yoke resting on her shoulders. As she approached the rear of the house, she heard her mother call to her.

"Elizabeth! Could you come over here please?"

She did as her mother had requested. "What is it Mother?" she asked.

"Now, I'm not saying that I believe them, but I just want to know from you if it's true or not," said Anne Lutkin in an uncomfortable manner. "But I've been hearing whispers about you meeting young Edward Allen about the village, up near Dobb's Beck. Is it true?"

Elizabeth was taken aback.

"Yes, it is true," she replied. "But it's not what people are thinking, I'm just teaching Edward to read and write."

"To read and write?"

Anne Lutkin sighed… "How long has this been going on?"

"Since about April. We crossed paths one Sunday afternoon and I showed him how to write his name. I've been teaching him to read and write ever since."

"Why didn't you say anything about it?"

"Because we thought that father wouldn't approve of him meeting me on Sundays. He'd also think that Edward was getting ideas above himself."

"He would at that!" said Anne.

"Look Mother, we've done nothing wrong and nothing to be ashamed of. He's learning really well. You've always encouraged us to read and write, why not Edward?"

"Edward is not my concern, you are and people are beginning to talk, albeit wrongly so you say, but they are talking nonetheless. This will have to stop before your father hears it, because if he does, there'll be big trouble."

"You won't tell him, will you? Please don't."

"Of course, I won't tell him girl, but it will have to stop. You say that Edward has learned well enough?"

"He has, he's learned very quickly."

"Then he'll have to read and teach himself alone, now that he knows how. You've done your bit, now let him carry on without you. Hopefully, he should get there all by himself."

"But we were doing so well. He just needed a little more time with me before he was ready to teach himself," said Elizabeth.

"God only knows what your father would do if he knew. You are to stop this now, and that's my final word on the matter."

Elizabeth ran into the house and up to her room, she began to weep, knowing she would have to tell Edward.

The following Sunday arrived, and as usual the same routine occurred. The parishioners all arrived to fill the church for the service to be greeted by the parson waiting at the church doors. Sermons were read, prayers were said and a baby boy called Thomas Lambert was publicly baptised. Once again, the reverend Jonathan Nash stood at the church door to bid the parishioners farewell after another Sunday service.

Elizabeth could see Edward a short distance away across the churchyard, and she discreetly broke away from her family and headed to a quiet spot a short distance from the church gate. She waited for him to look over to her, which after a while he did, and he discreetly smiled to her. With a quick movement of her head and an equally quick wave of her hand, she beckoned him over.

"Hello, Miss Elizabeth, how are you?" asked Edward.

"I need to speak to you," she replied.

Together, they walked just outside the church gate, out of earshot of anyone leaving the church grounds.

"People have seen us together, and they've been talking. My mother knows we've been meeting and why. She's forbidden me to see you again."

"She knows? Then she must know we've done nothing wrong."

"She does, and she said that she won't tell my father, but she's insisted that I'm not to meet with you anymore so as to stop people from talking. I'm sorry Edward, I don't know what else to do."

"It's alright, I understand," replied Edward. "But we've done nothing wrong other than being the people we are. Your father may not approve of me reading and writing just because I'm a farm hand, but we've done nothing wrong. To hell with 'em."

"I have to go now," said Elizabeth. "Please carry on reading and writing, you were doing so well. If you stop now it will have all been for nothing."

"I will, and I hope that maybe in time this will be forgotten and we can be friends again."

"I hope so too," said Elizabeth, and she turned to return to her family with a heavy heart. She had secretly enjoyed meeting Edward more than even she had realised, now it had to come to an end, she would miss his companionship and the charm that she had grown so very fond of in the time of their meetings.

Chapter Three

The months passed to mid-September 1776. Edward and Elizabeth had kept apart to prevent any scandal arising, and therefore George Lutkin was none the wiser of their secret rendezvous. Luckily for everyone concerned, news hadn't reached him, largely through the efforts of his wife Anne. Those who had been spreading gossip thought it a wiser option not to infuriate such an intimidating man as George, and consequently no one was brave enough to tell him. In time other subjects of gossip took over the conversations of the local villagers, which would liven up their otherwise uneventful lives, and Edward and Elizabeth's meetings were a soon forgotten topic. They did inevitably see each other at the farm in the course of their daily lives, and though their eyes did meet and formal polite pleasantries were exchanged, feelings were kept well hidden. There was no suspicion of anything untoward from anyone, even Anne Lutkin felt that everything had blown over.

Edward did carry on reading and writing as he had promised, and he learned well. Any piece of written word he could lay his hands on, he would use and read. Mainly prayer books were used, borrowed from the church from Parson Nash who was very helpful to him. Sometimes it was public notices posted either in the village or in Norwich. Whenever he visited the city, he would buy old copies of the Norwich Gazette or the Norwich Mercury. This all raised his reading skills to a higher level.

***

The harvest festival had been celebrated a week earlier, and Edward had been given the task of taking a cartload of produce and grain to Norwich market and the nearby corn exchange. George Lutkin, of course, was there to accompany his cart, it was his job to barter a good price with the market traders and the corn and grain traders. George was, in the course of his duties of negotiation, likely to accompany his trading associates into one or two of the many alehouses that were to be found in Norwich, as was his usual routine.

Edward had been chosen for this task because the usual carter Bill Comer was ill with dropsy, an ailment caused through fluid forming around vital organs such as heart, lungs and liver. It is more commonly caused by malnutrition. Not uncommon at the time but nearly always fatal. This reflected the lives of the peasant workers, though work was plentiful and many were housed in farm cottages on the estates, many still lived a life malnourished and in complete poverty.

George and Edward set off early in the morning just before dawn, so they could arrive in Norwich at the start of trade. Edward wasn't used to spending so much time in the presence of George Lutkin and the journey of six miles was to take just under an hour. Small talk with the governor was not something that Edward was looking forward to, especially in light of the gossip that until recently had gone around the village. But the cart did set off and Edward tried to make the journey a quiet one by not speaking. George, however, was not a man who enjoyed periods of silence, and soon began to try and raise a conversation at any opportunity. At first, a conversation was centred on Edward's family, and in particular his father.

"What's Nathaniel doing this morning?" George asked.

"Foreman's asked him to burn the stubble on the north field after he's brought the cows in for milking," Edward replied.

"He's worked for us for a long time now," said George. "Since he was a boy, when my father had the farm some thirty or so years ago. He met your mother here too, she worked as milk maid and helped with the harvests if I remember."

"She still helps with the harvest every year," said Edward.

"And your brother, he works here too, what is his name? I've forgotten."

"James."

"James! Yes, of course," said George.

Cutting through the village of Spixworth, which is next to Crostwick, almost joined to it, the cart then heads towards the larger village of Catton. There was another spell of silence on the journey until the cart entered Catton and passed Church Street.

"George Barrett!" Edward looked up Church Street in the direction George Lutkin was pointing to.

"George Barrett lives up there!" he said. "I used to be friends with him when I was about your age. We used to charm the girls and we had a merry old time in a few ale houses, I can tell you, boy."

George chuckled to himself as he reminisced old days of young single fun and frolics he had had in his youth. Edward smiled too. Then there was more silence as the cart left Catton and headed to Constitution Hill and then to enter the city through the Magdalen gate. Shortly after, they arrived at Norwich market just beside the ancient old, flint built Guildhall.

This was the city they knew so well, a fine, great city, England's second city at that time. Situated in the east of England and with a natural river port directly linked to the sea port of Yarmouth. Norwich had grown since the coming of the Normans, into a major player with the trade from the European mainland. Only London had a larger population, and Norwich's main trade was silk and textile weaving, using techniques brought over from Belgium and Holland over two centuries earlier. However, at that very time, the great canals linking the northern towns and the coal fields were being constructed which was to eventually cause the demise of Norwich in what was to become the industrial revolution.

Just eighteen months earlier, Parson James Woodforde had arrived at the city on the way to his newly appointed parsonage of Weston Longville, about eleven miles north of the centre of Norwich. In his diary dated 14th April 1775, he wrote that he had taken a stroll around the city and both he and his travelling colleague both agreed that it was the finest city in England by far. He described the old square Norman castle sitting high up on the castle mound, which commands a presence over the whole city. The thirty-six flint built churches he described as noble. He mentions the flint built city wall that surrounds the city, only stopping where the River Wensum forms a natural defensive boundary. From the high mound of the castle, he describes the many windmills seen on the landscape surrounding the city, and, of course, also seen from the castle, the great Norman cathedral with the second tallest spire in England, dominating the skyline of the city from miles around. James Woodforde was to spend the rest of his life living in Weston Longville and making frequent visits to the city. The diaries he wrote of his life in Norfolk until his death in 1802, were kept by his family and finally published in 1924, making him Norfolk's most famous diarist.

Amongst the hustle and bustle of the busy city, George Lutkin and Edward Allen set about doing their day's work and day's business. Edward's job was to carry baskets of potatoes, carrots and cabbages to the market as George led the way. He was doing all of the talking and haggling with the market traders until prices were agreed and all the produce was gone. Then the same again carrying grain bags at the corn exchange, until eventually, all that was left was an empty cart.

With business done, now came the most enjoyable part of George Lutkin's day, the alehouses and the inns, accompanied by his friends and associates from the corn exchange. This also left Edward with some time on his hands while George was busy sampling the delights of the local brew. Edward tied up the horse and cart to a post at the side of the market just outside the Guildhall. He strolled down the hill to see the sights of the city, not venturing too far so as to keep the horse and cart in sight, and just in case George emerged early from the ale house ready for his ride home. Looking towards the market from the Guildhall, Edward watched the traders at work selling fruit and vegetables. Rabbits and chickens were sold, both dead and alive. There was a separate fish market within the square, situated higher up the hill and divided by a row of shops, selling mostly herrings and oysters. There were also stalls selling tobacco with clay pipes for smoking. At the bottom of Guildhall Hill within the market square was Gentleman's walk, which had shops and inns of all kinds, shoemakers, tailors, wig-makers and hat shops. There were of course inns and alehouses, including the King's Head Inn where the mail coaches, carrying both mail and passengers from London and other major towns and cities would arrive. Their occupants would often stay overnight while making their journey to or from the city. There were even some newspaper printers within the square where copies of the Norwich Gazette or Norfolk Chronicle were printed.

Edward would often use a bookshop not fifty yards away down the bottom corner of Guildhall Hill towards the adjoining London Street. He quickly made his way down to look into the window to see the books. Maybe he would give a farthing for an old newspaper if they sold any, which more often than not they did. On this occasion, he was in luck and he came out of the shop with an old copy of the Norwich Gazette from over a month ago, from there, he made his way back to his tied up horse and cart. He climbed back onto the cart, sat down and began to read, just occasionally putting the paper down and looking at the sights of the busy city around him. An hour past, and Edward sat enjoying another brief reading moment when suddenly, he heard a man's voice coming from the other side of his newspaper.

"A cart driver who can read," said the voice.

Edward laid down his paper, and there stood a man of middle years, about five feet and seven inches tall. He wore a white wig, long at the back and tied with a black ribbon into a ponytail. On top of the wig sat a brown three cornered hat, his jacket was the same colour and he wore grey breeches with cream coloured stockings up to his knees. His face was round and had a reddish tinge to it, and he was smiling.

"Can I help you sir?" asked Edward.

"I just saw you reading your newspaper and I thought to myself that you don't see many carters who can read," said the man. "I hope I haven't offended you at all young man," he added.

"Not at all sir," replied Edward. "But I'm a farmhand, not a carter, and I'm still just learning to read and write."

"Even so, you don't see many farmhands reading and writing, and if you are still learning to read, then you must be doing all right if you can read a newspaper."

Edward paused for a moment. *'I suppose so'*, he thought. It hadn't occurred to him that his reading and writing had progressed enough to be to any kind of reasonable level, maybe this man had given him some food for thought.

"That's a good quality in a man, someone who's not afraid to learn new things, and is not scared to get his hands dirty through hard work either."

"Thank you for the compliment, sir," replied Edward. "I hadn't given it any thought about how good my reading is yet, I'm still learning."

"Well, read something to me from your paper," said the man. "And we'll see how good you are."

Edward did as the man asked and read a story of how, "The colonies of America had renounced their allegiance to the crown and dissolved all political connection between them and Britain. Their writing of declaration was entrusted to Benjamin Franklin, John Adams and Thomas Jefferson."

"That's enough!" interrupted the stranger. "Sounds like you are not learning to read to me, sounds more like you already know how to read, young man."

"Why thank you, sir," replied Edward.

The stranger offered his hand. "My name is William Burrell and I work for the King's mail office. I know you are already in employment at the moment but we are always looking for hard workers, especially those who can read and write. If you are ever looking for work in the future, just come to the mail office at Bedford Street, or just over there at the Kings Head Inn where the coaches run from, and ask for me by name. I've been very impressed by you, young man."

Edward shook the man's hand. "My name is Edward Allen, and I'm honoured sir."

"Likewise, Edward, and don't forget, ask for me, William Burrell, at the central mail office on Bedford Street, should you ever be looking for work."

"Thank you sir, you never know I might just do that one day," said a smiling Edward, and with that, William Burrell departed back to his nearby office.

A feeling of deep pride came over Edward, he could read well enough for the King's mail office. A thought came to him of how he would love to tell Elizabeth of what had happened today. She would have been so pleased and proud of what her pupil had been offered. Soon after, out of an alehouse appeared George Lutkin, slightly worse for wear. He staggered up towards the Guildhall of which outside his horse and cart and Edward were parked up.

"Take us home boy!" he slurred, and then climbed into the back of the cart. Within what could only be minutes, he was sound asleep. Edward untied the horse and set off, homeward bound.

Through the busy streets of Norwich and then through the gate at the city wall, to leave the city, the road became less busy as it merged into the countryside and the city lay far behind them. A mail coach passed them in the opposite direction heading for a coaching inn within the city, and Edward smiled at its passing. Along the bumpy, unmaintained dirt track of the North Walsham road, through Catton, then into Spixworth, and then finally into Crostwick, a journey of just under an hour was made. George Lutkin was still sleeping in the back of the cart when it passed through the gates of Spring Farm and finally stopped outside the farmhouse. Edward knocked on the door and Anne Lutkin answered.

"Mr Lutkin is in the back of the cart sound asleep, could someone help me to bring him in please?"

"Richard! Just help Edward to get your father out of the cart and into the house!" called Anne.

This was a situation that was not uncommon for Anne Lutkin, she had dealt with George returning home drunk on many occasions and usually after trading at the corn exchange. Both Edward and young Richard Lutkin managed to pull the large frame of George Lutkin to the edge of the cart, and with a pull on each arm managed to sit him up. This caused George to stir from his slumber. A groan came from his mouth and his eyes started to open, albeit in a very slanted sort of way. With Edward on one arm and Richard on the other, they both managed to manoeuvre George into the house and on to an armchair that sat beside the fireplace in the front room.

"Thank you Edward, for bringing him home," said Anne Lutkin, with obvious displeasure written all over her face.

"I'll just put the horse away and then I'll be off home, Mrs Lutkin," said Edward, and he set off with the horse and cart to the back of the farm where the yard and the stables were situated. He unbridled the horse and led the animal back into its stable. Settling the horse down in fresh bedding and putting fresh hay into the feeding trough, a voice came from behind at the stable entrance.

"Hello Edward."

He turned, it was Elizabeth. He was dumbstruck for a moment. This girl who had been so beautiful and warm to him, who he missed intensely and had never stopped thinking of since their forced departure. Here she was stood before him.

"Did you get your father settled down alright?" he asked.

"He's fast asleep in the chair," she replied.

"Does your mother know you're here with me?"

"She's busy getting father something to eat for when he wakes up. I don't think she even noticed me leave the house, I don't think anyone did."

Edward gave an understanding nod.

"Are you still reading?"

Edward smiled. "I never stopped reading. In fact, I was offered a job at the King's mail office, today in Norwich. A man from there saw me reading a newspaper, he asked me to read it to him. He was so impressed he offered me a job."

Elizabeth stayed serious. "Are you going to take that job?"

"Maybe, I don't know, I wasn't expecting it so I haven't really thought about it yet. It felt really good being asked though."

Elizabeth's face dropped, she looked down towards the ground. Edward sensed her upset.

"I don't want you to leave here, I'd miss you," she said, raising her head and gazing into Edward's eyes. He edged closer and took her hand.

"I've missed you badly," he said.

He pulled her towards him, the way lovers do. They kissed, intensely, for what seemed a while but in reality, was just a moment. He pushed her up against the stable wall, his left hand on her waist and his right hand grabbing her rear. His knee pushed in to part her legs, still kissing with great passion. This was passion that neither of them had experienced before in their young lives, but had secretly wanted on their earlier meetings. Passion rippled through both their bodies until, after minutes of this intense experience, both passionate and arousing, the lovers finally let go their embrace, fully aware that someone could walk in at any time.

Edward checked the door to see the coast was clear. "When can I see you again?"

"I don't know, someone will catch us, I know they will."

"I never stopped thinking of you last time, and I'll never get you out of my head now. Do you want to see me again or not?"

She paused. "Yes... I do."

Edward grabbed her again, once more, they kissed passionately… "When can I see you?" he asked her again.

"Sunday afternoon. I'll go for another of one of my walks, they're not watching me anymore, same place."

"I'll be there," he replied, and with that, Elizabeth straightened her clothing and left the stable to head back to the house. Edward checked the horse had all its needs and was settled. Darkness was now approaching so he lit a lamp outside the stable and closed the door. He then headed to the gate to make his journey home. This was a momentous day in the life of Edward Allen, one that he would never forget for the rest of it.

Elizabeth entered the house, her father was still snoring in front of the fire and her mother was busy in conversation with her sister Martha. Neither had noticed that Elizabeth had been gone for any abnormal period of time, so no questions were asked. Later that evening, Elizabeth sat quietly deep in thought whilst around her, her family were preoccupied with their own thoughts and activities, completely oblivious to anything untoward from her. Anne Lutkin and Martha were both knitting socks for George and Richard, under the illumination of an oil lamp. Jane and Richard were both in bed sound asleep, having both had a hard day's work on the farm. In time George stirred from his slumber and quietly smoked his pipe from the comfort of his armchair.

"Are you well, Elizabeth?" asked Anne, "You're very quiet this evening."

"I'm fine Mother," she replied. "I'm just a bit tired. I think I'll go to bed now."

She rose, kissed her mother and father goodnight, and then retired for the night.

Edward had arrived home in the darkness earlier that evening, his father Nathaniel, was not at home, he was at the local village alehouse, enjoying an after work ale with other farmhands from the village.

"Hello, Edward, had a nice day in Norwich?" asked his mother Mary.

"Not bad at all, Mother," he replied, smiling. His mind not completely focused on the single event of his trip to Norwich.

"Your food's on the table."

That night, the lovers both lay awake in their beds thinking of the moment of passion that had overpowered them both. Pleasurable feelings of desire oozed through their bodies and the excitement of the thought of their next meeting was with them for the rest of their conscious hours, until fatigue finally overpowered them to sleep off their eventful day.

***

Thursday, Friday and then Saturday dragged by, the lovers to be occasionally snatching glances towards one another whenever the chance arose when no one was looking. No smiles were exchanged just an occasional quick wink from Edward was the only communication between them, subtlety was the order of the day and they needed no words, their thoughts were the same.

At last, Sunday came, a cloudy but dry day. The usual ritual was performed by the parishioners of Crostwick, the trek to the church to be met at the church door by a smiling reverend Nash. As usual prayers and sermons were read and another baptism was held, that of a baby boy named Thomas Thacker. Then there were the usual pleasantries after the service before the trek back home. Again, there were fleeting glances between Edward and Elizabeth that had gone completely undetected but time couldn't go quick enough for the couple. Their last encounter being their first experience of almost erotic pleasure with a partner that either of them had ever known, the coming rendezvous was an excitement they yearned for, but also a nervousness of the unknown. Sunday lunch came with neither of them having much appetite, just an overwhelming desire to leave the house. Finally, the afternoon came, the time they had both longed for, and they made their journeys to their secret rendezvous at Primrose Hole.

Elizabeth was the first to arrive at the secluded wooded dell, the very same place they had secretly met in the past during Edward's reading lessons. The dell was ideal, not only for its seclusion but also for its shelter in bad weather, and though they had been seen walking in the area of the meadow and the stream, no one had ever seen them together in their quiet little wood. She waited twenty minutes, then thirty. She was shaking with nerves, the time seemed endless to her, the uncertainty of the outcome was also weighing heavy on her mind. Then at last, there in the distance, approaching along the outer fringes of the meadow was Edward, he smiled as he caught sight of her and her heart raced even more.

"Hello," he said.

"Hello," she replied with a half-smile, an uneasy smile. Edward immediately sensed the uneasiness within her and pulled her close to him.

"I'm scared too you know," he said, trying to sound reassuring.

Then Elizabeth broke into a full smile. "You know they'd kill us if they knew we were here." She looked up into Edward's eyes.

He kissed her, softly at first, their mouths together slightly opening until their tongues met, winding around one another. The nervousness that they had both been experiencing had all but gone and the lovers were now focused on each other, nerves were now being replaced by arousal and pure passion. They kissed harder, more intense and Edward pushed Elizabeth up against a tree, again, he moved his knee forward and Elizabeth parted her legs to allow him closer. As they continued to kiss ever more passionately, Edward raised his hand and placed it on Elizabeth's left breast. The feeling of softness and roundness in his hand had never been experienced by this young man before and he felt fully aroused. She was breathing heavily; the feeling of Edward's knee pressing hard between her legs was highly pleasurable to her, even through the padding of her dress. The couple then lay on the ground. Elizabeth's left hand was behind Edward's head, pulling him closer to her as they kissed more intensely. Her left leg climbed over his right leg as he lay on his side and he grabbed her rear and pulled her evermore tightly to him. More and more became the intensity of the lust between them. Edward moved his hand down to the bottom of Elizabeth's dress, which by now had slightly hitched up and he felt the smooth skin of Elizabeth's right leg. Caressing her, his hand slowly worked its way up to her thigh, reaching her cotton underdress, as his hand reached the top he felt a warm moistness and a heavy sigh was heard.

"No, we can't!" she cried out, still overcome with the passion, she grabbed his hand and pulled it down from her dress.

"I'm sorry," said Edward and the lovers let loose their grip from each other, still breathing heavily with the excitement of their first meeting as lovers, albeit heavy petting.

"Don't be sorry," said Elizabeth.

A smile emerged on her face, "I enjoyed it."

Edward smiled too.

The couple lay together, enjoying the tenderness after the passion, Elizabeth rested her head on the left shoulder of Edward who was gently caressing her face and left arm.

"What are we to do? How will they be if they find out?" she asked.

"I don't know," said Edward. "I hate to think what my father would say. I think that maybe he'd throw me out. He'd be scared for his job, that's for sure. Your father would probably throw me off his land. Maybe even my family from their cottage, who knows?"

There was a realisation between the couple of just how serious a situation they had put themselves in. There then presided a moment of silence and deep thought… two minutes passed… then three, as they pondered upon the consequences. Eventually, the silence was broken by Edward.

"Do you want to put an end to this now while no one knows?"

There then came another moment of silence before Elizabeth's reply.

"No, I still want to be with you again, if you still want to see me?"

"Of course I still want to see you," he replied.

Then the lovers kissed once more.

Edward rose up from the ground. "We must never speak of this to anyone, not our closest friends, family, anyone, there's too much at stake. My family could lose their home and their living if your father was to find out, do you understand?"

"Of course I do," she replied.

Lust and passion had taken over the young lovers as to take such a huge risk. Their fear of the consequences had been laid aside, such is the way that young people do with strong wills and almost reckless desires in their journeys of life, and their excitement of forbidden pleasures. The lovers brushed themselves down, removing grass and leaves from their clothing.

"Next week, same place and time?" asked Edward.

Elizabeth kissed him on the lips, "See you then, lover," she replied with a broad smile, and with that, they parted and returned back to their lives with their families, and their deep secret.

Chapter Four

Nathaniel Allen opened the bedroom door, in which slept Edward and his younger brother, James. "Come on boys, up yer get!" he called. It was early, dawn was rising and the sound of cockerels crowing their first calls of the day could be faintly heard from the distant farms and home dwellings of the village. They were of course the alarm clocks of their day to the population of rural workers of the villages, and equally of the urban workers of the towns and cities. The boys, however, struggled to get up as young men often do, but they had learned not to cause their father to have to call them a second time.

Their mother, Mary, had already risen with her husband, and was in the kitchen preparing her husband and sons some bread, and a boiled potato each to take to work with them for their lunch. For breakfast, she toasted a few cut rounds of bread, to be washed down with a cup of warm milk. The family sat quietly at the table eating their toast, the boys were still trying to wake up. Nathaniel had woken early; a lifetime of early rising had made him naturally wake up at that time of the morning, as working men of middle age and long experience often do.

He looked to Edward. "What are you doing today, boy?" he asked.

"As far as I know, I'm ditch digging at the south field, half of the old ditch is silted up and overgrown," Edward replied.

"And what are you up to?" he asked, looking towards James.

"Mucking out the pigs and the cow sheds this morning." James replied.

He was sixteen years old and looked similar in appearance to Edward, only slightly shorter and thinner, but it was clearly visible that the two were brothers.

"Are you ploughing again today Father?" James asked.

"I'm on the south field too. So I'll keep my eye on you, boy," he said jokingly to Edward, who returned a smile back.

The three men rose from the table and picked up their prepared food parcels which were neatly packed up in linen by Mary. The two young men kissed their mother and headed for the door. Nathaniel kissed his wife. "See you tonight," he said, and joined his two sons to head off for another day's work at Spring Farm.

The three men set off towards the farm for their day's work and were almost immediately joined by other workers from Spring Farm heading on the same journey. Soon, the group of three farm hands had grown to eight workers, all heading in the same direction. In the opposite direction passed workers from Greys farm, the other main Crostwick farm. Pleasant acknowledgements were made to one another and arrangements to meet at the local pub later that night were made by some of the men. Joining Nathaniel, Edward and James on their trek was Jim Yallop, and his eldest son, Billy. Billy Yallop was eighteen and was Edward's best friend in the village. The pair had known each other since childhood but recently, saw less of each other as Billy had become fond of a local girl called Marion Davey. Alf Chapman was there too, he was another experienced middle-aged worker who had worked with Nathaniel for close to twenty-five years and they were good friends. He had fathered three daughters and so, consequently, no sons were there to accompany him to work. The Dawson brothers had also joined the group. Charlie Dawson was the eldest at twenty and George the younger at seventeen. The two were the main providers for their family of five children and their mother as their father had died three years earlier from consumption. Of the five children, only three were of working age, their sister Sarah was fifteen and worked on Greys farm as a milkmaid.

The group neared the farm, to find in the distance the workers foreman Albert Yates standing outside the stable yard waiting for them to arrive, ready to dish out the orders for the day. Many of the hands already knew what they were to do this morning, it had already been discussed during the course of the previous day.

"Morning, boys!" said Albert, as the group arrived. "Hope you didn't have too many ales last night," he added.

There was laughter amongst the group as many had indeed enjoyed a few ales the previous night. Albert had been made works foreman or charge hand some ten years earlier. He had worked with Nathaniel, Jim Yallop and Alf Chapman for more years than they could count, ever since they were all young men themselves. They were all good friends and Albert was well respected by all of the farm hands, both young and old.

"Nathaniel and Edward, you already know what you are doing today, working in the south field. Billy, you can help Edward to dig out the ditches."

Billy smiled at the prospect of working with Edward, his best friend.

"Alf, you can help Nathaniel with the ploughing and pegging the lines. If you've time, you can help these young-uns with the ditch digging."

He continued his orders. "James, you and young master Richard can muck out all the stables and pens."

There were no smiles from these youngsters at the thought of this job.

"Charlie and George, you two can bring in the cows for milking, and then feed and water all the livestock, and Jim, you can run the harrow over the small field that Nathaniel ploughed yesterday."

With the mornings orders complete, the group dispersed to carry out their duties.

Whilst these orders were given by Albert, George Lutkin was still in his bed, about to rise. He had had his days of early rising and back breaking work. Now being a man of position, he could allow himself an extra hour or two in bed, should he feel the inclination. After all, he had the men to do the work now.

***

Billy Yallop and Edward Allen were the first to arrive at the south field. They were equipped with two shovels, a hand scythe and a wooden rake, along with their food and water for the day. Meanwhile, Nathaniel and Alf had the horse to hitch up to a cart to carry all the necessary equipment needed for their job. The arduous task of digging out ditches began. At first, Billy and Edward had to clear all of the overgrown areas using the hand scythe whilst Edward followed on by raking up the cut grass, nettles and wild flowers into piles to be cleared later. Half an hour of this preceded when came the arrival of Nathaniel, Alf and the horse, pulling a two-wheeled cart. The cart contained the plough, a shovel, a small barrel filled with water and a bucket, a bag of oats for the horse, and the worker's food parcels prepared by their wives that morning.

The plough and the rest of the equipment were lifted off the cart, and the cart was then unhitched from the horse and set aside out of the way of their work, it was then parked up at the field entrance. Nathaniel then led the horse over to the front end of the plough and began to attach the draught chain to the large leather horse collar worn around the animal's neck. Meanwhile, Alf was busy heading to the far end of the field where he gathered a number of tall wooden stakes taken from young trees and saplings of approximately five feet tall. He then pushed the stakes into the ground leaving a space of five feet between each one. Altogether, ten marker stakes were pushed into the ground and a piece of white cloth was tied to the top of the first stake. The cloth was used to make the stake more visible to the ploughman, giving him a clear sight to aim the horse to and keep the furrows in a straight line. The process was then repeated at the other end of the field.

Alf and Nathaniel were to share both the job of ploughman, and stake marker. The marker having the job of tying the white cloth onto the next stake after the furrows were completed between each one and to reposition the stakes after five stake widths had been ploughed. Together, they worked a shift system of about two hours give or take, swapping from ploughing to stake marking from one end of the field to the other. Many miles were to be walked and ploughed today. Many occasions would see the ploughman working alone and having to stop to mark out his own stakes when the other farm hands were too busy to help.

Meanwhile, Edward and Billy had completed their cutting, and raking of a thirty-yard section of the ditch so now the real work had to start, the digging. At first, the top of the ditch was dug, this was the dry part of the job where the turf was skimmed to a depth of about three feet. Then below came the damp soil and then eventually, mud and water. This part was left to last as it meant shoes off and breeches rolled up above the knees to enter the muddy water of the ditch. It was by far the most unpleasant part of the job.

The work was hard and physical and the young men laboured intensely with their digging, but they still talked and laughed and joked as they worked. Mid-morning came, and the two senior farm hands whistled to the younger ones and beckoned them over to the field entrance where the cart was parked. It was time to stop for some food and a drink. The two young men immediately put down their tools and made towards their elder workmates, carrying their food parcels and a clay bottle of water each.

"How are the ditches going?" asked Nathaniel to his son.

"Not too bad, we're still digging off the top, but we've still got the mud to do this afternoon."

The two elder hands chuckled, it was a job they had both experienced many times themselves, but now they were higher in the pecking order, thankfully, it was a job only seldom done by the experienced hands.

"I'll ache tonight, I think," said Billy.

They all agreed, a day's hard digging ditches would make the most hardened man go home with an aching back.

The four men sat down around the parked cart. The horse had been temporally unhitched and brought over, and a nosebag full of oats was strapped from his neck with a bucket of water placed beside him. As the men ate and drank together, they began their usual working man's small talk.

"I heard there was a fire in Norwich at Whitefriers the other day, a cabinet makers shop went up and took three houses with it," said Alf.

"I saw that in the Norfolk Chronicle," replied Edward. "It happened about six days ago, no one was killed though."

Nathaniel smiled with pride at his son and his newly learned ability.

"I heard that you'd learned to how read and write," said Alf. "I suppose you'll soon be too clever to be working on an old farm."

Edward just returned a smile.

"How did yer learn?"

Edward had thought about the answer to that question a while ago and had already thought of a plausible explanation. "A friend of mine taught me at first, and then I used prayer books, posters and newspapers and taught myself," he said.

Now these were times of naivety where education was concerned, and Edward knew that the 'taught myself' part of that statement was the part that was most likely to be remembered by anyone asking who knew nothing of literacy that is, but this sounded the most impressive. The part of the statement, "A friend of mine taught me at first," was more likely to be ignored. Nathaniel had thought Parson Nash had taught Edward at first because of the borrowed church books. He could see no harm in it other than keeping it secret from George Lutkin who may think it was not a farm hands place to know how to read or write.

"He'll be leaving for Norwich soon to start his new job as a clerk or a lawyer!" laughed Billy. The group all found that remark very amusing, including Edward.

"You'll have to find yourself a rich and educated young lady to marry," Alf joked. "Speaking of which, are you two courting any local young maidens at the moment?"

"You're seeing Marion Davey, aren't you Billy?" asked a grinning Edward.

Billy coloured up. "None of your business," he replied, and again, there was laughter amongst the men.

Alf carried on the banter.

"How about you, Edward?" he asked. "There must be someone in your life, there's plenty of fair young maidens in this village or Spixworth, or Horsted or St Faiths?" (These were the closest neighbouring villages).

Edward smiled again, treating the conversation in the jovial spirit that it was meant.

"There's no girl at the moment but I'm sure there will be someday," he replied.

At this point, Nathaniel, who until now had sat quietly listening and chuckling to the comical conversation, cut in to the chat himself.

"It's about time you found a girl, you'll be of age in two years, and it'll be time to be married and start a family of your own."

"Then there's still two years' Father, thas plenty of time." replied Edward.

Once again, laughter came from the group of workers.

"Right! We'd better get back to it before the governor turns up," said Nathaniel, rising to his feet.

The rest of the group followed suit and made their way back to their place of work.

Edward and Billy returned to their arduous task of ditch digging. Another hour of digging of the higher and dryer soil of the top of the ditch was completed by the pair, but then came the time they had dreaded, it was time to get their feet wet in the mud and silt of the lower level of the ditch. At first, the pair reluctantly dug out the mud, from standing just above the mud line and struggling to keep a firm foothold, but this soon proved too difficult, and inevitably, the time came to remove their shoes and socks, and roll up their breeches to above their knees and enter the mud and the water. With a wet gurgle, in went the bare feet of both the young men into the muddy water of the ditch. Digging mud was especially difficult due to the mud sticking to the blade of their shovels, every three or four shovelfuls of mud that were dug, the shovels had then to be cleaned in the surface water of the ditch, using their bare hands. On and on this laborious task continued, another two and a half long and hard hours past of dirty and wet, back-breaking work. Both Edward and Billy were heard grunting, and groaning and swearing in the process of this awful job as the horse and plough neared, which in turn caused a smile from Nathaniel and Alf. Then, later, at last, in the distance came another whistle from Nathaniel and Alf, it was time to stop again for a food and water break. The two young men were glad of it.

Again, the hands gathered around the cart at the field entrance for a well-needed half-hour break. Edward and Billy were covered in mud, and the sight of the filthy young men caused the elder hands to laugh.

"You look as if you're really enjoying that job," said Nathaniel.

Billy and Edward looked at each other, a slight grin was forced out with a shake of the head from the pair.

"I'll be glad when this one is over," said Billy.

"Yeah, me too," said Edward, causing laughter from Alf and Nathaniel.

"I hope your day's going as well as ours," said Edward.

"It is, very well my boy, very well," replied Nathaniel. "Should be done early, I think."

Then, Albert Yates appeared entering through the field entrance.

"Everything alright boys?"

"Hello, Mr Yates. Yes, everything's alright here," replied Alf.

Albert looked at the two muddy young men and smiled. "Yes, I can see that," he laughed. "I can see the ploughing is going well too, should be done early, I reckon. I'll find a nice clean job for you two after this one, I can see you've earned it."

"Thank you," replied Edward, and a smile broke from his muddy face.

"Well, I'd better be off, lots to do. I'll see you boys later," said Albert.

The group all knew what he meant, it was Albert's job to call the workers in at the end of a working day. They all bid him goodbye and off he went to visit the other workers situated around the other areas of the farm. Shortly after, lunchtime was over and the farmhands rose up to continue their afternoons work.

More field was ploughed and miles in distance was covered. Though the job was not as unpleasant as the ditch digging, ploughing was a long laborious job nonetheless. On and on the furrows were ploughed, until finally, Alf and Nathaniel had completed the task they had been set. It was time to pack up and take the horse and plough back to the stable yard and as they left the field, a loud whistle was blown from Nathaniel's lips and he and Alf waved to their young colleagues in the distance. Edward and Billy returned a wave back.

Another hour and a half of back breaking mud digging was worked by the young men until a call in the distance from Albert Yates beckoned the two to stop digging and pack in for the day. At last, it was over. The two moved further up to the un-dug section of ditch to use the cleaner, settled water to wash the mud off from their legs, arms and faces. Once clean, they put on their socks and shoes and headed back to the farm, carrying their shovels and the rake and scythe. Dusk began to settle and the two young men, having put away their tools then headed back home tired and aching, knowing they would have to do it all again tomorrow.

Chapter Five

"I'm going out. I'll see you later, Mother!" said Edward as he headed towards the door.

"Where are you going?" asked Mary.

"Just out for a walk," replied Edward.

It was Sunday, not long after lunchtime and another secret rendezvous with Elizabeth awaited.

"I'll see you later!" he called and the door closed behind him.

Edward knew he must try to avoid being seen as he headed towards Dobb's Beck. His pace hastened with his eagerness to meet her, he had longed to see her all week since their last secret liaison. It was Sunday and a day off for most, and there were people around. But the young people of the village mostly congregated around the green, just adjacent to the village pub, and many of the elder villagers were at home resting. Therefore, Edward, ever careful, made sure to avoid the green and headed around the village rather than go through it. As he made his way towards the meadow, he would on occasion see people pursuing leisurely activities, rambling or hare coursing with dogs. He kept a considerable distance from them, so as to not be seen or recognised.

At last, he reached his destination of the secluded wooded dell of Primrose Hole. He was the first arrive, and waited some fifteen minutes or so, until finally he saw in the distance, and hurrying towards him, Elizabeth, equal in eagerness to meet her lover. She looked up and caught sight of Edward, smiled and ran the short final distance straight into his arms. The lovers kissed and embraced.

"All week I have longed for this," said Edward.

"Me too, I can't stop thinking of you."

The lovers kissed once more and laid down at the foot of an old oak tree, the very spot where they had lain a week before. They kissed passionately, embracing tighter and tighter, his right hand lifted and cupped her left breast, she sighed and kissed him open mouthed, her tongue entering his mouth. They rolled over, Edward lying on top of Elizabeth, who manoeuvred her legs to accommodate him. His hands moved down and pulled up the hem of her dress, exposing her leg in white stockings, and her thigh in white linen petticoat underwear. He grabbed her buttocks and she wrapped her leg around him. The young lovers were now fully and uncontrollably aroused. Elizabeth then pulled up her dress at the other side, both legs now fully exposed and now wrapped around Edward who was rubbing himself against her.

"Do you want me to stop?" Edward called out in a husky whisper.

"No," she replied in heavy breath.

Edward then pulled down his breeches and tried to position himself somewhat clumsily. Elizabeth didn't need to remove anything; underwear of the time was just a petticoat. She then helped her lover to get correct position using her hand to guide him and which at first was unsuccessful, but after another attempt, he entered her. Elizabeth's virginity made the two lovers efforts difficult at first but in the course of time, the full experience was achieved. Pain was felt by Elizabeth but her desire for her lover overcame the discomfort. Together, they had made love, not for long, Edward lacked experience too and the feeling of absolute pleasure proved too much for him in a short time, as so many young lovers do find on their first experience of physical love. But they had experienced physical love for themselves nonetheless.

Having now made love for the first time in their lives, the lovers lay together silently in each other's embrace, caressing one another in deep thought, until Edward broke the silence.

"Did I hurt you?" he asked.

"Only a little," she replied.

"I thought you'd tell me to stop. I didn't think we'd go all the way."

"I did, I'd been thinking about it all week and I made the decision to go through with it... because I can't stop myself from thinking about you... I love you."

"I love you too," he replied. "Where does it go from here?"

Elizabeth kissed her lover. "I don't want to change anything right now, just carry on as we are with no one knowing anything and just looking forward to stealing moments with you, especially here every Sunday."

Edward looked deep into the eyes of his lovely fair young maiden. "You are the most beautiful girl I have ever known. Just being here with you, I wouldn't change a thing."

The pair kissed and caressed for another hour. Out of sight from prying eyes until it came time for the lovers to return to their lives and their families, but to meet again the following Sunday afternoon. Their virginity gone, and with the depth of their feelings towards one another, things would never be the same again, for both the lovers, and unknowingly to their families too.

The pair returned to their homes and their families with much on their minds. They both lay awake that night thinking of the events that the day had brought, and what may happen in the future, especially if their families were ever to find out. The biggest threat obviously being George Lutkin. However, this was a young couple in love, and young lovers do what their hearts tell them where love and passion is concerned, with a recklessness harder to comprehend in later years. These two were not going to let anyone, including George Lutkin, drive a wedge between them and their desire for one another. So the lovers carried on, secretly meeting and making love on Sunday afternoons, and making discreet smiles and winks from a distance during the working week. Sometimes, stealing quiet moments together at the farm when no one was around to see them.

***

Two months passed since the lovers first time, never failing to turn up for their secret weekly rendezvous unless severe weather made it too difficult for a meeting. It was now the end of November 1776, and the shorter days and the colder nights had arrived. Leaves were falling off the half bare trees and the wildlife in the countryside was thinning down due to hibernation, migration and mortality of the coming hard times. Elizabeth shivered with cold one frosty midweek morning. The cold had penetrated into the rooms of the house while a draining feeling of nausea had come over her. '*I must be coming down with something*', she thought. An extra blanket lay at the foot of the bed, left there by her mother who had a habit of always being prepared for all eventualities, especially with the coming of winter. She pulled the blanket over the bed, and then pulled all the existing blankets and the extra completely over her, submerging her to gain maximum warmth. Still she shivered, she had butterflies in her stomach, a sickly shivering feeling that made her stomach heave. At once, she threw off the bed covers, and reached down to under the bed where her chamber pot sat and quickly made a grab for it. She sat on the side of the bed with the pot placed on her knees, bent over, her stomach heaving to vomit, but nothing came out except a little green liquid. Her stomach was empty, it was early in the morning, before breakfast. The noise of Elizabeth soon woke her sisters sleeping in the same room.

"Are you alright?" asked Martha.

"No," replied Elizabeth. "I feel sick."

"Do you want me to get Mother?" Jane asked.

"No, I'll be alright."

Her stomach slowly began to settle and she laid the chamber pot back beneath the bed. Another hour passed and daylight began to shine through the thin cracks of the drawn curtains, and the three girls began to rise for the coming day.

"How are you feeling now?" asked Martha.

"A little better," said Elizabeth. "I don't know what came over me."

"Maybe you've got a tummy bug, or something you've eaten didn't agree with you. It'll be with you for a couple of days I should think," said Martha.

A porcelain bowl and jug of water a sat on the dresser. The girls washed and dressed ready for the proceeding day then descended downstairs to join their parents for breakfast. George and Anne Lutkin were already at the table. Toast and tea sat in front of George, his clay pipe lying beside him, ready to be lit as soon as he had finished his breakfast. Mother was busy toasting more bread using a wide toasting fork specially made by the village blacksmith to enable two rounds to be toasted at once.

"Can you take over the toasting Martha, while I make more tea?" she asked.

Martha immediately took the fork and continued with the toasting. Anne Lutkin then took the kettle which had been hanging from a spit just over the hot coals of the fire, which was beginning to boil. She poured hot water into the teapot on the table containing tea freshly imported from the East India trading company.

The family sat down to eat. Martha had by now toasted enough bread for two rounds of toast each, and the tea Anne had made was poured out into everyone's cup. It was not long into breakfast as the family quietly ate when, to everyone's surprise, Elizabeth suddenly rose to her feet and made a dash towards the back door. Quickly, she opened the door and made an exit, whereupon within just a yard of the door, she promptly proceeded to vomit onto the rose beds. George, still sitting at the table, looked towards Anne in complete surprise, but Anne, however, had already risen to follow her daughter outside, and she was also followed by Martha and Jane.

"Are you alright, girl?" asked Anne, but Elizabeth didn't answer she was too busy heaving to give a reply.

"She was ill this morning before we were all up," said Martha. "I think she has a tummy bug."

Anne stood at the door watching her daughter until it was clear that the sudden bout of illness had all but ceased. She took Elizabeth by the arm and led her back inside the house.

"Are you alright, my girl?" said George.

"No, Father, I feel sick," said Elizabeth. "I think I'll go and lay down for a while."

She left the room and headed back upstairs to the bedroom that she had left not thirty minutes earlier, and laid back down upon her bed.

"I'd better go and pick some rhubarb from the garden," said Anne. "It always helps an upset tummy."

"I hope it's not catching," said Jane. "That's all we need, everyone going down with tummy sickness."

"She'll have that for a day or two, I reckon," said George, lighting up his pipe. "These things always last a day or two."

Anne Lutkin stayed expressionless, a deep feeling of foreboding had come over her, a feeling she didn't want to share with the rest of her family. A mother's intuition maybe, but it was a feeling that she hoped she was wrong about.

Two hours passed, and Elizabeth still lay on her bed. She was occasionally visited by her mother till, eventually, the nausea passed and she finally felt well enough to return downstairs to her family, who by now were busy doing household chores. Anne was kneading dough to make bread in the kitchen. Martha was washing clothes in a large wooden tub filled with warm water and wood ash alkali to remove grease. She was treading on the washing like a winemaker crushing grapes. Jane was busy dusting and sweeping both the inside of the house, and sweeping the outside yard.

"Feeling better now, dear?" asked Anne, as Elizabeth emerged into the kitchen.

"I'm feeling much better now," she replied. "Do you want me to fetch more water for Martha?"

"Yes please," said Anne. "You can lay out the washing in front of the fire when you get back."

Elizabeth set off to the well with the wooden yoke and two pails resting on her shoulders.

The coming days saw Elizabeth in and out of states of nausea, but nothing more than slight sickness. The family shrugged off the illness as nothing more than a stomach bug that could be helped with a dose of rhubarb. Anne Lutkin, however, still had an uneasy feeling about her that all was not as it seemed, though she said nothing to anyone. Eventually, the sickness passed and all was quickly forgotten, tummy bugs were not so uncommon to folk living a rural life.

Chapter Six

The cold short days of December had come, and the countryside looked bare and almost devoid of visible wildlife. No birds sang, just occasional crowing of rooks and crows was heard by day, the hooting of a tawny owl by night, and ghostly shrieks from foxes at dusk was occasionally heard. The sounds of the domesticated farm animals, the crowing of cockerels in the morning, and the sounds of cattle, pigs and sheep would break the winter silence, to resonate in the cold air across the Norfolk fields.

Work on the farm was limited, winter wheat had already been sown and late crops such as swedes and turnips had already been harvested. Only the care of the livestock and the general maintenance of the farm buildings, fence and hedge repairs, were the tasks given to the farm hands. This gave everyone more time on their hands, so workers were given two days off a week instead of the usual one day. Sunday was, of course, taken by everybody, but the farm hands had to take their extra day off in turns, as some staff was still needed for the care of the animals. Edward used his spare day off, a Wednesday, to go on a trip to Norwich to see the sights, and maybe buy some old newspapers and some tobacco for himself and his father. He set off on foot for the six-mile journey to the city on the cold dull December day.

Elizabeth kept herself busy around the farmhouse helping her mother and sisters with housework, and some preparations were being made for the coming Christmas. The Lutkin family were to spend Christmas in the traditional way, church in the morning and resting at home after feasting. With the family's comfortable lifestyle, a few token presents were given to one another, a privilege not known by ordinary working people. Elizabeth had been feeling very tired recently, although this went largely unnoticed by her family. Winter time had a habit of making the body tired after a hard day out in the cold air, only to return home to sit in front of a warm fire and nod off.

George Lutkin continued with his duties of landowner farmer, overseeing his farm business and ensuring his stature was maintained as a pillar of the community of Crostwick. Things, however, were now beginning to develop in George's mind; an idea was being hatched concerning Elizabeth, unbeknown to her. Recently, he had visited a gentleman farmer, landowner, some would say a country squire, from the nearby village of Horsted. His name was Jeremiah Watts, and his wealth and position was all that George had aspired to be. His family had close links with George through his father, William Lutkin. Jeremiah's father, Alfred, had befriended William Lutkin a generation earlier and had given William a mortgage to buy Spring Farm. Though not close friends, George and Jeremiah had stayed acquainted, fully aware of the friendship the two families had once had. In the course of their meeting, Jeremiah happened to mention that his eldest son John had now turned twenty years old and that he would like very much for a young lady suitor to be found for companionship and maybe a view to marriage. Jeremiah Watts had farms and properties far out-sizing anything of George Lutkin, so this was a great opportunity to match or even marry his eldest daughter into a wealth greater than his own. So a suggestion was made to Jeremiah by George that maybe an introduction could be made between the two young people.

"That would be agreeable to me," said Jeremiah, secretly concealing that he already had Elizabeth in mind for the pairing; her being from a family of some wealth, and attractive at that. "Perhaps, you and your good family would care to join us for tea on Saturday, and maybe an introduction can be made."

"Would be an honour and a pleasure, sir," replied George, trying to lose his Norfolk accent, which, though not strong, still carried the reminder of his working past.

"Anne! We've been invited to Jeremiah Watt's house at Horsted," he told his wife on his return home. "The whole family are invited for tea on Saturday, so tell the girls and Richard to make sure they are clean and well turned out for the day. Especially Elizabeth, I want her to meet his eldest son, John. He's now twenty and he'll be looking for a wife soon, they may be a good match together I think."

Elizabeth was told of the invitation the following day at breakfast.

"I don't want to be matched to a complete stranger. I'm not going!" she said angrily.

"You will do as you are told young lady!" said George with equal conviction.

"I don't want to meet him. I'll find a husband myself without anyone's help. How dare you do this to me!"

"If you talk back at me again, you'll feel the back of my hand! Now you're coming with us and that's final girl!" barked George.

Then Anne Lutkin interrupted, to calm down the volatile situation she could see was unfolding.

"All you have to do is come with us for tea at their house. No one is saying or making you do any more than that. Just see it as it is, this family is just visiting the Watts family and having tea with them, that's all."

Elizabeth didn't reply, it was no use anyway, her father had already spoken and she wasn't to disobey him, such were the times.

It was Friday, the day before the pleasant family outing. It was the end of what had been a normal workday, except that on this occasion, Edward and Elizabeth had managed to steal a moment alone together, once again, in the stable when Edward was putting away the cart and bedding down the horse for the night. Elizabeth had entered the stable in much the same way as she did on the occasion of their first passionate embrace, and this time the lovers quickly stole the moment for a passionate kiss. Elizabeth then told Edward of what her father was putting her through. They talked of their own secrets and their own on-going events to come, their desire to meet again at the usual place and make love in the open air of the wooded dell. Then, with a kiss, the lovers parted to continue with the tasks of their daily lives.

***

The following day came, Saturday, the day of the outing to Jeremiah Watt's house at Horsted. It was another cold December day and the first snows of the winter were soon to come. George had given Edward the task of hitching up his four-wheeled chaise to two of his horses and saddling up his own grey mare for riding, while George and family were busy inside dressing in their Sunday best attire. George had given his wig a fresh dusting and had put on his finest green jacket, brown waistcoat and his beige breeches with white stockings. His shirt was white and a black neckerchief was worn between his collars. Anne Lutkin also wore a silver wig, not as tall and grand as the nobility would wear, but a subtle fashionable item displaying a woman of her years and of reasonable wealth. She had a large bustling green dress, and a crimson shawl was draped around her back and arms.

The three girls had put on their best dresses. Elizabeth wore light blue, Martha wore yellow and Jane pale pink. All wore bonnets to match and all, like their mother, were wrapped in crimson shawls to keep out the cold winter air. The younger generation, however, were not in the habit of wearing wigs, these were not fashionable to them. Young Richard Lutkin wore the plainest clothes of the group, opting to wear his usual brown jacket with black waistcoat, green breeches with cream stockings. On his head, he wore a black three cornered hat, his long dark hair tied at the back with a black ribbon.

Then, at last, came the time for the family to depart. Edward had led the horses and carriage to the front of the farmhouse on the drive leading to the gate. He knocked on the front door to announce the arrival of the family's transport. The four ladies came out first and Edward helped them into the carriage, with Anne leading the way and Edward helping her in with a gentle push to her lower back. Then the same for the three young ladies, Martha, then Jane and then Elizabeth; brief eye contact was made but discretion was kept by both. Young Richard mounted one of the two harnessed horses that were to pull the chaise and thus steer the horses. George Lutkin mounted his grey mare. Together, the family set off on their short journey to the large dwelling of Jeremiah Watts at Horsted.

River Manor was the abode of the honourable Jeremiah Watts esquire, it was a large dwelling consisting of the main house and adjoining outhouses of mainly staff dwellings. It was situated by the river Bure just past an old water mill. The main house was rectangular with a large central front door, black in colour, to which the long driveway directly ran, and beyond, running parallel alongside the river. On the rear gable wall, high up above a bedroom window, the builders of the house had built in iron work shaped to the year of its construction, which was 1736. Below the gable wall were separate out-buildings to accommodate the staff, they were L shaped and formed a small separate courtyard, with the cook's kitchen being part of the group but also attached to the main house.

As the guests arrived, waiting at the main front door was Jeremiah, dressed in a grand light blue coat and matching waistcoat with cream breeches and stockings, and a fine silver wig sat upon his head. Behind him stood his wife, Mary, who was equally well dressed in emerald green, adorned with a cream shawl and was also wearing her silver wig. Jeremiah welcomed his guests into his house. "George, my man, how wonderful to see you, welcome to my home!"

George responded by tipping his hat.

"Jeremiah, thank you it's an honour!" he said and the hosts led the guests into the house.

George and his family were brought into the main sitting room which was beautifully decorated in lime green. Tapestries and paintings hung on the walls and grand Georgian furniture adorned the room. Velvet armchairs were positioned around an oval coffee table which was situated in front of a large York stone fireplace with a log fire already burning brightly within it. To the left and to the right of the fireplace sat two elegant couches, both upholstered in crimson red, and able to seat three people on each. The guests were seated and Jeremiah took his favourite armchair in front of the fireplace, George sat facing opposite him from the other end of the oval coffee table.

Mary Watts left the room for a brief moment and then returned with her three children. Her eldest son, John Watts, was twenty years old, tall with brown hair tied at the back. He had a sturdy face with thick cheekbones, he was not handsome, but equally was not ugly either. He had a slim build and wore a fine deep blue jacket, and cream waistcoat and breeches. With him was his sister, Charlotte, she was eighteen, a pretty girl with fair hair under a crimson bonnet and adorning a pink dress. The youngest was their brother, Arthur, who was sixteen, he seemed young looking for his years, also with brown hair like his elder brother John, and was dressed rather much like young Richard Lutkin in brown and green.

Introductions were made with especial attention made to the introduction between Elizabeth and John Watts.

"Please to make your acquaintance," said John with a slight bow.

"Likewise," replied Elizabeth with a slight curtsey, and then the pleasantries began.

A maid brought in a large tray containing tea cups and saucers, a small milk jug, and a hot steaming tea pot, all in beautifully illustrated blue coloured china.

George began the chat with compliments to Jeremiah of how wonderful River Manor was and asked about the size and general running of the farm.

"About two hundred or so acres with ten workers' cottages and thirty workers on the farm, more at harvest time," said Jeremiah. "Maybe you would like to take a walk and see some of the grounds?"

"Yes, I'd like that very much, thank you," replied George.

"Do you ride horses Miss Elizabeth?" asked John Watts.

There was a silence in the room from the two families, hoping for an enthusiastic response from Elizabeth.

"No, I'm afraid I don't," she replied.

"Yes, you do! I've seen you ride," interrupted young Richard Lutkin, who naively put his sister in an embarrassing situation. Martha discreetly kicked Richard in the lower shin.

"Well, I can ride but I prefer not to," said Elizabeth.

"Why is that, may I ask?" said John, puzzled.

"No reason, I just don't like riding horses, that's all."

Jeremiah cut in. "We've got a small buggy you can use if you would like to see the grounds together?"

Elizabeth stuttered. "Well, I…"

Then Martha cut in. "I would love to see the grounds in the buggy, Mr Watts."

This took Jeremiah by surprise, this was not what he had wanted and neither did George, but not wanting to look foolish, he turned to his son.

"Would you like to accompany Miss Martha in the buggy to see the grounds John?"

"Of course, it would be an honour," replied John, ever the gentleman. "I'll just arrange for the buggy to be hitched up." And with that, he left the room.

George Lutkin gave a cold look at both his daughters, this wasn't how it was meant to be. Elizabeth, however, was greatly relieved and thankful that her sister had rescued her from this awkward situation.

"Well, let's all take a short stroll out and see the grounds," said Jeremiah. "We oughtn't to go too far, it's very cold out there today."

After tea, the hosts and the guests rose to make their way outside. Then a member of Jeremiah's staff appeared leading a single horse pulling a small buggy able to seat two young people. John politely helped Martha into the carriage and then climbed aboard himself. With a flick of the reins, the pair set off, Martha tightly wrapped in her shawl to keep out the cold. The rest of the party strolled down the track alongside the river.

Young Richard Lutkin and young Arthur Watts seemed to get on well as the group strolled. Arthur told Richard about how they had netted the river and had caught some large pike and trout, and also of how they occasionally hunted otters with dogs. This fascinated Richard.

Elizabeth talked to Charlotte Watts. The two girls being close of age seemed to get along well, although she thought what a pity that Martha wasn't here, she was sure that Charlotte and Martha would have become good friends, both being of the same warm character, she knew they would have had a lot in common.

The adults talked amongst themselves of farms and land as they walked. Young Jane Lutkin milled around the two groups, almost seeming unsure where she belonged, she had a desired connection to be with the two young ladies of Elizabeth and Charlotte, but also to be with the two youngsters of Richard and Arthur who were nearer to her own age. As the party strolled, they could see in the distance the buggy carrying John Watts and Martha Lutkin heading around the perimeter of a large field on a surrounding dirt track.

"Well, let's be making our way back to the house for a nice hot cup of tea and a warm in front of the fire," Jeremiah suggested.

Everyone agreed.

Thirty minutes later, the buggy carrying Martha and John arrived back at the house, from where the party had already arrived some fifteen minutes earlier and were already seated in front of the fire with hot tea being poured.

"Did you have a nice time, dear?" asked Anne.

"Yes, Mother," replied Martha. "It was delightful. Such a big farm and John was a charming guide."

"Why thank you," he replied slightly blushing. "It was my pleasure too."

This seemed to please the whole group including George.

Another hour passed. The party all seemed to enjoy one another's company, especially the younger members of the group. Sure enough, Elizabeth was right, Martha and Charlotte did get on very well, and were most likely to become friends, however, Elizabeth did keep herself distant from John Watts and always tried to dampen down any conversation that may begin to arise between them both. This didn't go unnoticed between George Lutkin and Jeremiah Watts.

Finally, the time came for the guests to depart.

"Well, we must be going now," said George. "Thank you for your wonderful hospitality. It's been a lovely day, of which I've thoroughly enjoyed. I thank you, Jeremiah and your dear lady wife, and I hope that we can return your kind hospitality by inviting you and your good family over to our place at Spring Farm one day. You'd be made most welcome."

"That's very gracious of you, sir, I'm sure that we'd all love to come, we'll have to make arrangements," replied Jeremiah.

"That we will sir! That we will!" said George, and the Lutkin family rose up and wrapped up for the cold journey home. The two families made their way to the Lutkin's chaise and they all bid their farewells. With a flick of the reins, the Lutkin's set off on their journey back to Spring Farm.

It was late afternoon when the family arrived back at the farm, and there was little daylight left. Edward Allen was still working, whilst also waiting for their return so he could put away the chaise and see to the horses. The chaise pulled up outside the front of the farmhouse, and the family all dismounted and disembarked, then made their way into the house, leaving Edward to do his last job of the day. Inside the house, a heated conversation was about to begin.

"I suppose you think you were being very clever, don't you my girl!" snarled George at Elizabeth.

Elizabeth was shocked, she hadn't expected a verbal attack from her father as soon as they had walked through the door.

"What do you mean?" she replied.

"You could have at least tried to like him; he didn't seem a bad fellow to me."

"I'm sure he is a fine fellow, but I don't want to be paired up by anyone or be made to like him."

This angered George, he wasn't a man who was used to defiance by anyone.

"You'll be here when they come to visit us, and that's an order. And you will try to get along with this lad!" he snarled.

The rest of the family stayed silent, not wanting to be drawn in, including Anne. They stared at George and Elizabeth, wondering what would be said next.

"I'm going outside for some air! It's getting very stale in here," said Elizabeth, and she turned towards the door.

Suddenly, there was a loud smack, as George slapped Elizabeth across her face.

"Don't get clever with me girl!" shouted George. "I'm your father and you'll do as I say!"

Elizabeth ran to the door crying and slammed the door behind her as she left, and ran outside. It was at this point that Anne decided to intervene and grabbed George as he turned to follow her.

"George!" she shouted. "Leave her!"

George stood still in his tracks; the shock of Anne shouting at him had startled him. He took deep breaths as he attempted to regain his composure. By now, Jane and Martha were both in tears. Shaking his head, George lit his pipe and made his way to the fireplace where he began an attempt to light a log fire; he stayed silent. A quiet atmosphere filled the room for the rest of the night.

Edward had just finished putting up the horses and was then leaving the stable. It was near dark and he held a lighted lantern in his hand. Then Elizabeth emerged from the darkness. He gazed towards Elizabeth's face glimmering in the lantern light from the near darkness of the twilight, and he could see that she had been crying. She took the lantern and laid it down on the yard floor, she pulled Edward towards her and the lovers kissed.

"Oh Edward, he's trying to marry me off to a man I neither know nor will ever love."

Edward kissed her again and smiled. "We both know that he'll never be able to do that."

They kissed again and then Elizabeth left to go back to the house before any concern for her absence was raised. Problems had come into their lives that sooner or later would have to be dealt with, but would have to wait till after the coming Christmas celebrations and the New Year. '*May God give us strength*', they had thought, knowing the hurt that could be inflicted upon those close to them.

Chapter Seven

The following day, Monday, was Edward's turn to have his extra day off, which he was to spend the same way as his last, a trip to Norwich to see the sights, and to bring home some extra food from Norwich market for the coming Christmas, only two days away.

His journey to Norwich was a relaxed affair, walking a route through Spixworth and Catton and through the more built up areas of the outskirts of Norwich, eventually passing through the city wall at the Magdalen gate. He browsed along the shop windows looking at the latest goods for sale, and enjoyed taking in the sights of the busy city life all around. The traders at their stalls and shops, and the workers going about their tasks and trades. Horse traffic of carts and coaches, and of course, shoppers and visitors to the city, very much like him.

He took time to look at the cathedral and at the two large gates of Ethelbert and Erpingham which stand outside the great building at Tombland. He had passed the great cathedral many times but had never actually looked that hard at it. He thought that maybe, one day, he would go in to see the great building from the inside.

He turned right, up towards London Street, and passed through to enter Gentleman's Walk and into the market square. It was within the square that he spent most of his time conducting his day's business, only to return back on his journey home some four hours later with a sack laden with food, tobacco and goods strapped across his back. This time, he changed his route home to make a change, leaving through the city wall, again at the Magdalen gate but heading through Sprowston, bypassing Catton before entering Crostwick. The walk seemed long on such a cold winter day, made harder by the weight of his sack, but at last, after a journey of an hour or so he arrived home exhausted, and with only a few hours of daylight left.

The following day arrived, it was Tuesday and it was Christmas Eve. Edward arrived at the farm at dawn, along with his father and brother, James. As usual, Albert Yates stood waiting at the yard to give the men their orders for the day ahead.

"Morning boys," said Albert.

"Morning," they replied.

"Nathaniel, can you start by going to Bill Hapton's with the hand cart and pick up a couple of wheels he's made for the governor's chaise."

"Will do," he replied and made off towards the handcart parked at the rear of the stable. Bill Hapton was the village wheelwright and farrier, and regularly did work for Spring Farm.

"James, can you take out the feed to the cattle and the sheep?"

James nodded and then set off to the hay store.

"Edward, can you check all the fencing around the sheep? Two got out yesterday so there's a hole in there somewhere, I need you to find it and fix it."

Edward was about to reply when he heard footsteps approaching from behind. He turned, and saw it was Billy Yallop and Alf Chapman heading up the drive towards them.

"Mr Yates, could I have a quiet word with you in private sometime today?" he asked, quickly before his workmates arrived, and within earshot.

Albert was taken aback, surprised.

"Why of course lad, is everything alright?"

"Yes, fine," said Edward. "Just a quiet word alone if you get a chance to see me later, if you don't mind."

"I'll come out and see you shortly," said Albert, realizing that whatever Edward had to say, he didn't want anyone else to hear.

The day dragged on, and another hard day's work in the biting cold of winter was endured, but tomorrow was to be Christmas day which was always special, and with just basic work duties to perform. Mainly, it was just the care of the farm animals early in the morning, then to go home to wash and change ready to go to church. This was an event the whole village was to participate in. Later and with the day's work done, the workers set off back home as darkness arrived, not much conversation was had between Edward, James and Nathaniel as they walked, they were all tired, and eager to get home out of the cold to a warm house and a hot meal. Soon, they arrived home. Mary Allen had anticipated their arrival and was in the process of dishing out their food at the table. The three men took off their coats and boots and quickly warmed themselves in front of the fire then sat down at the table to eat their meal of vegetable stew and dumplings. The meal was quickly devoured and the family sat relaxed at the table, Edward and Nathaniel both lit their clay pipes. Then, there came an unexpected announcement from Edward.

"I've got something to tell you all," he said. "Today, I gave my notice at the farm, I'll be leaving there for the New Year."

"You've done what?" said Nathaniel, hardly believing what he was hearing.

"I've quit the farm. I'll be leaving in the New Year to start a new job in Norwich."

"What new job?"

"I'll be working on the mail coaches from Norwich to London. They're paying double what I earn here because they need men like me who can read, drive horses, guard the carriages and also don't mind hard work in all weathers. They'll sometimes need me to work in the mail office too."

Then, Edward delivered the final blow.

"I'll be leaving here and taking a room in Norwich, so I'll be closer to the mail office and the King's Head."

Mary Allen's face reddened and tears started to run down her cheeks, she was horrified at the thought of losing her first-born son. "Do you have to leave? Can't you stay here?" she choked.

"I'm sorry, Mother, but it's time for me to leave and make my own way in life, and this is a chance I can't let go. It's nothing you've done, far from it. It's hard for me to leave you all, but it's my time to go."

"What did Lutkin say when you told him?" asked Nathaniel.

"I told Albert, then he told Lutkin and then Lutkin came out to see me. He was surprised, he didn't know I could read and write, at first, he was angry, saying that I had ideas above myself. But he eventually calmed down and had to accept it. He realised that this was an opportunity that I had to take. He wasn't happy when he left though, but he'll soon find someone to replace me and he knows it. He was never going to pay me what the mail coaches pay."

Nathaniel sat silently staring at Edward until he had said his piece and he had heard everything. He had a stern expression on his face but tried to keep his composure when he eventually gave his opinion on the subject.

"Now I'll tell you this!" he said. "It's not that you're just up and leaving, and upsetting your poor mother that makes me angry, it's the fact that you couldn't even talk to any of us about it. How long have you known you were leaving and when did you get offered this job?"

"I first met the boss at the mail office in September," said Edward. "He offered me a job when he saw me reading a paper in the cart. That time when Lutkin went to the corn exchange, when Bill Comer was ill and I drove the cart. Two weeks ago, I went to the mail office to see him to find out more about the job, how much it paid and if it was still open to me. He told me it was, and he told me what the job was, and how much I would be earning, so we agreed it all then. I've been finding a place to live ever since then and now I've found a place, it's time for me to tell you all about it."

"But why the secrets?" asked Mary.

"Because I didn't know if the job was still there for me and if so, how much it would pay."

Nathaniel let out a deep sigh. "That's still no reason to keep it all secret from us. Look at your mother, can't you see what you've done to her? You should be ashamed of yourself, boy."

"I'm sorry Ma, I didn't mean to upset you but I wasn't even sure that I would be leaving until recently," said Edward, hugging and trying to comfort his distraught mother.

"Well, thas it!" said Nathaniel. "I need a drink."

And with that, he put on his boots and his jacket, and made for the door, slamming it behind him. He headed in the direction of the village inn. The rest of the evening was spent by both Edward and James, the task of consoling their poor mother Mary, who was clearly upset at the future loss of her son from the warmth of her home.

***

The Lutkin household, however, was preparing for a Christmas feast and celebration, they were a relatively wealthy family and were able to make the day special. Dried fruit and nuts were brought to the table and a meal of roast beef and vegetables was planned for Christmas day. George and Anne Lutkin had presents for their children even though this was still not yet common practice for most households of lesser means. The women of the house were all seated but busy with their own individual tasks. Anne Lutkin was knitting a sweater for her eldest son, George. Martha was embroidering a pink rose onto a delicate cotton handkerchief and Elizabeth was reading a book by Daniel Defoe she had borrowed from Charlotte Watts the week before.

The door of the house opened and in entered George Lutkin from the coldness of the outside winter air. Anne smiled to her husband as he took off his hat and coat, and then sat down in his chair to take of his boots.

"Busy day dear?" she asked.

"The usual," came his reply. "However, we did have a hand give notice to leave today, young Edward Allen."

Elizabeth looked up but stayed silent.

"Really?" replied Anne. "And what reasons did he give for leaving?"

"Turns out, he's learned to read and write and he's got a job with the mail coaches. He's going to live in Norwich too. I think the boy's got big ideas above his place, but it's up to him if he wants to go, who am I to stop him?"

Elizabeth still stayed silent and listened with interest to the conversation that was unfolding between her parents. Still pretending to read her book. There was no emotion shown, but there was deep thought working within her mind.

"Never mind," replied Anne. "I'm sure you'll replace him easily enough and I'm sure he'll do well in his new job in Norwich, though it must be a worry for his poor mother."

"I suppose so," replied George.

Anne continued with her knitting, and momentarily, her eyes lifted in the direction of Elizabeth, almost as if to expect some kind of reaction. Elizabeth, however, stayed in a fixed position of hiding behind her book where no reaction could be detected, and there she stayed for the rest of the evening.

Chapter Eight

Christmas had finally arrived. Celebrations would begin with midnight mass on Christmas Eve night, attended only by those not fatigued enough to stay up that late on a winter's night. Then would follow the big day itself, of which for most usually consisted of work early in the morning, then to return home to change for the Christmas service at church, usually held at mid-morning. For this, nearly the whole village attended. Many workers were to have the remainder of the day off, but a chosen few would have to return to see to the livestock. Only the wealthy gave and received Christmas presents, the rest just brought extra food into the house if they could, bringing a welcome relief from the meagre diet they were usually accustomed to in daily life.

Elizabeth and her family were of those luckily enough to have given and received gifts. Elizabeth, Martha and Jane all received new bonnets and shawls. George Lutkin (the younger) and his wife Sarah, received a new table for their cottage on the Grey's Farm estate. Richard Lutkin received a knife with a carved bone handle. Their mother, Anne, had a new dress with matching bonnet, whilst George had a new pipe with a large pouch of tobacco from the children to go with a large keg of ale from Anne. Both George and Anne also received embroidered handkerchiefs from the three girls. After the church service, there was feasting, this was followed by resting, or sleeping off the meal.

At the Allen household, things were not quite as grand. Edward and Nathaniel rose at dawn to do two hours' work at the farm, which was mostly feeding the livestock. Later, they returned home to wash and change ready to go to church for the Christmas service. This they attended, along with James and Mary Allen and most of the village of Crostwick. Thereafter, they returned home for lunch, which consisted of vegetables and a small loin of pork and fat which was bought especially for the occasion, and was washed down with some ale. The meal was consumed with great enjoyment and satisfaction, and two hours were spent after the meal sleeping and digesting. Edward and Nathaniel were the chosen men of this year and so returned to the farm to feed and water the animals and change to fresh bedding where needed. After, they returned home to clean up before settling down in front of the fire to enjoy a cup of ale or two and a pipe of tobacco. The following day, Boxing Day was business as usual for both the workers and the gentry.

***

With Christmas over and then the New Year coming into being, life quickly returned to its harsh normality. Life was a matter of working and living in the bitter cold now that the snows had arrived. Water froze, food froze and farm life became a battle with the elements, only to return home after a day's work in the early darkness of winter. Some relief was had at home in front of the fire in the early evenings, but at night, the houses turned cold once more, and at times, the cold got so intense that even chamber pots would freeze under the beds. The harsh cold living conditions were suffered not only by the poorer working families but by the wealthier families too, whose larger houses could get equally as cold. The only difference was that the poor were nearer to starvation.

Edward had by now left the village to begin his new life working on the mail carriages, which were still running despite the snow which had not yet closed any of the main turnpike roads. He was living in a rented room of a building situated at St George's Church Alley, in the Tombland area of Norwich and within sight of the great Cathedral. The building was shared by four other tenants all with their own room. One room housed two masters from the Norwich School and the three other rooms housed three young families. Edward had managed to secure the smallest and the cheapest room from the building that was available for rent. At the back of the building was a small square courtyard where children played out in the cold air around rubbish and the contents of emptied chamber pots. The smell of the city was not at all like the smell of the farmlands of Crostwick. Hidden in the back yards and alleys of this fine ancient old city was destitution, sickness, and starvation. The smell of wood smoke and human excrement was all around, and the filth of the living conditions together with the waste of the textile factories, the skinners and the dyers all flowed into the River Wensum. Some streets were paved and cobbled whereas others were not. Some of the streets were just of compacted earth with thick tufts of grass growing in the untrodden areas. Along with the snow that lay around the streets, the whole place had become a cold slushy mess. Everyone longed for the end of winter, for the warmth of spring to arrive, just to give relief from the awful living conditions made worse by the cold. This was not only felt in the city but in the rural areas too.

Edward, though not having lived in the city before, was not in the least bit intimidated by the new life that had bestowed him. He was a strong young man both in body and mind, and dealt with every situation put in front of him confidently. He quickly got to grips with his new job on the mail coaches, which at first stayed local, transporting mail and passengers to Yarmouth, and sometimes the smaller market towns within Norfolk such as Fakenham and Aylsham. Of course, his job would include him having to sleep overnight at various coaching inns, but as time wore on and more experience showed, he found himself accompanying the longer distance coaches to Ipswich and London. This often meant several days away from home, sleeping in the inns or sometimes travelling at night. He would visit his family on Sundays if the weather was not too harsh and still make his usual rendezvous with Elizabeth at their secret meeting place in the afternoon.

Weeks passed and the snow cleared. Crocuses and snowdrops began to emerge in the countryside, and in the woodlands. At the farms, the lambs were being born and fields were being fertilised and ploughed ready for seeds to be sown. The winter fodder was now thinning out, though not enough for any concern as spring was clearly just a short time away.

***

"We've been invited to Horsted again by Jeremiah Watts!" said George to his wife Anne.

The Lutkin's had received the Watts family as guests during the Christmas period and a jolly time was had by all. All except for Elizabeth who once again had bore the brunt of an attempt at matchmaking by the heads of each household, then to be out-manoeuvred once again by both Elizabeth and Martha who again invited John Watts for

51

a tour of the grounds, this time at Spring Farm. Elizabeth sat in a chair reading another book she had borrowed from Charlotte Watts, a novel by Henry Fielding. She could overhear the conversation between her parents.

"When are we to go?" asked Anne.

"A week on Saturday," George replied.

Two days passed and it was Sunday again, the usual ritual was performed by all. Parson Nash greeted the parishioners at the door of the church, whereupon sermons were said, prayers were read and a baby girl called Hannah Middleton was publicly baptised. The parishioners then left for their homes and lunch and then the lovers secretly met at Primrose Hole.

Elizabeth explained to Edward that once again her father was planning a match making.

"What day?" he asked.

"Saturday," she replied.

The couple discussed the situation and hatched another plan to outfox George. They then kissed and made love among the snowdrops before departing, having already arranged their next rendezvous.

"Is everything alright with you, Elizabeth?" asked Anne Lutkin, one mid-week morning when the house was all but empty, leaving mother and daughter alone.

"Yes, Mother, I'm fine, why do you ask?"

"You just haven't been yourself lately and you're looking tired all the time. I've never seen you like this before."

"I'm fine, Mother, I've just been a little tired, that's all. It must be that the winter months have been hard on me, nothing more."

"If there's anything you need to tell me, you know you can, I'll always be here to listen and help you. You know that don't you? It's what mothers are for."

Anne stared deeply into her daughter's eyes as if detecting something hidden. Elizabeth's eyes started to glisten as if hiding a deep emotion.

"I'm fine, Mother, no need for you to worry."

Anne squeezed her daughter's hand and then left the room to carry on with her daily chores as a mother and wife. A deep longing was within her urging her to ask more from Elizabeth, but a fear held her back. Her intuition was telling her that events may be coming to Spring Farm.

Saturday arrived and the Lutkin family rose for breakfast. It was their big day out at Horsted with the Watts family, but one family member was missing at the breakfast table.

"Where's Elizabeth?" asked George.

"She's still in bed, she's not feeling well," replied Jane.

"What's wrong with her?"

"She's feeling sick in her tummy, almost throwing up like she was the other week."

This provoked a response from Anne to the situation. "I'll go up and see her," she said, and she hastily made her way upstairs to see her daughter, who was still lying in her bed on her side.

"Are you alright dear? Are you not feeling well?" she asked.

"I feel sick to the stomach and I'm shivering with cold," replied Elizabeth.

Anne put her hand on Elizabeth's forehead. "You haven't got a fever but you are a bit cold."

Suddenly, Elizabeth quickly reached for the chamber pot from beneath her bed and started to heave into it, but nothing came out of her mouth.

"I'll get you some rhubarb preserve. I suppose you'll have to stay at home today," said Anne, whose concern for her daughter's condition was slightly tinged with a suspicion of maybe something else. She returned downstairs. "She's not well, she'll have to stay at home today."

"What! But I was hoping that she would finally get to know young John Watts today," said George. "She'd better not be putting this on," he added sternly.

"No, I think she really is ill, she was heaving over her pot a minute ago, and she's cold and shivering. I'm going to give her some hot tea and some rhubarb preserve on some bread. That should help."

"Hmm!" grunted George, not overly convinced.

After breakfast, the family proceeded to get dressed in their best clothes. An hour later, they were ready, and they climbed into the carriage and George mounted his horse. With a flick of the reins, the family all set off on their journey to Horsted to enjoy another day out with the Watts family.

Once again, the two families had a pleasant day. Martha once again took a ride with John Watts in the buggy around the boundaries of the manor estate. Cards were played, along with other games such as dice and blind man's bluff. Tea and cakes were served, and the younger ones took a stroll out in the garden along the river. Martha and Charlotte Watts were ever increasingly becoming friends, being completely in tune with each other's thoughts and opinions. John Watts was ever the gentleman with Martha and equally enjoyed her company. Richard and Jane played in the garden with Arthur Watts almost like children half their ages. The adults were also enjoying the day, proudly watching their offspring getting on so well. George and Jeremiah talked of farming and land management, and of the old days when they were both young. Anne Lutkin and Mary Watts talked of children and families and gossiped of locals known to them both. After another delightful day between the two families it was time to return back to Crostwick.

"Thank you for another wonderful day," said George to Jeremiah.

"You are very welcome, sir," was his reply and with that, the Lutkin family departed on their journey back home.

After the short journey back to Crostwick, they all arrived back at the farm. Charlie Dawson was working in the yard, and was at once ordered by George to put away the chaise and bed the horse down for the night, which he proceeded to do quickly as night was beginning to fall.

"That's strange," said Anne. "I would have thought there would have been a candle lit and a fire alight. Where's Elizabeth?"

"Maybe she's still upstairs in bed," said Martha. "She could be asleep if she's not well."

"I'll go and see," said Anne, and she made her way up the stairs to the girls' room... The room was empty... Then she checked all the other upstairs rooms... They were empty too... she returned downstairs. "She's not here," she said, clearly concerned as she looked to George. Then, something caught her eye, sitting on the mantle of the fireplace sat a folded piece of paper.

"She's left a note."

Anne made for the fireplace, and grabbed and unfolded the note that had presumably been left by Elizabeth. By now, George had lit a candle and he passed it over to Anne for enough light to read. There was a silence as she read...Then, the colour seemed to drain from Anne's face. She dropped down into a chair. "Oh my God!" she said.

"What is it?" said George, realizing that something serious had happened. She handed the note to him. He read the words:

My Dear Mother and Father,

By now, I am long gone so please do not come looking for me. These past few months I have been seeing a man whose identity I cannot and will not disclose. I love him very much and he loves me, so we are running away together to live as man and wife. This we are doing not only for our love for one another but because I am with child and soon it would have been impossible to conceal.

I am sorry for the pain and hurt that I have now caused you and the family, I didn't mean this to happen but I hope that maybe one day you could feel it in your heart to forgive me.

Please forget me now and don't look for me, it would only cause more pain for everyone. Again, I am truly sorry for what I have done to you and I do love all of you. Elizabeth.

George said nothing, he just laid the note down and made for the front door.

"What is it Mother?" asked Martha.

Anne handed her the note, which she read…

"My God…What are we to do?" she cried.

"I don't know," replied Anne, who was herself now in tears.

Outside, George headed towards the stables where Charlie Dawson was closing the stable door after putting away the horses. "Charlie!" he shouted "Charlie!"

"Yes, sir!" Charlie replied.

"Did you see Elizabeth at all today?" said George.

"Miss Elizabeth?"

"Yes! Miss Elizabeth!" barked George. "Did you see her at any time today?"

"This morning, just after you left, sir," replied a surprised Charlie Dawson. "She was walking towards the gate carrying a sack over her shoulder."

"Which way did she go after she walked through the gate?"

"I think she went right up towards Dobb's Beck, Mr Lutkin, but I can't be sure," he replied, very confused.

George then turned and headed back to the house, saying nothing more. He entered the house to be greeted by a now crying Anne and Martha Lutkin. Richard and Jane had also by now read the note, and were sitting in a stunned silence.

"Well, it looks like she had it all planned out!" snarled George.

"What do you mean?" asked Anne

"She was seen leaving this morning just after we left for Horsted. She was carrying a sack, full of clothes I shouldn't wonder and she headed towards Dobb's Beck. It makes sense, she's cut across country so no one in the village would see her… and her fancy man, whoever he is!"

George was shaking with rage. He sat down, almost falling onto the chair at the head of the table. His elbows rested on the table and he buried his head in his hands.

"Shouldn't we go out and look for her?" asked Martha.

"Now? Out in the dark?" snarled George. "She's had a full day's head start on us. And where do we look? She knew exactly what she was doing and where she was going. She had it all planned, I expect her and her fancy man are tucked away in bed this very moment we speak!"

"George! Don't say that in front of the children!" shouted Anne.

"It's true, isn't it? She's expecting his bastard child and she's known for a while I expect. Yes, she's planned all of it alright."

George then turned towards Anne. "Did you know anything?"

"No, I didn't," replied Anne. "Though I did wonder, the other week when she was sick that morning."

"Morning sickness! Of course, it all makes sense now!" The rage was by now written all over George's face.

"Well, that's it, I'm finished with her, she's no daughter of mine anymore. Bringing shame to my house. I'll kill her bastard of a lover if I ever find out who he is!"

"What are we to tell people?" asked Anne, as she mopped the tears from her eyes with her handkerchief.

"Now hear me well, everyone!" announced George Lutkin. "From now on, if anyone asks about Elizabeth, you're to tell them that she's gone to stay with cousin Edith and her family in Ipswich, and you don't know when she'll return. Have I made myself clear?"

"But George, that's what everybody says when a girl in the family has got into trouble," said Anne.

"Even so, that's what you are to tell them. Have I made myself clear?"

Everyone nodded. "Now there'll be no more talk about Elizabeth in this house anymore, I wouldn't help her if she was starving in the streets. That's what happens when you bring shame upon this family."

A silence fell upon the Lutkin family for the rest of the night. Everyone was in deep thought of the events. There was none more upset than Anne Lutkin, who, under her husband's command, had just lost her eldest daughter. Little sleep was had by all this night.

Meanwhile, Edward and Elizabeth lay together in deep embrace. This was their first night together and their first time making love in a bed, almost as if man and wife. To them, it felt as it should be, with the shackles of Christian morals cast aside, a feeling much as newly married couples experienced on their first night of their newly found freedom. However, the day's events were so life changing for them that little sleep was ever likely to be achieved. Together, they lay wondering what had been said at the farm, especially the reaction to Elizabeth's pregnancy from her father.

It was true what George Lutkin had said, everything had indeed been planned by the lovers. From the moment they knew of the expected child, they had decided to run away. Edward's job offer at the mail office had come luckily only a short while before Elizabeth had fallen pregnant, so Edward had made subsequent trips to Norwich to both secure a job and to find them accommodation. They had, as George had said, arranged to meet that morning of the Horsted excursion at Primrose Hole and Elizabeth had indeed filled a sack full of her clothing, which she carried over her shoulder. They carefully chose their route to Norwich by skirting around the villages and not through, so as to avoid contact with anyone likely to recognise them. No one did.

Now they were together, to start a new life very different from the life they had known. With the love they had for each other and the baby on the way, an exciting time lay ahead, full of wonder of what the challenges of their new adult life would bring.

Chapter Nine

Edward and Elizabeth settled down quickly and well into their new life. Country living and city living were worlds apart but these were two young and determined individuals who were both able to deal with testing situations put in front of them. None more so than the situation they had just been through. Edward continued his work on the mail coaches, often spending two or more nights away on the long distance runs, which was usually to London and back. But sometimes there was work in Norwich if any of the staff from the mail office were absent, or if a man was needed to work on the counter. These times Elizabeth loved, enjoying the welcome company of Edward at home from the otherwise lonely spells without him. She still, however, had to keep a low profile, for fear of being seen by anyone likely to be in contact with her family back in Crostwick.

The days were long while Edward was away. Elizabeth's main problem was boredom, she had made few friends in the area, and mostly spent her lonely days sewing and knitting tiny clothes for the new baby to come. She missed her family dreadfully, especially the female companionship she had enjoyed with her mother and her sisters. She was inevitably growing bigger as the time of the baby's arrival neared, and she began to wonder who she could turn to and what she would do when the big day was finally to come. She hoped Edward would be there if the mail company proprietors would allow him to stay local at the due time.

One morning, just after Edward had left for work to travel a two-day run to London and back, Elizabeth, noticing that water was getting low at home, decided to take a walk down to the local pump at Tombland to fill a pail. At the pump, she found, as usual, that she had to queue behind four other local women, all about the same task and all carrying their own empty buckets ready to fill. She joined the queue and waited for a short moment, when all of a sudden, she heard a voice came from behind...

"That baby of yours is not gonna be long coming, is it?"

Elizabeth turned and immediately she recognised the face of being one of the mothers of the three young families that shared the building in St George's Church alley where she lived. Her name was Catherine Ellis. She was older than Elizabeth, being of twenty-six years of age. She was of medium height, with brown eyes and had a rosy complexion about her face. Her brown knotted hair was mostly covered by a dirty cotton bonnet, and her dress was dirty and worn, but she was not a fiercely ugly person, just plain. She was the mother of three young children and the wife of Chris Ellis, a weaver from one of the city's textile factories. His name, Chris, was short for Christmas, as he was born on Christmas day, and was so named as was the tradition.

"It won't be long, just a few weeks away," replied Elizabeth. "And I'm scared to death."

"I'm sure you'll do just fine," said Catherine. "I've noticed you're often alone all by yerself. Have you sorted who'll be there with you when it comes?"

"Only my husband, Edward, and that's what I'm worried about, he works on the mail coaches and is sometimes away for two or three days. I'm scared that the baby comes while he's away."

"Have you got family? Mother or sisters who can help?"

"No," said Elizabeth. "They live miles away in a small village. I'll have to find a local midwife if I can... Do you know who the local midwife is?"

"I do know her, Rosie Craske, lives up at Ten Bells Lane."

"I'll have to go see her, let her know I'm nearing my time," said Elizabeth.

"Who's gonna fetch her if you're unable to, and all alone. And what if she's already with someone else? She's a very busy woman round ere, you know."

Elizabeth was stuck, she didn't know what to answer. "I, er... I don't know. I hadn't thought of that," she said.

Catherine frowned. "I din't think you had. I can see this is your first baby and you're still very young."

Again, Elizabeth had no answer.

"Look," Catherine continued. "When that baby's ready to come, you call me, I've been through it enough times myself and helped my sisters through it too. You can't go through childbirth on your own, girl."

The pair filled their buckets and headed back to the alley.

"Are you sure you wouldn't mind?" asked Elizabeth. "Because I don't think Edward would know what to do if he was with me alone. I'd prefer a woman with me."

"Of course you want a woman with you. You can't have a man there, they're no good at that sort of thing. Look, maybe it's time for you to get to know Marion and Susan, they're the two other mothers who live in the house, I'm sure you'll get to like 'em."

Elizabeth had seen the two other mothers that Catherine was referring to, she had politely said, "Good morning" to them, but hadn't held any real conversation, or had been formally introduced. With the baby nearing its time, it was wise to make all the friends she could, especially ones living in the same building. They arrived back at their home at the alley and took their water back to their rooms. Shortly after, they met again, in the back courtyard where the children played, and the other mothers were there too.

"Do you know," said Catherine. "I don't even know your name yet. Aren't I the fool."

"It's Elizabeth," she replied, chuckling.

"Well, Elizabeth, I'm Catherine, but everyone calls me Cath for short. This is Susan, and this is Marion."

"Pleased to meet you," said Marion.

"Me too," said Susan.

Marion Webb was a mother of three, with two boys, one aged ten, the other eight, and a four-year-old daughter. She was thirty-two years old, medium height with brown hair and hazel eyes. Her husband was Robert Webb, and he was a bricklayer.

Susan Edwards was twenty-seven, and a mother of two girls, one was seven years old and the other was five. She had blond hair tucked away underneath her bonnet and she had blue eyes. Both women were untidy in appearance and were showing signs of premature ageing. This was common among working families, caused by harsh living.

"This poor girl is due to have her baby at any time and her husband works away on the mail coaches. Her mother lives miles away and she's got no one to be with her when the baby comes."

"Well, you've got us now, my dear," said Susan. "We can't have you going through that alone. If something happens, you'll need help and guidance."

Elizabeth smiled. "I've got some tea inside, do you all fancy a cup?" And with that, the group, having accepted Elizabeth's invitation, came inside to cement their new friendship. A great weight had been lifted from Elizabeth's mind as to who would support her on the arrival of her first-born child. She had always supposed her mother and sisters would be there for her one day, but clearly, circumstances had now made that impossible.

Tea was a luxury item, but Edward and Elizabeth had treated themselves to some for special occasions, the celebration of the birth of their new child being what they originally had in mind. Elizabeth knew that with the voluntary help from the neighbours, Edward would not have minded. Some tea was a small price to pay for such a kind and helpful gesture. The four women sipped their tea, and talked of their own lives and families.

"What's your full name Elizabeth?" asked Marion, she was of course referring to her surname.

"Elizabeth Allen," was Elizabeth's reply, but she was careful not to tell of the true circumstances of her being there. To them, she was a married woman.

She had never heard her name said with Edward's surname before. *'Elizabeth Allen, I like the sound of that'*, she thought quietly.

From that moment, life for Elizabeth ceased to be so lonely. She had made friends with her neighbours and now she had companionship while Edward was away. She would often help the mothers to look after the children, giving her valuable lessons in childcare. Edward was delighted that she had made friends so close to home and soon got to know the families in question for himself. Sometimes, on warm summer evenings, while the children played in the courtyard, the men, namely Edward, Chris Ellis, Robert Webb and Joseph Edwards, would sit out in the yard, and enjoy a smoke and a chat in the evening sunshine. Sometimes sharing a jug of ale bought from the local alehouse.

Time drew closer for the birth of the new baby, and Edward had explained his situation at the mail office, where it was agreed by the manager, William Burrell, that Edward was to be kept working local, either driving on the Yarmouth run or working in the mail office until the baby had arrived. Then, two days into August, Edward was working at the counter of the mail office at Bedford Street, when just before lunch, entered a small boy of about ten years old. Edward immediately recognised the boy as being Billy Webb, the eldest son of Robert and Marion Webb.

"Hello Billy," said Edward, knowing why Billy had come.

"Ma'am told me to tell you to come home quickly, the baby's coming!"

Without hesitation, Edward called out to Mr Burrell, who responded immediately. "Mr Burrell, this young man has just come with a message for me to come home at once, the baby's on its way."

William Burrell smiled. "Then you had better make haste and get home quickly, my man, I'll take over at the counter, and good luck Edward, I hope it all goes well for you."

"Thank you, Mr Burrell, you've been so kind," said Edward, and with that, he and young Billy Webb dashed out of the office to head back home to the alley in Tombland.

On their arrival Marion Webb stood outside the entrance to Edward and Elizabeth's room waiting.

"How is she, can I go in?" Edward asked.

"She's fine, she's doing well. Catherine and Susan are inside with her. She's in good hands, we've all been through it before. Just let nature take its course."

Marion was of course attempting to reassure Edward, but was equally aware that childbirth was a dangerous affair, for both mother and baby. Edward could hear the cries of distress coming from Elizabeth from behind the door.

"Can I go in?" he asked.

"I don't see why not," Marion replied. "I'm sure she'd love to see you for a moment, if not to give her strength."

Edward entered the room. Elizabeth was on the bed, in obvious pain and discomfort, and sweat was pouring from her face.

"I'm here, my love," he said, and sat beside her and held her hand. Elizabeth didn't answer, she had other things to deal with, but she nodded in acknowledgement of her lovers return. Together, hand in hand they sat as the discomfort troubled Elizabeth more and her contractions became more frequent.

"It's getting close now, my dear," said Catherine Ellis. "You'll soon feel the need to push."

Edward looked towards Catherine. "Shall I leave the room now?" he asked.

"Just leave it to us. We'll call you when it's all over," said Catherine, as she ushered Edward to the door.

Edward sat outside the room on a chair, smoking his clay pipe and listening to whatever sounds were coming from within. Occasionally, he paced up and down, not knowing what to do next. Marion was in the combined duties of observation inside the room and keeping Edward informed of any events occurring. But as time wore on, Elizabeth began screaming and straining as she began to push harder, Edward could easily hear from behind the door. She screamed, more and more, and Edward at this point became anxious. Suddenly, there came the unmistakable cry of a baby, it was all over.

More time passed as the placenta was expelled and the umbilical cord was cut. Mother and baby were cleaned up ready for presentation for Edward, who was by now pacing up and down eager to see Elizabeth and his new child, and to know that they were both alive and well. The door opened and Marion looked out.

"You can come in now Edward," she said smiling.

Edward entered the room to the sight of Elizabeth looking exhausted but cradling her new-born baby in her arms. She smiled at Edward. "This is our son," she said and she held him forward to face his father.

A tear ran down the side of Edward's face as he gazed down towards his new-born son for the first time. He was wrapped in a woollen blanket his mother had knitted especially for the occasion of his arrival. Elizabeth handed their baby over to him; his tiny eyes were open and he was looking all around as he experienced light for the first time. His mouth opened and closed and he occasionally popped his tongue in and out, and little sounds of whimpers came from him as he drew in his first breaths. His tiny hands were opening and closing as if grasping some imaginary item. On his tiny hands, Edward could see the minutest finger nails on the end of the tiniest fingers. His hair was still wet and so looked dark, time would tell his hair colour when it dried. He was the most beautiful thing that his father had ever set eyes upon. More tears rolled down his face. "Hello my son," he said quietly and proudly. "Jacob," he said. This name had already been agreed by Edward and Elizabeth some weeks earlier.

Edward then carried the new-born infant back to his mother and placed him back in his mother's arms. In the background, tears glistened in the eyes of Catherine, Marion and Susan who, had been such a rock of strength and help for Elizabeth. They quietly left the room for the couple to enjoy their moment together. Edward sat down beside his love and their child, he put his arm around Elizabeth and kissed her on her cheek.

"Our son, he's beautiful," he said.

Elizabeth, with tears running down her face, kissed her new baby and pulled him to her breast; the baby immediately began to suckle. Cradling her new-born, the mother and baby bond of love was made, and was never to be broken.

***

On the 24th August 1777, a baby named Jacob was baptised at St George's Church Tombland, Norwich. Son of Edward and Elizabeth Allen, and was entered in the church records.

Chapter Ten

Jacob grows bigger and stronger day by day, with the care and love from Elizabeth, who has taken naturally to motherhood. Edward works harder and longer to fulfil his responsibility as provider for his family. Some six months after Jacob's arrival, the young family have moved into larger dwellings within the same building block at Tombland. They live within a three-room apartment with a larger kitchen parlour, and with two separate bedrooms. This apartment was previously occupied by two masters at the Norwich school, situated close to the cathedral. They had been allocated living quarters within the school grounds and, therefore, no longer needed to rent their rooms. This suited Edward and Elizabeth much better, and the lodgings, though higher in rent, were still affordable to Edward. Literacy and hard work had its advantages, and better wages was one of them.

***

It was late February 1778, on a cloudy but mild Thursday for the time of year. Edward was busy working on the coaches doing the London run and was likely to be away for a couple of days or more. Elizabeth was keeping home as usual in his absence. She was now weaning the baby onto solid food, feeding him mashed potato or mashed turnips or swedes whenever he was willing. On this day, she happened to notice that potatoes were getting in short supply, so a visit to the market was needed to restock the potatoes, as well as other goods. So she set off to Norwich market, not a quarter mile walk away from their home, her baby strapped to her chest within the top section of her apron, wrapped warm within her shawl and a basket hanging from her arm. After five or six minutes' walk she arrived amidst the hustle and bustle of the city shops and stalls. She strolled around, not buying much, she already knew what she needed and where to get it, but she just browsed anyway, taking in the sights and looking at what the stalls had to sell. Maybe she would buy something nice on a later trip if anything took her fancy. She made for the stalls she knew so well where she would buy the food items she had come for, potatoes and a cabbage from one stall, and a shinbone from a bullock on another. The shinbone was full of marrow, and a small amount of meat was still left on it. *'Ideal for a stew'*, she thought.

After purchasing her goods, she then made for the outer edge of the market to head home, exiting from the right side at Guildhall Hill to head down towards London Street, just at the bottom of the hill. As she left the last stall to make the journey home, something caught her eye from across the road, outside the Guildhall itself, a person was standing and staring at her. It was a woman instantly recognisable, and who she had not seen for over a year… her own mother, Anne Lutkin.

She was alone, just standing and staring at the daughter she had lost, not knowing what to do or how to react. She longed to run over to Elizabeth and embrace her, but dare not.

Elizabeth stood shocked, also not knowing what to do. She looked around for her father, who she expected to be accompanying her mother, but he was nowhere to be seen. The pair, both mother and daughter stood motionless, staring as if waiting for something to happen... then finally Elizabeth seized the initiative and crossed the gravel road to stand face to face with her mother... trembling.

"Are you alone?" she asked.

"Your father's in the corn hall, and will probably go to an alehouse afterwards. He's with Billy Yallop, he's driving the cart... My girl, come here, I've missed you so much!"

Anne pulled Elizabeth to her, and the pair embraced, tears running down both their faces.

"Come, girl, let's get out of sight," said her mother.

They made for the other side of the market where there was situated an alleyway leading to an area known as the Haymarket, next to the large church of St Peter Mancroft. They were out of sight from the traders and the shoppers, but most importantly, well out of sight from where George Lutkin and Billy Yallop were conducting their business in the corner of the square. Anne looked down at the baby strapped to his mother's chest.

"This is your grandson," said Elizabeth. "His name is Jacob."

Anne gazed in delight at the sight of her first-born grandchild, and the baby gazed back as if in wonder of who this stranger was.

"He's beautiful," she said, her eyes glistening with tears. She kissed his head and gently held his tiny hand with her forefinger and thumb. "Same colour hair as you, Elizabeth," she said, as she studied the child before her.

Elizabeth smiled with pride.

"So," said Anne. "Are you well?"

"I'm well, we're not starving, and as you can see the baby's in good health. His father works hard and provides for us, so we're doing well enough, there's no need for you to worry."

"Do you want to tell me who the father is now?" asked Anne hesitantly.

"I'm sorry Mother, I can't do that, there have been enough tears and I don't want to cause anymore."

Anne Lutkin gave an understanding nod.

"How are the family?"

"Well," replied Anne. "Your brother, George and Sarah are expecting their first child in May."

"Oh that's wonderful," said Elizabeth, smiling with joy.

"And your sister Martha is about to announce her engagement to John Watts from Horsted."

Elizabeth was almost speechless with delight.

"It's true, they seemed to get on very well when they first met on those buggy rides around the grounds that you were meant to go on. They started to court one another soon after you left. That pleased your father I can tell you. Mind you, that Albert Nobbs from the village inn was not pleased. He'd hoped to marry her someday."

"I'm so pleased for her," said Elizabeth... Another tear ran down her face... "I do miss you all very much you know... I'm so sorry."

Anne hugged her daughter. "My child, I've missed you terribly. My heart was broken thinking that I may never see you again."

After a brief period of tears and hugs, Elizabeth composed herself.

"How was father when he read the letter?"

"As you would expect, he was furious, and now we're not to even mention you in the house. He told everyone that you had gone away to stay with relations."

"Just like him," she said. "Richard and Jane, are they well?"

"Still the same, just growing quickly. Jane's looking more like a woman every day."

Anne momentarily stared and smiled at baby Jacob… "You know, he's got his father's eyes."

Elizabeth was taken aback. "You know who his father is?" she asked, in disbelief.

"Of course I do," replied Anne. "I had my suspicion that you were pregnant before you wrote that note, and I had worked out who the father was too. It was all very convenient that Edward had left Crostwick to get a new job and lodgings elsewhere, just a short while before you left that shock on our doorstep. It is Edward Allen, isn't it? I can see his eyes in the baby. He is the father, isn't he?"

Elizabeth paused for a moment and thought very carefully of her reply…

"If father was ever to think that Edward was the father of this child, he would turn Nathaniel Allen and all his family out from their cottage, and he would dismiss both Nathaniel and James Allen from the farm. The whole family would probably end up in the workhouse, and they are all innocent. He must never know who the true father of my child is."

"Well, my girl, he must never know then. If I am correct and you are living here in Norwich with Edward, then sooner or later, you're going to be seen by someone from the village, and word will soon get out. So what I'll tell him, if heaven's above word does get to him, is that the child's real father left and abandoned both you and the child, leaving you both in destitution. Later, while on your way to the workhouse in Norwich, you happened to stumble across Edward, who lives and works here in the area. He takes pity on you and takes you both in, where he soon falls in love with you, and you with him. So you marry and live together as a family… That story should do the trick I think," said Anne, with a smug smile.

"You would do that; you would tell him that?" said Elizabeth.

"I would. There's no need for innocent people to be caught up in this, and be turned out of their home. Let's hope it never comes to that and your father never gets to know."

Elizabeth hugged her mother. She had always feared the consequences that could have been inflicted upon Edward's family should they ever be discovered. A great weight had been lifted from her.

Both mother and daughter talked for another hour of times gone and of the life and events that were happening in Crostwick. They were rebonding from times lost, a world apart from the life that Elizabeth was now living, but one that she still missed none the less.

"I had better get back to the cart," said Anne. "Billy Yallop's driving it and your father will soon be coming out of the alehouse I expect."

Elizabeth embraced her mother once more.

"If you ever need to get a message to me, leave a letter for me at the mail office or the King's Head where Edward works."

Anne nodded and kissed her daughter and grandson, then she departed back towards the Guildhall while Elizabeth and Jacob headed in the opposite direction towards the far end of the market square to avoid a worse for wear George Lutkin. As both Anne and Elizabeth walked away, they turned and looked to one another for one last glimpse of each other, never knowing if it may be the last time they were ever to see one another again.

Elizabeth made her way home, carefully avoiding the alehouses in the area of the corn exchange. She strolled home beside the castle mound, she passed the Shire hall to King Street which met Tombland at its end. Two days later, Edward returned home and was immediately informed of the events that had unfolded, to his relief also. In the due course of time, there were indeed letters for Elizabeth by her mother left at the mail office, informing her of any family news that may have arisen.

Elizabeth's elder brother, George and his wife, Sarah, did indeed have their first baby, a girl they named Anne after her grandmother. A year later, a wedding between Martha Lutkin and John Watts was held at St Peter's Church Crostwick, thus uniting the two families as both George Lutkin and Jeremiah Watts had so wished. Still there was no mention of Elizabeth allowed in the Lutkin household; a rule strictly enforced by George himself. Anne, however, kept her secret from him.

Chapter Eleven

It is Saturday July 23rd 1785, Edward and Elizabeth, and their seven-year-old son, Jacob, are enjoying a family day out in Norwich to witness an event in the city. Seven and a half years have passed since Jacob's birth, and he is still Edward and Elizabeth's only child. Since his birth the couple have tragically lost three siblings to their son. A year after Jacob's arrival, Elizabeth gave birth to a stillborn daughter who was to be named Martha after Elizabeth's sister. Two years later, a baby boy they named Thomas was born eight weeks premature. Survival of premature babies in these times was very uncommon and sadly, Thomas didn't make it. On a warm spring night in 1783, Elizabeth, now on her fourth pregnancy, miscarried a baby girl and she has not fallen pregnant since. The family, though deeply saddened by the dreadful events, carry on with their lives regardless and are in fact enjoying life as a small family. In these times of high mortality, and living for the moment and enjoying the time given is the only option.

So, on this day of July 23rd 1785, Edward, Elizabeth and young Jacob are in a busy Norwich, standing among a large crowd eagerly waiting for the major event of the day, to view a gas balloon that is due to fly high in the air above the city whilst carrying men on board. It was just a few weeks earlier on June 1st that another manned balloon flight had taken place in Norwich, the first in the city's recorded history. James Decker flew from Norwich at Quantrill's gardens, though the balloon sustained slight damage upon take-off, it still managed to fly a distance of ten miles, and flew over a thunderstorm in the process. Eventually, Decker's balloon came down to land just a short distance from the small market town of Loddon within the county. Many people witnessed the take-off and the flight until the balloon disappeared into the clouds of the oncoming storm. But many missed the flight as it was held on a midweek working day, so, on this occasion, the flight was held on a Saturday to accommodate a larger public viewing. Consequently, a very large crowd had gathered around the surrounding area of the same gardens to witness the event.

Three men were due to ascend in the balloon that afternoon. The owner of the balloon, Mr Lockwood, his friend, Mr Blake and Major John Money who was a local man from the village of Trowse, situated just outside the south-east of Norwich. Major Money was an adventurer, an army man of early middle age. He was also a wealthy landowner, living in a large country manor, and he managed a large farm within his estate. All three had flown before in the same balloon a month earlier in London, but on this occasion, they had brought their balloon to Norwich to raise money for the still relatively new Norfolk and Norwich hospital, as this was a charity close to the Major's heart, with him being a local man and all.

Crowds watched from any vantage point they could muster, walls, trees, rooftops and windows, but most, however, were blissfully unaware that the crew were experiencing problems trying to inflate the balloon. They had found it could not be sufficiently inflated with the hydrogen gas and air enough to take the weight of all three of them. With the dilemma of abandoning the flight altogether and therefore forfeiting any money raised for the charity. It was decided that Major Money would take the balloon up solo and fly a short distance to the outskirts of the city, and to land in a convenient field wherever possible. The balloon did, however, appear fully inflated to the gathered crowd who were none the wiser to the problems. Inflated, the balloon had grown to a height of about twenty-five feet which made it clearly visible to the surrounding crowd. It was white in colour with four red stripes running horizontally across it. Its outer membrane was made of silk and was sealed with an elasticated gum to make it air tight. It had a net draped over the top and rope supports hung down from the net through an iron hoop called the basket ring, which then attached to the boat or carriage below. This was made of light soft wood and was gondola shaped. Major Money, being an army man, was in full uniform, silver wig, black hat and long red army coat, and was easily seen from a distance by the spectators.

At twenty-five minutes past four in the afternoon, the balloon was released, but only being partly inflated it struggled to lift the weight of the Major who was by no means a small man. However, the balloon did slowly lift, and drifted towards a tree, where in turn got entangled. The Major promptly disentangled the balloon and released some ballast bags; he then threw off his large red coat which also contained small ballast bags in his pockets. This caused the balloon to raise clear from any obstacles, rising gracefully above the west end of Quantrill's gardens. Outside the gardens were crowds of people who could ill afford the entrance fee to be within the immediate vicinity of the balloon's ascent. Amongst them were Edward, Elizabeth and young Jacob. Edward lifted his son onto his shoulders to give him a better view while the crowd cheered as the balloon came into their view for the first time.

As the balloon rose higher, it caught a wind currant, changing its direction back towards its original starting point at the west end of the gardens, and giving the crowd within a wonderful view once more. Major Money waved down at them, and they in return waved and cheered back to him as the balloon then headed in a north-easterly direction.

Higher and higher it slowly rose, until it entered clouds for the first time, occasionally re-emerging to full view in the cloud breaks. Money looked below to view his hometown and the surrounding landscape as he had never seen it before. As expected, the cathedral and the castle were the most visible though never seen from that angle. He was able to identify other smaller buildings and streets around the city by using the two great buildings as points of reference. He could see for miles across the landscape, looking down as he worked out what villages lay beneath him in the surrounding countryside. He saw windmills dotted around the countryside surrounding the city, and square grids of beige wheat fields, and green grass meadows which were in turn grazed by tiny figures of livestock.

The balloon drifted over Wittlingham, and Money could clearly see his own house below, Crown Point, in the neighbouring village of Trowse. It was at this point that he decided to deflate the balloon to descend back to land, as this was only meant to be a short demonstration excursion and needed to land fairly close to the city for the balloon's easy retrieval. He tugged at the chord which was attached to a valve at the top of the balloon and was designed to release the gas. Money then found to his dismay that the valve had held tight. The sun's rays in the cloud clearings had caused the balloon to expand and thus tightened the valve outlet. He became frustrated and anxious and he made repeated attempts to open the valve, but to no avail. Shortly after, he drifted over nearby Surlingham and could see people below him in the neighbouring village of Kirby Bedon. Two residents had strong telescopes trained on the balloon to observe him and they called to him using cylindrical loud hailers, or speaking trumpets as they were so called. Money responded to their calls by waving a bright yellow flag back at them. He could hear their calls but could not make out what they were trying to say, but he felt, however, that he should respond to their calls nonetheless as it was the polite thing to do. From Surlingham, the wind took the balloon eastwards towards Yarmouth, and the sea.

It was obvious to him that being situated on the top of the balloon, the valve was clearly unreachable. His only option left was to keep pulling as hard as he could on the chord, and hope that it would eventually free itself and release the gas. So, using all his strength, he continued to pull hard on the valve chord. He checked down below to work out his position and could see the Burgh Flats beneath him. The Flats were a large expanse of marshland situated between Acle and Yarmouth, and was easy to identify. To him, the land below seemed to be getting closer and he mistakenly thought he was finally descending, until he reached another patch of clouds of which he had thought were above him, only to find they were in fact beneath him. To deal with this problem, Money had earlier on preparation made a device of his own invention fixed to the balloon carriage, and was now to be tested for the first time. Thin pieces of linen, a foot long, were tied to a wire hoop of about three feet in diameter, light enough to rise above the hoop when the balloon was descending, but stay hanging when ascending. The device was to be attached to a pole set up to overhang the balloon carriage. Now was a good time for Money to test his theory. After securing his invention, he could see the linen strips were still hanging, indicating the balloon was unfortunately still rising.

At this point, Money decided to try and cut an opening into the side of the balloon, thinking that pressure could be released and thus deflate the balloon sufficiently for descent. So, using his knife, he made a small cut to release the gas. He then again checked the pieces of linen hanging from the hoop. It was no use the balloon was still rising. Just heavier air from the bottom of the balloon had escaped and not the lighter hydrogen gas that was still causing him to rise. His cut was clearly not high enough, and far from air whooshing out, the cut just seemed to hiss a little, and stayed fairly well closed. His only option left was to continue to pull with all his might on the valve chord and hope it would eventually pull free from the top.

It was half past five when the balloon reached the east coast and Money had surmised that in the event of the balloon reaching the coast, he would ditch the balloon in the water as soon as possible as there was likely to be more sea traffic hugging the coastline, giving more chance to be rescued. He could see ships and small boats sailing down below, one in particular caught his eye, a ship that seemed to be following his very direction, as if chasing him. He hoped this was the case, making rescue a possibility. Again, he pulled harder and harder on the chord using both hands, pulling with all his might. After some time, he put his ear up against the balloon to hear if any air may be escaping... Then... to his great relief, he could definitely hear the unmistakable whooshing sound of air escaping, the valve had opened. It was now late afternoon and with the sun being less so intense, along with the cloud cover, the balloon had cooled enough for the valve to finally loosen. He looked over to the wire hoop and saw that the linen was rising above the hoop indicating a descent. At last, he knew that he was heading downwards.

As the balloon descended more and more, Money quickly took out his pocket watch and put it in his top pocket of his uniform jacket which had a button attached, to protect it should he have to enter the water. As he did this, he checked the time, it was close to six o clock. Moments later, the balloon hit the surface of the sea... At first, it rebounded off the waves and was then dragged by the wind a distance of about forty feet until it finally rested stationary in the water. The boat, or carriage, that had housed him, was tipped and had begun to let in water at one end. Money quickly stood on the edge of the boat at the opposite end to even up the weight.

With the balloon still inflated and floating, he knew that his best chance of survival was to stay with it and try to ensure that the balloon didn't leak. Unfortunately, it did leak, at the point where he had made the cut earlier to let out the gas, in his attempt to help him to descend. To combat this, Money was able to stand on the attachment ropes to reach the cut opening, and was able to pin the cut together using pinned badges from his uniform jacket. It still leaked but thankfully slowly. Two hours passed and water continued slowly leaking into the carriage, which was not designed to repel water, it was now up to the Major knees. He could see the coast of England in the distance and some boats sailing around the coast. He called to them, but to no avail; they were all well out of earshot. Darkness would soon be approaching, and Money, already fearful of his life, was not relishing a night in the water.

Suddenly, in the twilight just before darkness fell, a large wave hit both the balloon and carriage, and flattened the lower end of the balloon, swamping it with water and causing it to drag the carriage down with it. He quickly grabbed the swamped end of the balloon and stood up on the edge of the carriage and the lent back, pulling with all his might. As the canvas lifted, the water that had swamped the lower end of the balloon then began to run off back into the sea, saving the carriage from sinking.

Darkness came and Money's worst fears seemed to be coming true, no vessel was likely to rescue him in the darkness. There had been a glimmer of hope earlier, when just before the balloon's descent, he had spotted a ship in the distance that seemed to be following him, but now it was dark, he feared the ship must have given up as it was much harder to be found in the vastness of the sea with no light to mark his position. Equally, there was no response from the ships seen in the distance hugging the coastline, he had called out to them in hope but they were much too far away to hear anything. He still fought to nip shut the cut in the balloon that he had made and pinned back together. It was still leaking, so prolonging the balloon's floatation until daylight was his best chance.

Eventually, the sky finally cleared of cloud, exposing a near full moon which illuminated the surrounding sea, outlining a silhouette of the balloon that could be clearly seen for miles. "Maybe I'll be seen at last," he told himself, ever hopeful of rescue. But alas, more hours passed. By now, he was getting exhausted, still holding together the cut he had made in the canvas. It was now a full five hours that Money had been in the water, and some time since he had seen any passing boats in the distance. Cold and fatigued, he was beginning to think the worst was more likely to happen to him.

Then… suddenly… a light caught his eye. He hadn't seen it earlier as it had approached from behind him. He called to it… "Helloooh!" he shouted… Then… to his great relief, there was an answer.

"Yoh! Hello there! How many are there of you?"

Money could hardly answer he was so overcome with joy and relief, but an answer did come.

"Just me, I'm alone!" he called.

The ship anchored close by and sent a small manned boat alongside to bring him aboard. They attached a rope to the balloon and carriage which was still surprisingly undamaged, apart from the cut that Money had made on the side. The ship then proceeded to tow the balloon on its journey back to dry land.

The vessel that had saved him proved to be The Argus, a revenue cutter from Harwich that was on the lookout for smugglers. Its commander was one Captain

William Haggis and he had been chasing the balloon for some time. It was clearly the same ship that Money had seen earlier on his descent but had thought had given up the chase. In fact, the cutter had chased the balloon long before darkness had fallen. It had turned out that they knew that it was a balloon that they had spotted and they also knew that it had landed in the water. Studying it through the captain's telescope, it was thought that the balloon and carriage was empty and so, no urgency to recover the balloon was made, otherwise, Money would have been rescued some hours earlier.

Greatly fatigued and near exhaustion, Major John Money was taken to the captain's quarters where he quickly took of his wet clothes and went straight to bed. After what had been one of the longest nights of his life, he slept soundly. While he slept, the crew on the Argus dried his clothes ready for his journey home the following day.

According to the captain's log, the Argus had picked up Major Money at a bearing of west by north, eighteen miles off Southwould, on the Suffolk coast. He was taken back to the port of Lowestoft, where the Argus arrived at about eight in the morning. From there, he hired a chaise back to Norwich and to his house at Crown Point in Trowse. There, his arrival was greeted with great pleasure and relief by his family and friends who by now had feared the worse.

Word of his adventure and eventual rescue to safety soon circulated around Norwich, eventually, even reaching Edward, Elizabeth and young Jacob Allen who had been among the crowd in the streets cheering and waving to Money as he ascended on his epic adventure. Edward Rigby, reporter of the Norwich Gazette and Norfolk Chronicle wrote a fully detailed article on the Majors' journey, and paid tribute to his courage and heroism. He was certainly a hero of Norfolk and especially Norwich and he was to be recorded in the history books as a great adventurer of these pioneering times of the earliest aviation.

Chapter Twelve
Jacob's Story

We often reflect back at our lives and recall our fondest memories from our earliest years, when life seemed so uncomplicated and every issue was simple black or white. Fond memories of playtime and laughter with family, and the comfort of a mother's cuddle when things seem so bad. A problem remedied with a simple call for help to one's parents, who would always be there and thus become a problem no more. Memories of when the sun always seemed to shine in the summer months and crisp white snow lay in the winter ready for play. For young Jacob Allen, these were such times. His earliest memories were now forming; memories of the love and affection from his mother and father. Times of playing in the yard with other children at the dwelling where he lived, and the memory of the day he witnessed a huge balloon carrying a man, soaring high into the sky while a large crowd cheered as he sat on his father's shoulders. He is now nine years old, bigger, and now more adventurous enough to leave the protection of his mother, and to play out onto the streets and alleyways of the city with his young friends. To experience for the first time, the reality of the outside world, albeit still under the shadow of the great cathedral, just a couple of hundred yards or so from the dwelling place he calls home.

His parents, Edward and Elizabeth, like so many parents, have striven to give their only child the best they can within their own resources. They have taught the little one as much as necessary to give him all the advantages needed for survival, including reading and writing, deemed most important to both parents. Elizabeth is teaching the boy while Edward is away at work, and thus following a family tradition that was also strictly enforced by her own mother, Ann Lutkin. As for Edward, no one knew more than him the advantages there were to be gained from being literate. The very skill he had learned from Elizabeth and had enabled him to break free from the shackles of his own family tradition of farm labouring and giving him a taken opportunity to take a higher paid job working on the mail coaches.

Both Edward and Elizabeth have dreamed that if possible, their own son could break through the social barriers of the times, and maybe in the future, become a clerk, a doctor or a lawyer. This, however, was unlikely as these were not times of social equality, and though his literacy was still likely to be an advantage among the poorer classes, it was still more probable he would be kept in working class life. Only rarely did the working classes make the upward leap into the realms of the wealthier classes. Of course, Jacob's great grandfather, William Lutkin, was one of those rare exceptions to the rule. He had managed to befriend local landowner and country gentleman, Alfred Watts, who in turn loaned him enough money in the form of a mortgage. Enough money to purchase his farm and begin his transition towards a higher social standing.

So, Elizabeth set about the task of teaching her son to read and write from an early age. Despite protests and an unwillingness that are often found in little boys who are more interested in playing than learning their ABCs, perseverance did prevail and young Jacob began well on his way to a basic education. Yes, these were happy times for Jacob, and Edward and Elizabeth, who were proudly watching, doting and enjoying the presence of their only child.

***

One morning in mid-July, as Edward was preparing to make his way to work at the Kings Head ready to embark on another two or three-day excursion to London and back, a question came to him unexpectedly from his son.

"Could I come and ride with you on the mail coach?" he asked.

Edward stopped and looked to Elizabeth, who was busy in the process of preparing Edward's packed lunch for the journey. A potato, some bread with cheese and a small bottle of cider.

"I'm sorry, but your father's going to be away for two, maybe three days, that's far too long for you to be away. Maybe when you're a bit bigger you can go."

"Maybe," said Edward, smiling with pride at his son. "Maybe one day you can come with me on a run to Yarmouth. It would be a long day, but at least you'd be home at the end of the day to sleep in your own bed."

Elizabeth looked to Edward. "Would they let you do that?"

"I think so; we've had children on the top before. Mr Burrell's grandson, Tommy, came with us once and Richard Moore's son, Robert. I'll ask Mr Burrell if it's allowed."

Edward then kissed his family goodbye and then set off for another journey away.

Two weeks passed since that morning conversation when Edward left for the London run, which did indeed last two and a half days. In fact, within those two weeks, Edward made three London runs, two Yarmouth runs and two Fakenham runs, and back.

"Is he still asking about coming on the coach with me?" asked Edward one evening as his son slept.

"No," Elizabeth replied. "I think he's forgotten all about it, he hasn't said anything."

"Pity," said Edward. "I've got a Yarmouth run the day after tomorrow and Burrell said it would be alright for Jacob to ride on top. He can come along if he likes."

Elizabeth smiled. "I'll ask him tomorrow, I know he would love to go with you, but promise me you'll keep him safe for me."

"He'll be fine as long as he sits tight, which I'll make him do. He'll be up top with me and Tom Elmham, there should be enough room."

The following morning, Edward, as usual, was the first to rise even though it was his day off. Elizabeth, knowing she didn't have to rise early to prepare Edward's food, had taken the opportunity to have an extra hour in bed. Next to rise was Jacob, he had woken earlier but stayed in bed for a while, not quite finding the energy to rise until the sound of his father in the adjoining room, and going about lighting the stove had prompted him to get up and join Edward. He entered the parlour and sat down in a chair beside the table and opposite his father.

"Morning son," said Edward.

There was no reply, just a distant stare into oblivion from a little boy who hadn't quite fully woken up.

"Sleep well?"

Still, there was no reply. Little boys often need a little prompting to finally acknowledge the existence of those around them when first up early in the morning.

"Would you like to come with me on the mail coach tomorrow son?"

Jacob's head turned in surprise. "What, to London?" he asked.

"No, to Yarmouth and back, should take a full day. Would you like to come?"

Jacob smiled and nodded, then ran into the bedroom where his mother lay, still half asleep in bed.

"Ma! Father's taking me on the mail coach tomorrow!"

Elizabeth, her eyes still shut, smiled. "That's wonderful, darling," she replied. Her eyes opened and gazed towards her son.

"I did already know, your father and I had talked about it earlier. Now you be good and do exactly as your father tells you to do."

Jacob nodded and ran back into the living room, where Edward sat in the process of filling his clay pipe, ready for his first smoke of the day.

"Where will I sit? Will it be inside the carriage?"

"No, on the top with me," Edward replied.

This was just the beginning of a bombardment of questions to Edward on the subject of the forthcoming day. His eagerness was so apparent, his father quietly chuckled, in pride of the joy that he had obviously brought to his son. However, this was also to be a valuable lesson to Jacob on what his father did to make a living and what a day's work entailed. At this time, children were often made to work at an early age, especially among the poor. This fate, however, was not likely to befall upon Jacob, his father was making a comfortable living, so was deemed unnecessary. But Jacob had been given chores to do around the house as a preparation for the beginning of his working life, which was still early. Working life usually began at nine or ten years old, so when his time was to come, he would be a child thrown into an adult world.

The following morning arrived. Edward, as usual, was up early and had to wake up his son for his big day, an introduction into the daily life of a mail coach driver. Elizabeth stirred early too, she wasn't going to let her son leave without a meal in his belly so made breakfast of toast and warmed milk. After breakfast, she prepared their lunches for the day, of bread and cheese and a bottle of water for Jacob, and bread and dripping, and a larger bottle of cider for Edward. Soon after, both Edward and Jacob put on their hats and coats, and kissed Elizabeth goodbye. Her eyes glistened slightly as she kissed her son but she kept composed. Since Jacob had been born, he had barely ever left his mother's side, so this was an emotional time for her albeit unbeknown to Edward and Jacob. Jacob, however, had the excitement of the coming day on his mind and consequently, wasn't fazed at all on leaving his mother behind.

The pair left their home and made their way to the Mail office which was just a short walk of about five or ten minutes or so, and was situated at Bedford Street, close to the market square. On their arrival, Edward entered the post office with his son in tow, to be greeted by his boss and general manager, William Burrell. The very same man who years earlier had spotted Edward reading a newspaper whilst sitting in a cart outside the Guildhall.

William Burrell smiled at the sight of young Jacob, who stood at his father's side.

"Good morning, young master Jacob. I hope you're all ready for your trip to Yarmouth."

Jacob smiled back and nodded shyly.

"This'll be a new thing for him to see. Thank you for letting him have a ride, Mr Burrell, he'll remember this for a long time to come I think."

Burrell laughed. "That he will. Hope you enjoy your day, young man."

"Right, I'd better get ready and head up to the King's Head before the Diligence arrives from London, then we'll be heading for Yarmouth."

The Diligence, that Edward was referring to, was the London to Norwich mail coach. The Yarmouth coach always departs upon the arrival of the Diligence, to transport any passengers or mail whose final destination is upon route. Then the Yarmouth coach would leave at three o'clock for its return journey back to Norwich. The Diligence would then set off back to London upon the Yarmouth coach's arrival at the King's Head.

Edward went into a back room where his King's mail uniform hung, a smart blue coat with white breeches and a black three cornered hat. After putting on his King's mail clothes, he then picked up a sack containing the day's mail and newspapers, all destined for Yarmouth, and he and Jacob set off on the short walk to the King's Head where the coaches arrived and departed. On arrival, the pair entered the courtyard of the inn via a wide arched opening, wide enough and high enough for the mail coaches to enter and exit. The archway led into a long cobbled courtyard just wide enough to turn a mail coach round to the right direction, and at the rear of the yard stood a black and yellow coach, as yet to be loaded and horsed which was to be the transport for their Yarmouth run. Within the cobbled courtyard, the stables were situated, for the horses that were kept for changeover. There was small forge and workshop for the resident farrier and also an entrance to the inn itself. Working at the yard were two stable lads as well as the farrier who could be heard working in his forge. The Kings Head was known as a coaching inn. It was most commonly used by travellers to and from Norwich or passing through to the various small market towns and villages in Norfolk or North Suffolk. Many travellers would stay in rooms at the inn overnight to break up their long journey.

As driver, Edward was one of a team of three. The other team members were the post boy, who would ride on the back of one of the lead horses. It was his job to help steer the team of four, helping the driver keep easier control. Seated at the rear would be the guard, armed with two pistols and a sword. He also carried with him the mail horn; a long bugle of about a yard in length, meant to warn pedestrians and traffic in the visible distance of the approaching coach.

"Morning Tom," said Edward as he entered the yard.

Tom Elmham was the post boy, though hardly a boy, he was a man in early forties, small in stature as all post boys were expected to be for the sake of the horses. He also adorned the uniform of the king's mail, of blue jacket and black hat, though grey breeches were worn instead of white like Edward and the guard. This was to hide any mud or dirt picked up on the journey. He always joked that it was to match the colour of his hair.

Then, there was Bill Anderson, he was the guard. A large man both in height and stature. At thirty-five years old, he was still a force to be reckoned with. With long dark hair and stubble on his face, he looked every bit intimidating as was his job to be. He had served ten years as a foot soldier with the South Lincoln regiment in his younger days.

The mail and parcels that were to be delivered on the Yarmouth run were put in a compartment situated beneath the driver's seat. Luggage was strapped to the top of the carriage and often, passengers would sit amongst the luggage if all the outside seats were taken. There was also a small luggage compartment situated beneath the rear guard seat.

At last, the Diligence carriage from London finally arrived, having travelled through the previous day and most of the night, with regular stops every ten or fifteen miles or so to change to fresh horses. On this journey, two drivers were used along with the post boy and guard. This was often the case on the long runs, though not always.

The team was well known to Edward; he had taken over their runs many times in the past. Often, during the night on the long runs, the teams were changed as well as the horses, enabling both sets of teams to get some rest in rooms at the inns. This particular team that had arrived were all local men to London.

The passengers from the Diligence disembarked from the carriage; it was journeys end to all but two of them. They were to join Edward's coach and carry on their journey to Yarmouth. They were quickly joined by the passengers from Norwich who were heading to Yarmouth. They had been waiting patiently inside the King's Head for the Diligence to arrive. The luggage from the two passengers from the Diligence was soon transferred onto the Yarmouth coach and the passengers climbed on board. Horses were brought out from the stables, four in all, and were hitched up to the Yarmouth coach by the two stable lads. In total, a group of eight passengers were to be taken. The two from London were a middle-aged husband and wife who were visiting relatives at Gorleston, next to Yarmouth. There was a family who were from Yarmouth, a mother and father and two young children. They were returning home after a sight-seeing visit to Norwich. These two groups were to travel inside the carriage, but two more passengers were to travel up top on seats behind the driver and co-driver (in this case, Edward and young Jacob). The two outside passengers were a lawyer and his clerk on their way to Yarmouth to conduct some business, drawing up an export contract to ship some of the first convicts to the new colony of Australia. They were employed by the prison authorities at the Norwich castle.

Having shown the passengers to their seats, the team climbed on board themselves to take up their positions ready for their journey to the Star Inn in Yarmouth. Jacob sat up front beside his father and then, at approximately nine o'clock King's Head time, Bill Anderson sounded the horn of the King's mail coach.

"Hold on tight, son!" said Edward, and with a flick of the reins and a crack of the whip, the coach set out on its journey to the east coast of Norfolk, destination Yarmouth.

At first, the team travelled at a slow pace through the streets of Norwich for safety sake along the surrounding road of the market square, and then up towards the cathedral at Tombland where Elizabeth was waiting to wave off her man and their son. A broad grin greeted her from Jacob as he caught sight of his mother. Both Edward and Jacob waved to her before the coach turned to head toward the Bishopgate Bridge to exit the city. Having made the crossing over the River Wensum, Jacob was already beginning to experience sights new to him. He had never ventured outside the city before, and now he was to go further in his life than he had ever known.

The team of four horses had at first to climb the steep road that entwined the hills of Mousehold Heath, which, once at the top, commanded the most breath-taking view of the city that he'd ever seen, and which would ingrain itself upon his memory for the rest of his life. From there, the team quickened its pace on the more level ground of the road to Yarmouth. The sound of the mail horn was constantly heard, blown to warn anyone seen in the distance. This was the King's mail and it stops for no one.

Jacob was holding tight, just as his father had instructed, the horses were by now in full canter and the carriage was now bouncing on the bumpy road. He was fascinated by the scenes that were before him, he had never seen the countryside properly before, the trees, the fields and the country villages. Little Plumstead and Salhouse, through Panxworth, to South Walsham and then finally to Acle, where the coach was to stop at an inn for a fresh change of horses.

At Acle, the passengers left the coach for refreshments within the inn, while the crew were busy with the horse change and mail deliveries for that area. Jacob stayed sat on the coach, he could gain a greater vantage point from there and he was happy to take in the sights around him in this unfamiliar place. He noticed as he looked in the distance how this place seemed to be flat and with windmills dotted around in the distance, some still under construction. He looked across the flat marshland that had been so easily identified by Major John Money as he flew high above in his gas balloon three years earlier.

"Do you need a wee son?" asked Edward as he led a new horse to the coach to be hitched up. Jacob nodded and climbed down, where upon his father led him to the back yard of the inn where a small brick latrine was situated. (A hole in the ground, bridged by a wooden bench with convenient round holes directly above). When the deed was done, Jacob then made his way back to the coach which by now had two new horses hitched up. He climbed back on board, and found the bread and cheese that his mother had made for him wrapped in a piece of linen cloth, together with his small clay bottle of water.

Bill Anderson and Tom Elmham led the last two fresh horses to join the team. Jacob sat watching them being hitched when his father emerged holding a tankard of ale in one hand and a small clay bottle in the other.

"Here, son, this is for you." He handed over the bottle. "It's ginger ale."

Jacob smiled, this was a drink he only had occasionally as a treat and enjoyed very much. Edward climbed up to join his son and reached for the food that Elizabeth had prepared for him. Father and son sat side by side enjoying the early autumn sunshine with food and drink.

"Look Father! They're building a windmill over there."

Edward looked towards the direction Jacob had been pointing and there in the distance, he could see a half built windmill, one of the many dotted around in the distance.

"They're building lots of 'em, son, to drain all the wet land over there."

Edward pointed to the vast expanse of flat land in the distance. He was referring to the marshland of the Burgh Flats, which was in the slow process of being drained by Dutch workers and engineers. They were using drainage ditches and newly built windmills to pump water into the river Bure to eventually flow out to sea.

Soon after, the passengers were led back out to the carriage by Tom and Bill, to continue their journey. Edward lent forward to grab the reins, as he did this his coat fell open exposing a belt around his waist. Tucked into the belt were two flintlock pistols. This caught Jacob's attention immediately and he nudged his father.

"What are they?" he asked.

Edward looked to his son. "They're pistols, son, this is the King's mail coach and so it is in our charge to keep it safe. It has an armed guard and an armed driver, just in case anyone is daft enough to try and rob it, that's why I carry the pistols. If a highwayman tries his luck, both me and Bill are paid to shoot him."

"Have you ever had to shoot anyone?" was the inevitable question from Jacob.

"No, I never have and I hope I never have to," replied Edward.

He was never likely to either, with a team of four horses pulling a large enclosed carriage at high speed and with two armed guards, the King's Mail coach stopped for no one. Any budding highwayman would find the mail coach a particularly dangerous target to rob. Better to rob a private, smaller and less armed road traveller and lessen the chance of either being shot or being caught, to be hung from a hangman's noose.

Leaving Acle, the coach crossed the river Bure on a wooden ferry specially built for the mail carriages and funded by tolls to the general public. The road then continued to skirt around the marshy Norfolk wetlands of the Burgh flats. Jacob looked in wonder, though a flat landscape, it was beautiful nonetheless. There were expanses of grasses and reed sedges and glistening watery dykes with windmills alongside. It was a scene that could only be found in the eastern region of this country, from South Lincolnshire to the fens of West Norfolk and Cambridgeshire, and on the Broadlands of Norfolk and North Suffolk.

The coach continued through the countryside to the village of Billockby.

"You'll soon see two huge lakes with a road and a bridge running through the middle of 'em son," said Edward.

Not long after, two, maybe three miles later, Edward's words came true, a huge lake could be seen to the right of the road, with sedges all around its banks. Moments later, from behind some trees and hedgerows, emerged another lake on the left. The banks of the two lakes seemed to draw closer together on either side until for a brief moment, just the road seemed to separate the huge expanses of water. A small wooden bridge appeared ahead and as the coach reached and crossed the bridge, Jacob could see that the two lakes were in fact joined by a small channel of which the bridge crossed. The two lakes they had encountered were in fact broads. Rollsby Broad was on the left of the road and Filby Broad was the lake on the right. Soon after, the coach sped through the village of Filby itself.

"Won't be long son, you'll soon see the sea," said Edward.

Jacob had been looking forward to that, he had heard stories of the sea, and of naval ships and of fishermen, but he had never actually seen any of it other than the fish being sold in the market or the occasional sailor on leave walking the streets back home. The coach, however, continued on through the village of Mautby and soon after, as his father had predicted, Jacob saw the sea for the first time in the distance, thanks to a convenient nudge from Edward who knew exactly where and when the first sight was going to be. In this case, just as they were approaching the coastal village of Caister. On entering Caister, the coach then linked onto the main coastal road. Jacob was in awe of the vastness of the sea. He had thought the two broads they had passed earlier were a vast expanse of water unlike anything he had ever seen, but this was even better. Vast blue water broken by white patches of surf and large sailing ships in the distance. Fishing vessels hugging the coastline. He asked his father what the white patches were, having never seen surf break before. Edward smiled and replied, "They're white horses, son, they're the backs of white sea horses that swim in the sea and are only ridden by mermaids."

Jacob, being young and none the wiser, took his father to his word.

Onwards they travelled, closer to their destination on the coastal road. This time, the sandy beaches and dunes caught Jacob's eye, but he also looked to his right, inland at the vast Burgh flats, this time from the other side of them. In the distance, the unmistakable sight of Yarmouth lay ahead and as they approached the town, in the distance to the right of the buildings was another expanse of water. This time, it was the estuary of the river Yare and the river Bure, forming a huge flood marsh called the Breydon Water.

The coach arrived at Yarmouth at approximately half past one. It turned right off the coast road into the town and to the Star Inn which was just fifty or so yards down the high street and was the main mail coach inn in the town. Jacob noticed how, though the building looked different, the general layout was the same as the King's Head in Norwich. There were stables and stable staff, the inn itself and the dwelling rooms up top. Meanwhile, Edward performed his duties of mail delivery and helping the passengers to disembark whilst Bill and Tom, along with the stable hands from the Star

Inn, saw to changing the horses. Jacob took a short moment to stretch his legs and take in the sights of Yarmouth, minding not to stray too far as instructed by his father.

He walked a short distance back up the high street and back to the coastal road where he could see the sea once more as this was more exiting to him. To his right, in the distance, he could see a large number of masts of fishing vessels, which had arrived at the port to land their catches of herrings, freshly caught from the vast shoals that inhabited the North Sea. It then struck Jacob that nearly everything that he could see along the coastline was fishing related. He returned back to the Star Inn where his father was and told him of what he had just seen. "All those ships at port," he said.

Edward smiled.

After an hour and a half, which consisted of a food and drink break, a new team of horses hitched up, a new set of passengers embarked and mail loaded up, everything was ready for the return journey back to Norwich. The coach set off and Jacob was to experience all of the wonders he had seen that day, all over again in reverse. The sights were just as wonderful to him the second time around.

After another trouble free return journey, the coach arrived back in Norwich just after seven in the evening when dusk was beginning to fall. It was another half an hour by the time the horses were stabled and the mail had been locked away to be taken to the post office the following morning. Edward and Jacob could now go home. Darkness had already fallen by the time they arrived back. Elizabeth sat by the fire waiting as they walked in,

She kissed Jacob. "How was your day?" she asked.

Both Jacob and Edward then proceeded to spend the next hour telling Elizabeth of the sights that Jacob had seen for the first time. Eventually and after some food and warm milk, Jacob finally settled down to bed, exhausted from a long day and he slept soundly.

Chapter Thirteen

The apparent recovery of King George III from his temporary bout of insanity has caused rejoicing amongst the general population of England, notably the aristocracy and ruling classes. The Prime Minister William Pitt is especially relieved, as in all likeliness would have seen his power diminish should the Prince of Wales become Regent. To the poorer classes, though a topic of conversation from time to time, they were indifferent to the situation, having more pressing problems in their lives, survival and the struggle to feed their families. In that same year of 1789, news began to arrive back to England of revolution in France. The peasant workers had stormed the Bastille Prison in Paris and many wondered if the same unrest would show itself here.

***

A twelve-year-old boy was working as an errand boy at the King's Head Inn in Norwich when talk of the rebellion began to unfold. To him, it meant nothing, he couldn't understand why the rebellion was so close to people's hearts when to him it all seemed so far away. The boy is Jacob Allen and he has been working at the inn for nearly two years. His father, Edward, had managed to secure his son with employment there due to his own connections with the establishment, however, Jacob's time as errand boy is soon to end. It has now been agreed by the proprietors, employers, and Edward, that Jacob should now begin an apprenticeship as a stable boy and trainee farrier. A trade destined to keep him in work constantly in the days when horsepower was king. Edward and Elizabeth's dream of their son becoming something higher in the social scale was now a forgotten dream as the realities of life comes to pass. Jacob's literacy was still an advantage nonetheless, and both parents feel fully justified in his tuition. As for Jacob himself, he was happy to comply with his chosen profession. He had helped his father with the horses many times since that first excursion to Yarmouth when he was nine years old. Indeed, most of his duties as errand boy included stable work, so this choice of career seemed an inevitability to everyone concerned.

***

Time moved on, and Jacob laboured around the forge at the rear courtyard of the King's Head. It was his job to work the bellows on the forge fire, whilst the farrier, namely Robert Langley, shaped the horseshoe. Langley, as well as being farrier, was in charge of the whole stable area. He was responsible for the welfare of all the horses. Which horses were to be used on each run, and which ones were rested. He was also in charge of all the stable hands, including Jacob. He was a short, stocky man of mid-thirties with fair hair which was beginning to thin. Though good at his job involving horses and the general running of the stables, he could be short tempered at times, often barking orders at the younger stable hands when irritated. He ruled the stables with a rod of iron, but as a consequence lost all respect from the staff.

Jacob was one of two apprentices learning their trade at the forge. The other was Ned Barrett, he had also worked as errand boy before being apprenticed two years before Jacob. The two had become friends while working together, having much in common both in mind and work. The pair, though respecting Langley's great knowledge of horse care, grew to despise the man as a person, having often borne the brunt of his irritations and aggressive mannerisms.

It had been another long hard day, but thankfully nearly over. Both Ned and Jacob were conducting their last chore of the day, that of clearing up the forge workshop and making safe the forge fire. This consisted of raising the fireguards around the forge to stop any coals from falling out and making sure the floor was swept clean from any flammable objects. It was late September and the nights were drawing in ever earlier. The two apprentices were eager to finish for the day and return home. It had been an ordinary but hard day for Jacob, much the same as the one before except for a small almost insignificant incident that Jacob had paid little attention to, and which had occurred earlier that day in the courtyard of the inn. Jacob had been busily leading and hitching fresh horses to the Diligence, ready for the London run, when he noticed a woman standing at the yard entrance, and staring towards him. She was older, in her mid-fifties, and she was wearing a silver wig and a crimson shawl. Jacob, though a bit bemused why the woman should find his work so fascinating, smiled and nodded to the woman. He uttered a polite "Hello" to her, but took little notice and continued with his work. Many people looked into the yard as they passed and this was just another passer-by he thought. For nearly five minutes, the woman had stood staring at him, this was strange, they didn't usually stare for so long. Jacob looked back... Had he seen her before? He couldn't be sure, there was something familiar but he didn't know what it was. Then, in a moment, she was gone, back to the busy streets of the city from whence she had come.

Finally, with the forge cleaned and swept and the yard given a quick sweep, it was time to finish for the day. Jacob and Ned put on their jackets, and bid the staff inside the inn a farewell, much as they did every day when they left off. There was a call from Ben Sharples who worked inside the inn.

"Jacob, there's a letter here for your mother. A lady brought it in to give to your father, but as he's in London you can take it home to her."

This surprised Jacob, it was not a usual thing for his family to receive mail. Just occasionally, Elizabeth would receive a communication from the Lutkin household, left either at the mail office or the King's Head, as instructed by Elizabeth all those years ago. It was down to Jacob to be the courier of important family news this time. Taking the letter, he immediately set off on his short journey home to Tombland, where on arrival, he handed the letter over to his mother, and of which she immediately read. The letter contained these words:

Elizabeth,

My darling daughter, it is with great sadness I write to you today to inform you of the passing of your dear father. He had become ill some two months ago and his illness became worse in the passing of time. He finally left us yesterday morning and his funeral will be at the church here in Crostwick on Thursday at 12 noon. Please come, there is much to talk over, and bring Edward and Jacob if possible. We would welcome you all gladly.

Your loving Mother.

A tear ran down the side of Elizabeth's face as she held the letter.

"Are you alright?" asked Jacob, clearly seeing that something had upset her.

"My father... Your grandfather has died."

She buried her face in her hands and began to sob. Jacob immediately put his arms around his mother to comfort her from her loss and distress. He had never heard much talk about Elizabeth's parents in the house before, or Edward's either. Very little talk of his grandparents was ever said whenever he asked of them as a child, the conversation was quickly changed. Sometimes, if Jacob asked where his grandparents were, Edward and Elizabeth would tell him that they lived a long way away, too far to go and visit them. Being a child, he had never questioned their words.

After a while, Elizabeth composed herself.

"You alright now?" Jacob asked once again.

"I'm fine now," she replied. "It was just a shock, that's all."

However, Elizabeth still looked visibly upset.

"Was the letter from your mother?" Jacob asked.

Elizabeth nodded. "She must have delivered it by hand at the King's Head, or sent one of the family."

A sudden realisation came to Jacob of the small incident that had happened to him that day as he worked.

"There was a woman at the King's Head today, she was staring at me as I worked. She had a silver wig and wore a crimson shawl. Did your mother know I worked there?"

Elizabeth nodded, she had on occasion kept her mother informed of her family life by leaving a letter at the post office via Edward, which Anne Lutkin would collect on her occasional visits to the city. Likewise, Anne would also leave news via Edward, either at the post office or Kings Head.

"I saw her," said Jacob. "My grandmother."

There followed a short period of silence, a time of deep thought and reflection from both mother and son as they pondered over events that had been, and of events yet to come. Elizabeth sat thinking of the childhood she had with her father now gone, and how the events of her life had turned that previous life upside down. The result being that she may never really enjoy the company of the ones that she had loved ever again, or be at her father's side at his very end. Jacob sat in sympathy for his grieving mother whilst reflecting upon his encounter with his grandmother for the first time. With it came the realisation that his family could be more than just his mother and father.

Elizabeth broke the silence. "The funeral is on Thursday. Mother wants us all to come."

Jacob looked to his mother but said nothing.

"I wish your father was here." she said.

At that time, she needed a strong mature shoulder to cry on, but Edward was away and wouldn't be returning until later the next day, she would have to manage without him for the time being. The rest of that evening returned to the deep reflections of the events in hand. Edward returned home the following day, and upon hearing the news, did what he could to comfort and support Elizabeth. He agreed that the family should be at Crostwick to attend George's funeral and maybe try to heal old wounds.

***

The day of the funeral service came just a day after Edward's return. Permission for a day's absence from work was sought and granted at the post office early in the morning before they were to set off for Crostwick. This was to make good time to spend with Elizabeth's family before the church service. Thoughts of what reception lay ahead from the family they had left so long ago weighed heavily on the minds of

Edward and Elizabeth as they journeyed on. Neither one knew how the family would react after such a long time, hostile or kind? Elizabeth, however, had no doubt that her mother, Anne, would greet her with open arms, but the doubt lay with her siblings, and of the shame and scandal that she and Edward may have caused them. Jacob was, of course, unaware of any this and looked forward to meeting his new-found relatives for the first time.

The journey seemed to go quickly in the morning summer sunshine. For Jacob, this was another new experience for him in the storybook of his life, and he was excited at what lay ahead and eager to learn more of his mother's family. They arrived at Spring Farm at eleven, and Edward and Elizabeth surveyed the surroundings of the place that had played such a big part in their lives so many years ago. Not much had changed at the farm from the time that they had left Crostwick twelve years earlier, but then things never did when the pace of life was so much slower. As the three walked up the path leading to the front door of the farm, the door opened and Anne Lutkin emerged from the doorway. She immediately made straight for Elizabeth to embrace the daughter that she had lost all that time ago. Mother and daughter hugged, and cried for the lost years of love, while Edward and Jacob looked on not quite knowing what to do or say. Then, from behind Anne Lutkin, came out of the house Elizabeth's sisters, Martha and Jane, who joined Anne and Elizabeth to form a communal group of emotional women, full of hugs, kisses and tears.

There was a brief but great outpouring of emotion from the four women reunited once again after what had seemed an eternity of lost companionship and love. Then, Anne turned and looked to Jacob.

"I know who you are but you don't know me, do you Jacob?"

Jacob smiled. "You're my grandmother, and I saw you the other day at the King's Head."

"That's right," said Anne. "Come into the house, it's good to have some happiness on what is to be a sad day."

As they entered the house, Elizabeth noticed that her brothers, Richard and George, were standing at the doorway. They had been watching the reunion of their mother and sisters, and now the whole family was reunited for the first time in many years. No ill feeling seemed to be shown towards Edward and Elizabeth from anyone. This was a relief to them both as neither wanted a scene in front of their son. Jacob was introduced to the Lutkin family for the first time, uncles, aunts and cousins that he had never met. Indeed, there were nephews and nieces that Elizabeth had never seen. Jacob did, however, notice how his father seemed quiet and stayed in the background away from the family gathering. That was until Martha showed her usual warmness and decided to include Edward in the reunion.

"Edward, can I get you some tea?" she asked. "You must all be tired from the walk from Norwich."

"Thank you, that's most kind of you, Mrs Watts," he replied.

Martha smiled. "You can call me Martha; you are family you know."

This statement struck a chord with Edward and he almost instantly felt more at ease within his surroundings.

"Thank you Martha," he replied.

Twelve years had gone, and now all of Elizabeth's family were married with children of their own. They had been told the real story of Edward and Elizabeth's affair by Anne who thought that now was the correct time for the family to hear the truth now that George Lutkin was gone. Both of the brothers, Richard and George, were not entirely happy of what they had heard, but thought that accepting the situation after such a long time would be in the family's best interest. Elizabeth's sisters were not fazed one little bit. They thought the whole story extremely romantic and even quietly envied her a little. Anne Lutkin, however, had given strict instructions that her husband's funeral was to be a dignified affair and that no disputes were to be allowed. Elizabeth and Edward were married with a son, what was the shame in that? Only Edward and Elizabeth actually knew that they weren't really married, and they would never let that secret out for the sake of their son.

In the front room of the house, resting on two purpose made benches lay the casket containing the mortal remains of George Lutkin. Elizabeth was led into the room by her mother to see the coffin.

"This is where your poor father is, at peace now," said Anne.

"Did he suffer? What ailed him?"

"His lungs," she replied. "This last year saw him coughing and gradually getting worse. These last two months saw him virtually bed ridden. He got thinner and thinner, till he was just a shadow of the man he used to be. His end was a kind release by God I think."

"I wish that we could have been friends, he would have loved Jacob. I'm sure of that."

"I think so too," replied Anne.

"You were still never to talk of me, right to the end?"

Anne shook her head, almost with a feeling of guilt of the abandonment of her daughter. Though Elizabeth felt no malice, these were circumstances brought on entirely by both her and Edward, and there was nothing that Anne Lutkin was able to do.

The time came for the casket to be taken to church for burial. The male family members, namely Richard and George Lutkin, John Watts, and Jane's husband, Francis Watling, carried the casket out to be placed into a black funeral carriage, hired from an undertaker from Norwich. Then there was a slow march from Spring Farm to the church. George and Richard Lutkin walked ahead of the procession, and the rest of the family at the rear behind the carriage. This included Edward, Elizabeth and Jacob, upon Anne's request.

Like the Sunday services he had held without fail, Parson Nash stood at the church ready to greet his parishioners, who were to mourn the passing of a major citizen from the parish of Crostwick. From the carriage, the aforementioned pallbearers brought in George Lutkin's casket and laid it on two benches at the front of the church before the altar, and in full view of the mourners. Due to the importance of this respected parishioner, the church was almost full. At the back of the church were a large group of farm hands and their families, all from Spring Farm. Among them sat Nathaniel Allen with his wife, Mary and son, James, who in turn was accompanied by his own wife and two small children. Towards the front were the landowners and local gentry, all respectful of the passing of one of their colleagues, and of course, George's own family sat at the immediate front.

The service was held, prayers were said, George Lutkin the younger read a tribute to his father, and finally they laid George Lutkin to rest within the churchyard. His resting place was marked with a beautifully carved headstone. Outside in the churchyard after the service, the Lutkin family thanked everyone who had attended to pay their last respects. Edward and Elizabeth kept discreetly in the background of the family group so as not to cause any embarrassment or gossip. Even so, Edward slipped away from the group to speak to his own mother, father and brother, who having spotted Edward in the church, beckoned him over from across the churchyard.

He hugged them all. "I'll be coming to see you later at the cottage, but for now, I'll have to stay here."

"Please come, son, promise me," said Nathaniel.

"I promise," he replied and made his return back to his family of the present.

After all the thank you and farewells to the friends and parishioners, the Lutkin family returned back to Spring Farm for the afternoon. Edward explained to Elizabeth that he would have to go and see his parents, and therefore leave the gathering for a short while. Also that he would like to bring his family with him. This was a rare opportunity for Nathaniel and Mary Allen to see their grandson and Elizabeth as they had rarely seen him since he left for Norwich twelve years ago. Elizabeth agreed and begged her family's pardon for a while, whilst they visited Edward's family, everyone fully understood.

A short walk from the farm and a knock on the door was greeted by a smile and "Come in son," by Nathaniel Allen as he answered the door. On entering the cottage, Edward was hugged by his mother and warmly greeted by his brother, James. Edward noticed how much older and frailer his parents were now looking but said nothing. It is a sad but inevitable fact of life we all have to endure watching loved ones' age, made more noticeable for Edward after such a long period of time apart.

"This is my wife, Elizabeth, who you already know," said Edward. "And this is our son, Jacob, your grandson."

"Hello Jacob," said Mary Allen warmly. "We haven't met before, I'm your grandmother, and this is your grandfather and your uncle James. We're very pleased to meet you."

Jacob returned a smile, which was then returned with a hug from his grandmother. Elizabeth, however, was treated with a cautious politeness. It was difficult for Edward's family to know how to react to her, being from the family of their employers. Nathaniel handed out tankards of mild table beer to all including Jacob, as table beer was allowed to children. Questions were then asked of Edward's life. "Where are you living? Are you living well? Is work good?" And so on. In turn, he also caught up with family news. James was now married to a local girl from the village and they had three children and another on the way. A short period of family gossip was interrupted when Edward took a stroll outside in the garden to answer a call of nature. The deed done in a bush, he turned to head back to the cottage, to be greeted by his father Nathaniel who had followed him out.

"Don't go back inside, son, I need a quiet word alone."

"I know what you're going to ask. How did I end up with Elizabeth and have a child?"

Up to that point, Edward, on his rare and brief visits to his parents, had only told them that he was living with a woman and her child. He had never let on that it was Elizabeth for fear of reprisals from George Lutkin should the news ever leak out.

"Did you ever wonder what happened to Elizabeth? Why they said that she had left to live with relations elsewhere?" Edward asked.

"Well, I had an idea that maybe she had got into trouble but I never thought that you had anything to do with it."

"It was me, that's why I had to leave. We both ran off, because if George Lutkin had have found out that I was the father of the child she was expecting, you would all have been thrown off the farm and out of this cottage. Anne Lutkin knew it was me but never said anything. She had a story made up if George or anyone else found out we were living together. She was going to say that another man was the father and left her in destitution, and that I took her in and married her. She did that to protect all of you."

Nathaniel gasped in shock of what he had just heard, but was unsure how to react. He could be angry at Edward for taking such a huge risk that would have jeopardised the well-being of the family, but it had all happened twelve years ago and they had got away with it, with no harm to anyone except themselves enduring their own isolation.

"So you are married then?"

"Yes, we are," Edward replied, knowing that this was a secret best kept for the sake of everyone, especially his son.

"I have to tell your mother about this, you know that don't you."

"You can tell her if you like," said Edward. "The Lutkin family all know about it now and nothing is gonna happen. I suggest you keep it quiet from everyone around here though, so as not to upset Elizabeth's family, they don't want this gossiped about again."

"I'm not stupid, son," said Nathaniel. "I'm just relieved you got away with it. If anyone asks, I'll tell 'em the same story Anne Lutkin had ready for 'em."

Edward agreed and the pair returned back inside for the family reunion. After the brief visit, it was time for Edward and family to return back to Spring Farm to re-join the Lutkin family briefly before their return to Norwich. Farewells were said with hugs and kisses especially from Mary Allen to her new-found family. With that, they departed.

The return back to Spring Farm was all too brief for Anne Lutkin, she desperately wanted Elizabeth to stay longer. She had missed her daughter badly over the years and now it was time to catch up.

"You don't have to walk back to Norwich, I'll get Charlie Dawson to take you home in the chaise if you like. You can stay a little longer then."

This took Edward by surprise. He was to be ferried home in a private chaise with a driver to take him there.

"That would be very kind of you." he replied.

"Not at all, you're family," said Anne.

Shortly after, Edward stole a quiet moment with Anne Lutkin while she was out of earshot from the rest of the family.

"You know, I never got to thank you for what you did for us back then. Elizabeth told me how you already knew but said nothing and how you were willing to cover for us, should your husband had ever have found out. For that, I sincerely thank you."

"You know," said Anne. "Elizabeth looks happy, and you both have a fine son. Look after them both and it will all have been worth it."

"I promise I will," Edward replied.

Chapter Fourteen

With the passing of time, a boy has become a young man. It is 1796 and Jacob is now nineteen. With the same colour dark hair as his mother and the tall solid stature of his father, Jacob has become every bit the young man their parents had hoped for. The years have seen revolutionary France execute its reigning monarch, Louis XVI and his wife, Marie Antoinette, later to declare war on Britain. A major naval victory is won for the British at Ushant by Admiral Jervis, and the hero of the battle is a young commodore by the name of Horatio Nelson, a Norfolk born man educated at the Norwich school.

***

"I want one of you two to take the small cart to Sprowston and pick up two wheels for the Yarmouth Flyer. Which one of you is it to be?" asked Robert Langley one mid-week morning.

Both Ned and Jacob looked at each other. "I'll do it!" they said in unison.

"It won't take two of you to pick up a couple of wheels now which one of you is it to be?"

Both Jacob and Ned were eager to escape the monotony of the stables and forge for a while, and have a break from the miserable character that was Robert Langley.

"I'd like to go," said Jacob.

"So would I," said Ned.

"You two had better stop pissing me about and decide. Now come on, who's going?" barked Langley, his face starting to glow red in irritation.

Jacob looked at Ned. "Toss for it?" he said.

Ned smiled and nodded. Jacob produced a halfpenny coin from his jacket pocket, he tossed it. "Heads!" called Ned.

The coin spun and was caught and covered by Jacob... his hand lifted... he smiled. "Its tails," he said.

"Shit!" growled Ned, his hopes of a welcome change now dashed.

"Right," said Langley. "I want you to go to Sprowston. When you get there, you turn left at Church Lane, just before the Blue Boar Inn. Go down the lane towards the church, about a hundred yards on your right is Bill Fox's place. You'll see it cos he's got a carved wooden Fox sign hanging from outside his gate. Here's a purse with the correct money, and I don't expect you to be too long."

Jacob nodded and took the purse which he buttoned up in his jacket pocket. He hitched up the small two-wheeled cart up to a brown mare from the coach teams and then began his journey to Sprowston. He had planned his route to pass his own house at Tombland before heading down Magdalen Street and towards the Magdalen gate, which was one of the last surviving gates left at the old city wall. Since 1791, a plan of demolition had come into effect of the gates of the surrounding wall to allow the increasing coach and cart traffic to pass safely through. This was especially important for the priority of the king's mail coaches, which were the main link to the outside world. The demolition program came into its peak in 1793 seeing the end of four of the main city gates.

After exiting the city at the Magdalen gate, Jacob took just a short while to reach Sprowston on the main turnpike road eventually leading to Wroxham and the Broadlands. He travelled into Sprowston for about a mile or so, to eventually turn left onto Church Lane as instructed. He continued down the lane for a short distance until he saw to his right a carved wooden fox, just as he had been told by Langley. He pulled up beside the fox sign and peered in at the property he had been directed to. It was a thatched cottage built of wattle and daub. To the right of the cottage was a track or drive, easily wide enough for a cart to pass through which led down to a back yard with surrounding outbuildings.

Jacob climbed down from the cart, tied up the horse to the post of which the fox sign hung and walked down the drive to the yard. Ahead, and in the far left hand corner of the yard was a small empty stable, suitable for one horse, and which was in turn adjoined by a shed containing hay and bedding for a horse. A small two-wheeled cart stood beside the fodder shed in an open fronted shed of its own. To the right of the cart shed adjoined and reaching to the right hand corner of the yard, stood another outbuilding that was obviously a carpenter's workshop. The outbuildings to the immediate right and leading back towards the drive was a small blacksmith's forge with a smoking chimney on the roof, and beside this was an open fronted and roofed wood store full of seasoned timber of mostly oak, ash, beech and elm. Leaning up against the cottage wall were a large number of wooden cartwheels of various sizes and in the yard itself stood a four-wheeled cart that was clearly in the process of major repairs from a skilled carpenter.

There was no sound of any activity within the yard so Jacob called out... "Hello!" There was no reply. He knocked on the workshop door and looked in... there was no one there either, so he checked the forge... still no one.

'Maybe there's someone in the cottage', he thought. The back door was situated on the side of a lean-to rear extension to the cottage and which formed the left hand corner of the yard. Jacob approached the door and was almost at knocking distance when suddenly a figure appeared, startling both Jacob and the stranger at the door, who happened to be a young girl. She screamed, "Aaagh!" which in turn made Jacob jump with fright.

"Oh...You made me jump!" said the girl.

"You made me jump too!" said Jacob.

A moment of regained composure was then followed by laughter. Their sudden shock seemed hilarious all of a sudden.

"I'm sorry about that, I don't usually go around trying to scare girls wherever I go. Not intentionally I don't."

The girl laughed again. "Who are you?" she asked.

"I'm Jacob. I'm from the King's Head in Norwich where the mail coaches are and I've come to pick up a couple of wheels that were ordered."

"Oh," said the girl. "You want my father, he's not in."

"Is your father Bill Fox? That's who I was told to collect the wheels from."

The girl nodded. "Yes, you've got the right place," she said.

"I've been given the money to pay for 'em. Do you know which ones they are?"

"I've no idea which ones they are, he makes lots of wheels for lots of people, could be any one of those that stand there," she said, looking to the large group of wheels.

"Well, when is he likely to be back?"

"Not long I shouldn't think, he often goes out and then is back within an hour or so. I don't know where he's gone, he left without saying."

Jacob sighed, he didn't know what he should do next, return to the King's Head empty handed or wait for the girl's father to return and collect the wheels as instructed. That was until the girl made the decision for him.

"You'll have to wait," she said. "I'm sure he won't be too long."

Jacob studied the girl. She was a pretty thing of roughly his own age. Maybe waiting wasn't such a bad idea after all.

He smiled. "I'd better wait here then."

The girl of whom he had found so pleasing to the eye had fair shoulder length hair, blue eyes, and fair skin with a hint of rose coloured cheeks that dimpled as she smiled. Her small petite frame was nicely proportioned, just how he liked a girl to be.

"There's no one else here who'd know which wheels are for me?" Jacob asked.

"No, everyone's out. Mother's gone out to Manor farm with my sisters to get milk and potatoes. My father's out somewhere with my brother, Edmond and I'm the only one here."

"Do they often leave you alone here whilst they all go out?"

"No," said the girl. "We take turns to look after the house if everyone has to go out and this time is my turn."

Jacob smiled at the pretty young girl. "You know I'm talking to you but I don't know your name yet."

She smiled. "It's Sarah, Sarah Fox."

"My name's Jacob, Jacob Allen and I'm pleased to meet you."

"I suppose you must live in Norwich if you work there?" said Sarah.

"Yes, I do, I live nearly opposite the Cathedral at Tombland."

"I like to visit Norwich from time to time, and see the shops and the market, but I don't know if I'd like to live there. It seems too busy and smelly to me."

"It's not that bad," Jacob replied. "If you know where to go or what to do. It can be a bit rough sometimes when men come out of the alehouses worse for wear."

Sarah chuckled. "They come out of the alehouse just the same here too you know."

"You're right about the smell though." said Jacob. "Can be a bit ripe in the summer."

Sarah laughed.

"You're from a big family then?" Jacob inquired.

"Fairly big, I'm the middle one of five children, I have two sisters and two brothers. How about you, do you have any brothers or sisters?"

"No, I'm an only child. The brothers and sisters I had died when I was small, I can't remember 'em."

"That's sad," said Sarah. "It must be lonely for you at times."

"Not really, you don't miss what you've never had. Often it has its good points too."

"Really?"

"Yes, it does. Tell me, did you ever argue or fight with your brothers and sisters when you were young?"

Sarah chuckled. "All the time. In fact, we still do."

"Well there you are then," said Jacob. "I never argued or fought with anyone at home aside my parents from time to time. I was never bossed around by any elder brothers and was never irritated by any younger brothers or sisters. I just picked my own friends. That's not such a bad life, is it?"

"I suppose not, I never thought of it much like that before," she replied.

She was beginning to find this young man quite fun to talk to.

"Is there much to do here, it seems a bit quiet?"

"Everyone's working on the land. It gets busier in the evenings and at the weekend when everyone's at home and away from work. The Blue Boar gets busy at night when the men get back from the fields. The women and girls are always around during the day looking after the little-uns. Many of us meet up at the village green, us younger ones that is."

"How old are you?" asked Jacob.

"I'm eighteen, how about you?"

"Nineteen," he replied.

"Sometimes there are small village gatherings or fairs on the green and sometimes there are barn dances held to celebrate the harvest or Christmas or Easter or the coming of spring, so it's not always quiet here. There's a barn dance this week at Manor Farm, everyone will be there, why don't you come along and see what village people do to enjoy themselves?"

"I could come along I suppose," said Jacob. "I'll see if Ned wants to come too. He's a friend of mine who works with me at the King's Head. When is it exactly?"

"It's on Saturday evening."

"Then I'll do my best to be there," said Jacob. "But on the condition that you'll have to show me how to dance, because I've never been to a barn dance before and I've never danced with such a pretty gal before."

Sarah blushed at this young man's cheeky comment. "If you come, I'll teach you how to dance," she chuckled.

"I'm looking forward to it already," said Jacob.

Girl and boy both smiled. An attraction had clearly formed between them, maybe a friendship or even more. As the pair chuckled during their flirtatious conversation, Sarah's mother and two sisters arrived into the yard.

"Hello," said the mother. "What's all this laughing then and who is this young man who's making my daughter giggle?"

The two sisters laughed at catching their sister with a young man.

Sarah smiled. "This is Jacob, he's come to pick up two wheels from father for the mail coach at the King's Head, but father and Edmond are both out."

"I know," said Sarah's mother, her name being Anne Fox. "He's gone to the rectory to fix Parson Sutton's small chaise; he shouldn't be long."

"I'll have to wait a little longer then," said Jacob.

"Would you like some warm milk, Jacob, while you wait?" asked Anne.

"I'd love some warm milk, thank you."

Anne Fox went inside the cottage.

"Do you work for the mail office, Jacob?" asked Beth, who was Sarah's elder sister by two years. She was a pretty girl just like Sarah and she also had fair hair like her sister. Though not closely identical in appearance to Sarah, she bore enough resemblance to establish that they were in fact siblings.

"I work for the proprietors of the King's Head Inn, who manage the mail coaches to and from Norwich. My job is the horse care at the stables. I'm a shoe smith or farrier, or whatever you like to call the job."

"Do you ever travel on the mail coaches to London or Yarmouth?" asked Annie, Sarah's younger sister by three years. Annie, at fifteen, looked slightly different to her sisters. She had brown hair and had a different face structure, but her eyes gave away the identity of her being a sibling of the other two though it was plain to see that she was a pretty girl in the making.

"I've been to both London and Yarmouth on the coaches," Jacob replied. "But only a few times."

Nonetheless, this seemed to arouse a great interest from the three sisters who until now had never ventured far outside the village and only travelled to Norwich a few times a year.

"What's London like?"

"Did you see the King?"

"Did you see the bloody tower of London or travel over London bridge?" were some of the questions that were instantly fired at Jacob from the three sisters.

"I only travelled to the White Horse Inn at Fetter Lane. I did see London Bridge though, and the Bloody Tower from a distance, but I didn't see the king."

"Oh," said a disappointed Annie.

"So do you drive the mail coaches?" asked Beth.

"No, my father does, he's taken me to London and Yarmouth a few times, but not often."

"What's Yarmouth like?" asked Sarah.

"I like Yarmouth," said Jacob. "It's not as busy and dirty as London and smells completely different."

"Smells different?" asked a confused Sarah.

"Yes," said Jacob. "London smells a bit like poo, fire smoke and something gone rotten, whereas Yarmouth's got a salty fishy smell to it, especially around the docks where the boats are moored. The docks are a bit of a mess but the sandy beach and the sand dunes are really nice to see."

"I'd love to see it, I've never seen the sea before," said Sarah.

"You'd love it, it's beautiful, especially on a sunny day."

Anne Fox emerged from the cottage carrying a mug.

"Your warm milk," she said, as she handed a small tankard to Jacob.

"Thank you most kindly," he said and continued his conversation where he had left off.

"There's a really good fish market at the docks, you won't get fresher fish anywhere, sold where they're landed. Father often brings back fresh herrings when he's been on the Yarmouth run."

It was just then that two figures arrived down the drive leading to the yard. They were carrying a box of tools and a tray of nails, and were leading a black and white mare, obviously the occupier of the empty stable. It was Bill Fox and his youngest son, Edmond. Edmond was a lad of seventeen years of age. He resembled both his father and his younger sister, Annie, having brown hair and a similar shaped face. Again, the eyes gave away the siblings resemblance, they all had the eyes of Anne Fox.

"Hello," said Bill. "Who's this fellow who seems to be charming my three gals?"

Bill fox was a thin man, not very tall and of middle age. His hair was the same colour brown as Edmond and Annie though with a few grey streaks to add. He wore clothes of a working man, long cotton breeches, brown in colour with tough leather shoes. He had on a grey shirt and a green jacket. Upon his head, he wore his black three cornered hat. By nature, he was a calm, easygoing man who would always reason things out before acting and he was a highly skilled wheelwright.

"This is Jacob, Father," said Sarah. "He's come for two wheels that were ordered for the mail coaches in Norwich."

"Ah, I see, Mr Burrell sent you, did he?"

"Yes," replied Jacob. "Two wheels to pick up for the Yarmouth coach. I've been given the money to give to you."

"You must work with Robert Langley if you're from the stables at the King's Head."

Jacob nodded. "He the man in charge, he sent me here."

"I bet he's a real pleasure to work with, I've had a couple of run-ins with him."

Jacob smiled but said nothing, the smile was enough for Bill Fox to interpret. Then Bill walked over to the group of wheels that were leaning up against the cottage wall and separated two that were together at the right hand side of the group.

"These are yours," he said.

"And this is yours," said Jacob as he handed over the purse of money.

The wheels were rolled to Jacob's cart and loaded onto the back, Jacob then climbed on board. Bill Fox and his family stood watching from the drive and Sarah Fox walked up to the cart to bid the charming young man farewell. Jacob looked down the drive to the Fox family.

"Thanks, Mr Fox, for the wheels, and thank you Mrs Fox, for the milk."

He looked down to Sarah who smiled to him. He smiled and winked to her. "I'll be seeing you later I hope."

"Saturday evening at the Manor Farm barn dance," Sarah replied.

Jacob nodded, and with that, set off on his journey back to the King's Head. Sarah returned back to her family.

"I can't work out if that boy's taken a shine to you or you've taken a shine to him," said Bill.

Then a voice came from behind.

"They've both taken a fancy to each other I think!" said a smiling Anne Fox.

Sarah just blushed.

Chapter Fifteen

Jacob had arrived home before his father from his day's work at the King's Head. He had finished at five in the afternoon but it was six thirty in the evening when Edward had arrived back home after what had been a busy day doing the Yarmouth run. On entering the house, he sat down at the table to wait for his evening meal, which Elizabeth was busy preparing. Jacob entered the room freshly washed, hair brushed and wearing his Sunday best outfit ready to go out for the evening.

"Where are you going?" Edward asked.

"I'm going to a barn dance in Sprowston," said Jacob.

"On your own?"

"No, I'm going with Ned."

"Sprowston?" asked Edward. "Why Sprowston? Why walk all the way out there?"

"I was kind of invited," replied Jacob. "I went there earlier this week to pick up two wheels for the Yarmouth coach and I got talking to some of the villagers who told me about it and wondered if I'd like to come along."

Edward smiled. "Villagers? They wouldn't happen to be pretty young girl villagers, would they?"

Elizabeth smiled as she dished up Edward's meal from the other end of the living room.

"She was a pretty young villager now that you come to mention it," replied Jacob. "She told me how the locals all get together and have fun at the dance, and she wondered if I'd like to see for myself. She's the daughter of Bill Fox, the wheelwright, who made the wheels. He seemed a nice enough bloke, so did all his family for that matter."

"I don't think I've ever met him," said Edward. "You've got a fair walk there and back, you'll be late home I reckon."

"If I can find somewhere to get my head down for the night, I'll stay there and come home in the morning. Maybe I'll go to Crostwick and visit Granny Lutkin. It's not all that far from there."

"Oh, that would be a good idea," said Elizabeth. "She would love that. She hasn't seen any of us for quite a while now. Edward, we must go and see her, it's been too long since we last saw her."

"We could go tomorrow and meet Jacob there if you like, I'm sure she'd like to see all of us." said Edward.

Elizabeth agreed. This was a day she would look forward to.

"Right, I'll be off then. I'll see you tomorrow at Crostwick if I can find a place to sleep that is," said Jacob, as he made for the door.

"See you later." said Elizabeth.

"See you later son, and good luck with the wheelwright's daughter," said Edward.

Jacob smiled as he left the house.

After meeting Ned outside the cathedral at the Erpingham gate, the pair made their way to Sprowston, leaving the city at the Magdalen gate on the main turnpike road to

Wroxham, which was a fifty-minute walk. They reached Sprowston just as light was beginning to fade. The local villagers were all making their way up the main road, passing nearly all the way through the village until they came to a barn situated just off the turnpike road on the outer fringes.

On entering the barn, both Jacob and Ned surveyed the scene. A large number of candle and oil lamps hung around the surrounding walls, giving off a soft and even illumination all around. At the end of the barn and tucked into the far left hand corner were the musicians. A fiddle player, a drummer with one long drum and a singer, who as well as singing, would compare the whole event by announcing each dance and directing the dancing groups as they danced. In the right hand corner, there stood a large wooden table from which behind stood a bar maid who was serving ale and cider from the fully laden table of barrels and tankards, for those who desired some liquid refreshment. Along any available wall space were placed planks of wood that sat on anything available to support them, bricks, pails, small barrels etc. to act as seating benches. Many of the women were indeed already sat upon them in small groups of families and friends. At the back of the barn stood the local men who were in larger groups and nearly all were holding tankards of ale. Those feeling inclined would join the women later when the music began.

Jacob looked around to see if there was anyone who may be familiar to him, namely Sarah Fox and her family. Neither she nor her family were anywhere to be seen, but there was a man in the barn that Jacob did recognise as regularly coming to the King's Head whenever there was entertainment within the venue such as bare-knuckle fights or cock fighting. He also noticed that one or two of the young men happened to be glancing in their direction. This was their village after all and strangers were likely to be noticed immediately, Jacob and Ned were to be no exceptions to the rule. They made their way to the ale table to buy some drinks and waited behind a small queue of men who all had the same intention in mind. After a few minutes, they were served their ales at a farthing a head and as they turned to make their way to the rear of the barn. Jacob then noticed Bill Fox enter the barn alongside his wife, Anne and closely followed by his family, namely Beth, Annie and Sarah with sons Edmond, and eldest son, Will and his wife, Priscilla.

The Fox family made their way to the centre of the barn to get a good vantage point of the surroundings and to find any available benches to sit on, which, after a minute or so, they did. The ladies all sat together in a line; Sarah was sat on the far right hand side next to her sister, Beth, and Jacob pointed her out to Ned.

"That's the girl I told you about over there. The one on the right, the wheelwright's daughter, she's a looker, isn't she?"

"That she is," replied Ned. "The one next to her is not bad either."

"That's her sister, Beth," said Jacob.

But no sooner had the words left his lips, a tall fair-haired young man approached the pair and began a conversation with them both. Whatever he said seemed to amuse the two young ladies as they both began to laugh.

"Look out Ned, looks like we've got some competition."

For a full ten minutes Jacob and Ned watched as the young man talked to the two pretty young sisters, seeming to impress them both the more as time wore on, until finally, the man bid his farewells and re-joined his friends among the group of men standing at the rear of the barn.

After a short spell of chat with her sister, Sarah looked up and spied Jacob standing alongside Ned with their tankards of ale in their hands. She smiled and waved to him.

Jacob in return raised his tankard in a mock toast to the pretty girl who had just waved. She beckoned him over.

"You came then," said Sarah.

"Of course I did," replied Jacob. "I've got a dancing lesson tonight."

Sarah laughed, and so did her sisters who were both listening from their seats beside her.

"This is my friend, Ned, Ned Barrett," said Jacob. "Ned, this is Sarah Fox and family."

Ned smiled. "Pleased to meet you."

"You don't have to worry about me showing you how to dance, they tell you what to do as you're dancing, you just follow everyone else," said Sarah.

"I'll watch a couple of dances first so I get the hang of what I'm supposed to do."

"Good idea," said Sarah.

Then the music began to play, not to dance to but just as background music to get everyone into a good spirit. They opened up with a sea shanty tune and then followed with an Irish jig, and the crowd applauded after each rendition. Then the singer joined in for the third song, a merry song of which the crowd in the barn seemed to know. Many joined in with the sing-along.

Songs come, come my hearts of gold,
Let us be merry and wife, it is a proverb of old,
Suspicion hath double eyes,
What'er we say we say or do, let's not drink to disturb the brain,
Let's laugh for an hour or two, and never be drunk again.

The villagers applauded, and then the singer announced the first dance of the evening and called for any budding dancers. The first group formed three circles, even numbers in men and women all holding hands, man, woman, man, woman. As the music began to play, the circles turned with the music, both men and women dancing in a skipping motion. At first, the circles turned in a clockwise motion, and then turned anti-clockwise at the singer's command. Then again at the singer's command the circles broke and formed a line of dancers, one by one and hand in hand heading to the next circle, and slowly replacing the circle with the dancers of the next. The result being that each circle of dancers has changed position with the next. As the music played, the crowd clapped their hands, Sarah Fox and Jacob Allen included, until the dance finally came to an end and to the sound of applause.

"Do you think you can do that?" asked Sarah.

"Looks easy enough to me," said Jacob.

"They're doing the same dance again with different dancers, why not have a go?"

Jacob grabbed Sarah's hand. "Why not then," he said, and led Sarah to the floor and to the smiles and laughs of the onlooking Fox family.

Once again, three circles were formed. Jacob and Sarah stood hand in hand in one of the circles. Jacob spied Ned Barrett in the next circle with a girl from the village who had obviously joined him in the group. In the third circle, Sarah's sister Beth had joined in with her promised man, Herbert Middleton. Once again the music played, and the group danced and the crowd clapped. Jacob danced easily with the others of the group, skipping to the music wasn't difficult at all to him, all he had to do was follow the rest. The young pair smiled and laughed. They were often hand in hand as they danced, then skipping and turning and clapping until the music finally stopped playing. They then returned back to the bench where Sarah's family were seated, still smiling from the fun they had both enjoyed together.

The next dance was called the Festival circle. A double circle is formed, ladies in the inside circle facing out to the men who were in the outside ring. The facing couples danced right hand turns to the music and then clapped, then the same again with a left hand turn and a clap. Both Jacob and Sarah enjoyed the experience of this dance, facing one another.

"You dance well for a beginner," laughed Sarah.

"Thank you," replied Jacob. "I think I like this dancing face to face with a pretty girl."

This made Sarah blush a little. Again, two groups danced to two renditions of this, before there was a short break from dancing while the musicians played and sang songs.

Another dance called The Circassion Circle came into being. This consisted of a large group of couples all joining hands and forming another large circle, this circle took up nearly all of the dancing area. The circle turns to the left and then four steps are made into the middle and then four steps out. Then the circle dances to the right and then four steps in and out again as before. Then the ladies took four steps in and out, followed by the men who took four steps in, jumped and punched the air and roared before returning back. Jacob got the first jump, punch and roar wrong but excelled on the second attempt to the joyful laughter of Sarah. Then, once again, when the dance had finished, they returned back to the bench with Sarah's family.

The musicians played and sang a love song which seemed to captivate the audience and many gently sang along.

A courting I went to my love,
Who is sweeter than roses in May,
And when I came to her by jove,
The devil a word could I say.
I walked with her into the garden,
There fully intending to woo her,
But may I be ne'er worth a farthing,
If I love, I said anything to her.

As the song played, Jacob held Sarah's hand. The pair smiled in a gentle but brief tender moment, in flow with the mood of the moment.

Shortly after, Ned came into view, and signalled to Jacob that he was about to buy another ale from the bar and would he like one? To which came a reply of a nod of the head and a thumbs up. Then the singing compare called for dancers to come to the floor for a dance called the love knot. Sarah immediately grabbed Jacob's hand and led him to the floor. Two groups of four women in a line faced four men in a line. The music began, and the ladies line danced around the male line and back to the place of start. Then the men's line did the same around the ladies' line. The singer then directed the top couple to weave down the opposite line until they reached the end; the result being the girl ends up in the men's line and the man in the girl's line. The next couple follows this procedure and so on until the two lines of men and women have completely changed positions. This cycle was repeated twice until the music finally finished and the couples who were facing one another bowed to their partner and the sound of applause ended the dance. Both Jacob and Sarah walked hand in hand back towards the bench.

Suddenly, there was a commotion heard from the corner of the barn where the ales were served. Jacob looked and to his dismay, he saw two young men who had obviously been fighting, being pulled apart by the surrounding group of men. One of the two fighting men was Ned Barrett. Jacob let go of Sarah's hand and marched up to the trouble spot in aid of his friend.

"What's going on, Ned?" he asked, but before Ned had time to answer, a voice came from the crowd of local lads who by now had rallied around the other young man who had been fighting with Ned.

"You stay out of this or I'll bloody well hit you too!"

"This bloody idiot just hit me from behind when I was getting a beer!" said Ned.

Jacob stared hard at the local lad. "Is that true?"

The young man that he was addressing was a local lad by the name of Jim Barber, a fair haired and slightly spotty individual of average height, smaller than Jacob, but then, Jacob had inherited his tall stature from his father. But Jim Barber had obviously gathered enough courage under the influence of the ales that were being sold in that very corner.

"Yes, it is true," said Barber. "He's been hanging around our women all night and so have you. You two can piss off back to the city where you came from, if you don't want a hiding that is!"

Jacob laughed. "You're gonna give me a hiding, are you boy? Go ahead, see what happens to yer!"

"We'll give yer a fuckin hiding," said Barber as he gathered his three friends around him.

At that moment, two elder local men stepped in, and Bill Fox was one of them.

"Take this outside boys, there'll be no trouble in here."

Nobody argued with him, they all headed straight outside the barn and one of the local lads grabbed a lamp from the wall as he exited.

The very moment everyone was outside of the barn, without hesitation, Jacob turned and punched Barber clean in the face, on his nose to be exact, knocking him backwards to the ground and splitting his nose, which bled profoundly.

Barber's friends came to his aid as he lay on the floor. "Are you alright, Jim?" they asked as they lifted the dazed figure of Barber to his feet, giving him a second or two to regain his thoughts. The four local lads stood face to face with the two city boys.

"You bastard!" shouted Barber.

Then suddenly, out of the darkness came another figure, a large strapping man with dark hair.

"Four onto two. I think you two could do with some help," the man said.

The four local lads looked on with fear. They had recognised the man as being Thomas Walker, a local farm worker who was not one to be trifled with. He was known as a local hard case of the village.

"This has got nothing to do with you," said Barber. "These two city boys have come here trying to be a couple of charmers to our girls."

Thomas laughed. "That's more than you'll ever be Barber. I saw you hit that man from behind, you're a brave one, aren't you? Now we're all facing you and the numbers are a bit farer with one in your favour. Do you want to try it now?"

Barber stayed silent, and so did his friends.

"No, I didn't think you would, now piss off!"

Knowing what would happen to him if he stood his ground, Barber decided to opt for safety instead of valour and he and his friends walked off into the darkness not to be seen again that night by any of the locals.

"Thanks friend, it was good of you to do that for us." said Jacob.

"I never did like that pratt Barber, it gave me great pleasure seeing him and his mates whimper away like that."

95

"It gave me great pleasure knocking him on his arse too." said Jacob.

"Is everything alright Thomas?" asked a girl who emerged as a silhouette from the light of the barn doorway. Thomas gently put his arm around her waist, pulling her towards him.

"I'm fine, Keziah," he replied. "It's that idiot Barber, had too many drinks and was trying to start some trouble with these two, along with three of his friends behind him that is. They've gone now, we convinced them not to try anything."

The girl who had come to Thomas Walker's side was Keziah Woodrow, and she was his intended. She had promised to marry him next year when she came of age and the pair were seldom seen apart since that promise. She was a thickset girl who also had dark hair, and it was of the general opinion that they were to be a perfect match.

Jacob offered his hand to Thomas,

"Thanks again, my name's Jacob Allen."

They shook hands.

"My name's Thomas, Thomas Walker," he replied.

The group then returned back into the barn where the musicians were beginning their last song of the night, a love song to mellow the mood for the end of the evening. Jacob and Ned made their way back to the bench where the Fox family sat. Sarah's face was one of concern for Jacob.

"Are you alright?" she asked.

"I'm fine," Jacob replied.

"I heard you knocked Barber on his arse," said Bill Fox.

"I did," said Jacob.

"Good," said Bill, who was obviously another of the locals who was not at all a fond admirer of Jim Barber.

"You walking back to Norwich now?" Bill asked.

"I was hoping to find a barn or stable to get my head down for the night. My grandmother lives at Crostwick and I was hoping to see her tomorrow morning while I was in the area."

"I've got a fodder store next to my horses stable, there's plenty of hay and straw to make a bed if you want. It's not much but it's somewhere to get your head down."

"Thank you most kindly," said Jacob. "That would be exactly what we're looking for."

Sarah smiled, it was obvious that her father liked Jacob, and so did she.

It was just a short walk to the Fox household and comfortable bedding was arranged of straw and hay in the fodder shed. Both Jacob and Ned settled down for the night where they enjoyed a relatively comfortable night's sleep.

The following morning came, and Jacob and Ned were awoken to the sound of a cock crowing from the next-door property, and light was shining through the cracks in the door and the gaps in the roof tiles from above. When they emerged into the morning light outside in the courtyard, it was obvious that no one else was up yet, it was Sunday after all and they had been out till late drinking ale. Having scouted their surroundings, the pair quickly used a small privy situated between the cottage and the stable, and had a refreshing drink of water from a barrel used to catch rainwater from the guttering of the cottage. They were after all somewhat dehydrated from the ales consumed the night before.

"Shall we go now before everyone's up?" said Ned.

"You can if you like, you've got further to go than me. I'm going to Crostwick to see my grandmother, but I'd like to thank these people for putting us up before I go."

"Will you thank them for me? I've got a fair walk home and I'd like to get an early start."

"Yeah, of course I will," replied Jacob. "I'll see you at work tomorrow morning."

With that, Ned bid his farewells and set off on his walk back home to Norwich. Jacob returned back to the fodder shed where he lay for another hour until the sound of footsteps could be heard coming from outside. He quickly rose and opened the door to see who it was… it was Sarah.

"Good morning, did you sleep well?" she asked.

"Slept like a log," he replied. "I must get a fodder shed of my own someday."

Sarah laughed.

"Mother's up, she's warming up some milk for you. Where's Ned?"

"He's already gone, he asked me to thank you all for putting us up for the night."

Sarah smiled.

"And by the way," said Jacob. "Thank you for a lovely night last night, I really enjoyed myself. Never danced before but would love to do it again."

Sarah smiled again but said nothing, she had enjoyed the night too, especially in Jacob's company.

"I'd love to see you again. That is if you'd want to?" he asked.

If he had known her thoughts, he wouldn't have asked so hesitantly. She was as taken by him as he to her and there was never any doubt that she would accept.

"Yes I would," she replied. "When?"

"How about next week? Sunday after church? I'll come here to Sprowston, and we can spend the afternoon together."

"That's fine by me." Sarah replied.

Then, Anne Fox emerged from the cottage carrying two cups of warm milk.

"Where's your friend gone? I've got some warm milk for him."

"He's already gone, Mrs Fox, he asked me to thank you for your kind hospitality but he had to go because he had a fair walk home ahead of him."

Anne handed the two cups to Jacob and Sarah, and then Bill Fox emerged from the cottage.

"Good morning, young man, sleep well?"

"Very well, thank you," replied Jacob.

"Do your knuckles hurt after knocking Barber on his arse?"

Jacob smiled at Bill's joking comment.

"You know I never could stand that Jim Barber. We've had a bit of trouble with im around here. He'll think hard before starting trouble again I reckon," said Bill.

"I hope so," replied Jacob. "I don't want trouble every time I come to Sprowston."

"Oh I'm sure it'll all blow over in the end. Where's your friend?"

"He left early and told me to thank you for your hospitality."

"Why didn't you go with him?"

"I'm not going to Norwich, I'm going to Crostwick to visit my grandmother."

"Oh good for you," said Bill. He liked that, a young man who still took the time for his family, this was a good quality in his eyes. Jacob finished his milk and handed the cup back to Anne.

"Thank you very much, I'd better be on my way now. Again, thank you all for your kindness and hospitality."

"Give us a look if you happen to be in Sprowston again," said Bill.

"That I will," said Jacob as he smiled with a quick glance towards Sarah, who smiled back. And with that, he began his walk to Crostwick and waved goodbye to the Fox family.

"So when are you seeing him next?" asked Bill.

"Sunday after church," replied Sarah.

"Thought so," said Bill.

Anne Fox smiled.

Chapter Sixteen

It was a quarter past the hour of nine in the morning when Jacob arrived at Spring Farm. His knock on the door was welcomed with great pleasure and surprise by the Lutkin residents, who, at that very moment, were dressed in their Sunday best outfits ready for the forthcoming church service. Living at, and running the farm was Elizabeth's elder brother, George, along with his wife, Sarah, and their three children, Annie Lutkin who was eighteen, Robert Lutkin who was seventeen and their youngest child, Amelia, who was fourteen. Of course, Elizabeth's mother, Anne Lutkin, was also living at the house with the family. She was now an elderly woman and was being cared for by George's family, as she had inevitably become frailer with age. It was a rare occasion to see Jacob and everyone were pleased to see him, especially his young cousins who were more of his own age.

"Jacob, my boy, it's good to see you, what are you doing here?" asked George.

He was now the proprietor of Spring Farm who by tradition as eldest son was destined to inherit his father's estate.

"I was at a barn dance in Sprowston last night and some friends of mine put me up there for the night. I thought that while I was in the area, I should pay a visit; it's been a while since I saw you all."

Anne Lutkin, though now frail, hugged her grandson. "Well, I'm glad to you came to see us, it's always a joy to see you. I wish you would come here more often. How are your mother and father?"

"They're fine Gran, in fact, they're coming here too. I should think they'll be at church if they don't get here before."

This news pleased Anne Lutkin immensely, today she would have most of her family around her, all except for Martha who was still residing at nearby Horsted. She still stayed in touch with her family and visited Crostwick at least once a week, never losing her closeness to her mother in the passing of time.

Ten o'clock arrived and the family began to make their way to church in their Sunday best. As they left the farm through the main gate and onto the road leading towards the church, a call was heard in the distance. The group turned and looked, and there in the distance was a couple waving to the group, it was Edward and Elizabeth, they had just made it in time for church. They met the group there were hugs and kisses and joyful greetings among them all. Anne was especially overcome with joy, ever since her daughter's departure all those years ago, too little time had been spent with her. She had always regarded the years of Elizabeth's absence as lost years, but now, they were over she still only saw her on occasions and longed to see her daughter more.

The group finally arrived at the church yard where the locals of Crostwick were making their way up the path leading to the church entrance, there to be greeted by a young country parson, who, only a year earlier had taken over the parsonage of Crostwick following the sad passing of the Reverend Nash, who had faithfully served the parish for well over twenty-five years.

Inside the church, the Lutkin family sat in their usual place second row from front. Behind in the third row, already seated, sat Richard Lutkin with his wife and two children, and Jane Watling (formally Lutkin) with her husband and their two children. Edward looked behind to the back of the church where, as he had expected, sat his brother James, with his wife and four children. They smiled to one another; Edward signalled that he would take time to see them later that day. James acknowledged the communication with a thumbs up.

Prayers were said, sermons were read and a baby girl called Mary Carter was publicly baptised, before the village congregation were to finally leave the church to return to their homes and enjoy a lazy Sunday afternoon of rest. After the service, the young parson stood at the church door to bid his parishioners farewell. The Lutkin family, including Richard and Jane's families, all returned to Spring Farm to enjoy a Sunday afternoon of which food and drink was consumed and everyone sat together to reminisce of happy times of old. Of times when they were young in childhood growing into adolescence, fun had playing together, and of the good times they had enjoyed with their parents. Stories came from Anne of how she and George had married and started a family, raising the children and running the farm together when they were just young adults themselves, not much older than the very grandchildren that sat around her. They were happy times indeed. For a short while, tears welled in the eyes of Jane and Elizabeth, but especially they welled in the eyes of Anne Lutkin, who, though with the absence of Martha, could see that this rare occasion of the family being together could well be the last of these moments to occur in her lifetime.

After a while, Edward begged pardon for a short absence as he left to pay his brother a visit at his cottage within the Spring Farm estate. In these last five years, both Edward and James had to endure the sad loss of their own elderly parents. Nathaniel Allen was the first to depart this earth in early December 1791, catching a winter chill from which he found unable to endure and which finally overcame him. Not eighteen months later, Mary Allen passed away having become frailer since the passing of her husband. Some say she died of a broken heart, but who will ever really know what Mary Allen was feeling in both her mind and body.

Edward reached his brother's cottage in just a few moments. It was situated in the same block of terraced cottages, and four doors away from the very cottage that was the home of his parents, where both he and James had grown from children to men. Upon his arrival, Edward hugged his brother, it was good to see the man of who he had grown up with and had played with as a child. With their parents now gone, and with the preoccupation of their own new families to deal with, encounters between the brothers had become all too rare, and with the passing of time were more unlikely ever to improve.

James was now head of his own household. His wife, Millie, was a local girl from Crostwick, she had known James nearly all her life since childhood. Together, they had four children which they had named after the four members of the previous Allen family. The eldest son, as was often the tradition, was named after himself and was affectionately called Jimmy. The second child was a son he named Nathan after his own father. Then there was his only daughter named Mary, and his youngest son he called Edward to the delight of his namesake and uncle. For nearly an hour, Edward sat at his brothers table enjoying his family's hospitality and they too reminisced of stories of old when their family of birth were together. They enjoyed talking of treasured moments that were to be firmly ingrained in their minds until the time of their own final demise. Though the two men hid their emotions as grown men were expected to do, a tear could have easily been shed of the memories of those innocent times of when they were both small children and Nathaniel and Mary Allen were both young parents themselves.

Edward and James hugged once more upon Edward's departure and he returned back to Spring Farm. He neared the farm gate, and there saw a small two seated buggy pull into the track leading to the front door. As he approached, he smiled upon the realisation that the occupants of the buggy were none other than Martha and her husband, John Watts. Elizabeth would be beside herself with joy at seeing Martha, he thought.

Edward entered the house just behind John and Martha, and as predicted, Elizabeth was beside herself with joy at Martha's arrival, but the most pleased was, of course, Anne Lutkin. For the first time in many years, all her children were together again all in the same room. She couldn't remember how long it had been but the moment seemed all so special. Unknown to all those around her, she had a deep suspicion that this time would be the last full family gathering that she was to witness.

Another two hours passed of this family gathering, and the special feeling of joy and happiness that the gathering had brought, until finally, Edward, Elizabeth and Jacob had to bid their farewells and make their journey back home to Norwich. After their walk back, they settled down exhausted and retired to bed early to gather strength for the working day ahead the following morning. Fond memories of that day were to stay with them all to the end.

Not one month later, news came from Crostwick to Elizabeth that Anne Lutkin had passed away in her sleep. She was found lying peacefully in her bed by her family in the morning. Once again, the family reunited to pay tribute and respects at her funeral. Though sadness and grief was with everyone present, her family had the comfort of knowing that not long before her passing, she was reunited with them all for one last time.

Chapter Seventeen

The war with France had come to the city of Norwich during the year of 1797. After the naval battle of Camperdown against the Dutch fleet, which was led by Admiral Duncan, the victorious fleet sailed to the port at Yarmouth where many of the wounded were brought back to the city to be treated at the Norfolk and Norwich hospital. On February 14th, a British fleet under the command of Admiral Jervis successfully defeated a Spanish fleet of twice its own size just off the Cape of St Vincent. A young commodore named Horatio Nelson, who was from the Norfolk village of Burnham Thorpe and educated at the Norwich school, was the hero of the day having successfully split the Spanish fleet by sailing through the middle of them whilst on the attack. A week later, he was subsequently knighted and promoted to Rear Admiral. The battle had ended with the surrender of the Spanish Rear Admiral Don Xavier Wynthuysen who presented Nelson his sword. Nelson was later to present the sword to the city of Norwich. He wrote in his journal that he knew of no place where it would have given him and his family more pleasure to have it kept than in the capital city of the county of which he had the honour to be born. As a result, he was given the freedom of the city.

Meanwhile, close by, a fond relationship had blossomed between a young man and a pretty young girl. The pair would meet regularly every week when the working week was finished. Jacob would journey to Sprowston on Saturday evening to stay overnight as a guest at the Fox household, strictly chaperoned, of course. Bill Fox had, in the course of time, become quite fond of Jacob and had no problem foreseeing him as a son in law in the making. That was only if Jacob would finally work up the courage to pop the question. Jacob, however, continued in his employment at the King's Head and was by now, along with his friend Ned Barrett, a fully trained and working farrier. He worked not only on the horses of the King's mail coaches, but to a quite successful horse shoeing business based and owned by the same establishment, namely the proprietors of the King's Head Inn.

***

It was late May, almost into summertime, on one midweek morning that Jacob arrived at work on what he thought was to be an ordinary day. After feeding and watering the horses that had stabled up at the Inn overnight and which were ready to be harnessed up to the Yarmouth coach, Jacob and Ned set about preparing the forge fire ready should any customers arrive wanting to have their horses shod, which in due course did happen. An uneventful morning went by of usual chores which consisted of Jacob and Ned juggling jobs of horse shoeing with the daily business of dealing with the mail coaches. Robert Langley had disappeared during the late morning and Ned and Jacob had a good idea where he was likely to be. He often disappeared in the time period leading up to lunchtime and would often return at mid-afternoon with the strong odour of ale about his person. Needless to say, not much work was carried out by Langley for the rest of the day.

Sure enough, at about two in the afternoon, Langley returned and settled down on a chair that stood in the corner of the forge with a strong smell of ale wafting off his breath. He had a face of thunder about him, something or somebody in the alehouse had clearly annoyed him, but to Ned and Jacob, this was not unusual. Robert Langley was a man of very unpredictable mood swings and had a very short fuse, especially under the influence of ale.

As Ned and Jacob continued their day's work, Langley nodded off in his chair, dribbling and snoring in the process. An hour had passed when a regular customer to the forge came in, a malt house manager called Herbert Bawdswell brought his horse in which was in urgent need of a new shoe, so naturally, Ned and Jacob immediately set to work. After tying up the horse outside the forge, Jacob began the job of removing the old shoe by straightening the clenches. These are the nails securing the shoes which are bent over at the side of the hoof wall to prevent from moving. Once straightened, the old shoe can be removed by using a pair of pincers. Meanwhile, Bawdswell left the two farriers to see to his horse and entered the inn to have an ale as he waited. Ned worked the forge, pumping the bellows to create more heat in the coals and thus heating the metal strip so hot as to be pliable enough to shape to the desired shape and form the new shoe. Jacob trimmed the excess growth of hoof using hoof cutters and levelled off using a rasp. Finally, he tidied up the hoof wall and any ragged pieces of the sole using a drawing knife.

Ned had heated up the already half prepared shoe which was nicely bent to the rough shape but it still had to burn onto the hoof to find the final shape which would then be finely tapped. He pulled the shoe from the hot coals using large metal tongs, and as he snatched the shoe from the forge, a hot coal flew out, landing squarely on the lap of the sleeping Robert Langley, who was seated not a yard away from the forge fire. Just at the very moment when Ned passed through the door to hand a waiting Jacob the tongs and shoe, an almighty shriek resonated from within the forge. Ned looked back to see Langley jumping up from his chair in a state of panic, frantically brushing the hot coal off his now smoking breeches at groin level.

"You stupid bastard!" screamed Langley, as he hastily patted down his smoking groin.

Ned turned his head away from Langley to hide a fit of laughter that, with closed mouth to muffle the sound, was now completely overwhelming him.

Jacob, seeing that something funny had obviously happened by the expression on his friends face, started to chuckle himself. He asked Ned what had happened knowing from the sound of the shriek that something unpleasant had obviously happened to Langley. Still trying to hold back the laughter Ned replied, "A hot coal landed on Robert's lap." This in turn had the effect of both Ned and Jacob trying to suppress an unstoppable fit of laughter.

With the hot shoe held to the hoof and burning the desired pattern onto it, still laughing, Jacob made the finer adjustments to the shoe to get the correct shape. He finally cooled the shoe in water and nailed it to the hoof and cut off the nail ends. Jacob had found this one the hardest horseshoes he had ever changed. He fought to suppress the laughter as he filed the nail ends and the edge of the shoe and bent the nail ends round to form a new clench.

Langley by now had extinguished his smoking breeches and was beginning to boil in a fit of rage at the laughter that was being had at his expense. The hilarity of the moment was about to be ended in one quick instant, for as Ned returned back into the forge, he was greeted by a loud and painful smack across the side of his face. Langley had hit him with a leather horsewhip. Ned, after momentarily recovering, then lunged forward, knocking Langley backwards and up against the wall behind him. He then pinned Langley's head tight to the wall, his left forearm up against Langley's throat and snatched the whip away with his right hand.

"That's the last time you'll ever hit me, Langley!" snarled Ned. "You pathetic pratt!"

He then pushed Langley away, he turned and headed back towards the door and towards Jacob who, having heard the commotion, stood at the door watching in disbelief. Suddenly, Langley grabbed a hammer from off the anvil and made for Ned who was unaware as his back was turned from him.

"Look out!" shouted Jacob, and he rushed past Ned, straight at Langley and grabbed the now raised hammer, pulling it from his hand and throwing it to one side. Then, a loud smack was heard as Jacob hit Langley square in the face, knocking him down to the floor.

"The bastard was going to hit you with that hammer!" shouted Jacob to a now horrified Ned. "Go and get Jackson and tell him there's been trouble at the forge."

The man who Jacob was referring to was Charlie Jackson, the manager of the Post office and the mail coaches based at the King's Head. He had succeeded William Burrell as manager two years earlier after Burrell had sadly passed away after serving over twenty years for the proprietors. Ned returned back with Jackson after just a couple of minutes. He was a short stocky man, middle aged and smartly dressed, and wore a silver wig. He was a man who had settled in well into his new position and was clearly in charge.

"Now, what's going on in here?" he asked.

"It's these two," said Langley. "Thought it was funny to put hot coal on me, and this one hit me." He pointed towards Jacob.

"He was going to hit Ned with a hammer!" shouted Jacob. "He could have killed him."

"Is that true Robert?" asked Jackson.

"No, it is not!" Langley replied. "These two have never liked me and this time they attacked me."

"He's a liar!" shouted Ned. "The coal was an accident, and he hit me across the face with a horsewhip. When I took the whip from him, he came at me from behind with that hammer, and Jacob grabbed it from him and hit him."

Jackson stood silent, pausing for thought of what to do next. Seconds passed to what seemed like minutes to Ned and Jacob.

"You two," said Jackson. "You two can go home right now, and I want to see you both here first thing in the morning."

No reaction was made by the pair, just stunned silence.

"And you Robert, can stay here and cover for these two for the rest of the day, until I come to a decision of what to do with you all in the morning."

Jackson, being a rational man, had decided that more time was needed to give this situation more thought. He could see the red mark across Ned's face where Langley had hit him with the whip and could also smell the odour of ale upon Langley's breath. He surmised that an element of truth had come from Ned, but never the less, he needed more time.

Jacob and Ned grabbed their belongings and left together while discussing the events of what had just happened, and what the reactions of their families were likely to be, should they lose their jobs. Above all, they vented their anger at Langley who had clearly lied.

"You're home early, is everything alright?" asked Elizabeth upon Jacob's arrival.

"No it's not," replied Jacob and thus began to tell Elizabeth the whole story.

"Father will be furious, won't he?"

"Maybe," replied Elizabeth. "Let's see what happens first. I'm sure Mr Jackson is wise enough to let this go, and I'm sure he won't want to lose you or Ned. Who knows? He might even get rid of Langley. We'll cross that bridge when we get to it."

Jacob didn't sleep well at all that night, with the thought of the oncoming decision from Charlie Jackson and the reaction from his father who was due to arrive back on the Diligence from London the following morning. When the morning finally came, after a long night, Jacob set off full of uncertainty of what events might unfold. He met Ned at the corner of the market square which was just a short distance from the King's Head.

"My father told me that if I lose my job, I had better find another job within a week or I'll have to leave home. He says he's not feeding anyone old enough to earn their own keep," said Ned.

"My mother said wait and see, but I don't know what my father will do or say when he gets back from London," said Jacob.

Moments later, they arrived at the King's Head where they were greeted by Charlie Jackson who led them into a room at the rear of the Inn used for administration and financial affairs.

"Good morning, you two," said Jackson. "Right, let's get down to it. I've had time to think about what's happened, and the way I see it is that I can't prove either way that you put that hot coal on Robert's lap deliberately, or as you say it was an accident. Equally, I've only his word that he didn't come at you with a hammer, whereas you say he did. Either way, I can't see how you could possibly work with Robert Langley again, or him with you. Either he will have to go or you two will."

There was a brief pause, followed by a deep sigh from Jackson.

"I have to tell you now that my decision is based entirely on the fact that Robert has a wife and two young children who are still not yet at working age, whereas you two are young and have no dependants. I'm sorry but I'll have to let you both go."

"But it was his fault, he attacked Ned!" yelled Jacob.

"I'm sorry young man, but that's my decision. I'm sure you'll both find work soon enough, you're both young and strong but Robert has a family to support and I wouldn't want that on my conscience. I'm sorry that's all I have to say upon the matter."

Jacob and Ned left the King's Head furious with Langley, and with Jackson who had made the decision albeit for honourable reasons.

"There's gonna be some squit now when I get home," said Ned. "What the bloody hell am I gonna do?"

"Me too, my father's gonna go mad," said Jacob.

Indeed, later that evening, Edward returned home having already heard what had supposedly happened when he arrived at the King's Head, but he waited to hear Jacob's side of the story. He stayed calm but was nonetheless deeply disappointed with him and was a little angry within, but unlike Ned's father was unlikely to throw out his only son. Jacob told his story and explained why Jackson had come to the decision he had. On that account, Edward agreed that Jackson, given the circumstances, had made what he thought was a logical decision and held no blame towards him. He was, however, quite eager to speak to Langley on the subject.

Chapter Eighteen

Jacob had suddenly found that he had nowhere to go when he rose the next morning at his usual time. Both Edward and Elizabeth also rose at their usual early hours. Elizabeth warmed up some toast and milk for breakfast.

"Where are you going today?" she asked Jacob.

"To find a job," he replied.

"Where might that be," asked Edward.

"I don't know yet, I think I'll try all the smithy's and stable yards. If I don't have any luck there, then I'll go outside the city and get farm work, it'll be harvest time soon."

"In two months it will," said Edward. "You'd be better off sticking to your own trade, though out of the city may be a good idea. Most of the smithy's around here are family run, sons are working for fathers and they're unlikely to employ anyone outside the family."

"I'll try anyway," said Jacob. "I've got nothing to lose by asking, and besides, it'd be better to find a job around here."

So Jacob set off on his mission to find a job, and so did indeed spend his time visiting smithy after smithy to find, to his great disappointment, that his father was right all along. Most of the farrier positions were indeed taken, or were kept closely within the family of the businesses concerned. Meanwhile, while Jacob was in the process of his fruitless task of job seeking, his father returned back to work at the King's Head to begin another three-day shift on the Diligence to London and back.

"Where's Mr Jackson?" asked Edward to a stable lad who was bringing out one of the horses for the Diligence.

"He's already been and gone," replied the lad. "He dropped off the mail and returned back to the post office."

Edward surveyed the surroundings of the stable yard. Everyone was doing their duty ready for the coach's departure, which was scheduled to depart in about an hours' time. He checked the forge, it was empty, so he entered the staff room to put on his King's mail coat and hat and gather his work equipment. He then returned back to the stable yard where two more horses had been brought out. At last, he saw what he had been waiting for, Langley emerged from a stable and headed back into the forge alone. He quickly entered the forge just behind Langley and closed the door behind him.

Langley turned in surprise. "What do you want?"

"I've come to see you Langley," replied Edward.

"What for?"

"You know what for. You cost my boy his job with your lies and deceit."

"No, I didn't. One of them put a hot coal on my lap while I sat in that chair and the other one hit me," stuttered Langley.

"I heard you picked up a hammer and made for young Ned from behind."

"He's a liar!" Langley shouted.

"No he isn't, there was a mark on his face where you hit him with a horse whip. We all know what you are like with the young-uns, you're a cowardly sack of horse shit."

Langley stood silent.

"You ever cross me or my boy again, I'll fucking kill you, Langley, do you hear?"

Langley again didn't reply. He was a younger man than Edward by about ten years or so and was a man who was used to bullying young boys rather than being threatened himself, which he didn't find to his liking. It therefore came to him that he might possibly get the better of this older man if the opportunity should arise, if he should happen catch Edward unawares, and that moment suddenly came. Edward, having said his piece, then turned back to leave the forge, he had his back turned, so Langley seized his moment. He grabbed a horseshoe and threw it at Edward, just grazing the side of his head, luckily for Edward, not full on. Langley's aim was not good unluckily for him, because with that, Edward lunged towards Langley and hit him hard in the face, then, to Langley's great surprise, followed on with a left hook and then a right. The older man was faster than he had anticipated. Langley fell back on the floor in much the same manner as Jacob had left him two days earlier.

"Is that all you've got, you pathetic little shit!"

Langley however recovered, and this time, he picked up an iron bar from the workbench.

Then… to Langley's horror, there was a sound of the click of a flintlock pistol, and the pistol was pointed directly into Langley's face.

"Try it, Langley and I'll blow yer fucking head off!"

Edward stepped forward and Langley retreated backwards until he was backed up against the forge wall. Edward then put the barrel of the pistol into Langley's mouth, he shook uncontrollably in mortal fear for his life.

"You know, Langley, anyone who harms my family, I would gladly swing from the gallows for, so just give me half a reason to pull this fucking trigger."

Langley dropped the bar. The shock of having a loaded and cocked pistol pointed at his face caused him to suddenly experience an uncontrollable bodily function. Red faced and shaking, his breeches started to moisten with the wetness of his own urine which had trickled into a small puddle on the floor at his feet. Edward, on seeing what had happened, continued to hold the pistol motionless for more than four seconds before he finally lowered it. He then slowly turned to exit towards the door and as the door opened, Edward began to chuckle, and his chuckle turned into full laughter as he left. Langley, however, dropped down to his knees, still shaking, and kneeling in his own piss.

The following morning, Jacob took it upon himself to visit his sweetheart Sarah Fox in Sprowston as he had decided that he would take advantage of his hopefully brief time of leisure. The fifty-minute walk to Sprowston was greeted by Bill Fox who was working out in the yard with his son Edmond.

"Good morning, Jacob, why aren't you at work today?" he asked.

"Because I've lost my job at the King's Head," he replied.

"Why, what happened?"

"It was that Langley, the yard foreman, he had a fight with Ned. He hit him with a horsewhip so Ned pushed him up against a wall and took the whip from him. Then Langley came at him with a hammer."

"You're joking."

"I wish I was," said Jacob. "Ned had his back to him so I hit Langley and knocked him down on his arse and took the hammer from him, he would have killed Ned

107

otherwise. Both me and Ned lost our jobs because of it. I spent all yesterday looking for work in the city with no luck so I thought I would come out here and see if there's any farm work to be had, and pay you all a visit while I'm out here."

Bill smiled, "She's inside with her mother and sisters. She'll be glad to see you."

Jacob entered the cottage to the expected greeting of "What are you doing here?" from Sarah and her family. He told them the whole story of what had happened and how he was now looking for work. The women showed great concern for his situation.

"Oh my word, you poor thing, what are you going to do now?" was the predicted response. Jacob enjoyed the attention, and sat with a cup of warmed up milk that Anne had prepared for him in her usual polite and customary way. An hour passed of this pleasant social visit with his sweetheart and her family before he finally rose to continue his quest of searching for work. His intention being to seek out employment at one of the larger farms, especially Manor Farm, whom he thought would welcome a young farm hand who was a trained farrier. He kissed Sarah goodbye and arranged their next meeting at the usual time and place, namely on Saturday and into Sunday. Leaving the cottage and the women behind, he would just take time to say goodbye to Bill who was in his workshop with Edmond.

"I'll see you later, Mr Fox," said Jacob, as he stood at the workshop door.

"Where are you going?" asked Bill.

"I thought I'd try Manor Farm. They're bound to need extra help with the coming of harvest, and besides, I'm an experienced farrier, that's bound to be useful to 'em."

"You know," said Bill. "You know that Walter Fairclough died of dropsy last month."

"Who's Walter Fairclough?" asked Jacob.

"Walter Fairclough was the blacksmith of Sprowston. The entire village and the farms around here used him, and passing travellers on their way to Wroxham, Stalham and Caister."

"Really?" said Jacob.

"Now Walter didn't have any sons, he had three daughters who have all married, so there's no one to carry on the business. He lived just off Blue Boar Lane."

"Did he?" replied a still confused Jacob.

Bill continued. "Since he died, anyone who needs their horse shoeing now has to go to Graver's place at Catton. It's the nearest to here but it's still nearly two miles away, and on the wrong turnpike road."

"Really?" said Jacob who was still lost at the point that Bill was trying to make.

"Well, don't you see? Sprowston needs a smith. You're a shoe smith and I've got a forge and a yard. This is a good opportunity for the both of us, we could double up as a wheelwright and smithy. You could learn a thing or two about making wheels and Edmond could learn horseshoeing as well as his own trade. It would be a good business; everyone would come here. Why not come and work here?"

Jacob didn't need to think about Bill's offer, it made perfect sense to him, but the details of the arrangement would have to be sorted out. The wages, would he be working for Bill or was it a business arrangement?

"How about we divide the horse shoe business a third to you, two thirds to me. That's to cover the use of my forge, and the coal and metal. When you're working for me making wheels, I'll pay you sixpence a day," said Bill.

"Sounds good to me. Are you sure about this?" said Jacob.

"It'll either work or it won't," said Bill. "There's only one way to find out."

"When do we start then?" asked Jacob.

"Well, why don't you start now, by making up a sign to hang out the front showing there's a smithy here and also one for the main road with an arrow pointing the way to us. Then come here tomorrow and we'll see if anyone shows up. I'll put the word out in the village too."

Without hesitation, Jacob set about the task of sign maker. A simple horseshoe was nailed to a plank of wood and was hung underneath the fox sign out the front. Then, a similar sign, cut arrow shaped and nailed to a wooden peg was driven into the ground on the side of main turnpike road, just yards from the turn off for Church Lane where Bill Fox's place was situated.

"We're going to open up a smithy right here. It was your father's idea," said Jacob to a clearly happy Sarah.

"That's wonderful," she replied. Now she would be able to see Jacob every day.

A second arrow shaped sign was then made and placed at the main road just yards from Church Lane in the opposite direction to cover any traffic coming the other way. Jacob then bid his farewells and headed back home to Norwich, where on his return he told his mother of the events that had unfolded. Elizabeth, though slightly fearful of the possibility of a failed business venture, was pleased that Jacob had found a venture to pursue and she wished him well. She was bound to worry, she was his mother after all.

On his arrival back from London the following day, Edward also greeted the news warmly. This to him was a great chance for his son to make something of his life. Should the venture fail, he knew that both he and Elizabeth would always be there for him. There was laughter between father and son later, when Edward, who had waited for Elizabeth to be out of earshot, told Jacob the story of what had happened between him and Langley. How Langley had been knocked down and pissed himself at the sight of a pistol pointed at his head. Jacob laughed, he was very proud of his father.

Chapter Nineteen

Bill had made a special trip that evening to the Blue Boar Inn. "I've got to put the word out that we're now a smithy," he told his wife, Anne. It was refreshing for him to have a real excuse to have a few ales at the Blue Boar Inn with his mates. The news was received with great interest too, it had been an inconvenience to the farms and villagers having to travel two miles to Catton to shoe a horse or repair a broken tool. Every village essentially needed a smithy; Bill had recently filled a small gap in the market by occasionally making nails and metal straps for the local builders and farmers. Now he was to replace the old smithy of Sprowston on a permanent basis, and just in time too, for unknown to Bill, Manor Farm was on the verge of creating a smithy of its own.

Jacob turned up for work early and eager the following morning.

"Right, Jacob, until we start getting a few horses in, you can help Edmond prepare and fit some iron rims that are ready to fit on them there wheels I've already made. Welcome to the world of wheel making," said Bill, smiling.

Jacob didn't need much guiding either, he was used to working around a forge and his trade of farrier wasn't just limited to horse shoeing. He had learned to make basic tools and repair them, along with forging tie straps and nail making almost like a basic blacksmith whose metal working skills were far more advanced than a farrier. This new environment was sure to teach him new metal working skills and maybe even teach him some carpentry skills as a wheelwright too.

It was nearly ten o'clock when the first customer came in with a horse to shoe. Albert Broom, a farm hand from Manor Farm, came in with one of the large working horses, a Shire and Suffolk Punch cross.

"Morning Bill," said Albert. "Told the foreman about your smithy this morning and he told me to bring this beast in to be shod. He needs two, one front and one rear. Said he was glad someone close by could do it at last."

"No problem Albert, I've just the man for the job, he'll get to it right away," said Bill.

Jacob needed no orders, he immediately got on with the job at hand and had the horse sorted in no time. Albert returned to Manor Farm a happy customer. The next hour, Jacob spent preparing for more horse shoeing that might happen to be needed. Strips of steel were cut to various lengths, ideal for horseshoes and stored in a corner of the forge ready for the next jobs. Then he returned back to helping Edmond with the wheel rims. Welding the metal hoops together using hot molten iron and eventually fitting the red-hot hoops to the wooden felloe rims, where they would contract and tighten as they cooled as soon as water was thrown on, thus pulling the wheel and spokes tightly together. Shortly after, another horse was brought in, this time from Church Farm which was situated at the far end of the same road as Bill's place. Word was getting out already and once again Jacob shod the animal.

Jacob continued to labour between wheel making and horse shoeing as the day progressed, until finally he had shod four large working horses from three farms, and had helped with the fitting of four metal wheel rims as well as the preparation of the shoe steels and some shoe nails were made for future horses. It had been a busy day. Sarah came out with a tray of three tankards containing weak table ale for the three working men.

"How was your day?" she asked Jacob.

"Fine, as I expected," he replied.

"Four horses shod on the first day," said Bill, smiling. "I think this smithy is gonna be a busy one."

This made everyone feel happy. Jacob returned home, exhausted after his day's work and with nearly an hours walk back home to Tombland.

"How did it go?" Elizabeth asked.

He told her, and it was clear to her that work was there to be had, and that though she initially worried of the venture, maybe her son had made the correct decision. Jacob settled down in his father's chair in Edwards' absence, of course, only to be disturbed some forty minutes later when there was a sudden knock at the door, which in turn was answered by Elizabeth.

"Is Jacob in?" said a voice coming from the door, a voice Jacob immediately recognised.

"Yes he is, come in," replied Elizabeth. "Jacob! Ned's here to see you!" she called.

Jacob sat up. "Ned, what brings you here tonight?"

"I've come to say goodbye, old friend."

Jacob looked puzzled, "Goodbye? Where are you going?"

"British army, I've signed up. I'm taking the Kings' shilling, I've had to."

Jacob was shocked. "Why?" he asked. "You're not a soldier, you're a farrier, what did you go and sign up for? It's bloody dangerous being a soldier."

"I've been thrown out by my father. He said he's not supporting a grown man and that I'll have to make my own way in life. I've looked everywhere for work and I've been sleeping rough in the streets these last two nights."

It was at that point that Jacob noticed how Ned seemed to be looking rather gaunt, rough shaven, and he noticed that his clothes seemed grimier than normal.

"I've only two choices, the army or the workhouse, and the army will feed me and pay me, especially in these times of war."

"But you might be killed," said Elizabeth, who was listening with equal interest and surprise.

"I'll probably die here in the streets of starvation or in the workhouse if I don't. I reckon I've a better chance with the army feeding me. They might just have me looking after the horses instead of fighting, especially if they know that I work with horses and can shoe 'em. I might not do anything thas too dangerous."

Jacob understood, he had looked for work himself in Norwich to no ends. It was only luck through his own connections with Bill that had created his fortunate circumstances.

"When was the last time you ate?" asked Elizabeth.

"I ate the last of the food my mother gave me yesterday."

"Why didn't you come here earlier? We could have put you up for a short while till you found work."

"No, ya couldn't," replied Ned. "You've enough problems of your own with Jacob out of work, and besides, I don't want to intrude. This is my problem to sort out not yours, but thanks for offering none the less."

"We couldn't leave you to starve on the streets, Ned, not a friend," said Jacob.

"I'm sorry, but I've got my pride and I'm not imposing myself upon you kind people, it just wouldn't do."

"Well, at least we can give you some food now," said Elizabeth.

She made straight for the larder to find some bread, cheese and cider.

"When do you leave?" asked Jacob.

"I join up tomorrow at the Guildhall. The local militia are calling for volunteers to join the King's First Dragoons. I'll take the King's shilling then. Spoke to a recruiting sergeant today and they'll be expecting me there tomorrow bright and early."

"Do you know where they'll send you?"

"No, I don't," replied Ned. "Got to train first, then I'll go wherever they tell me."

Elizabeth brought the food and drink she had prepared.

"You'll stay here tonight, Ned," she said.

"Thank you, Mrs Allen, you've been most kind, I won't forget this. The nights are hard sleeping rough on the streets."

"You know, Ned," said Jacob. "Things are not quite as bad here as you may think. I've found work with Bill Fox in Sprowston. He's opened up his forge to take horse trade and wants me to shoe the horses and help with wheel making, I started today in fact."

Ned smiled. "I'm glad for ya, old friend. You know you'll have to marry Sarah now, now that yer working with her father!"

"That's right Ned, you tell him!" laughed Elizabeth.

"Maybe someday, who knows?" said Jacob. "Besides, she may not wanna marry me."

With that, everybody laughed.

Both Ned and Jacob retired early to bed, they both were exhausted after what had been a long eventful day. Jacob was fatigued from his first days' work at Bill's forge and Ned, having his first decent night's sleep after living rough in the streets of Norwich. The following morning, they both rose early, to eventually leave in different directions, and maybe to never see one another again. They stopped at the bottom of the alley at Tombland and the friends shook hands.

"Goodbye old friend and good luck," said Jacob. "Don't go and get yourself killed, just go and give them Frenchies hell!"

Ned laughed. "That I will! And you make sure you marry that gal of yours and raise a family with her. You're both meant to be, you know that."

Jacob smiled. "I will. You have a good life."

Ned patted Jacob's shoulder. "You too," he replied.

And with that, the friends parted, not knowing what future lay before either, but there was a feeling within both of them that this would be the last time they would see each other again.

Chapter Twenty

Work progressed well at Bill's forge. Word was getting around, and consequently, more trade came in, steadily the horse trade became regular. In time, the locals came to using the forge for more specialised work such as tool making and repairing. Knives and chisels were sharpened and even plough blades were forged. The smithy was evolving to not just a smithy and wheelwright's forge but into a fully functional blacksmith's workshop in its own right. The main customers were, as predicted, the surrounding farms and the passing traffic from the main turnpike road through Sprowston, and the business flourished. Jacob learned many more skills in his new environment, and as more work came in he found that he was making a better living than at his old job at the King's Head. This pleased his parents immensely.

***

It was a Wednesday in late January 1798, when on Jacob's arrival home from a day's work at the forge, his mother made an announcement.

"Your cousin, Robert, is getting married at Crostwick Church on Saturday and we're all invited. Are you coming?"

Jacob looked to his father who was sat in his chair in front of the fire quietly smoking his pipe. There was no real reason for him to look Edward's way, he was just curious to see what his father's reaction to the announcement may be.

"It would make your mother happy if you went," said Edward. "Why don't you bring Sarah with you? I'm sure the family would all like to meet her."

"I suppose so," said Jacob.

Then, he thought for a moment. "He's very young to be getting married, isn't he? Who's the girl?"

"Just a local girl in the village," said Elizabeth.

Both Edward and Jacob discreetly smiled, knowing that marriage to one so young, as in the case of young Robert Lutkin could only mean one thing, he had got this girl pregnant and a quick marriage was the solution to avoid any scandal. This was the way things were commonly done in such a situation.

"So, are you bringing Sarah with you?" Elizabeth asked.

"I'll ask her tomorrow," replied Jacob, and the following morning, he did indeed ask Sarah.

"Yes, I'd love to come," she replied.

Like so many young girls of the time, there was nothing they liked better than a wedding celebration. This for them was the time of romance and happy ever afters and celebrating, it was welcome entertainment in times when entertainment was scarce. The day was always special, not just for the bride and groom, but to the guests and family, especially the women. There was nothing they enjoyed more than to help with the celebrations and get together in the way only women do.

Saturday arrived. Jacob had already arranged with Bill to have the day off from what was by now a busy thriving business. Both Bill and Anne Fox had thought that Jacob and Sarah going on to a wedding might prod them in the right direction as to any future matrimonial endeavours. This thought had also crossed the mind of both Edward and Elizabeth Allen, who were very fond of Sarah. Jacob had brought his Sunday best clothes with him to work on the Friday and stayed overnight at the Fox residence, much as he usually did every Saturday. He slept in the room used by Edmond and formerly their eldest brother, William, who had by now married and left the residence. Sarah also put on her Sunday best dress, a cotton dress pale blue in colour. Not fancy, a dress of a village girl made special by her best cream coloured bonnet and a beige coloured shawl to wrap around her shoulders and thus keep out the winter chill.

Jacob's best clothes were mainly hand me downs from his father which had the distinct similarity of a mail coach uniform, namely a smart blue jacket and a black three cornered hat. However, his breeches were of a different colour from the uniform, these were grey. *'Better not to look too much like a mail coach driver'*, he thought. But despite the hand me downs, he did look very smart none-the-less.

Bill had allowed the couple the use of his horse and cart which he would usually use for working purposes. He didn't want Sarah to mess up her best dress on the muddy roads between Sprowston and Crostwick. Jacob was to meet his parents at the church, this was another chance for them to see Sarah who they liked very much but always felt they never saw enough of. This was due to Jacob always staying away at Sprowston at the weekends. Sarah had never stayed in Norwich at Jacob's home, it was not an acceptable thing for a young girl to do. But to Edward and Elizabeth, Sarah was the girl their son was most likely to marry, and like most parents they eagerly awaited a forthcoming announcement.

It was a quarter to eleven in the morning when the Lutkin family arrived at the church from Spring Farm. Edward and Elizabeth had already arrived an hour earlier at the farm having made an early start that morning on their trek to Crostwick. Fortunately, they had managed to hitch a ride on the back of a cart heading in the same direction for the last three miles. Rides on carts were common in these days of slow travel, it was second nature for a cart driver to offer a lift to a stranger who was walking the road the same way. Shortly after, Jacob and Sarah arrived on their borrowed cart. The service was due to be held at approximately eleven, so they had only just made it in time with little room to spare. Most of the guests and family had already entered the church as they drew up, only to be greeted by Edward and Elizabeth who were waiting patiently outside for their son's arrival.

"I didn't think you were going to make it in time," said Edward.

"I did," replied a smiling Jacob.

Elizabeth greeted Sarah with a hug and a kiss.

"Hello, Sarah," said Edward. "Lovely to see you again, you look lovely. We'd better go in quick before they start without us."

Inside the church, the family and friends sat as far to the front as they could, this was a rare opportunity to sit in the area usually reserved for the higher status villagers, although the Lutkin family were usually near the front anyway. Many of the friends of the young couple were used to sitting at the rear with their own families who were just working folk. This time, the Lutkin family sat at the immediate front three rows at the right side of the church to support young Robert on his big day. His bride's family and friends were seated to the left; it was this group who were not used to sitting up front. His bride was a young and pretty girl of eighteen called Caroline Jarvis, and she was the third daughter of one of the farm hands from Grey's Farm. Robert was marrying beneath his social standing within the village for obvious reasons, but neither family seemed put out by these events. No scandal was raised and the problem of the girl's pregnancy was being handled. The most important thing was that the young couple seemed very happy together. Robert Lutkin sat at the front eagerly waiting for his bride to appear. His best friend and best man sat beside him, who, to Edward's obvious delight, turned out to be Jimmy Allen, the eldest son of Edward's brother, James. It was obvious that the Lutkin family clearly didn't have the same social boundaries between classes that the late George Lutkin senior had so desired in his lifetime.

Everyone in the church stood as the bride entered the church and marched up the aisle. The congregation turned as she approached and Elizabeth immediately recognised the bridal gown that was worn by Caroline Jarvis. It was one of her mother's own dresses, crimson in colour, slightly altered and with a white linen apron at the front and white frilly cuffs and collars added in. Obviously, the women in the Jarvis family had been hard at work to make the alterations. Nonetheless, everyone was pleased with the result. Both the dress and the bride looked beautiful as she graced the church accompanied by her bridesmaids, namely her two sisters.

The usual wedding service was observed by the congregation, and after the short service, the bride and groom led the guests out to the churchyard where everyone gathered. Elizabeth's sisters, Martha and Jane, came over to see Edward and Elizabeth.

"Hope you don't mind us using Mother's dress for the wedding," said Martha.

"The poor girl had nothing nice to wear for her big day," said Jane.

Elizabeth smiled. "I recognised it instantly. I think mother would have been pleased and proud that the dress was used for such a good use. By the way, you haven't met Sarah, have you?"

Jacob and Sarah were standing behind, hand in hand but they had not gone unnoticed to Martha and Jane.

"Sarah, these are my two sisters, Martha and Jane, and this is Sarah, Jacob's young lady friend."

Both Sarah and Jacob blushed.

"Pleased to meet you, Sarah, and what a pretty girl you are too," said Martha.

Sarah blushed again.

"So, are there any plans like today for you two in the near future?" Jane enquired.

Sarah blushed once more, and Elizabeth smiled.

"Nothing's been planned yet, Aunt Jane," replied a very uncomfortable Jacob.

After the pleasantries in the churchyard, the relatives and friends of the bride and groom departed. Wedding gifts had already been brought to the abode of the happy couple a few days earlier. A group of immediate family of the couple then set off to Spring Farm to enjoy food and refreshments prepared specially for the occasion.

"So when are you getting married, Jacob?" was a question asked, four, maybe five times in the first couple of hours or so of the duration of the celebrations, especially as more ale was consumed. Even the bride and groom asked Jacob, to his great annoyance.

"If I hear anyone ask me that again, I'm leaving." said Jacob to his father, whilst standing in the corner of the main sitting room out of earshot from the guests.

"Well you can't blame 'em for that," said Edward. "You are a young couple at a wedding, and you've been together near on a year and a half now and you're both of marrying age. Course they're gonna ask you that."

Jacob didn't reply.

Another hour passed and fatigue finally set in to many of the guests, who began to leave in small groups. This included Jacob and Sarah, who hugged and kissed their way

115

out of Spring Farm. They kissed goodbye to Edward and Elizabeth who were to make their journey home mostly a different route towards Norwich, whilst they made for Sprowston. Their cart had left the farm behind a mile or so when Jacob finally let out his frustration to Sarah.

"All day, when are you getting married? Have you any plans for the future? That's all I've heard all day!"

Sarah just nodded quietly but didn't reply… this was followed a prolonged period of silence as the cart continued on its journey… which was finally broken by Jacob.

"Maybe it's time we did get married," he said.

Sarah smiled. "It's your fault, you haven't asked me!" she replied… then more silence…

"Well, I'm asking you now!" said Jacob.

"You don't ask a girl to marry you like that, Jacob Allen. You have to ask a girl properly."

Jacob stopped the cart and hopped over to the back of the cart. Sarah turned to see Jacob Allen get down on one knee… and from the back of the cart, he asked…

"Sarah Fox! Would you so please do me the honour of marrying me?"

Sarah burst out laughing and hugged Jacob.

"Yes, of course I will, I thought you'd never ask!"

At that point in time, a horse and cart coming up the same road in the opposite direction came past. Its three occupants, a man and two women all cheered. "Well done!" and "Congratulations!" they called as they passed, clearly seeing as they approached what event had just unfolded. This put both Jacob and Sarah into a fit of laughter and a smile beamed on both their faces for the rest of the journey home.

On arrival at the Fox residence, Jacob and Sarah entered the cottage. Sarah was almost bursting to tell her mother and sisters the news of what had just happened on their journey home. However, there was the expected tradition of asking the future bride's father for permission to marry his daughter.

"Father, could Jacob have a quiet word with you in private?" Sarah asked.

Everybody smiled, knowing that it could only mean one thing.

"We'll go out in the yard, my boy," said Bill.

On exiting the cottage and out to the yard, the noise of the women inside could be heard as they screamed with delight.

"Well, my boy, what can I do for you?" said a smiling Bill.

"You know what I'm gonna ask you," said Jacob. "Me and Sarah have been fond of each other for a while now and we'd like to get married. If you are alright with it, with your permission that is?"

"Of course, I'm alright with it, yer daft apeth. Congratulations, my boy, I thought you'd never ask her."

"Well done, Jacob," said Edmond, who had been standing unnoticed at the cottage door. With that, both Bill and Edmond shook the hand of their future family member and in-law. More ale was drunk in celebration that day, this time at the Fox household, and for Jacob and Sarah.

***

On a warm and sunny September's day of the same year, just as the harvest had been brought in ready for celebration, the Fox, Allen and Lutkin families joined together for a celebration of their own, to witness the marriage of Jacob and Sarah, which was warmly greeted by all those concerned. Typically, like the Sunday church services, he had constantly held for the parish of Sprowston, the Reverend Charles Sutton greeted the congregation at the entrance of the church and joined the happy couple in matrimony. After the ceremony, a family gathering was held at Bill and Anne Fox's cottage. It being a bright and warm day, everyone feasted and drank ale outside in the courtyard. A table was brought out from the cottage, along with chairs and seating benches, hastily made from cut barrels, timber and anything that was available. In the warm sunshine, it felt like the perfect day to all present, especially the happy couple. News of Nelson's victory at the battle of the Nile had only recently reached Norwich and so, consequently, was among the topics of conversations amongst the men. The more so as more ales were consumed.

The ladies stayed seated in small family groups together enjoying sweet conversations of marriages past and predictions of future weddings of younger family members. There were tales of love and romance from times old and new.

Edward and Elizabeth had already met Bill and Anne Fox before the joining of their children, and both parents had mutual respect for one another. Both were happy to welcome in their newest members to their families.

Chapter Twenty-One

A new chapter had entered into the lives of Jacob and Sarah Allen, a sweet time of young love and sexual freedom that they had never known before, but now enjoyed to the full as man and wife. The experience, however, was not entirely new to them as Sarah was no virgin bride. Jacob and Sarah had enjoyed quiet moments alone before matrimony, they were after all a normal young couple.

The newly-weds had found a cottage to rent just a short distance from Bill's place. It is a farm cottage within the estate of the rectory and Church Farm, made available to them by Parson Sutton himself. They had managed to furnish the cottage with the help of wedding gifts from friends and family and have settled into their new lives well, these are indeed happy times for them both.

Life has changed for Edward Allen too, he has now after twenty years of coach driving, been given a permanent position working in the main post office. His duties are of manning the counter and of sorting the increasing volume of mail as well as making deliveries to those wealthy enough to have their mail brought personally to their homes. This is much better for both himself and Elizabeth, as he is now permanently working in and around Norwich. His long hard days travelling to London and back are now over.

***

"Jacob! Can you come with me to the manor? They want me to look at a cart thas in need of a fix, and Sir James's coach door is hanging off its hinges. We've got a wheel for him for his small buggy too. Edmond, you can carry on turning those hubs till we get back. If you finish 'em before, then you can bend them there felloes."

Edmond acknowledged his father's orders with a nod.

Carrying some loose timber, metal plates and nails, along with a box of tools, Bill and Jacob set off on their short journey to Sprowston Manor. The manor was a large dwelling with adjoining stables and a farm within the estate. There had been a Sprowston Manor situated there for as long as anyone knew, as long ago as the sixteenth century or even earlier. The manor had once belonged to Miles Corbett, one of the 59 parliamentarian judges who had signed the death warrant of King Charles I. The Corbett family dynasty had lasted several generations before being sold to a number of wealthy dignitaries and finally ending up being owned by the wealthy Blackwell family. Sir James Blackwell was the present resident and owner of the manor but his dynasty was soon to come to an end. He was the last of three generations of Baronets to hold the manor, but being old, widowed and childless, the Blackwell reign was all but over, and everyone knew it.

As Jacob and Bill arrived at the manor, there to greet them was Sir James himself. He had happened to be outside in the stable yard at the time and was busily dishing out orders to his staff, namely to bring out his chaise and his two wheeled buggy for Bill's attention.

"Ah, Bill the wheelwright, just the man we were preparing for," said Sir James.

He was a man of the old times, still wearing his old style attire of silver wig, blue jacket with frilled cuffs and cream breeches and stockings. He was a man in his late sixties, which was deemed elderly for the time. After a lifetime of living as the local squire or lord of the manor, he had spent his entire life dishing out orders to the peasant classes and keeping up appearances to the local gentry. A fruitless task to a man in his autumn years who was devoid of remaining family and now had few friends left alive. Even the chaise and buggy that he was now to have repaired was seldom in use. For him, there was no one to see and nowhere to go. The man had nothing more to do than to keep up the appearance of the only life that he had ever known, to give orders and to stay in command, only to reminisce of the old and happy times that were once his.

"Well," said Sir James. "As you can see, this chaise has a broken door, if you would be a good chap as to repair it, and of course, there's the buggy with the wheel to change. When you've finished those jobs, I want you to go to the farm and see Mr Greenwood, he's got a cart for you to look at that's in urgent need of your attention."

"Very good, sir," said Bill, putting on his humble voice to keep his customer happy. With that, both he and Jacob set about the tasks in hand. The coach door turned out to be a minor repair, just a slight reposition of one of the hinges seemed to do the trick. Then there was the buggy wheel to change for the new one that had already been constructed by Bill and co, which caused no real problems to a man, who had changed hundreds in the course of his working life. With the two minor jobs finished, Bill and Jacob set off to the outer boundaries of the Manor grounds where the farm was situated. On arrival at the farm, Bill knocked on the door of the main farmhouse, which was answered by an almost elderly looking woman of late fifties, maybe sixties, it was hard to tell. She was craggy faced and looked like she had suffered years of hard toil.

"Good morning, Ma'am, there's a cart somewhere for me to repair, I've had my orders from Sir James," said Bill. "I'm to see Mr Greenwood."

"My husband's out on the fields somewhere," she replied.

She was obviously the farmer Greenwood's wife. Bill had never met her before but had, on occasion, had dealings with her husband from time to time.

"If you go round the back, one of the hands should be there to tell you what you need to know."

From there, Bill and Jacob did as instructed, and made for the rear of the farm to the back yard where a farm hand was leading out a shire horse from one of the stables.

"Morning," said Bill.

The worker looked up to see who was there. The farm hand was none other than Thomas Walker, the big farm labourer who had come to the aid of Jacob and Ned on the night of the village barn dance.

"Oh, it's you Thomas," said Bill.

"Morning Bill, what can I do for you?" he said, glancing in the direction of Jacob and instantly recognising him. He had not spoken to him since that night but had seen him about the village on various occasions in the company of Sarah. He nodded to Jacob in acknowledgement of his presence.

"Sir James sent me here to repair a cart. Do you know anything about it?"

"Follow me," replied Thomas.

Bill and Jacob were led along a track which took them to behind the stable yard where a large hay cart stood leaning at a thirty-degree angle and with a rear wheel almost hanging off. Bill surveyed the damage.

"New wheel and axle arm," said Bill. "Look, the axle arm must have hit something and broke and forced the wheel over and split the hub. Bet it was over loaded and hit a rock or a hole or somethun. I'll take the wheel off, and the axle arm, cos I need to use the arm as a pattern for a new one. The job'll take three or four days to make the wheel and arm, and then to come back with the new bits and fit 'em."

"I'll tell Mr Greenwood when he gets back from the fields," said Thomas. Then he looked to Jacob "Haven't had any more squit with that Jim Barber, have you?" he asked.

Both Bill and Jacob smiled.

"No, he's left me alone since that night, and so have his friends," Jacob replied.

"Now there's a bloke who needed hitting. I hear that you and Sarah are married now, and living at the Church Farm cottages?"

"That's right, Parson Sutton let us rent a spare cottage that had just come free. It's nice and handy, just up the road from Sarah's family and the workshop."

"You and me's gonna be neighbours then," said Thomas. "Sir James and the parson got talking the other week, and Parson Sutton 'appened to mention that his foreman's down with miller's lung and is not long to live. He didn't trust any of his hands with the foreman's job so they agreed between themselves to offer me the job, along with one of the cottages. Me and Keziah are getting married next week and will be moving in thereafter."

"Oh, well done Thomas, good to hear it," said Bill.

"It'll be good to have you as a neighbour," said Jacob.

"Thank you," said Thomas. "I'll be seeing you around when I start to move our things into the cottage."

The wheel and axle arm from the cart was taken away back to Bill's place where the task of the repairs was set about. As Bill had predicted, four days was indeed the time taken for the job when Bill and Jacob finally returned to fit the newly manufactured wheel and axle arm. Just a day after, Thomas Walker and his intended Keziah Woodrow, began moving old furniture and belongings into their vacant cottage. The following weekend, they married at Sprowston church just after Sunday service. Jacob and Sarah were invited, beginning a new neighbourly friendship of which unknown to them, was the beginning of a new chapter in all their lives, major events were to come and affect their lives in the most dramatic way.

***

The cluster of five farm cottages where Jacob and Sarah lived was one of two blocks of terraced cottages owned by the Church Farm estate. The other block was situated less than a hundred yards away down the same road, namely Barker's Lane, situated just off Church Lane and was within the grounds adjoining the church farmhouse itself. There were four cottages in that group and all of the cottages consisted of a small kitchen with a brick oven fireplace and parlour at ground floor with a fireplace located central to the end wall with a cupboard and shelves constructed to the left within an alcove. To the right of the fireplace was a door that hid a set of tightly compacted stairs leading to two bedrooms above. These rooms were both about ten feet square, and were separated by a single wall and linked by a door. In these small cottages, many of the farmworkers raised large families. Six to eight children were not uncommon. However, the survival rate of their offspring did not always supersede their numbers.

As one would expect, two recently married couples, both about to embark on the beginning of a new life of setting up a home and having babies and raising their families, who happen to live within close proximity of each other, were soon to become good friends. Ales were drunk out in their gardens on the warm summer evenings of 1799 and occasionally, Thomas and Jacob would go for a tankard of ale at the Blue Boar Inn. As the year wore on into autumn and then to winter when the nights drew in early, they would sometimes visit one another's cottage, and enjoy games of cards and dice and dominoes within the illumination of the candlelight.

Christmas came and passed, and then a new year and a new century arrived, bringing with it a new optimism of what life would bring for the two young couples. As for Jacob, the smithy business with Bill and Edmond thrived, as there was always work for the village blacksmith and wheelwright. Thomas Walker equally settled well into his new job as works foreman on Church Farm.

One day in the early spring of 1800, Jacob was working a busy day at the forge due to a large number of customers from the village and some unexpected road traffic custom that had come in to shoe their horses. This meant, consequently, that he had no time to help Bill and Edmond who were in the process of making a large number of ordered wheels. When Jacob had shod his last horse of the day, and had helped clear up the workshop and had made the forge fire safe, he returned the short distance home to find Sarah in the company of her sister, Beth, and friend and neighbour, Keziah. The three women all seemed in good spirits as Sarah prepared the evening meal of stew and dumplings.

"Well, I'd better be off and start getting Thomas's meal ready," said Keziah. "I'll be seeing you later," she added, and Jacob and Sarah acknowledged her farewells.

"Time for me to go too," said Beth, and she rose up from her chair and kissed her sister goodbye. Jacob acknowledged her farewell too with a quick wave. Shortly after, with their evening meal prepared and then eventually eaten to the usual small talk of the events of that particular day. Sarah cleared the table and washed the dishes in a pail of water. Jacob sat down in front of the fire and lit his pipe. The outside darkness of the evening began to draw in until the room was finally within the soft illumination of the log fire and a single oil lamp which rested on the centre of the table. Sarah joined her husband within the soft glow of the fire.

"We've got another order from the King's Head today, a complete set of coach wheels to lay spare in their yard, just in case they're needed. I'll be helping start them tomorrow if no horses turn up to be shod," said Jacob.

Sarah smiled. "Whilst you're working with all that wood, you can make a cradle for me, we're gonna need one for about November."

There was a momentary pause as Jacob took in the news... followed by a broad smile, as his surprise was replaced by euphoria. He embraced Sarah lovingly and kissed her.

"Are you sure, there's no mistake?"

"Of course not, I've had my suspicion for a while, and now I've no doubt, I've been getting morning sickness just lately and that confirmed what I'd already thought. If my sums are right, it should come late October or early November."

Jacob kissed Sarah again. "Does anyone else know, your mother or your sisters?"

Sarah nodded. "They all know, and so does Keziah. You know how us women talk to each other. Mother's beside herself she's so happy."

"Does your father know?" asked Jacob.

"No, none of the men know. Why don't you tell 'em?"

"I will, and I'll tell Thomas too if Keziah hasn't already told him. Come on, girl, let's go and tell everyone!"

With that, Jacob and Sarah got up and ventured outside into the darkness and made for the door of Thomas and Keziah Walker just two cottages away where they were greeted with joy by their neighbours. Thomas did know the news. Keziah had let out the secret at the table at mealtime, but Jacob didn't care, nothing could dampen his spirits that night. Soon after, they made their way in the direction of Bill Fox's cottage.

The news, though already known to the women of the Fox household and kept from Bill, was greeted with the expected joy and pleasure of a family receiving such news. Bill, however, was blissfully unaware that he was the one of the last in the family to know the news, a secret best kept by all. Though joyous, this was not Bill and Anne's first grandchild, as only a year earlier, Priscilla Fox, wife to their eldest son, William, had given birth to a son who in the family tradition they also named William.

After the news was delivered, Jacob, Bill, Edmond and Thomas Walker all set off to the Blue Boar Inn, and celebrated in the traditional way befitting such news. Many ales were consumed and all felt a bit under the weather at work the next morning, but no one cared, it was all for a good cause.

Chapter Twenty-Two

On their first opportunity, Jacob and Sarah made a trip to Norwich to see his parents and deliver the news of the forthcoming baby personally. Elizabeth was overjoyed at the thought of her first grandchild, as was Edward. However, there was the usual realisation of the risks that were involved of the dangerous task of childbirth. No one knew more than Elizabeth who had herself suffered the loss of three babies. The remainder of that year passed in good speed, but with enough time for Jacob and Sarah to make preparations for their new arrival. Jacob had noticed how his parents were now making trips to Sprowston more frequently as the pregnancy wore on. It was obvious to him that it was Elizabeth who clearly wanted be part of the event of the new arrival to come, such is the way of a mother.

The time finally came on November 5th, a night when traditionally the locals would all came out in the darkness of the early November evening to a meadow located at the end of Church Lane, to witness the lighting of a large bonfire to celebrate the failed attempt by Guy Fawkes to blow up the houses of Parliament two centuries earlier. An effigy of Guy Fawkes himself was made of weaved corn stems and straw to be sat on the top of the fire. There were no fireworks to be had but the locals enjoyed the celebration none the less. To them, not only was it a celebration of times long ago, but this was an event that was a break from the usual mundane evenings usually spent at home with little to do. This gathering was nothing more than a few words spoken from more senior members of the parish, and a recital of 'remember, remember the fifth of November', before the eventual lighting of the bonfire, which would bring on loud cheers from the villagers. The rest of the evening was usually spent just watching and enjoying the warmth of the fire in the winter air surrounded by friends and family. It was just cheap entertainment and something different to do. On this night, however, Jacob and Sarah had joined Sarah's family, all of them were there, Bill and Anne, Edmond, Beth and Annie, and also William had come along with his wife, Priscilla and their young infant son, William.

With the fire already lit and the straw Guy Fawkes already consumed by the flames, the family silently watched the fire burn... that was until the silence was broken by the heavily pregnant Sarah. A deep sigh was heard, which was followed by "Mother, I think my waters have gone."

"Come on, girl, we'll take you home," said Anne Fox.

She alerted the rest of the family to the situation and they left the gathering without hesitation, Jacob held tightly to Sarah's hand. Anne led the group back to the Church Farm cottages where Jacob and Sarah lived. This childbirth was to be done in the usual way with the female family members in direct attendance, and Jacob would be there only to vacate the birthing room at the correct moment, exactly as Edward had done twenty-three years earlier when Jacob was born.

Not much happened at the earlier stages of the birth, the pains of labour were brief at first between periods of less pain and less discomfort. This gave the women, namely Anne, Beth and Annie, time to prepare. Boiling water for cleaning both mother and baby after delivery and preparing the birthing bed and cradle, and warm blankets to wrap the baby should it survive. During this preparation, Jacob kept with his duty of comforting his wife best he could by keeping a tight hold of her hand and giving her words of reassurance.

"I'm scared," said Sarah.

"You'll do just fine," Jacob replied.

More time passed, and the pain increased for Sarah as her contractions increased. By now, Bill had returned back home to his cottage to grab as much of a night's sleep as he could. Both he and Edmond would still have to work in the morning, so there was no point in him being there, it was Jacob's job as expectant father to be in attendance.

Two hours passed, then three. It was now past midnight and into the early hours of the morning, Sarah was now near her time and was clearly in considerable distress.

"You'd better leave now," said Anne, and she ushered Jacob out of the door.

Jacob, though obviously concerned, was in complete agreement that this was a job for the women to deal with. He didn't know what to do and more than likely would only get in the way. There was a feeling of complete helplessness within him and consequently, a feeling of guilt for that very reason. He sat downstairs listening to the noises from above; the sound of the women guiding and supporting Sarah in her hour of need, and of course, there were the screams from Sarah herself. He lit his clay pipe and smoked it, and then again and again, continually smoking until the loudest scream of all came from Sarah shortly followed by the unmistakable cries of a baby as it drew its first breaths, and Jacob knew it was all over.

Another hour passed as the women dealt with the baby, namely knotting and cutting the umbilical cord, and cleaning and wrapping the infant. Sarah had to be looked after too, she washed herself and changed into clean and dry bedclothes whilst her mother and Beth dealt with clearing and changing the bedding, and Annie had to dispose of the expelled placenta by taking it out into the garden for later burial. Finally, Anne came down.

"You can go up now Jacob, it's all over and they're fine… and you have a son."

Jacob rushed upstairs and into the bedroom where Sarah lay exhausted but cradling her new-born son. She smiled at first sight of Jacob and handed the new-born to him. He held him, smiling but silent, completely overcome with joy at the first sight of his first-born. He kissed his new son's head, the baby just slept through it having already suckled for the first time at his mother's breast. He was wrapped tightly and warmly in his blanket that his grandmother had prepared for him. His parents had already decided that their first-born son was to be called John, and Jacob held John proudly in his arms and sat down beside his wife. He kissed Sarah.

"I love you," he said.

Sarah smiled in acknowledgement.

The following morning, Jacob rose later than usual, having had very little sleep, though not because of the cries and whimpers of his new-born son but because the major events that had just unfolded had left his mind alert and full of reflective thoughts. The event of John's arrival had only given him a couple of hours sleep at the most in the night. Sarah, however, slept heavily through sheer exhaustion.

He made a breakfast of toast and warmed milk which he took up to Sarah as she lay asleep in bed with the cradle containing baby John beside her. He looked at Sarah as she lay there, then he looked at his son sleeping in his cradle. No stage in his life had ever been so good, he thought to himself. Then Sarah stirred, gently awakening and Jacob joined her, sitting on the bed where upon they enjoyed their breakfast in bed, proudly unable to take their eyes off their new-born son John. As the morning light set into the room, they could see that his soft, downy hair was fair like Sarah's.

"Your mother should be here soon. I bet she didn't sleep much either," said Jacob. "I'd like to tell my mother and father that they have a new grandson, I'd like to tell them today."

"I'll be alright here with Mother, Beth and Annie if you want to go this morning," said Sarah.

"Thanks, I will. I won't be too long I hope. You know they'll want to see him as soon as possible."

"Tell them to come to church on Sunday for his christening," said Sarah.

"I will."

Then no sooner had they spoken, Anne Fox knocked on the door and entered the cottage, eager to see her daughter and new grandchild, and of course, Bill, Beth and Annie were there also.

"Congratulations, son, well done," said Bill. "We won't be seeing you at the forge for a day or two I expect."

"No," said Jacob. "Just a couple of days, but I'd like to go quickly and tell my parents the news, so I'll be away for a couple or three hours."

"You can take the horse if you like, you'll get there a lot quicker." said Bill.

"Thank you, I will if you don't mind," replied Jacob.

Then Bill was beckoned to come upstairs by Anne, so he left the room to see his grandson for the first time. Jacob bid his farewells and left for Bill's cottage to collect the horse, from there, he left for Norwich.

It was just a short time after that Jacob arrived in Norwich at his parent's house on Bill's horse, but he had not made it early enough to catch Edward before he had set off for work at the post office. Elizabeth was there, and the news of the birth of her first grandchild was greeted with the ecstatic joy expected.

"Let's go and tell your father at the post office," she suggested.

So they made for the post office at Bedford Street which was just a few minutes away by horse. Edward was taken aback in surprise at the sight of his wife and son at his workplace at that time of the morning but was overcome with joy at the news.

"Well done, son!" he shouted and shook Jacob's hand.

"He'll be christened on Sunday, you'll be there, won't you?"

Nothing would have stopped them, for on the following Sunday, which came four days later, the christening of John Allen was witnessed by the Sunday parishioners of Sprowston and the Fox and Allen families. An entry was recorded in the church records.

John, son of Jacob Allen and his wife, Sarah.

Born 6th November,

Baptised 10th November 1800.

Chapter Twenty-Three

A brief year of peace between Britain and France has existed but was thus broken in 1803 when Napoleon Bonaparte violates all peace treaty agreements and forces Britain to declare war on France once again. News of battles, both losses and victories continue to reach Britain, though in rural Norfolk, traces of the war only occasionally surfaces to pockets of the population. In Norwich, the sight of troops is sometimes seen moving supplies and equipment to the river port on its journey to Yarmouth and then to wherever needed. Otherwise, the war was just news from a distant land that would come in from time to time and would be the topic of conversation for the men to convey in the alehouses or at the workplace.

***

On a sunny Sunday in Sprowston, Edward and Elizabeth Allen have made the long walk from Norwich to visit their son and his family. Jacob and Sarah have by now increased the size of their family to three children, all boys, their eldest son, John, then William and baby Edward. This has now become a regular outing for Edward and Elizabeth who, being now in their late forties, approaching their fifties, are now enjoying their times with their grandchildren as the timepiece of their lives continues to tick by. After meeting at church, the family leaves to enjoy the summer sunshine in the cottage garden. Playing in amongst the group are the two children of Thomas and Keziah Walker who are very much the same young age and living just two doors away. They were always destined to be playmates with the Allen children throughout the duration of their childhood. Thomas and Keziah have a boy and a girl named after themselves, which was common practice of the times. All seemed calm and happy until the moment when some sad news came to Jacob by way of his father.

"Some news came into the post office the other day," said Edward. "Your friend Ned Barrett is dead."

Jacob turned in surprise. "What! Where did you hear that?"

"Bill Anderson came in for the mail to take to the King's Head, he told me that he'd seen Ned's older brother, and news of his death had reached them over a year ago, he had died in India a year before that so they say. I don't know how, I just heard he was dead, and that his family knows. One of his regimental pals, who joined up when he did, and came from Norwich, returned and gave his family the news. That's all I know and that's all Bill Anderson knows."

"Did you hear that, Sarah?" said Jacob. "Ned Barrett's dead, died in India."

"Oh no, that's sad. I liked him," she replied.

"Was he the one who came with you to the barn dance that night you hit Jim Barber?" asked Thomas Walker, who had been listening in the background as he sat with Keziah, keeping an eye on their children.

"That's him, we worked together at the King's Head. Poor Ned, that is a shame, he was my best friend."

Jacob then took hold of his tankard of ale and raised it.

"To you, Ned, my old friend, may you rest in peace."

This gesture inspired all of the other men in the group to follow suit and raise their tankards in tribute of a lost soldier and friend. Shortly after, Thomas Walker made his own announcement.

"While we're all raising a cup in honour, now is a good time to announce that me and Keziah are expecting our third baby, should be here in the spring."

Everybody gave a cheer and raised their drinks to toast the coming of another new arrival. The women gathered around Keziah, giving her support.

Now country life, in all its simplicity, slowly passes by in much the same way it has for hundreds of years, by following the seasons and performing the tasks that in turn follow with them. Just a month after the mentioned Sunday gathering, came the time for the harvest, when most of the villagers, no matter what profession, would come together to cut the sheaths of wheat and corn, and gather in the produce of the year as quickly as possible. Builders, smiths and wheelwrights, carpenters, millers and the women and children, all took part, and for a good reason too. A bad harvest would affect everyone, no matter who, it was to everyone's interest to take part or risk hard times or malnutrition. This harvest of 1805, however, turned out to be a successful one and was brought in in good time. The year moved on into late October and news came in of the greatest naval battle of all in British history, the battle of Trafalgar, and with it the consequent death of Lord Horatio Nelson himself. This news sent shockwaves across the whole of the country, and the following month of November saw a great period of mourning for Britain's finest and most loved hero, till his eventual burial at St Paul's in London in early 1806 before a huge crowd, all there to pay homage to Norfolk's own hero.

Spring approached, snowdrops and crocuses were giving way to daffodils and bluebells, and the sharpness of the cold winter air felt less intense. Fields were now being ploughed ready for early spring sowing, it was busy times for farmworkers to prepare for crop production. It was on an early spring night in the year 1806 when the sound of frantic banging on the door of Jacob and Sarah's cottage broke the slumber of the couple and their children. Jacob rushed downstairs and opened the door to find an obviously distressed Thomas Walker at the door.

"Jacob, the baby's on its way, we need help. Can you get Sarah?"

"Come in Thomas, I'll get her."

"No, I've got to get back to her, just tell her to be as quick as she can please."

"Of course I will," he replied.

Jacob returned to the bedroom to find that Sarah had heard the conversation at the door and was already getting dressed.

"Just see to the babies, will you? It's likely to be a long night."

Jacob nodded.

Sarah had agreed a while back to help Keziah with her birth when the time came, along with Keziah's mother who was staying with her daughter as her time drew nearer. She was dressed in a moment and hurried out of the door to help her friend in her hour of need. Jacob, having settled the children back down, returned to bed to let the women get on with the task that only they know so well.

The night wore on, and Jacob, having had his sleep interrupted, was finding it difficult to return back to the state of slumber from which he had left. He could hear distant screams coming from Thomas and Keziah's cottage between long periods of silence. On one occasion, he heard the sound of footsteps outside, quicker than usual as if running. Then later, footsteps returning, though this time more than one person was running back and voices were heard, although Jacob couldn't make out whose voices he was hearing or what they were saying. More time wore on… and then more distant screams followed by silence… eventually, the sound of the birds outside could be heard, beginning their dawn chorus as that day's sunlight began to emerge from behind the silhouettes of distant trees at the far end of the fields.

Must be over soon, he thought, *Sarah will be back soon.*

Lighter and lighter became the morning, and still no return of his wife… the youngest of Jacob and Sarah's three children, baby Edward began to cry for his mother. Though now partially on solid food, he would still cry for the comfort of his mother's breast. Jacob saw to his child, giving him some water in a small cup and putting his finger in the baby's mouth to encourage it to suckle, not very successfully though.

Wherever is she? Jacob thought. *There must be problems.*

Suddenly, the sound of the door opening downstairs could be heard and Sarah ran upstairs desperate to get to her own children, knowing that they would now be requiring her attention. She ran to the baby Edward and placed him to her breast.

"Is everything alright?" asked Jacob.

"No, it isn't," Sarah replied, trying to hold back tears that were beginning to well around her eyes.

"The baby was breached. We had a terrible time trying to turn it. I had to send Thomas up to mother's to fetch her. Me and Keziah's mother were running out of ideas of what to do next. Mother eventually turned the baby, it came out feet first… and dead… it was a boy. Keziah's lost a lot of blood, I don't know if she's gonna live or not. Thomas and the children are with her now."

Jacob sighed, completely flattened by the news of the tragedy that had just befallen their friends. All he could think of to say was that it was best to leave the family alone, and that now it was in God's hands.

Another hour passed. Jacob and Sarah were having breakfast at the table with the children when Anne Fox entered.

"How is she?" Sarah asked.

Anne shook her head… "She's gone."

Sarah immediately burst into tears. "Oh poor Keziah… the poor children, what will they do?"

"For the moment, they'll need time to grieve, and when they've mourned Keziah, they'll have to work out then just what they're to do next," said Jacob.

The remainder of the day was spent in deep reflection as Jacob and Sarah pondered on thoughts of the dilemma and pain that their good friend Thomas was experiencing, and the terrible thought of two small children who had just lost their mother. There were deep reflections of one's own mortality, and of how in one day, one's life can be turned upside down through reasons far beyond anyone's control. Jacob returned to work later that day having spent the morning helping to support his wife. Sarah had been through an awful ordeal herself spending the night trying to help Keziah, only to see her friend die in the most terrible circumstances. Then to go home after and try and look after three small children. She was a woman feeling the strain.

It was later the following day before Jacob and Sarah felt it the correct time to knock on Thomas's door to pay their respects and wish their condolences. They were greeted by a deflated Thomas who was clearly overcome by grief.

"I'm so sorry, Thomas, if there's anything we can do, just ask," said Jacob.

Thomas sniffed. "Thank you," he replied.

"Where are the children?" asked Sarah.

"With Keziah's mother. We thought it better to keep them away from all this. Her mother's finding strength to have the children around her."

Inside the parlour and sat on two specially built benches was Keziah's wooden coffin, hastily made by the village builder and carpenter. He also doubled up as the village undertaker as was commonly the tradition in the rural villages.

"She's being laid to rest tomorrow, I don't know what I'll do without her. How am I gonna look after the little-uns?"

"You'll bring them round to ours," said Sarah. "They can play together with our little-uns and I'll look after 'em while you're out at work. I'm sure that if we all pull together they'll be just fine."

"You'd do that for me?" said Thomas.

"Yes, of course we would," said Jacob. "It would be the only decent Christian thing to do."

"I know that my mother would help and so would Keziah's mother."

"Well there you are then, we can all help you. You just keep working and you'll all survive," said Sarah.

After an hour, Jacob and Sarah left Thomas to return home knowing that they had at least left Thomas with some answer to his problems. They had lifted some of the great burden upon his shoulders, though nothing could take the great pain away that he was now experiencing. The following day, Keziah Walker was laid to rest within the consecrated ground of Sprowston churchyard. In attendance with Keziah's close family were Jacob and Sarah and other friends and colleagues from the village. Such were the dangers of childbirth, many had paid their respects before to a lost mother, and no doubt would do so again someday.

As everyone had promised, Thomas didn't have to struggle alone as family and friends did indeed pull together to help him raise his motherless children, especially Sarah. Though initially grief stricken, Keziah's two children did continue to survive and managed to settle into their lives of being cared for by their grandparents and Sarah whilst Thomas was out working. Life became a big playground for them having Jacob and Sarah's three children to play with for long periods of the day. Life carried on in the situation that circumstances had left them with. Everyone knew that in these harsh times, they were never far away from yet another tragedy in life, and no one ever knew who was going to be next.

Chapter Twenty-Four

The last of the city gates was demolished, to widen for the increased traffic of horses and carriages and trade carts that were venturing in and out of Norwich for its daily business. This last opening was the closest and most used by the people of Sprowston as the Magdalen Gate was situated at the very end of the main turnpike road leading straight through their village, eventually, leading through Wroxham and the broads, and to the Norfolk coast at Caister near Yarmouth.

It is now 1808 and life is continuing in much the same way, however, Jacob and Sarah have since had another child, a boy which they named Vincent. Sadly, on this occasion, the baby breathed its last breaths just a few days after it had breathed its first. The arrangement between Thomas Walker and Jacob and Sarah continues, and his children still share their time with Jacob and Sarah and their grandparents. The Walker children now spend so much time together with the Allen children, both sets almost look upon each other as siblings.

In Norwich on the 9th April of this year 1808, a young man of twenty-four years of age is sent to the gallows at the castle gates having been found guilty of arson, that of deliberately setting alight a cart lodge, a barn and a stack of barley belonging to General John Money of Trowse near Norwich. This was the very same John Money who had made the heroic gas balloon journey over Norfolk in 1785, only to ditch into the sea eighteen miles off the coast at Southwould. The young man who was hanged was one Thomas Sutton, and was also from Trowse. Sutton had a family history of criminality; his father had been hung at Norwich in 1786 for horse stealing and his elder brother was transported to the colonies for the same offence. In 1800, hoping that he would join his brother in the colonies, he stole a pony from the estate of Money but instead was sentenced upon capture to seven years' hard labour at Woolwich. After his sentence was complete, General Money tried to help the young horse thief to get his life back on course. However, a relationship breakup and the death of his brother, who had been transported years earlier, had disturbed the young man to the extent to seek some kind of retribution towards General Money, prompting him to commit the arson attack on his estate. Money was saddened by the waste of a young life and felt that Sutton had done the deed deliberately almost as a kind of suicide.

***

On a normal day in early autumn, Sarah was busy performing her usual chores of housework and childcare, while Jacob was at his usual place at the forge, shoeing horses and helping Bill and Edmond with wheel making. Earlier, Sarah had brought the children to Bill's place to visit their grandparents and their father as he worked. This was common practice, living so near they visited almost every day and Jacob was always glad to see them despite his workload. Thomas Walker's young children, Keziah and Tom, were also there as usual playing alongside young John, William and baby Edward. An hour or so was spent there until Sarah finally returned back with the children to continue her chores at her home at the Church Farm cottages. It was about twelve noon when Joe Daniels came to Bill's place leading a large black shire named Sampson from Manor Farm.

"He needs a shoe, back left," said Joe. "I'd watch him if I were you, he's been a bit jumpy this morning, something seems to have scared him. Probably Mr Blackwell shooting those rabbits earlier, I reckon."

"You hold him up front and keep him steady, and I'll sort him right at the back." said Jacob.

So Jacob pumped the bellows of the forge fire and placed one of the larger pre-formed shoes onto the fire, where upon he set about the task of removing the old shoe and which he finally achieved in relatively short time, despite Sampson's obvious unwillingness to co-operate with the farrier. After cleaning up the hoof with his broad knife, he retrieved the now red-hot shoe from the forge fire to burn an outline of the hot shoe onto it, so as to know where the finer adjustments to achieve the correct shape were to be made. As he did this, the hot shoe touched the hoof, Sampson suddenly happened to jerk his hind leg just at the wrong time, causing the hot shoe to touch and burn the more sensitive sole of his hoof. Suddenly, Sampson kicked back at Jacob and reared at the front, causing Joe Daniels to pull hard at the front stirrups and which, in turn, the great horse pulled backwards, and pinned Jacob tight up against the forge wall. Sampson, now panicking kicked back, catching Jacob on his right upper leg.

"Aagh!" he cried out, in excruciating pain. Joe managed to pull hard at Sampson.

"Wooh! Wooh!" he called, and the horse, after a while, responded and began to calm down. Joe quickly led Sampson outside and out of the way from the injured Jacob.

"Are you alright, Jacob?" asked Joe, concerned but unable to help as he still kept a hold of Sampson. Edmond rushed over to Jacob who by now was doubled up in pain.

"Jacob! Jacob! Are you alright?"

Jacob coughed and then took a couple of deep breaths. "I'll live," he replied, "I'm gonna have a bleedin' great bruise on my leg, I can tell yer."

Jacob had been temporarily winded as the horse had pinned him to the wall and compressing his ribs, but after a minute or two of gathering himself up, he stood back upright.

"Right, we'd better have another go, this time we'll all hold him, but get ready to move quickly if he rears up again."

The second attempt proved to be more successful and the shoe was eventually replaced. Jacob spent the rest of the day working, though in some pain. He returned home at the end of the day after what seemed to him to be a long day having to suffer the discomfort as he worked. At home, he settled down after his evening meal with a tankard of ale to take the pain away from his leg and his ribs where the beast had pinned him to the wall. As he sat, two of his sons, John and William, though still small and young, came over to their father and jumped onto his lap like they had done so many times before either for comfort or to play fight, which were the usual reasons. On this occasion and to their unwelcome surprise, their father didn't come forward to either play or cuddle like he usually would but angrily cried out.

"Get off!"

Sarah looked in surprise, it was not like Jacob, he always had time for the children. The boys were obviously shocked and scared and immediately backed away from Jacob not knowing that they had just climbed upon the very sore leg and ribs that he had injured during the day.

"What did they do?" asked Sarah.

"I was kicked by a horse today and it pinned me up against a wall. I'm sorry, boys, but you sat on me right where it hurts the most."

"Let's have a look at your leg," said Sarah. Jacob pulled down the right hand side of his breeches, exposing a by now very bluey purple top right leg.

"Ooh that looks sore."

"It is," Jacob replied.

"You'd better let your father be, boys," said Sarah. "He's been hurt by a horse and it hurts too much to have you on his lap."

The boys didn't argue either, they were still shocked by their father's outburst.

The night wore on and the children were put to bed. Jacob drank another cup of ale to help ease the pain before he and Sarah eventually retired to bed themselves. Sarah slept soundly, but Jacob's night was one of discomfort, of which a full night's sleep was not achieved, consequently, the following morning he set off to work tired and still sore. The discomfort seemed worse on his upper side and he wondered if he could possibly have cracked a rib or two, but he soldiered on nonetheless and completed another day's work despite all until his return home in the late afternoon.

"How are you today?" Sarah asked as he entered the cottage.

"Still sore, especially my side. I think that horse might have cracked my ribs or something like that."

"Take your shirt off so we can see if you're alright."

Jacob took off his shirt, exposing a large bruised area at the right side where he was hurting.

"I think you could have cracked a rib," said Sarah. "It's certainly bruised enough."

"Wouldn't surprise me, it bloody hurts like hell."

"Maybe you need some rest," said Sarah. "If you're still in pain tomorrow, take the day off. I'm sure Father and Edmond will understand."

Jacob agreed, it was not like him to take a day off that easily but it was obvious to him that his discomfort was making it difficult to do his job. The following morning, he was still in pain, and took no hesitation in taking the day off and staying in bed as Sarah had suggested. She made a trip down the road to the forge to tell her father of Jacob's absence. Bill, having already heard what had happened to Jacob, had half expected him to stay at home, he could see on the previous day that things were not well for him.

"Tell him not to come back till he's well enough," said Bill. "Tell him we can manage just fine."

Jacob stayed in bed, trying to get back some of the sleep he had lost the previous night but with only partial success. Sometimes he would come downstairs and sit in his chair in front of the fire only to find that this caused the ache to get worse. Sitting upright and in a hard chair didn't help at all so he returned back to bed. The day ended and night came, Sarah joined her husband having put the children to bed. Still the pain continued and another restless night was had. By morning Jacob was finding himself coughing more frequently than normal, but he put it down to the boredom of the previous day that had caused him to smoke his pipe more than he usually would.

Another day in bed followed as Jacob had felt that his condition didn't seem to be improving as was expected. His cough began to worsen and so did the pain to his ribs the more he coughed. By the middle of the next day, Sarah was beginning to get worried. Jacob had taken knocks before and been ill before but he had always recovered quickly, ill health was something uncommon to him. She bathed his ribs with cold wet linen and also his head as his body temperature seemed to rise, causing him to sweat more.

The following day again saw no improvement. Jacob was now bedridden and didn't even find enough strength to get out of bed and come down to sit in his chair. The children came up to visit their father, aware he was not well but not realising just how serious things were beginning to look. It was then that Sarah took the decision to ask Edmond to make a trip to Norwich to tell Jacob's parents that their son was ill, possibly gravely ill. Edmond left immediately.

Elizabeth took the news badly as you would expect a mother to do on the news of her only child being so ill. She immediately ran up to the post office to inform Edward who left work without hesitation and with Elizabeth, made haste towards Sprowston to be at the side of their son.

On arrival at Sprowston, the two women in Jacob's life tearfully embraced and went upstairs to where Jacob lay. Edward stayed below to be with his grandchildren, who at this time were being watched over by Anne Fox.

"How is he?" asked Edward.

"I'm sorry Edward, he's not so good," said Anne. "I think he broke a rib the other day and it's done something to him inside. He's started coughing up some blood and his breathing's making noises like when you've got a cold or the flu. He's getting weaker."

Edward sighed and shook his head, holding his lips tightly together, his eyes glistened and a single tear began to run down his face. He knew what the outcome was likely to be so he made his way upstairs to join Elizabeth to be with their son. In the bedroom, Jacob lay asleep, his mother was sat beside him holding his hand, her face and her eyes were reddened by tears of distress she had shed just moments earlier. Sarah just stood motionless.

An hour passed and Jacob briefly woke from his slumber, having heard the voices of his loved ones as they talked together, in much the same way as one does when hearing the sounds in the morning from people already up and about their business. Slowly emerging through, from dream state and delirium, where the sounds around mingle with the dream itself, and then eventually to consciousness and awareness of the reality around.

"Mother, Father," said Jacob. "You've come to see me."

"Of course we have, my love," replied Elizabeth. "We'll always be here for you."

Sarah kissed her husband. "Can I get you anything, a drink or some food?"

"Just some water please."

She left the room, and returned a few moments later with a cup of water and with their three children, who were told that their father was now awake. Jacob began coughing again into a handkerchief where more blood was coughed up but quickly wrapped up in his hand and put beside him out of sight as not to scare his children who were standing behind Sarah.

"John, William, come closer so as your father can see you," said Sarah, still holding her youngest infant, Edward.

Both her eldest boys came over to see Jacob as requested. Jacob smiled to them and held their little hands.

"I love you boys, be good to your mother."

The boys both nodded, not fully aware of the circumstance that was unfolding around them being so young. His words to his sons brought tears flowing within the room. Elizabeth, Sarah and Anne Fox who were standing at the back, and then Edward finally broke down after trying so hard to hold his dignity together. Men weren't supposed to cry.

Jacob coughed again into his handkerchief and looked around again to his loved ones. A tear emerged from the corner of his eye.

"If anything should happen to me, I want you all to know that I love you all very much, and no man could have been happier with you all."

He took another drink of his water and lay back on his pillow. One by one his loved ones kissed him and squeezed his hand whilst slowly he drifted back into his state of delirium and back into his deep slumber. The hours wore on and the day faded into night. Bedding was made downstairs for Edward and Elizabeth who would not leave their son until things were to come to an end one way or another.

The night was long. Sarah sat beside Jacob on a wooden chair, helpless to do anything except watch her husband sleep and occasionally cough. She mopped the blood away from his mouth. The sound of Jacob's raspy, bubbly breathing could be heard through the cottage. Edward and Elizabeth lay below unable to sleep, listening to the painful sounds of their dying son from above. Thankfully the children slept, blissfully unaware.

Slowly fatigue got the better of Edward and Elizabeth, and they drifted into a brief light sleep of their own that was quickly ended by the developing daylight of the morning and the sound of the birds outside singing the dawn chorus. Then, there was the realisation by Elizabeth that she couldn't hear the sound of her son's breathing. It was a feeling she hadn't experienced for many years since her son was an infant when she would listen for his breaths at night to know all was well with him. This time, years later, she heard nothing and quickly sat up, which immediately stirred Edward.

"He's not breathing."

They both quickly rose and climbed the stairs and entered the bedroom. Sarah lay on the bed cheek to cheek with Jacob's face. All they could only see that she was crying, and then she rose and turned to them.

"He's gone."

Elizabeth immediately flung herself upon her dead son, her head laid upon his chest and sobbed uncontrollably. Edward was now in tears and held his son's lifeless hand. Sarah stood with her face in her hands crying for her lost husband and love of her life. Jacob had breathed his last just before the dawn of a new day. His children woke to the news that their father was gone. These were times of high mortality and at this time another young father was taken at the age of just thirty-one. Another mother's tears were shed, and a father's tears and a wife, and there were the tears of three small children who had just lost their father.

Chapter Twenty-Five

Jacob was laid to rest at the village church three days after his tragic passing, and the service was obviously attended by close friends and grieving family. After the service, Bill Fox and Edward Allen had a private word together and agreed that now it was time for both families to deal with the situation that has befallen Sarah and her three children. A meeting was arranged and subsequently, held at Bill's cottage two days later, between the Fox family, Edward and Elizabeth, and of course, Sarah and the children. Everyone sat around a large wooden table in the living room, made by Bill himself years earlier.

"Right Sarah," said Bill. "It goes without saying why we're all here, we're gonna have to work out how we're gonna help you and the little-uns now that Jacob's gone, God rest im. You can't end up in the workhouse so it's up to us as family to help yer."

"I think it should be easy enough," said Edward. "We'll work out how much money she needs for rent and food and split the cost down the middle, if you agree Bill?"

"Yes, thas the only way and it's fine by me."

"Thank you," said Sarah. "But I could always try and find some work on the farms, maybe as a milk maid in the dairy. That would help a little."

"Your job is to look after the little-uns my girl. You can't take them to no farm at their young years," said Bill. "Just you leave it to me and Edward, we'll see you alright."

"I could look after the little-uns while Sarah works if you like," said Anne Fox, who had until now been sitting quietly listening to what was being said.

"Well we'll deal with that if Sarah decides to get a job, till then we'll do what me and Edward agreed."

"Thank you," said Sarah. "That's taken a weight off my mind. If there's any way I can repay you I would."

"No need," said Bill. "Times like these mean we all have to pull together and help."

"We'll make a trip here every week to see you and the children and we'll bring our share of the cost with us," said Elizabeth.

"So it's all agreed then?" said Bill.

"Not quite," said Edmond, who had also been sitting quietly listening to the events at hand.

"I was thinking that maybe we should all be thinking about the long term," he added.

"How do you mean?" asked Bill.

"Well, neither of you are getting any younger and the children are still very young. What'll happen if, God forbid, anything should happen to you two. Who'll help them then?"

Bill looked at Edward. They were both unable to come up with an answer.

"This is what I think," said Edmond.

"At the earliest possible time, we should take young John on as an apprentice, and then William and then young Edward. They need to learn a trade so as they can earn their own living in the future, for the time when you aren't here to help them."

Bill looked to Edward, they both nodded in agreement.

"You're right, boy," said Bill. "We'll start John as soon as he's ten in a couple of years' time, he's still a little young right now."

Edmond and Edward both agreed. Then, Elizabeth voiced her opinion.

"I think it's important that the children should learn to read and write as soon as possible, right now in fact. I could teach them every week when we come here to visit. Sarah, you can read and write, can you teach them during the week if I show you what to do? I know how to teach, I taught Edward a long time ago."

Sarah and her sisters knew how to read and write to a basic level, though it was never put to any academic use. They still, however, didn't underestimate the importance of an education and were in complete agreement with Elizabeth that the children should indeed learn.

"Well, that seems to have covered everything," said Bill. "If all goes to plan, you and the children should be alright."

A tear began to run down Sarah's face. "Thank you," she said. "All of you."

The women rushed over and comforted Sarah who was still a woman full of hurt and pain. With the issues sorted out, the rest of the day was spent giving Sarah and the children much needed company and support.

Time passed by and the arrangement made on that day went exactly as planned, Edward and Elizabeth did set money aside to help Sarah and the children and every week, as promised, they made the trek to Sprowston to give Sarah her rent money. Elizabeth kept her promise to set about teaching the children to read and write, with support and help from Sarah. Bill and Anne Fox kept their promise too, and each week donated their half of the support money as well as any other extra help needed.

The loss of their son had hit Edward and Elizabeth hard despite the strength that was drawn by the company of their grandchildren left to them by Jacob. Sarah's plight, however, did give them both a feeling of purpose and a knowing that they were needed now just as much as when Jacob was just a child. Edward seemed to have a large part of his life ripped away from him through Jacob's loss and as time wore on, he seemed to look visibly older, even to Elizabeth who understood more than anyone what was within Edward's head.

***

Two years of this pulling together from the family passed until the time finally came for young John to take up his role as apprenticed wheelwright and farrier, which he did under the watchful eye of his proud grandfather Bill Fox. The boy had started as all apprentices do by being given the mundane tasks of sweeping up and pumping the bellows in the forge, as well as fetching tools and materials when told. It soon became apparent to Bill that he had a very obedient and responsible young man within his fold, who seemed to be a natural worker. *Must take after me,* he thought. But John laboured on doing just as he was instructed, and both Bill and Edmond became very fond of this little chap.

In January 1811, as the cold winter was claiming its usual victims of the young, weak, old and poor, Edward Allen set out to work in the morning as usual, as he had done for the last thirty years or more. He had missed breakfast that morning as he felt that he didn't have any appetite, however, Elizabeth had prepared some food for the day as she always did and kissed Edward goodbye. Edward was now working as letter sorter, desk clerk and local postman. He was never entirely sure what tasks were likely to befall him on any given day, especially in winter when absenteeism was common place from the harsh conditions, he would often find himself covering another man's job. Everything was as a normal day until late morning, almost mid-day, when there was a vigorous knock on the door at St George's Church Alley, and which of Elizabeth answered immediately somewhat startled at the ferocity of the knock. It was Percy Chamberlain from the post office.

"Mrs Allen, can you come quick, something's happened to Edward."

A sinking feeling suddenly dropped through the pit of Elizabeth's stomach. She trembled as she struggled to find her shawl and wrap it around her to make the journey to who knows where. As they left, she asked, "What's happened to him, where is he?"

"He was sent out to deliver some mail at Chapelfield, and less than an hour later a kind man brought him back to the office on the back of his barra cart. He's not well, I think it's his heart."

Elizabeth hastened her steps, eager to be with Edward as soon as possible. A feeling of impending doom came over her, she desperately tried to keep composed despite the near hysteria she was feeling in reality. In just a few minutes they reached the post office which was now situated near the market square. Elizabeth rushed in.

"He's in the back" said the desk clerk, and Elizabeth immediately went through.

Edward was sitting upright on the floor and propped against a back wall, his hand was upon his chest and he was breathing heavily. His face looked grey and he was sweating. Crouched beside him was another man who introduced himself as being a doctor, of whom his name was not paid attention to by Elizabeth.

"He's not good I'm afraid," said the doctor. "It's his heart. I'd better leave you for a moment," he added and left the room.

"Oh Edward, what happened?" she asked.

"I felt unwell this morning and there's something funny with my arm, like pins and needles. I just got to Chapelfield and I got a sharp pain in my chest and fell to the floor. A man brought me back here on a small hand cart."

Edward grimaced in pain as the pain intensified. Breathing more heavily, he looked to Elizabeth. "I'm going to die, aren't I?"

Elizabeth sobbed and tightly embraced her lover and partner of thirty-three years.

"Don't leave me, I love you," she sobbed.

"I love you more than you could ever know," said Edward, and the lovers embraced for a final time. Moments later, after suffering more pain in his chest, Edward slipped away from Elizabeth and then from life itself, he was gone…

Elizabeth held tight to the only man she had ever loved until finally she was led away by the doctor so as the office manager could organise an undertaker to take Edward away from the grounds of his majesty's post office.

Elizabeth returned home distraught, where she was comforted by her friends and neighbours from within the communal block of apartments from where she and Edward had lived for so long. Her long-time friend and neighbour, Catherine Ellis, asked her youngest son to make a trip to Sprowston to inform Sarah of the tragic news. This he did first thing the following morning and Sarah immediately returned back with him to be with Elizabeth, leaving her children in the charge of her mother Anne. Sarah spent the day supporting Elizabeth and making the arrangements for Edward's laying to rest. Three days later, the funeral of Edward Allen was held at the church which overlooked his dwelling and whose name was given to the alley where the dwelling was situated. Sarah and the children were there, as was Bill and Anne Fox, and many of the workers from the post office and the mail coaches. All there to pay respects to a colleague lost. After, the family, including Bill and Anne Fox returned back to Elizabeth's nearby home.

"What are you going to do now?" asked Sarah. "Do you want to come to Sprowston and live with us?"

Elizabeth shook her head. "You've the children to feed and your man's gone, you don't need me there, you've enough problems of your own."

"But what'll you do?"

"You forget I come from a wealthy family in Crostwick, my brother owns a farm and cottages. I'll go and see him and see if he'll help me, I don't think he'll want to see me end up in the workhouse. If he can't help me I'll try my sister Martha. If no luck there, then maybe I'll take your kind offer and come to you if you'll have me. I swear I'll not be a burden to you and I'll try and bring wages into the house some way."

"I'll come with you to Crostwick if you like," said Sarah. "If you come and stay with us at Sprowston for a few days, we can go there together in my father's small cart."

Elizabeth agreed and she joined Sarah and her family on the short journey back to Sprowston, where, over the next few days, she found being surrounded by Jacob's family very therapeutic. It temporally eased her pain and the loneliness that was likely to fall upon her. Then eventually, Elizabeth and Sarah made the trip to Crostwick to inform her family of the sad loss of Edward. The unexpected arrival of Elizabeth and Sarah was greeted warmly by George Lutkin the younger, however, his sister's arrival without Edward did raise his curiosity. He hugged Elizabeth at the front door of Spring Farm and ushered her and Sarah inside.

"It's lovely to see you after all this time," said George, "and you too, Sarah," he added.

Sarah smiled at George's kind words.

"Where's Edward?" he asked.

Tears once again began to glisten in Elizabeth's eyes. "He's gone, he died less than a week ago, his heart gave way while at work."

"Oh my God, I'm so sorry, so sorry."

Elizabeth began to cry, and George's wife, Sarah Lutkin, rushed over to comfort her sister in law.

"Oh you poor thing, your husband and your son gone within two years, I'm so sorry," she said.

She sat Elizabeth down onto an armchair in front of the fire. It was a chair that Elizabeth had spent many an hour in her past reading and embroidering when she was a girl. Then Sarah Lutkin left for the kitchen to put the kettle on the fire. A cup of tea was sure to help in a time of crisis.

"What will you do, how will you live?" George asked.

"Sarah has said she will have me at her cottage but she's enough problems of her own supporting the children without Jacob, I would just be a burden to her. I've come to you or Martha to ask you if you have a place I can live, an empty cottage or room or anything. I can work on the farm, do cooking, cleaning, dairy work and I can help with the harvest too. I just need a place to live."

At that point, Sarah Lutkin entered the room, having listened to the whole conversation from the nearby kitchen. In her hands was a tray of cups and a steaming teapot which she placed down on a nearby table. George looked towards his wife to evaluate her reaction of what Elizabeth had just said. She just shrugged her shoulders, indicating that it was up to him to make the decision. George took a minute to think before making his decision, then announced.

"Well," said George. "The children have all flown the nest and we have two spare bedrooms here. I'm finding that now as we all get older and our children are all busily working and raising their own families, they don't have the time on their hands for us. Maybe us older ones should all look out for one another. Martha and John often come here to visit and likewise, Jane and Richard still live in Crostwick, and we still see them. They come here many an evening and play cards and games, and we all share in gossip. We're all older now and I enjoy the company of my brothers and sisters, it reminds me of when we were young. You can come here and go back into your old room, and work in the dairy if you like, to give you a small income and some independence. If things don't work out, either me or Martha could find you a cottage or somewhere for you within our estates, I'm sure we could do that. Till then you're welcome here, I'm sure our dear mother would have wanted it this way."

Elizabeth hugged her brother, a serious problem had been solved, and she was now no longer to be a burden on Sarah and the children. She would begin to organise her move back to Crostwick as soon as was convenient to both herself and her brother George. Now the only other problem in hand was the lost income of Edward that was helping to support Sarah and the children. Things were likely to become a lot harder for them.

Chapter Twenty-Six

In the course of time, Elizabeth moved her belongings back into Spring Farm, the place where she had been born, spent her childhood and was filled with her own personal memories. Her grieving for the one love of her life was eased somewhat by the company of her brothers and sisters, who she was now seeing on a regular basis and within their childhood surroundings. She especially enjoyed the visits from Martha as they were close when they were young. Martha herself had a very kind and warm nature that Elizabeth found at ease with. In some ways, it was just like the old days but with mature years upon them. The important thing to Elizabeth was the feeling that she belonged there, equally her brothers and sisters almost seemed to need her there as much as she needed them.

Sundays were the most pleasant times when George's children and their families would visit, and occasionally Martha and her husband John Watts would visit too. Sarah Lutkin, Martha and Elizabeth would all work together in the kitchen preparing a Sunday meal for the large gathering and together enjoy gossip and women's chat as they toiled with the food preparation. With these pleasant Sundays and her work in the dairy, which also kept her mind busy within the company of the other dairy girls, Elizabeth found the whole situation an enjoyable experience and was able to cope with Edward's passing. Though at night, alone in her room, he was never far from her thoughts. She did, however, set time aside to visit Jacob's family at every available opportunity, regularly taking a walk to nearby Sprowston. She would always find time for them and loved to watch the children, who resembled her son so much, grow ever taller and ever wiser.

Things for Sarah Allen did indeed become harder because of the lost income from Edward. She was almost totally dependent on the help from her own family, Bill and Anne Fox, and her brothers and sisters. In time she learned to be more resourceful, she would throw out very little, repair and mend anything that needed it, and earn money wherever and whenever she could. Yes, times were hard but she and the children were still surviving.

It was later in that same year of 1811, just a short time after the harvest had been brought in. The harvest had given Sarah some welcome extra income as she helped on the fields with the large teams of field workers from the village. The talk of the time was of the King's on-going insanity which had forced Parliament to create his eldest son and heir, Prince Regent. The harvest festival had just been celebrated in church and there were social gatherings within the village and farms themselves. It was at just such a social gathering at Church Farm that great changes in Sarah's life were about to unfold. Word had already been spread that a farm-workers' celebration was to be organised and held at the rear yard of the farm. Ale had been brewed of three different strengths, and the local women and wives of the farm workers were to prepare food, enough for all who had taken part bringing in the harvest. Children were encouraged to accompany their parents to the gathering as indeed many had helped their parents in the fields themselves.

The sun shone on this mid-September day, possibly one of the last warm periods before the weather was to change to the coldness of the autumn fall. Straw bales and half barrel benched seats were laid out in the usual way for such events, and a local fiddle player was hired for country dancing and communal singing of old country songs. The proprietors were to be there, namely Parson Sutton and his wife and family. He was expected to make a speech and maybe raise a glass for thanks for the harvest. However, the main ale consumption of the men would have to be postponed until the Parson and his family had left to let the workers celebrate in their own way, as was customary for such an event.

Sarah came along to the celebration which was to begin at twelve noon, along with her two youngest children, William and Edward, and her neighbour Thomas's two children, Tom and Keziah, who she still cared for whilst Thomas was at work. They were to meet Thomas at the celebration later, being the foreman he still had work duties to do and would celebrate with the rest as soon as the jobs were done.

Everybody gathered together at the appointed time and Parson Sutton welcomed all of the workers and their families and thanked them all for all the hard work done. As expected from him, a prayer and a blessing was said which was received respectfully by all who had attended, this was not a gathering of atheists. Then he and his family raised a tankard of the more liberal strength of the three ales in honour of those workers who had toiled so hard to bring in the harvest. Everyone joined in by raising their tankards to toast the harvest, and with that, there was a brief period of mingling and pleasantries before the Parson finally left to let the real party begin.

Fiddle music began to play and the player began to sing to his songs to accompany his music. The crowd began to sing along to the tunes they all knew so well and some began to dance. Meanwhile, the mothers were busy making sure that their children were fed from the food table. This is what had kept Sarah occupied, feeding both her children and Thomas's. Soon after, Thomas Walker and a couple of farm hands finally joined the gathering having completed their tasks of feeding and bedding the livestock. He was greeted with great enthusiasm, as being foreman of Church Farm he was in close contact with nearly all present.

"Hello Sarah, I hope they've been behaving themselves." said Thomas, referring to his children.

"Good as always," was Sarah's reply.

The children were all happily tucking into the food on the table and listening to the music. The sound of musical instruments was a novelty to them, not heard very often, just the sound of somebody whistling a tune or singing a song was all the music they would usually hear. Food would be eaten by the adults once the children were sorted out and then the ales would begin to be consumed, especially by the male farm workers. The women watched and could see the effect that the ales were having on their men the more they drank, some of their faces had reddened with a glazed look in their eyes, and more and more laughter was heard between the singing of the songs as they accompanied the fiddler. Arms were put around the women and some were grabbed and pulled onto the dance area of the yard. Most joined in, they had enjoyed a small cup or two of ale themselves, it was a celebration after all. Those women who did not want the attention of the men who were under the influence of the alcohol just politely declined their dance requests and steered the men discreetly back towards the ale barrels or the dance area. This of course, included Sarah who despite enjoying the event, did not feel it was appropriate to respond to a man's friendly advances in front of her children.

The afternoon celebrations in the warm sunshine finally came to an end in what had seemed almost an instant to the revellers, but was in fact, five hours of celebrations that had come and gone, so now it was time to clear up and go home. There was still a little food left, so the children were allowed to take with them small amounts wrapped up in linen handkerchiefs. Thomas Walker strolled back to his cottage with Sarah and the children.

"Thanks again for all you've done for us all this time," said Thomas, clearly under the influence of the ales he had helped to celebrate with.

"You know I don't know what I would have done without you and Jacob when I lost poor Keziah. I don't know how I would have supported the little-uns."

"You would have done it fine," replied Sarah. "Your family would have helped you just like mine are helping me now."

"Are you finding it hard now that Jacob's family can't help?"

"Yes it's hard but we're still surviving and that's the main thing."

"You know Sarah, now it's you who needs the help. If there's anything you need, you only have to ask."

"That's kind of you Thomas, but we'll be alright."

The group approached their cottages and Thomas spoke again with a slight slur upon his speech.

"Well, thank you again, if there's anything, you only have to ask."

Sarah laughed. "I know, you said. Look, your two can stay at mine tonight with my three, I'll make them up a bed. You look like you could do with a night's sleep. I'll sort their breakfast out in the morning."

The suggestion didn't seem such a bad idea to Thomas. He clearly needed to sleep off the ale, and dealing with the children in the morning didn't seem all that appealing to him knowing how he was likely to feel when he woke up.

"Are you sure you don't mind?"

Sarah smiled. "Go on Thomas, you go and get a good night's sleep, you'll be better for it in the morning."

Thomas thanked Sarah again and retired for a night's sleeping off the ales whilst young Thomas and Keziah joined their young playmates for a sleepover two doors down from their house.

The following morning, Thomas rose at his usual early hours in the morning ready to go to the farm and see to the livestock. It was Sunday and most of the farmhands had the day off. He, however, was foreman and had taken it upon himself to be responsible for all of the livestock on Sunday mornings. He would go in for a couple of hours and give the animals enough feed for the day, enabling the rest of the hands to enjoy their Sunday off. This gesture by the foreman always gained respect from the farm workers. Though awake and able to work, Thomas could still feel the effects of the ales from the previous day. His head ached and he still had the usual collie-wobbles within his gut. Badly dehydrated, he made for the communal well, shared by all the farm cottages. Pulling up a bucket of water, he quickly drank a tankard full and poured the remainder over his head. This did the trick, making him feel more awake and he then made his way to the farm to perform his duties, of which, after two hours, he completed and returned back home to find his children playing together in Sarah's back garden.

"How are you feeling this morning?" asked Sarah.

"I'll live," said Thomas. "I did feel the ales this morning when I woke up though."

Sarah laughed. "That'll teach you."

Thomas smiled.

"I'd better get these two ready for church, and get washed and changed myself."

"We'll walk up there with you if you like," said Sarah. "My mother and father will stop by as usual and we can all go there together."

"See you then," replied Thomas, and he and his two children left to get ready.

All went to plan; Bill and Anne Fox did indeed turn up at Sarah's ready to go to church, and the group, who were all dressed in their Sunday best, stopped on the way for Thomas and his children to join them. The church was full as usual, and Parson Sutton welcomed the worshippers of his parish. Prayers and sermons were said, and a baby girl named Ann Thacker was publicly baptised, after which, everybody returned home to spend the rest of the day having lunch and resting on a lazy Sunday afternoon. Some of the villagers would pursue leisure activities such as hare coursing, hunting and fishing. Some would enjoy creative activities such as basket weaving, needlework or toy making for the children. For Sarah and the children, Sunday was spent having lunch at her parent's cottage before finally returning home later in the afternoon. On arrival home, Thomas and his children were already outside in their garden two doors away, and young Tom and Keziah rushed around to Sarah's to join their young playmates. Soon after, Thomas joined them.

"Have a good dinner?" asked Thomas.

"Beef stew and dumplings," Sarah replied. "How about you?"

"Boiled pig's trotter, cabbage and spuds," replied Thomas.

"Sound nice."

Thomas sat down on a wooden log as he watched the children playing in the garden. Sarah brought out a chair from inside and sat down beside Thomas.

"How do you find life now? Are you managing to cope alone alright?" asked Thomas.

Sarah smiled, she thought of the previous day when Thomas had asked that very question under the influence of ale, and now had forgotten having asked again.

"I'm coping and we're surviving," she replied. "Thanks to my family. Soon enough, the boys will be older and bring some badly needed wages into the house."

"Are you lonely? Is it still painful to think about Jacob?"

"Will! Stop that and play nicely!" shouted Sarah, momentarily distracted by the antics of her children.

"Yes, I still think of him and yes, I miss him, but there's too much to do, what with caring for the children. I just think of them and keep myself busy, there's no time to get upset... Do you think of Keziah much?"

"When the children are put to bed and I'm alone I think of her, and I miss her companionship, even when she got angry, I still miss that."

"Those are the moments when I sit and think," said Sarah. "Just those quiet brief times when the children are sleeping and I'm sitting alone knitting or sewing or repairing clothes."

A long pause of silence came over them as they watched the children playing in the garden.

"Do you think you'll marry again?" asked Thomas. "Is it too painful for you or... you know, is it too early?"

"I don't know, I suppose I will if the right man comes along who will want to take me on and my children."

"You know, Sarah, since Keziah passed on I've wondered how I was going to manage with the children with no mother to look after 'em. It was only because of you that I was able to carry on. I would never have been able to work and care for the little-uns alone, and for that I thank you."

"There's no need to thank me."

"No, hear me out," interrupted Thomas. "You've looked after my little-uns as if they were yours, and they look to you as the mother they haven't got, and equally your boys are like brothers to 'em. You need a man to look after you, you're still young enough to marry again… I could be that man if you so wanted. It would make sense for everyone, I can work and support us and you can care for the children and look after the home. I know you don't love me but at least we could all survive and live together as a family. It's got to be worth at least thinking about."

What Thomas had just suggested didn't entirely take Sarah by surprise. It was obvious to her that looking after Thomas's children whilst he was away at work seemed almost a step in that very direction now that Jacob was no longer here to be her husband. However, now the question was asked and now she had to deal with it. The trouble was that Thomas was right, she didn't love him, she liked him but not love. Any paring between them would have to be more like an arrangement for the benefit of all those concerned. She thought carefully before she replied…

"Thomas, I'm flattered that you would think that way and be willing to marry me and take on my little-uns, but I would have to think hard on it. It's not just me, I have the boys to think about."

"But you will think about it then?"

"Yes I'll think it over, but don't rush me, just give me time. This is a big thing and will have to be thought out properly."

"Take all the time you need."

A short time after Thomas left with his children, leaving Sarah to ponder on the events of what had just been said. Later, and with the children now tucked away in bed, she sat down in front of the fire imagining what life could possibly be like with Thomas Walker as her man. What would she do? It came to her that maybe she would ask for advice from family and friends around her, especially her mother and father and most importantly, the thoughts of Elizabeth Allen.

The following morning, Thomas's children came knocking at the door as they usually did. Their father had already risen some two hours earlier and was at Church Farm sorting out the day's duties for the workers as well as working manually himself. His children were quite used to getting up and dressed themselves for in these times children had to learn quickly. After Sarah had given all the children their breakfast, she and the children went to her mother and father's cottage, as Sarah's intention was to have a private word with her mother. Her children were always glad to see their grandparents and to see their brother John at work. He had already risen an hour earlier to start his working day as apprentice at the workshop and forge. Soon, he would be joined by his brother William, who would soon be ten years old and ready to begin his training.

"Mother, would you mind looking after the children for a while? I need to go to Crostwick and see Jacob's mother."

Anne was surprised, this was an unexpected trip that was not mentioned before.

"Of course I will, is everything alright?"

Sarah looked around to see that the children were safely out of earshot. They were, they had gone out in the back yard to watch the men at work and to feed the horse in her stable.

"Thomas Walker has asked me to marry him."

This news caused Anne Fox to raise an eyebrow, even though it wasn't a situation that hadn't crossed her mind.

"And what answer have you given him?" she asked.

"I haven't yet, I don't know what to do except ask for yours and father's advice, and Elizabeth's of course, that's why I need to see her. What do you think I should do?"

"Are you fond of him?"

"Yes, but I don't know if I love him," replied Sarah.

"It would make sense to marry him, if not for the sake of all the children, yours and his," said Anne.

"I know that but what do you think father would think of it all?"

Anne made for the door. "Let's ask him. Bill! Can you come here please?"

Bill was busily shaving some wheel spokes but immediately came into the cottage on Anne's request.

"What is it?" he asked.

"Thomas Walker's asked Sarah to marry him, what do you think?"

"Has he now?" said Bill.

"Well, what do you think she should do?" asked Anne.

Bill looked at Sarah. "I think you should marry im my girl. Those children need a father and he can support all of you. He needs a woman to care for and be a mother to his little-uns, so it would make sense to."

"I don't love him like Jacob though," said Sarah.

"Love's got nothing to do with it. It's about what you both must do for your children. Besides, you two both need someone for help and support. I think you should at least think it over. There you are, that's what I think, now if you don't mind, I've got work to do."

Bill's opinion certainly gave Sarah food for thought.

"I need to talk to Elizabeth," she said, and shortly after, set out on her journey to Crostwick to seek the advice of her mother in law. This wasn't going to be easy, Elizabeth wasn't likely to accept easily another man's advances towards her own son's wife.

She arrived at Spring Farm in less than an hour and was greeted warmly by Elizabeth although somewhat bemused. Why was she alone, where were the children? She asked that very question upon greeting her.

"I needed to see you privately to ask your advice on something," said Sarah.

Elizabeth nodded, half expecting to know what Sarah was about to say. It was something that Elizabeth had thought would happen sooner or later.

"Well," said Sarah, with slight hesitation. "A man's asked me to marry him, and I don't know what to do, so I'm seeking advice from close family, namely, mother, father and you."

"Who's the man who asked you?"

"It's Thomas Walker, the man who lives two doors down from me. He's widowed and has two children."

"The two children you look after during the day?"

"Yes," replied Sarah.

"Do you love this man or care for him?"

"He's a good man and I do like him, but I don't love him, not the way I loved Jacob. He knows that but he thinks it would be better for all of us if we married. Most of all, for the sake of the children."

Elizabeth paused for a moment as she thought things out. She was a woman of logic, a characteristic inherited from her own mother.

"Could you see yourself with this man, sleeping with him and bearing his children as his wife?" she asked. "Because he will expect this if he is to support you and your children."

"I think I could if he was my husband, I do like him." replied Sarah "He is a good man."

"Do your parents think you should marry him?"

"They think it would make sense to join the two families for the sake of all the children."

"I think I agree with them," said Elizabeth. "A child needs both a mother and a father and your children are no exception and neither are his. If you feel that maybe you could live with him as a wife, then maybe it's not such a bad thing to go through with. If it were me, I would do what I had to for my children."

Sarah had heard what she needed to hear.

"I thought you would be hostile to another man wanting me."

"Jacob's gone," said Elizabeth. "But his wife and children still live. They will live a lot better with a man to support them and be a father like Jacob would have been. We can't bring Jacob back, God rest him, but you must try to live and survive as well as you can. I think he would have wanted that for you and the children."

Sarah thanked Elizabeth and told her that she would hear soon of her decision before finally leaving for her journey back to Sprowston. The walk back seemed almost timeless, she was fixed in deep thought throughout the whole journey. She reached the far end of Barker's Lane, which linked up to Church Lane, then heard someone whistle loudly in the distance, which immediately broke her train of thought. She looked, it was Thomas, he had seen her as she neared the farm and came out to the gate to greet her.

"Thought it was you," he said. "Been somewhere good?"

"I've just been to see Jacob's mother. The children are safe, they're with my mother."

"Have you thought anymore of what I asked you?" asked Thomas.

"I have... and I will marry you."

This announcement brought a broad smile to Thomas's face and he grabbed Sarah and pulled her to him.

"You won't regret this, I swear you won't."

And with that, Thomas Walker and Sarah Allen shared their first kiss as future man and wife.

"Just be a good husband and father, that's all I ask."

"I will, I swear it," he replied, and he smiled and winked to her. This momentarily reminded Sarah of that time years back when Jacob had asked her to marry him on their journey from Crostwick to Sprowston.

Thomas bid Sarah goodbye and returned back to work, leaving Sarah to return back to her parent's cottage and to tell the family of the proposal acceptance. The news was gladly welcomed and came as somewhat of a relief to Bill and Anne Fox who had always feared of what would become of Sarah and the children, should anything happen to them and leave no one to support her. Two days later, Thomas and Sarah journeyed back to Crostwick to inform Elizabeth Allen of the news and to invite her to the wedding ceremony, which of course was accepted gladly. Weeks later, the families reassembled to the church to witness their union. An entry was made in the church records of the parish of Sprowston. Sarah Allen remarrying after being widowed, to a widower named Thomas Walker of the same parish. The marriage was formally witnessed by Bill Fox and Elizabeth Allen.

Chapter Twenty-Seven
John and Amelia

"We've got to go to Riverside timber yard John, to pick up some long lengths of pine to repair the roof on the stable and fodder shed. We also need some more ash and elm for the workshop. Can you come with me?" asked Edmond Fox to his nephew and work colleague, John Allen.

It is now 1817 and events have now moved on.

Bill Fox has sadly passed away having succumbed to a bout of influenza in the autumn of 1813. The business he had left behind was always destined to become Edmond's, and not his elder brother, William, as would have been tradition. William had chosen another trade, that of bricklayer, which itself was a respected trade, and one that had served him well in prosperity. Edmond is living back at the cottage that was once his father's, and is working to support his own family and his now elderly mother. He had briefly moved away to live in a cottage of his own after marrying his wife, Molly, in 1812. Molly has since born Edmond a son they have called Johnny, named after young John Allen, to his obvious delight. Johnny is four years old.

Sarah and Thomas Walker are living at the cottage that was once part of the Church Farm estate, and Thomas and Keziah's original marital home. The cottage, and Thomas's employment, has since been purchased by Sir Thomas Woodruff Smyth, the new owner of Sprowston Manor. The buildings and land have been drawn into the Manor Farm estate where Thomas Walker continues to work as foreman. There are two more additions to their family, Sarah has given birth to two more children, to add to the ones had from their previous marriages. James Walker was born in 1814 and his baby brother David was born earlier in the current year of 1817. The cottage they call home is now getting crowded and sleeping arrangements are difficult, but like so many large families of the time, they have to manage.

Elizabeth Allen continues to live out her autumn years in the company of her now ageing siblings at Crostwick. She still stays in touch with her grandchildren by letters to and from Sprowston. Occasionally, Sarah and John, Will and Eddie travel to Crostwick to pay her a visit, filling Elizabeth's heart with joy on seeing Jacob's image within the eyes of his children.

Jacob and Sarah's eldest son John is seventeen and his apprenticeship as a fully skilled wheelwright and farrier is almost over. His brothers are also serving their apprenticeships and all are working together helping Edmond run a thriving family business. John has kept a level head on his shoulders and has developed natural leadership skills. He helps Edmond with the general running of the business to the point that Edmond is almost completely reliant upon him. He works almost a full partner despite his young age. He has a strong community spirit within him, often helping with parish events, local celebrations and church services. The new clergy at the church has found John to be an invaluable help to his newly appointed parsonage. John has grown to become a tall young man at almost six feet tall, and he resembles both his parents. He has blue eyes and has facial features closely resembling Jacob but has his mother's fair hair and resembles her most when he smiles. He is a young man who already commands respect from many of the community despite his young age. There are some who think that John will, one day, become a man of substance, and a pillar of the community he lives in.

"Yes, I'll come," replied John. "I've just about finished Patterson's wheels, they're nearly ready for rimming. Will and Eddie can sort that out."

Edmond and John hitched up the horse to the cart, and climbed aboard and began their journey to Norwich. The trip to pick up the timber was not really a two-man job but Edmond liked the company rather than travelling alone and John enjoyed a welcome break from the workshop. Cutting through Mousehold Heath, their journey took barely twenty minutes as it was downhill most of the way. Their destination was the Riverside timber yard which was less than a hundred yards from the city's Foundry Bridge. Either side of the bridge there is a river port which receives imports directly from the sea port of Yarmouth, cargoes are brought in by river wherry to feed the city's needs of coal fuel and supplies. This of course includes imported timber, mostly pine from Scandinavia and Scotland, hence the convenient timber yard close by.

John and Edmond travelled alongside the river from Mousehold and passed the Foundry Bridge itself as they neared the yard. Just past the bridge a couple of Norfolk wherry sail barges were moored up, both with full cargoes of coal which had been loaded up at Yarmouth from sea fearing vessels and brought to Norwich. They were waiting to be unloaded by port labourers who were busy down river unloading grain from another wherry which had arrived earlier that morning. John and Edmond completely ignored the moored wherries, they were a common sight on the river. It was the vessel moored up past them that really caught the eyes of the two wheelwrights. Operating since 1813 was the first steam vessel seen in Norwich in these very early days of steam power. The Courier was a steam packet which ran a service of ferrying paying passengers to and from Yarmouth, a journey of three hours and fifteen minutes. It was a small paddle steamer almost the same length as the wherries moored close by, about forty feet long by thirteen feet wide. Two large grey paddle wheels were positioned both sides at mid-ship and just behind the paddle line stood a tall black iron chimney. At the bottom of the smoking chimney was the steam engine driving the paddles with an array of iron crankshafts hidden below deck. Behind the steam engine was a full coal bay doubtlessly brought to Norwich by one of the Norfolk Wherry's from Yarmouth that had been shipped down the east coast of England all the way from Newcastle. Covering the top half of the paddles were timber water guards painted white and displaying a painted sign in red lettering reading, Wright's Norwich and Yarmouth transport. Passengers of the ferry service were in the process of both queuing and boarding. It was Good Friday and paying guests were likely to make special visits to family and church gatherings for the Easter weekend.

John and Edmond continued past the steamer which was obviously due to depart for its journey to Yarmouth, they were nearly at journeys end themselves as the Riverside Timber yard was situated just fifty yards or so past the moored steamer.

"One day, I'll go on that," said John. "I've always wanted to go to Yarmouth. My father used to go there when he was a boy with his father on the mail coaches, so Mother told me."

"I remember hearing that too but from your father's own lips many years ago. Maybe I'll come along with you, I've always fancied going on that boat too. Costs too much at the moment though," said Edmond.

Moments later, their cart drew up at the Riverside Timber yard where a cart belonging to a local builder from Norwich was already being loaded up with various sizes and lengths of Scots pine by two labourers who worked at the yard. The owner and proprietor of the Riverside Timber yard was Walter Spooner, who, seeing that his yard staff were busy with the builder, came out of his wooden office to serve Edmond and John personally.

"What can I do for you?" he asked.

"Need about five ten foot lengths of two by four pine and a nine by nine of elm, also about ten foot. Oh, and I'll need some ash too, some four by four," said Edmond.

"Nine by nine elm?" asked Spooner. "What's it for, a beam is it?"

"No, we're wheelwrights. We'll get quite a few hubs outa that," replied Edmond. "The pines for some repairs around the cottage and the workshop and the ash is for the outer felloes of the wheels."

Spooner immediately checked his stock of elm. This was a large size of timber but he knew that he had some in stock and which he finally found underneath a small pile of smaller sized elm aside of two similar sized lengths. The three men all moved the smaller items off the desired nine by nine inch lengths and began to pull one of them free from the wrack from which it lay. A toot was heard in the near distance from the Courier as it began its departure to Yarmouth. Another heave and the three men began to dislodge the timber away from the pile.

Then suddenly, and to everyone's great shock, there was a tremendous bang... louder than either John or Edmond had ever heard in their lives... the sound of an explosion. Their horse immediately reared up in fright at the sudden loud burst of sound and shock wave that accompanied it. Edmond quickly grabbed the beast's harness and fought to calm it down, which after a few moments, he did. In the distance the sound of screams was heard. Everyone in the yard immediately rushed out to the riverside road to see what had just happened, knowing it was to do with the steam packet.

The scene that greeted them was that of sheer carnage and devastation. The Courier was almost completely destroyed. Its boiler had blown up but its hull still remained, just intact and afloat less than five yards from the bank. Debris was everywhere floating all around the river and was piled all around on what was left of the deck. Lying in amongst the debris were seriously injured passengers, some lying still and some awake and screaming in agony. Rising to their feet were the dazed and uninjured passengers, who could do little to help as the injured were mostly suffering fractures and bad scolds from the exploding boiler. There were bodies too, three men and two women lay dead on the deck, some had lost limbs and one man had lost half of his head. Blood was all over the place including over the screaming surviving women passengers.

"Throw me a line!" shouted one man on the bank. He was Thomas Agg, the next-door neighbour to the timber yard who was first on the scene and had only moments earlier been talking to the engine driver just before its departure. One of the survivors threw a line to Agg, and he and the two timber yard labourers pulled the vessel back to the bank and tied the line to a mooring steak. Over on the far side of what was left of the vessel and floating in the water were more bodies, that of two adult men and a small child who had been blown into the water and drowned, it was too late to save them. John jumped on board along with Thomas Agg, Walter Spooner and the two labourers from the yard.

"Bring your cart here!" shouted Spooner to Edmond. "We need to get the injured to hospital!"

Edmond immediately obliged, and ran back to the timber yard where his horse and cart were tied up. Meanwhile, on board the stricken vessel, John was seeing to an injured woman, he was reassuring her that she would soon be taken away to hospital. Then suddenly, he noticed laying on the floor close to the side of the vessel and beside what was left of the shattered seating bench was a weaved Moses basket containing a baby boy. He immediately rushed over and picked the basket up which in turn drew the attention of a balding middle aged man who happened to be one of the passengers to have come out unscathed.

"Is he dead?" the man asked.

John studied the baby but couldn't be sure, his eyes were shut and there was no movement. He couldn't hear if the baby was still breathing due to the noise of the moans and screams of the injured passengers.

"I don't know I can't tell," John replied.

"Try pinching his ear," said the man.

John did this... and there was movement from the baby as it stirred. John put his finger to the baby's hand and it wrapped its tiny hand around John's forefinger. A slight smile then came to John's face, even in amongst all the carnage that was around him.

"He's alive!"

Moments later, Edmond arrived with the cart. Two other carts were behind called over from the roadside to lend a hand from the by now large crowd that had gathered to both watch and help. Three injured women were loaded onto the cart and two unhurt male passengers who were husbands of two of the women. One of the women was unconscious.

"John!" shouted Edmond. "Quick, come here, we're going to the hospital!"

"Whose baby is this?" John called.

"It's hers and his!" shouted an injured woman who was in the process of being helped off the stricken vessel. She was pointing to a man kneeling on the deck who was holding a dead woman in his arms, and was sobbing for his dead wife. Beside them was the lifeless body of the small boy, about four years of age, who had just been pulled out of the river and laid down beside his dead mother. The baby in the Moses basket had slept through the whole ordeal not knowing that his mother, who was called Mary Bleasey, and his elder brother, John Bleasey, had both died.

"John! Where are you? Hurry!" shouted Edmond.

John handed the Moses basket to the uninjured man whose attention had been caught when finding the baby.

"Can you give his son to him when he's ready?"

The man nodded and took the baby from John.

John quickly jumped ship and boarded the cart of which sped away abruptly in the direction of the St Stephen area of the city, the location of the Norfolk and Norwich hospital. They were followed by the other two cartloads of injured passengers with some of their friends and relatives. Ten minutes later, Edmond and John arrived at the hospital and John ran inside and alerted the medical staff to the emergency that had just unfolded. The response was immediate, doctors and orderlies dropped what they were doing where possible and came out to the carts with stretchers to bring the injured in for immediate treatment. Very soon after, the three carts were emptied and the injured passengers were brought in.

A worker from the hospital came over came over to John and Edmond who by now were standing among a group of fellow rescuers who had also rushed injured passengers to the hospital in their carts.

"What was it like down there at the river?" he asked.

"I never want to see anything like that again in my life," said John.

"It was terrible," said Edmond. "Blood and death everywhere. There was a man lying there with half his head blown away and a man crying for his lost wife and little boy."

"The boat didn't look like a boat anymore. It was in pieces, but was still floating. It was like gun powder had gone off in it," said John.

The worker gave an understanding nod. "You're good people, all of you for bringing them here and helping them."

"I never got to know any of their names, those who we were carrying that is," said John.

"Don't suppose we ever will know or what happened to 'em," replied Edmond.

"It'll be in the papers I suppose, maybe it'll say more of what happened and why. There'll be a list of the dead and injured I should think," said John.

Edmond agreed

"What do we do now?" asked John.

"We'd better go back to the timber yard and pick up that timber we pulled out."

"It'll be crowded around there," said John. "Maybe it is best if we head back home and pick the wood up tomorrow."

Again, Edmond agreed. So they headed back home to Sprowston without the desired timber they had made their journey for in the first place. Unknown to them both, the unconscious woman who had been put into their cart sadly died while in the Norfolk and Norwich hospital. On return home, the pair told family and work colleagues of the tragic ordeal they had just been through, and news of the disaster quickly spread around the village. The following day, John and Edmond returned back to the timber yard to pick up the timber from the day before. Scores of people had come to see the remains of the steam packet, some were watching from on the foundry bridge and others were at the riverbank. It had turned out that the timber yard's neighbour Thomas Agg had only moments earlier been talking to the engine driver, who was one of the vessel's crew of two. He had boasted that he would get her steam well up to give her a good start. Over the course of the next week, the newspapers did indeed report the facts of the accident and stated that very fact of the engineer's boasts, however, he had paid dearly with his life as he was one of the victims killed in the tragedy. Amazingly, six people on board remained completely unhurt and one of them was actually standing over the boiler when it blew. A list was published a week later of the dead and injured in the Norwich Mercury, they were:

Killed or died later as a result of the tragedy
John Bleasey age 4 John Marron age 55
Mary Bleasey age 40 Richard Squire age 30
William Battledor age 50 Thomas Louis age 53
Elizabeth Stevens age 50 William Richardson age 25
Diana Smith age 60

The following persons were conveyed to the Norfolk and Norwich hospital:

Sarah Smith (24) of Norwich; fractures to left leg. Susan Carr (22) of Hingham; wound to the head. Mary Harrison (50) of Norwich; fracture to right arm and wound to face. Esther Welton (50) of Acle; compound fracture to right leg. Martha Dredwell (58) of North Creak; wound to the head and Mary Shepherd (36) of Yarmouth with compound fractures to both legs and wound on thigh.

A subscription of £350 was later raised by charitable citizens of Norwich and Norfolk to help the families of those who were caught up in the tragedy. Valuable lessons were learned as to the dangers of over pressured steam engines due to the publicity of the disaster that had reached the whole country in the network of newspapers. In Norwich, a complete generation never forgot what had occurred on that day on Good Friday April 4th 1817.

Chapter Twenty-Eight

The long reign of George III had finally come to an end upon his death in January of this year of 1820. Despite his son ruling as regent since 1811 due to the king's bout of madness, it was time for the unpopular Prince George to take over the role of monarchy in his own right, long live King George IV.

***

John Allen, now nineteen years old, has become a virtual partner at the forge in all but name. He is equally running the business with Edmond and with the help of his two brothers, Will and Eddie. All three brothers are by now fully skilled wheelwrights and farriers. It is Sunday morning, and his family are preparing for their usual visit to St Mary and Margaret's church in the village. The family has increased in size again by two more children under the surname of Walker. Robert Walker was born in 1818 and Elizabeth Walker is the newest arrival at just two months old. Sarah now has three children by Jacob Allen and four by Thomas Walker. Thomas's eldest two children from his first marriage, Tom and Keziah, are also still living at the cottage and things are getting more strained within the small cramped abode. The eldest children are by now all young adults and help their parents with the younger ones whenever possible.

"It's Parson Banfather's first Sunday service alone, so I want you little-uns on best behaviour," said Sarah. "John, are you helping him?"

John nodded. "He's got a baptism, I'll fetch the register for him and fill the jug for the font, but otherwise, he's doing it all alone."

Henry Banfather was a young vicar just recently given his new parsonage within the Sprowston parish following the death of Parson Sutton. He had been helped into the job with the aid of Parson Williams who was a stand in chaplain sent from Norwich Cathedral, and whose job it was to fill the gap of transition.

The large family of Walkers and Allen's left their cottage to make their way to church. They were joined on their journey by Edmond Fox and his wife, Molly, son, Johnny, and his now elderly mother Anne Fox, who was always happy to be surrounded by so many of her family.

"Can I have a quiet word with you after church Edmond?" John asked as they walked.

Edmond agreed.

On arrival, the new parson stood waiting at the church doors to greet the parishioners as they entered. The church was full this Sunday, it was a novelty to have a new parson and most were keen to see him officially begin his duties. As usual, prayers and sermons were said, but on this occasion, hymns were sung for the first time. Henry Banfather had brought some new ways of delivering Sunday service with him. However, as one might expect, whenever there is change or something new added, some would enjoy the change and some would not. A baby girl named Martha Davidson was publicly baptised and the baptism was recorded within the church register by the new parson. Soon after, the service was over and Henry Banfather bid his parishioners farewell as he stood once again at the church door to see his flock vacate the church. Meanwhile, John cleared up the prayer books and the new hymn books, though just only a few had been used as literacy was not so common amongst the farm workers and labourers. Shortly after, and with the books put away, he left the church and hurried to catch the family as they walked their short journey back home. In just moments, he had caught up with the rest, and Edmond, knowing that John needed to speak to him, let the family go ahead and joined John two or three paces behind the group.

"You wanted to speak to me?" he asked.

"Yes, I did," John replied. "What I wanted to ask you is a big thing that I was hoping you might consider. As you know, mother and father now have a larger family, what with four little-uns and us five older ones, it's getting overcrowded and very uncomfortable to live there."

Edmond agreed, and had a very good idea as to where this conversation was leading.

John continued. "Me, Will and Ed were wondering if you would consider renting a room out to us at your cottage. I know the spare room was meant for Johnny but it'd be an extra income for you and it'd only be until we're all ready to marry one day. It would take the pressure off Mother and Father now they've got their new family to look after. We could help you look after Granny Fox as well."

Edmond continued walking, he didn't reply at first, he just kept walking as he pondered over John's request.

"I can see your problem John, but it's not just you three I have to consider, there's Molly and young Johnny and my mother. They'll have to be spoken to first and see if they agree. We were going to put young Johnny in that room soon, we'd have to put that off for a while longer. I'll have to talk it over with them when we get back home."

John agreed, and moments later, the group arrived at the Fox cottage and smithy, whereupon Edmond, Molly and their son, Johnny and Anne Fox said goodbye to the remaining members of the group. Thomas, Sarah and their family headed back to their own cottage while John stayed with Edmond knowing that he would have to be there when the question was put to Molly and his grandmother.

"Are you coming to have lunch with us, John?" asked Anne Fox, who was slightly confused as to why John had come to their home at Sunday lunchtime.

"No Grandma, I'm not," he replied.

Then Edmond cut in. "John's here because he has a problem that needs sorting, which may concern all of us."

This confused Anne Fox even more, as did Molly. The family entered the cottage, and all sat down at the dining table to begin their discussion. Edmond began the proceedings.

"John, Will and Eddie want to know if they can live here, and pay rent to stay in the spare room. It's too crowded up the road for them and it'll also give Thomas and Sarah more room for their little-uns... What do you think?"

There was a moment of silence and looking at one another for reaction, which was eventually broken by Anne Fox.

"I think that it's not a bad idea, it would help Sarah with her new family."

Molly looked to her husband trying to work out where his opinion lay, she pressed the issue further by pointing out a possible problem.

"Johnny would have to stay in our room for much longer," she said.

"I know," said Anne. "But he likes all of them elder boys and it would be good for him to have their company and learn off 'em. It'd only be until one of 'em finds a wife and marries, and they're all close to marrying age now, it shouldn't be for long I expect. Then he can share with the other two, he'll be older then and shouldn't mind."

Molly was still unable to work out Edmond's opinion on the matter so decided on the only option, to ask him outright.

"What do you think Edmond?"

"I think that they do have a problem, it is crowded at Sarah's and there is space here. This is also their place of work and family must help each other when in need… and their need is now. I say we let them come here and see how it goes. If it doesn't work they'll either have to go back, or better still find a place of their own to live. They should be able to manage with three wages coming into the place. At the moment we should give it a chance and see. That's what I think."

Molly reluctantly agreed. She wasn't either a selfish or vindictive woman, she was just a mother and a wife who would always think of the interests of her husband and child first. However, and unfortunately for her, these were days when the man of the house usually had the last word. So, with the decision made, John left for home to tell the news to his brothers, and to Thomas and Sarah that they would soon be leaving home. The news was received well by Thomas, but to Sarah, it was a moment of mixed emotions of losing her three eldest children to make way for the upbringing of the younger ones. But common sense told her that this was the right thing to do for all. There was, however, the lost income of her three elder boys to consider, it was to be easier with more space but tougher for the family financially, but later that week, the three brothers packed their belongings and moved into Bill Fox's old cottage and smithy that was their place of work.

The following Sunday, the Walker and the Fox family, accompanied by the Allen branch of the family, returned back at church for the usual Sunday service. Once again, John helped in the affairs of the service, fetching and passing out the new hymn books and the old prayer books as well as registering a baby boy named Walter Greenbough who had been publicly baptised by the new parson Banfather. After the service, the new parson bid his parishioners farewell as usual from the church doors, whereupon he re-entered the church after the last worshipper had left, leaving John the only one left inside clearing away the books and the collection takings of the day.

"Ah, John," said the Parson, "Just the man I wanted to see. I just wanted to say to you that it's good to see that you keep a keen interest in helping with the service every Sunday, and for that, I thank you."

This surprised John, he had not expected thanks from the new parson, he had been helping with Sunday service for some time now having struck a friendship with the late parson Sutton and the church sexton, George Manthorpe, years earlier. It was a job that he had done for so long that it was just expected that he would be there to help things along.

Henry Banfather was a young parson only a few years older than John himself, in his mid-twenties. He stood at medium height about five feet eight tall and had dark hair and brown eyes, and wore the traditional clothes of the clergy, black waste coat and jacket, black breeches and white stockings. He was considered a relatively handsome man by the local women and girls of the village, but was clearly unavailable being married to his wife, Mary Anne, who had born him two young sons.

"Thank you," John replied. "But it's nothing that I haven't been doing for four or five years now since I was a boy."

"Nonetheless, it is kind and very public spirited of you to help and that's why I wanted to talk to you. I don't know if you know that George is thinking of giving up his duties as church sexton. He feels he's getting too old to look after the church, especially the burials he is expected to oversee. Frankly, I agree with him, I think the job would be better suited to a younger man. Both George and myself think that you would be the right man for the job. Would you be interested in taking that job?"

John was taken aback with the suggestion, which seemed to have come from nowhere. He didn't know that George was thinking of leaving his post, there had been no mention of it to him despite working alongside him for countless Sundays. He had always thought that George would be sexton of the church till his dying day. But it was an honour to be asked such a thing to a man so young, and John was fully aware of that.

"I, er, I don't know what to say. This has taken me completely by surprise. I didn't know that Mr Manthorpe was thinking of leaving, how will he live now?" John asked.

"He says that he's a man of independent means, and that he and his wife are able to support themselves into older age. He also has four children who can help when they become frailer with age. Anyway, you haven't answered my question, are you willing to become the new church sexton?" asked the parson.

"I don't know," replied John. "I would have to give it some thought. I have a job and I help to run the business too. How will I have time to do these duties?"

"Any time that you spend on church duties will be paid for. We're not asking you to do this for nothing. Each parish church is run like a business, we get income from the tithes collected from every landowner and farmer within the parish as well as from the collections of each service. From that, we can pay your wages for any work done, it's all kept on the accounts, which in turn are sent to the bishop at the end of the year. Any time taken from your place of work will be fully compensated. I have noticed in my short time here how much you like to help within the affairs of this community. With your ability to read and write and your mature state of mind combined with the physical strength of a young man, I think that you would be a very good keeper of this church."

John thanked Henry Banfather for his kind remarks and told the parson that he would need a short time to decide whether or not to accept the position offered. He had already surmised for himself that Henry Banfather was likely to be a man that he was able to work with. Yes, it was true to say that he liked Henry Banfather from his first few encounters with the man. Banfather was a man not many years older than himself but clearly seemed to have a wise and mature head upon his shoulders. John left the church feeling full of pride, and he headed straight to his mother's cottage to tell her the news first.

"What are you going to do then, John?" Sarah asked on hearing the news later, and feeling pride at the offer to her eldest son.

"I'm going to do exactly what I told him, I'm going to think hard on it and give my decision in a few days."

"They're paying you for it, aren't they?"

"They will be paying me for all work done at the church, that is cleaning, maintenance of the building, and organising and helping with services. It will be my job to toll the bells and dig graves at burials. It's the time taken from my job at the forge that I'm concerned about, that's why I have to think about it. I'm gonna talk to Edmond about it when I get back."

Sarah agreed that this seemed to be the most sensible course of action, and shortly after, John returned home to the Fox cottage where Edmond was given the news and of John's misgivings at the offer.

"If they're gonna pay you for keeping the church I can't see what your problem is," said Edmond, who himself was of a logical nature.

"I agree," said Will. "There's three of us here to manage while you're doing the church work and you'll still be here all the other times. You should easily be able to manage the work in both places. I'd take the job if I was you, the extra income would always be welcome."

"Maybe you're right," said John. "But I'm still gonna give it some thought."

It was two days later when John returned back to the rectory to inform Reverend Banfather of his decision to accept his kind offer, but on a trial basis of about two to three months to see if the post would indeed interfere with both his duties and living made by his chosen profession. Henry Banfather gladly accepted his terms and with that the position was secured.

***

Three weeks after John's appointment at the church, a visitor from Crostwick came calling to Thomas and Sarah's cottage.

"Cousin Sam! It's been a while since we last saw you," said Sarah. "Come in."

Cousin Sam was led inside.

"John, Will and Eddie are just up the road at the forge if you'd like to see 'em."

Samuel Lutkin was the third son of Robert Lutkin, cousin of Jacob and whose wedding Jacob and Sarah had been to when Jacob proposed to Sarah all those years ago on their return journey home.

"No thanks," said Sam. "I'm not here for a friendly visit, no offence meant. I'm here because my father sent me here to tell you that great Aunt Elizabeth is ill. She's not likely to recover and father says you'd better come quick before she leaves us."

Sarah's heart sank. "Oh no, we had better go to her. I'll tell the boys right away. Thank your father for us and tell him we'll be right along."

With that, Samuel Lutkin departed back to Crostwick. Sarah rushed to the forge to inform her three eldest sons of the grave news of their grandmother. On hearing the news, John, Will and Eddie agreed that they should all make haste to see Elizabeth one last time before her passing. The horse was quickly hitched up to the cart and Sarah and her three boys climbed on board, and immediately set off on their short journey to Crostwick. Before long, the cart was on the main turnpike road to North Walsham that would pass through Crostwick on its way. On arrival into the fringes of the village, it was noticed there were now slight changes to the old place that Edward and Elizabeth had once known. An old oak tree that had stood at the side of the main road for as long as anyone could remember had been felled to make way for an entrance to a new inn that had been recently built, the inn was called The White Horse. Sarah looked at the new building as the cart passed by and wondered if time had changed the village and farm much since she had last been there, which was soon after she and Thomas had married. The cart turned off the main road and drove through the village itself, eventually turning off to the entrance of Spring Farm which was nearer the outskirts of the other side.

Elizabeth's brother George, had passed away three years previous but his wife Sarah still lived and resided at the farm. Together, she and Elizabeth had been living out their later life in the company of, and being cared for, by George and Sarah's eldest son's family who now ran the farm themselves. The knock on the door was quickly answered by Sarah Lutkin who was expecting them. She showed them into the house.

"Thank you for coming so soon," she said. "You're her direct family, the last link with Edward and Jacob. She'd be overjoyed to see you if she wakes up."

"She's asleep?" said John.

"She's been asleep for a day and a half and she doesn't know who's around her. I'm afraid she's slipping away. Come, I'll take you to her."

Sarah Lutkin led the group upstairs to Elizabeth's bedroom. The very room from where Elizabeth had slept in her childhood and into young adulthood. This was the room where she had returned to live out her autumn years until her end. Sarah, John, Will and Ed stood around Elizabeth's bed and watched her as she lay in her deep sleep. Her features were gaunt and her hair was thin and white in colour, that of an old woman in her final years. She had lost weight, almost that she was beyond all recognition. The sounds and sight of her breathing were clear and her aged hands were slightly aloft while her fingers opened and shut as if grasping, very much as like a new born baby feeling and testing its new surroundings. One by one the group came over and held Elizabeth's hands even though she was unaware of their presence. They said nothing but all wondered what could be going through her mind as she slept and edged away. Could she be close to God or maybe in the presence of the spirit of her dead husband and son? Could her mind be full of the memories of a life that none of them knew as they looked down at this dying old woman? Maybe it was a time of a pretty young girl who had fallen in love with a tall and strong young farm worker, and the love affair and the secret liaisons along the meadow and the stream of Dobb's Beck. The memory of teaching Edward to read in the Dell of Primrose Hole and of how she would leave her loved ones to live, give birth and raise a son with her lover. All these memories were to go with Elizabeth and were to be a forgotten memory to those few who were there to witness her story. The loved ones she had left could only grieve and hope that she would re-join the loves of her life, Edward and Jacob. Soon after, Sarah, John, Will and Eddie left knowing that they had seen her for the last time. The following day, word was sent from Crostwick that Elizabeth was gone. She was laid to rest four days later in the very churchyard where her family had assembled every Sunday when she was young and where she had smiled to Edward and secretly signalled her plans of meetings to the love of her life. All her surviving family were there to grieve her loss.

Chapter Twenty-Nine

The illumination of gaslight was seen for the first time at night in the centre of Norwich. The newly formed Norwich gas company had installed a piped gas supply to their 'Gasolier' a tall lamp standing approximately twenty feet tall and which fed four separate hanging gas lamps. This Gasolier was to light up the centre of the market square and stand there for the next sixty years, thus becoming a familiar sight for a whole generation of the Norwich population. This population of the city had increased significantly as the industrial revolution had changed the country from a society dominated by farm and rural life to a faster moving urban life as more work was found within the cities and towns.

Sprowston was also to be affected by the ever-swelling city of Norwich. It sees its own population double within less than twenty years as new arrivals move closer to the city to earn a living. At the fringes at what was once a village and has now become a hamlet, a new industry has moved into Sprowston and replaced the farms as the dominant place of work. A number of brickyards have appeared around the city to supply its demand as it expands and two brickyards have opened within the boundaries of Sprowston. One of the yards is situated at the north end of the village where the church, old village and farms have stood for hundreds of years. The other is to the south where Mousehold Heath separates the hamlet of Sprowston from the city of Norwich.

**

"Here's more new arrivals," said Edmond.

Edmond and John are in their cart heading for a quick visit to Norwich to pick up more timber. They see in the near distance another cart heading the opposite direction filled with a family's belongings. Sitting up front with their hired carter are three women, and walking alongside are two men who are clearly father and son.

"Good morning!" John called as the two carts approach each other.

The three women acknowledge the young man's politeness with smiles and a polite, "Good morning," back as the carts pass. One of the women in particular catches the eye of the polite young man as she smiles. She is a young girl who is obviously close to his own age and is alongside what are obviously her mother and her sister. However, both carts continue on their journeys in opposite directions and John soon puts the girl out of his mind. So many times before he had spied a fair maiden who was pleasing to the eye and that he was never destined to meet or know.

The family continued their journey for another hundred yards before their cart finally pulled up to their destination which is a small cottage built of wattle and daub and has a thatched roof. The cottage is situated on the main road that runs through the hamlet and is known as Blue Boar Road or the Wroxham Road (Wroxham is one of the road's destinations). The family enters the cottage to survey their new home.

"Looks a bit run down," said the mother, whose name is Elizabeth Metcalf.

"It'll tidy up and feel warmer when our stuff's in it, especially when we've got a fire going. I see there's still some wood left in the wood shed," replied her husband. His name is William but is better known as Billy to his friends.

For the last year, Billy Metcalf had been working at one of the brick makers at the edge of Sprowston. Cannell's brickyard was the one situated at the north of the village between the church and the North Walsham road known as Barkers Lane. Billy had found he disliked the long walk to and from work every morning and evening. He himself lived at the Duke Street area of Norwich which was some four miles or so from his place of work, so moving to Sprowston was a necessity for him, as well as a welcome relief from living amongst the squalor of the crowded city streets. With him and his wife Elizabeth, were his now grown up children of two daughters and a son. His eldest daughter is Beth, so named after her mother and is twenty-four years of age. She is betrothed to a cloth dyer from the city and is not expected to live at the new dwelling for very long. Then there is her sister, Amelia, she was the girl who had momentarily caught the eye of John as they passed on the main road through Sprowston. She is twenty and is hoping to find employment within the immediate area to avoid having to walk back to the city to work at her current job as a laundry worker for a small business that washes bedding to a number of hotels or coaching inns. Both sisters carry the features of their mother who has dark brown hair and hazel eyes. Neither girl is a stunning beauty but they both carry a charm of their own and are still pleasing to the eye none the less.

The youngest of the Metcalf children is Simon Watling Metcalf. He carries the middle name Watling after his mother's maiden name, which he is proud to carry. He is sixteen and is working with his father at the brickyard. He is an intelligent boy and has his sights set on using his literacy to eventually work up to a job within an office as a clerk or eventually manager within Cannell's brickyard itself. He is of average height, has brown hair like his father and has only a slight resemblance to his mother and sisters, that of their hazel eyes.

The family soon set about off-loading the cart and Billy paid the carter for his services. The women swept and cleaned each room before Billy and Simon Metcalf brought their belongings into the cottage and into the correct rooms where their furniture belonged. After four hours of toil, the family were pretty much satisfied that they had done enough to begin living at their new home and any major changes or repairs could be done all in good time. The family stopped for lunch then rested before preparing their rooms for their first night's sleep in the Sprowston cottage. Later, when it was early afternoon, it was felt by all to be a good time to survey their new home and its surroundings.

"Well, this is gonna be alright," said Simon. "We've got a garden to sit in on a summers evening. It's a world away from that yard we just left."

Everyone agreed, the little cottage they were to call home looked like the beginning of much nicer times ahead.

"Let's go for a stroll around Sprowston," said Billy. "I never get a chance during the week at the yard, we only get a half hour lunchtime."

This seemed like a good idea to everyone so the decision was made to stroll down to the older end of the village where Cannell's brickyard was, and the Blue Boar Inn and the church. These were places that they all knew that they were likely to visit now that they resided in the area. So, they walked down the main road for half a mile or so passing Church Lane and the Blue Boar Inn and headed for the Manor which they could see in the distance and seemed an interesting start to their exploration. Very soon they were at the gates of the manor itself and gazed in awe of the wonderful red brick building before them.

"Thas where the money is," said Billy. "Might be work for yer there, Amelia."

"Could be," she replied.

"Doesn't look too bad," said Beth. "Shall we go down that lane we passed where the inn is? I think the church is down there somewhere."

"It is, and the brickyards further down that lane too," said Simon.

The family doubled back from whence they came, a distance of a quarter of a mile or so, then past the inn once more and turned right into Church Lane. They passed fields and a few cottages as they strolled eventually reaching a cottage on their right with two signs displaying out front, that of a fox and of a horseshoe. The Metcalf's peered in on hearing the sounds of banging and clanging from the tradesmen inside the workshop, who were going about their business of horseshoeing and wheel making.

"Well, there's the local smithy," said Billy. "Must be there that Cannell's go to shoe their horses and fix their carts. Never see that in the yard, Neville Pierce the carter sees to all that."

They continued down the lane until, in the near distance, the church bell tower became visible from behind some oak trees. Making their way further down the road until they reached a junction of which to the right led straight to the church, and straight ahead became Barkers Lane where Thomas and Sarah Walker lived and where Cannell's brickyard was situated further down. The road would eventually lead down to the main North Walsham road where Crostwick was situated some three miles away. The Metcalf's turned right and headed towards the gates of the churchyard of which when reached emerged the full view of the church itself. The church was of old flint construction and was average in size, however, the square bell tower was built in more modern red brick. Unknown to them but apparent at sight, the church tower had been built just a hundred years earlier in the early eighteenth century with locally made bricks following the collapse of the old flint tower. Overall, the church was an average looking one just like the many others that were dotted all around Norfolk.

In the distance to the far right of the churchyard, a man was backfilling the fresh grave of a poor child who had passed away in the week and whose funeral service had been held just an hour earlier to the dismay and grief of its parents and loved ones. The Metcalf's entered the church doors and surveyed their surroundings. Overall, they found the interior of the building quite pleasing to the eye. There were two Gothic stalls which were separated by a central isle with oak pews on either side. To the far wall opposite the entrance were placed a number of beautiful monuments which made the otherwise ordinary church into a memorable one. Some of the memorials were dedicated to the Corbett family who had been lords of the manor generations before. One such lord had been Miles Corbett who had sat as one of the judges and signed the death warrant of King Charles I. After the restoration of the monarchy, he fled to the Netherlands, and was later arrested by the English ambassador and was later executed in 1662. Another monument in alabaster paid tribute to Sir Thomas Adams and his wife. Adams had become lord mayor of London in 1645 in his lifetime but upon his death in 1668, was buried in the church which was situated within his estate. On the monument there was an inscription written in Latin that unknown to most of the parishioners read that Sir Thomas had died of a kidney stone weighing 25oz.

The most beautiful monument located in the far left isle was of white marble and was of a family still residing in Sprowston. The Micklethwaite family had owned large swathes of farmland of which were leased and rented out to tenant farmers and smallholders. They themselves lived in a large lodge situated just off the North Walsham road and ran a farm of their own within their own estate.

"This one's beautiful." said Elizabeth Metcalf.

The family gazed at the beautiful sculpture. The monument depicted Lady Wilhelmina Micklethwaite, who had died in childbirth in 1805, returning to see how her child was faring. The wet nurse sees the apparition and holds the baby out to the spirit of its mother.

Then, from behind, the group were interrupted by the figure of a man entering through the open doors of the church, silhouetted by the bright sunshine from behind him.

"Good afternoon," said the man as he entered the church. It was the man seen in the distance backfilling the child's grave whose funeral had been held earlier that day, it was John Allen.

"Good afternoon," replied Billy Metcalf. "We were admiring the lovely monuments you've got here. You don't see many like this in small village churches like this one."

"There have been and still are some important people who are from this village. The Corbett family lived here for many generations and one of 'em signed the death warrant of Charles I after the civil war," said John.

"What about this one?" asked Elizabeth Metcalf, who was pointing towards the beautiful Micklethwaite monument. "This is the one we like."

"Oh, that's Lady Wilhelmina Micklethwaite, she died in childbirth over twenty years ago, her family still live here. They were rich landowners who moved here nearly fifty years ago from the Lenwade area."

John caught sight of Amelia momentarily and tried to think where he had seen her before. He couldn't put the face to anyone he had ever met before. However, both Amelia and her sister Beth were silently impressed at this young man's knowledge of the monuments.

"You work here at the church do you? Only I couldn't but help notice that it was you we saw as we came in, filling in that grave," said Elizabeth.

"I'm the church keeper amongst other things," John replied.

"Well, you keep a nice church here, young man," said Billy.

John just smiled but didn't reply to the compliment, he was far too modest for that.

"Are you visiting the churches around this area?" John asked.

"Only this one," replied Billy. "We've just moved in today and we thought we'd explore the area we're now gonna live in."

"Oh, that's nice," said John. "Welcome to Sprowston, I hope you get to like it here."

The Metcalf's acknowledged the young man's welcome with a polite thank you.

"Have you moved from far away?"

"No, we're from the city, around the Duke Street area at St Mary's. I work at the brickyard, so we've come here to save me the long walk to and from the place. I've always seen this church from the yard but never really had time to come and see it properly. We've only half an hour lunch so there's no time."

Then the penny dropped in John's mind. He then realised where he had seen the family before, he had passed them on the road earlier that day as he headed to Norwich to pick up supplies of wood. He especially remembered Amelia, the girl in the cart who had caught his eye.

"Haven't had time to meet anyone from around here yet," said Billy. "There are one or two of the local builders who come into the yard that I know and one or two who work at the yard. There's Ted Fisher, our foreman, and Wally Blake and Tommy Land."

"I know Tommy Land and Ted Fisher. Ted lives up Barkers lane near the yard and the Land family live on the main road. A lot of the old local families are at this end of the village, most of 'em are farm hands from Manor Farm, Lodge Farm and White House Farm."

"How about you?" asked Billy. "Do you just do church work or have you got another job as well?"

"My family all work at the local smithy. I'm a wheelwright, farrier and carpenter."

"You must be a busy man," said Amelia. "What with the church work and all."

John smiled and once again stayed modestly quiet at the compliment paid, but he was flattered nonetheless, especially from a girl that he found pleasing to the eye.

"If you need food you can buy it straight from the farms and the mill is down the road for the flour you need," said John. "There's a coal seller near the Black Horse on the way to the city if you need it and there's three village wells for water, one at this end, one the Norwich end, and one in the middle just off the main road. Where do you live?"

"We live on the main road at the middle," replied Billy.

"Most of the new arrivals are moving in at the Norwich end and the old regulars are at this end where the old village is. The place is getting bigger."

"Must be the brickyard workers moving in," joked Billy.

"In June, we have the Magdalen Fair which is held on the meadow on the main road opposite Church Lane. Everyone comes here from the surrounding villages from miles around, it's very popular. There are barn dances at some of the farms two or three times a year, and in November we have a bonfire on Guy Fawkes Night, all the village comes out to that too. I help organise most of 'em," said John.

"Proper village person this man," said Billy. "Every community needs one. What's the Blue Boar like? I like an ale or two from time to time."

John smiled. "The ales good and the floor is a lot stronger than that City of Norwich pub."

Everyone laughed. What John had been referring to was a topic of conversation that had been on the lips of most around the Norwich area at the time. Just a month earlier in Norwich, a congregation of a religious sect commonly known as the Ranters assembled in a fifteen feet square room for divine worship in a pub called The City of Norwich, which was in the St Stephen's Street area of the city. Just moments earlier, a barmaid had been down the cellar below to fetch a keg when, no sooner had she returned, the floor gave way plunging the revellers nine feet below and crashing into the cellar itself. There was panic and many were injured including women and children, some of which had broken limbs and severe lacerations. One man from Yarmouth had a compound fracture to a leg which had to be amputated immediately at the Norfolk and Norwich hospital. However, despite the injuries and the loss of the poor man's leg, many found the story quite amusing and there were many discreet jokes cracked about the incident. This happened to be one of those times.

"Well, we'd better be off now, we've still got a bit to do at our new home. I expect we'll be seeing more of you from now on, especially if you work at the smithy and the church. You must know most of the village I expect."

John laughed. "Thas true I do," he replied.

Billy held out his hand to be shaken. "My name's Billy Metcalf and this is my wife, Elizabeth. This is Beth and this is Amelia, and this is Simon. Pleased to meet you."

163

John shook Billy Metcalf's hand. "My name's John Allen," he replied, and with that, the Metcalf's left the church and the company of the young church sexton. As John watched them leave, his eyes momentarily fixed on Amelia, who turned and smiled as she left.

Chapter Thirty

The following Sunday began with the warmth of spring sunshine as John tolled the church bell to summon the local parish worshippers to the church to begin another Sunday service. Henry Banfather, once again, greeted his congregation as they arrived while John passed out prayer and hymn books as usual. Starting from the front row, he handed books to each row of the right hand aisle till eventually reaching the back row and where, to his pleasant surprise, sat the Metcalf family of whose company he had enjoyed just days earlier.

"Good morning John, nice to see you again," said Billy Metcalf.

"Likewise," replied John. "I hope you're settling in well."

The family smiled in acknowledgement whilst John moved over to the left hand isle to repeat the process of handing out the books. For the Metcalf's, it was nice to see a familiar face in their new surroundings. Once again, a service was held as prayers and sermons were said, and hymns were sung. A baby girl called Alice Gately was publicly baptised and John fetched the church register for Reverend Banfather to fill in the details. After the service and whilst the congregation were leaving the church, John quickly gathered up and put away the books so as to join his family and friends outside in the churchyard as it was such a pleasant morning. He knew that everyone enjoyed being out in the sunshine among the spring flowers to exchange pleasantries and chat after a service as this was always a social time. He also made a special point to come over and talk to the new arrivals of the village, not least because of the girl who had caught his eye on their previous meetings. The Metcalf's had already spoken to Henry Banfather who had welcomed them into his parish, and neighbours who lived nearby took their opportunity to come and speak to them for the first time, more out of curiosity rather than the welcoming motives that they had pretended to convey.

"Must be a lot nicer only having to walk a short distance to work this week," said John.

"It is," replied Billy Metcalf. "I wish that I'd have moved here a year ago. It's not so mad here either like it is in the city."

"The only trouble is I have to walk into the city to go to work," said Amelia. "I work at a launderer that wash bedding for the inns and boarding houses in the city."

"Where in the city do you work?"

"Fishergate," she replied. "At least it's this side of the city, it's not too far. What I'd like to do is find work around here like Father and Simon."

"I could ask around if you like, I know and see a lot of people around the village. You're willing to do most things like farm work, dairy work or whatever?"

Amelia nodded. "Yes, anything."

"You could try the Manor if you're a launderer, it's a large place and a lot of people live there. The owners and the servants all have to have their clothes and bedding washed and cleaned. I could speak to Mr Marler, the chief butler, if you like and see if they need anyone. I can't say that he would employ you but I am going there tomorrow. If I see him, I'll ask him for you."

"Would you do that for me?"

"I would, but I can't promise anything. If he agrees to see you, I'll let you know straight away, but I don't know exactly where you live, other than somewhere in the middle of the village."

"We live on the main road, Blue Boar Road. Ours is the little thatched wattle and daub cottage with a small pile of flint stones in the front garden," said Billy.

"Oh you mean old mother Lacey's place. She died not a month ago. You're there, are you? I know the place well. Knew old mother Lacey well too, sad to see her go, God bless her."

"Then I hope to hear from you," said Amelia.

It was mid-morning the following day when John did indeed go to the Manor with two wheels for Mr Woodruff Smyth's chaise. As was usual, he was led to the rear of the property where the stables and outbuildings were situated and where he quickly set about his task of replacing the two front wheels of the carriage. The old damaged front pair were to be taken back to the workshop and repaired to be kept as spares in case of any future problems. Less than an hour later, the job of replacing the wheels was finished and it was time to be paid. The stable lad, who had led John to the chaise and had helped him support it for the wheel change, quickly set off to fetch Mr Marler. Marler was the head butler whose responsibility it was to see to the upkeep and repairs of the Manor and its equipment under the authority of Mr Woodruff Smyth himself. He came out to the stables immediately on hearing of John's completion of the job from the stable lad.

"Well, Mr Allen, how much do we owe you?" he asked as soon as he had inspected the work, pretending that he knew all about carriage repairs, which he didn't.

"Two pounds and six shillings please," said John.

Marler paid the bill with the cash that Woodruff Smyth had allocated him for the job.

"Thank you, Mr Marler," said John. "We'll bring back the old wheels when there fixed for the agreed price we said earlier."

Marler nodded.

"While we're here, could I have a quiet word?" asked John.

Marler was slightly surprised. "Yes, what can I do for you?" he replied.

"I happen to know a young lady who has just moved into Sprowston, she lives just up the road and she's looking for work more local to her new home. At the moment she is working as a laundress for a business that washes and cleans bedding for inns and boarding houses. I told her yesterday that if I saw you I would ask if you may need to employ such a girl. I know myself that she is a hard worker and will do other work aside from laundry duties."

"Hmm," said Marler, as he took a moment to think hard on John's request. "As a matter of fact, it just so happens that Ellie, the scullery maid, is in the family way and will soon have to leave, along with Jack the footman who got her that way."

John smirked a little but not too much as not to antagonise the butler whose favour he was now asking.

"Tell the girl to come here round the back entrance at eleven o clock tomorrow so as I can meet her and speak to her, and see if we think that she would be suitable for the pending position."

John thanked Marler, bid farewell and set off on his short journey back to the smithy. However, no sooner had his cart reached the end of the manor's long shingle drive at the gateway at the main road, the thought came to him that he would tell Amelia now before returning back to the smithy. So he headed back from whence he had come, but instead of turning right at Church Lane where the smithy was, he carried on up the main road past the Blue Boar inn for another half mile to mid-village where the Metcalf's cottage was. On his arrival and after tying up the horse, he knocked on the front door... there was no answer... he knocked again... still no answer. *'I'll come back later'*, he thought, and returned to his tied up horse and cart.

"Hello!" called a voice from behind. John turned to find that it was Amelia's mother, Elizabeth Metcalf. She was looking slightly shabbier than the times that John had seen her before but he surmised that she had obviously been busy working outside in the garden as she was holding a spade in her right hand.

"Oh hello John, I wondered who was there. I was digging the back garden, we're going to grow some taters and beans. I appened to catch sight of you just now as you were leaving. What can I do for you?"

"Is Miss Amelia here?"

"No, she's at work in Norwich at the launderers. Is there anything I can help you with?"

"I've just spoken to the head butler at the Manor. I told him that Amelia was looking for local work and he told me that he would soon need a scullery maid, cos their maid is leaving."

"Oh she would do that alright, I know she would," said Elizabeth.

"Can you tell her, that if she's interested in the job, she'll have to go to the back entrance of the manor at eleven tomorrow morning and speak to Mr Marler, the head butler. He'll be expecting her."

"Oh I will," Elizabeth replied excitedly. "She'll be happy about that if she gets the job, I know she will. Thank you John, it was kind of you to ask for her."

John smiled. "Tell her good luck from me."

"I will," Elizabeth replied.

John mounted the cart and set off back to the forge.

It was lunchtime the following day. John, Edmond, Will and Ed had stopped for their usual lunchtime break and meal of bread and a cup of ale. All were grabbing their brief moment of relaxation and were quietly seated inside the workshop. John and Eddie were eating bread, while Will and Edmond were sitting on their wooden chairs head down and eyes shut in a state of light slumber, much as they always did at that time of the day. Their break, however, was to be interrupted by the sound of footsteps coming from outside in the yard.

"Sounds like we've got a customer," said Eddie.

John rose and went out into the yard to see who was there, but it was not a customer, it was Amelia.

"This is a surprise," said John. "You got my message yesterday I presume."

"I did and I've come to thank you for being so kind," she replied. "I've just got back from the manor where I met Mr Marler."

"How did it go?"

"It went well," she replied. "He said that he would let me know when he had spoken to the master of the house. He said that what he had found most convenient was that I was local and didn't need to live in the servant's quarters, as he didn't feel quite right turning that poor girl out onto the streets. He wanted her to have a little more time for her and her man to do the right thing and to marry and find a place of their own. Till then, he said he would find me work around the place, mostly laundry work and kitchen work, and sometimes work in the dairy room on the adjoining farm if they need me. If the master approves, they'll want me to start within a month."

John smiled. "Sounds like he's already made his mind up. Can't see why the master shouldn't approve. They always listen to their butler's advice when it comes to the servants. Well done Miss Metcalf."

"You can call me Amelia, and thank you for what you did. It wasn't a small thing you did it was a kindness with no reward. I won't forget this."

John modestly smiled again but didn't reply.

"Well, I'd better get back home, I'll be helping mother with the housework I expect. Goodbye, and again thank you."

John watched Amelia turn and head for the gate. He stood watching her as she left with a quiet feeling of pleasure within, he had obviously made an impression on this charming girl. It was the following Sunday at church that John heard the news from Amelia that the master of the house Thomas Woodruff Smyth had given his consent upon the advice of his head butler and that she had indeed been taken into the employment of the Sprowston Manor estate.

Every Sunday the Metcalf's would turn up at church and would always exchange pleasantries with John as he performed his church duties. The times when their paths crossed in the village were times that always brought pleasure to John. It was clear that both John and Amelia now regarded themselves as friends, and her family, like many in the village, now held John with regard and respect.

***

It was mid-June and time for the annual Magdalen Fair which was always held on a fallow field known as the meadow, the very same field that was used for the November 5th celebrations. As usual, John played a big part in its organisation, he was one of a small committee of locals who always took charge of the event. His job was to go to Norwich and seek out and recruit some entertainment for the event. He would go to various inns and taverns that were known to have entertainment of their own and see if any of their performers were either interested or available. Sometimes he would recruit street entertainers from around the market square if they were a good enough act. This year he managed to recruit a juggler and acrobat who had agreed a fixed sum that would be paid for from the takings from the pitch rents that stall holders and traders would pay for their pitches. As usual there was to be music. A local fiddle player and singer would play to the crowd accompanied by a drummer and penny whistle player. They were regular players in the area, often playing the barn dances held in the village two or three times a year.

"If there's anything I can do to help, you only have to ask," said Amelia at church the Sunday before.

The event was to be held the following Saturday and Amelia always had Saturday's free from her work at the manor, leaving her with enough time to help. John thanked her and said that he would let her know if she was needed, but unknown to him, Amelia was determined to return the favour of the young man who had helped her to gain employment at the manor.

Saturday arrived and John rose early for his busy day ahead. He was to join a small team of villagers who were to run the whole show, and the first of the team was the owner of the field, farmer Robert Welton who owned a smallholding called Blue Boar Farm. His field was annually cropped in late summer for winter hay but on special events such as this he would put a flock of sheep onto the field to crop the grass short for the event. On John's arrival at the field, he found that some of the traders had already arrived and were setting up their pitches under the direction of Robert Welton.

"Morning John," said Robert. "I'm putting the traders on the south side and the entertainment stalls opposite as usual. Henry Cappendell from the Blue Boar Inn will be setting up his ale stall at the road boundary and that should leave the middle for your entertainers if you're happy with that?"

"Sounds good as usual," said John. "I've worked out an order of who and when the entertainers are going to perform. The musicians will be playing on and off all day between breaks. The juggler and acrobat will be on at midday and then again at two. Harold Stringer and his dog will be on at ten in the morning and at one o clock and the Burlingham dancers will be on between acts when it suits 'em. There's also a man with a peregrine falcon on display which I thought we could put amongst the entertainment stalls. He said that he might fly it if there's enough room."

"Sounds like you know what you're doing John. Can't wait to see the acrobat and juggler," said Robert. "I'll leave you to it then. I can see more traders coming up the road, I'd better go and sort 'em out."

With that, the pair went their separate ways to continue in their rolls as fair organisers. In less than an hour most of the traders and stallholders had set up their pitches for the day. There were food sellers selling bread and pies, and cheese and shellfish and apples. The Manor Farm had donated a small pig for a hog roast, and of course, there was the Blue Boar Inn's stall selling ales, cider and ginger beer to refresh the thirsty revellers. Aside from the organised entertainment, there were fair trader stalls all hawking for a farthing here and a halfpenny there. There was a stall with an archery set and a target. A bullseye could win you a shilling at a penny a go, though the target was a considerable distance away and not many shillings were likely to be paid out. There was a stall of throwing a wooden ball at some wooden skittles at a halfpenny a go, and the usual gypsy caravans were there reading palms and predicting all kinds of futures whilst another was to hold an arm wrestling competition for the young men.

Just before ten, there was a rush of local fair goers entering the meadow all eager to enjoy the day and they were just in time for the day's first entertainment event. John used a cylindrical loud haler to announce the act so as everyone could hear, though many still couldn't.

"Ladies and gentlemen!" he called. "It is with great pleasure that I introduce to you, Harold Stringer and his outstanding dog, Tilly!"

The crowd, though still small as yet, applauded. For those who were local to Sprowston, the man and his dog were well known. Harold Stringer and his Border collie bitch, Tilly, were from the village. Stringer was a shepherd from Lodge Farm who had trained his dog from a pup for his job in shepherding, but he had also added a few extra tricks to entertain friends and neighbours and of course, children. Dogs that could play dead, roll over and fetch under disciplined instruction were very popular. Stringer had made a wooden jump for Tilly to leap over when fetching a wooden ball and of which he made her do numerous times and commanded her to lie down straight after the ball's retrieval. As usual, she was obedient as ever and complied fully with her master's commands. Various amazing tricks were performed similar to sheep driving but Tilly's grand finale was to dance on her hind legs whilst Stringer held his hands aloft. Unknown to the audience, he had hidden in his hand a scrap of beef, causing Tilly to jump and spin for her reward. The crowd cheered and clapped at the clever dog and her master as they bowed to the audience and exited from the centre of the field.

By now the field had become more crowded as revellers came from the surrounding villages as well as Sprowston. Some even came from the city to enjoy the day. The musicians began to play, the fiddle player and his accompaniment of a drummer and penny whistle player played a mix of country dance music, sea shanty's and occasionally Irish jigs, which conveniently led into the male dance troop of the Burlingham dancers. The troop wore green jackets and white breeches and stockings and each one of the six dancers wore a black three cornered hat. They had bells at their knees and carried battens that they would hit together as they danced. Mostly, they danced old English tunes that had been passed down from generation to generation and were widely known amongst both musicians and dancers. The style of the Burlingham dancers had evolved from country dancers dating back as far as the fourteenth century to evolve into troops of Morris dancers.

As the day continued, John began to mingle with his friends and family whenever he found time between the organising and announcing of the events. He came over to greet his mother Sarah, who had arrived late morning with Thomas and their new family of siblings to John. John was greeted with the usual joy, tenderness and respect that his mother and family all held for him as the eldest brother. Later, he joined Will and Ed at the ale stall of the Blue Boar Inn. He just had a small weak strength tankard of ale with them as today was not a day to get under the influence, there was far too much to do.

"Hello John," said a voice from behind, as he enjoyed his brief ale break with his brothers. It was Billy Metcalf and his son Simon.

"I thought you'd be too busy to be drinking," said Simon.

"I am, this is just a quick one with my brothers. I've got to get back to it in a moment, the jugglers are coming on. Where is your wife and the girls?" asked John, the question being directed at Billy.

"Oh, they're about somewhere. Last saw 'em looking at that stall selling jam and preserves. You know, the one that's run by them local women."

"That's Esther Land and her daughters, they make jam of all kinds, mostly when apples and blackcurrants and raspberries are in season, all specially for this day… Right! I'd better go, I've got to announce the juggler and his brother."

"No peace for the wicked," joked Billy.

Using his loud haler, John called for the attention of the crowd.

"Ladies and gentlemen! Now for our main event of the day. We have performers here who regularly show their skills in such establishments as the Maid's Head and The Angel and once in the Theatre Royal, all within our great city of Norwich. A man whose skills in juggling are second to none and along with his brother, are the most brilliant acrobats that you are likely to see within this fair county. I would like to introduce to you, the outstanding Samuel DeVellera and his brother Joe!"

The crowd cheered as the acrobat ran onto the centre of the field, cart wheeling and flipping to a magnificent somersault entrance. His brother quickly followed to throw the skittle shaped juggling clubs one by on to him so as to begin his act. The two brothers were of muscular build though quite short in stature. They wore tight breeches and stockings, cream in colour and red waistcoats with no shirt beneath. Both had long dark hair partly covered by tight red headscarves and both had black moustaches. With large gold coloured earrings hanging from their ears, they were very gypsy like in appearance. The crowd were amazed to see Samuel DeVellera juggle three clubs, then four and then five as his brother Joe threw more to him. As he juggled, his brother fetched a barrel laid upon its side to which he at once jumped upon and manoeuvred forward as he juggled the five clubs. The crowd, mesmerised at such a sight, clapped and cheered, especially the children who had never seen such a thing done in their lives. John was equally amazed, he had heard of the juggler but had never actually seen him perform before. The act continued and DeVellera one by one swapped the clubs for coloured balls thrown to him by his brother as he continued to juggle, when five balls all of different colours were being juggled, his brother Joe then laid back on the floor and positioned his legs half bent and in the air with his feet square on. Samuel jumped onto his brother's awaiting feet so the two men were feet to feet, one brother perched up high and standing on his brother's soles whilst he continued to juggle to the obvious cheers of the crowd. Throwing the balls away one by one, Samuel then slowly bent over to replace his feet that were upon his brother's feet with his hands, and slowly raise his own feet high into the air to form a perfect hand stand upon his brother's raised feet to the sound of a drum roll from the musicians and the cheering of the crowd. Then slowly he returned back to his original position of standing upon his brother's feet where upon came the grand finale. His brother Joe gave an almighty push with his legs, causing him to perform a backwards somersault to land on his feet and take his final bows to the audience, who by now were cheering and clapping once more at the wonderful spectacle they had just witnessed.

After the show, John returned to mingling with friends and family for a short while. Once again he came across his mother Sarah and the rest of the family.

"What did you think of the show Mother?" he asked.

"Best one yet," she replied. But then again she always said that at every show he had organised.

"How on earth did he do that balancing thing on his brother's feet like that and then flipping backwards like that?" said Thomas Walker.

"You'll be stopping the little-uns trying that for the next few weeks." John laughed.

"When will we be seeing you next?" asked Sarah. "This week I hope, the little-uns always like to see you."

"I'll be coming round one night this week Mother, or maybe a couple of times who knows."

There was a tap on John's shoulder from behind, it was Amelia Metcalf.

"I thought that I would come and see you for a quiet word Mr Allen," she said. "You told me that you would let me know if you needed any help with this fair of yours and I never heard a word from you."

John smiled. "I'm sorry Amelia, I got so caught up with so much to do, what with this, the church and the smithy, I completely forgot. I would much rather that you enjoy the day here with your family than have to work here on the event."

"I still haven't forgotten what you did for me, helping me get the job at the manor, and I insist in helping you in some way, it's the least that I can do."

"It really wasn't anything that I did, you got that job on your own merits."

"I insist," said Amelia.

"Well," said John. "If you insist on helping, you could always help me with clearing up the meadow when the event's nearly over."

"I'll go and tell my parents that I'll be helping you later, and I'll see you when you begin to clear up."

John smiled but didn't reply, he just watched Amelia disappear back into the crowd to seek her family who at that time were watching some locals trying their luck at archery. Sarah, however, had been listening to her son's conversation with this nice young girl but said nothing, she just smiled discreetly.

The day continued much as it had begun, the musicians continued to play sometimes between acts and sometimes with them. Harold Stringer and his dog Tilly returned to do a second show of the same tricks to the enjoyment those who had missed the earlier show and to the young men of the village who were by now under the influence of the ales served up at Henry Cappendell's Blue Boar Inn pitch.

Grey clouds broke into white clouds and broken sunshine, making the whole day a delightful experience to the many families with children, of whose special day would be ingrained as a cherished memory. Late afternoon came verging into early evening. The entertainment had run its course and many of the revellers had by now gone home. The traders and the stallholders began to pack away the remains of their stock to return home after another day's trade. Amelia joined John as she had promised knowing it was soon time to help with clearing the field.

"Where shall we start?" she asked.

"We can help some of the remaining traders load their carts and then clear the field," John replied.

Amelia immediately set about the task at hand, and John followed suit by helping Henry Cappendell take his casks and tankards back across the road to the Blue Boar Inn. This was no job for a young lady other than an experienced serving wench, and John didn't want Amelia around any drunken young men who happened to still be waiting around the area hoping for any freebies as the stall was cleared. Within an hour the field was empty of revellers, leaving John, Amelia and Robert Welton to clear a field of widely scattered rubbish.

"I've got some sacks to put the rubbish into," said John. "We'll bring them over to the field gate."

Amelia took a sack and immediately set about clearing the field, John cleared close by, and Robert Welton cleared from the opposite end not wanting to intrude upon the young ones.

"You know you really didn't have to do this," said John, as they cleared. "I really didn't help you that much, I only asked Mr Marler if he would see you, the rest was up to you. It was you that made the good impression upon him."

"Nonetheless, it was a kindness that should at the very least be appreciated. It's the proper thing to do and I always do what I think is the right thing, it's called good manners."

"Can't argue with that," said John. "That's a good quality in a person. I find that so many people today seem to think that good manners or politeness is a weakness in a person rather than the strength of character that it really is."

Amelia agreed. By now they had both filled their sacks with rubbish from the field and headed for the field gate to leave the sacks and begin clearing new areas of the field with new sacks.

"The sun's going down," said John. "There's not too much more to clear, I think we'll get done while there's enough daylight. Your parents won't worry if you're out in the dark, will they?"

"There should still be some daylight left when we're finished, I'm sure there will. Besides, they know that I'm with you and so trust you to keep me safe. They do like and respect you."

"Respect me?" asked John curiously.

"Yes, respect you, just like so many in this village do."

John didn't reply, he just kept on walking and picking up rubbish as he strolled. He was far too shy with women to reply to Amelia's compliment.

"You're blushing, aren't you?" said Amelia, who was smiling at John's inability to reply.

"No I'm not, I just didn't know how to answer to that, I wasn't aware that I was respected."

"Well you are and you should be," said Amelia. "Whenever there's something going on in this village you are nearly always the one who either organises it or helps with its being. You are one of those people that every village needs, a man who is in the centre of the community. That's why people respect you."

John continued to clear the field slightly embarrassed, but he enjoyed the company of Amelia nonetheless, and this time, he did reply.

"Why, thank you Miss Metcalf, that were a very kind thing of you to say."

Both laughed.

The golden glimmers of light dusk saw the last sack filled and the field cleared.

"It's too late for you to be walking home on your own. Would you mind if I accompanied you home safely?" asked John.

"Thank you, I would like that very much," Amelia replied.

The couple left the field after bidding farewell to Robert Welton who himself was likely to end his day within the establishment of the Blue Boar Inn. They strolled back up the road towards Amelia's house which was about half a mile up the very same road.

"I've embarrassed you, haven't I?" said Amelia.

"No, no you haven't," John laughed. "More like flattered me."

Amelia laughed "I always say too much. I take after my father I think."

The pair both chuckled until eventually fading into a silent stroll which was eventually broken by John.

"Amelia, I respect you too, and have done since the first time that we met. Since then, I have become very fond of you. I hope I'm not offending you?"

"No, no not at all," she replied.

"I… I would just like to ask you if you would ever consider being courted by me?"

Amelia smiled in the twilight.

"Yes, I would consider being courted by you Mr Allen, in fact, I would be very proud to be."

John smiled and held Amelia's hand.

"In that case, Miss Metcalf, I will be calling round at your house tomorrow at seven if you have no objection?"

"That would be fine by me," said Amelia who by now had developed a broad grin upon her face.

The couple reached the gate of the Metcalf's residence and John turned and kissed Amelia's hand. "I'll see you tomorrow then."

Amelia kissed John's face. "See you then," she replied and skipped up the drive towards the back door. John turned to return home. It was almost dark by now and no one could see the smile that was upon his face for most of the entire journey home.

Chapter Thirty-One

John continued a busy life of juggling his time between church and community work as well as making a living at the smithy with his brothers and uncle Edmond. Now, however, he had the help and support from Amelia. She would faithfully spend whatever spare time she had to be with John to help at church and community events in any way she could. The November 5th celebrations came once again, and as usual, the local community came to the meadow to see the lighting of the bonfire and burning of the Guy. Many would enjoy roasting potatoes on sticks and some would light coloured lanterns. The numbers were greater than years before, the hamlet had expanded both in population and size. Weeks later came the celebrations of Christmas which always kept John busy, not just the various services and events that were held at the church but the larger number of burials to perform at that time of the year. Winter was always a time of high mortality, the cold and the harsh conditions claimed many a life of the very young, old and weak. These were church duties that Amelia stayed well away from, leaving John to deal with in his own private but respectful way. With the coldness of winter came the new year of 1824, and the bond between John and Amelia had grown stronger, and with the blessing of both the families concerned. John's mother, Sarah Walker, and her husband Thomas were both thrilled that John had found a partner who was more than willing to shoulder the heavy burden of the responsibilities that he had laid upon himself and they were very fond of Amelia. Equally, the Metcalf's were respectful of John. To them, this was a man of substance who was courting their daughter, a man who was becoming a pillar of the community and a highly skilled young man at that. They had liked him from the very start and could see no better man in their mind that Amelia could have befriended. Both families knew that it was just a matter of time when the pair would be joined officially.

"I thought that I would go to Norwich on Saturday," said John, one mid-week evening whilst visiting Amelia at the Metcalf's abode.

"There's a tailor I know who's not too dear. I want him to make me a new coat and breeches for my church work. Would you like to come with me? I thought that we could have a nice day together looking around the market square and maybe eat at an inn somewhere if you want to."

"I'd love to," Amelia replied. "I haven't had barely a day to myself to go to Norwich ever since we moved here, what with helping you and working at the manor."

It was settled then, John and Amelia were to have a day out together in the city, and there were no social or official events to intrude upon them as there usually was.

"Is the cart free on Saturday? Me and Amelia are going to the city for the day," John asked the following day whilst at work.

"We need it to take two wheels to the riverside yard for their cart and we'll get some pine while we're there," replied Edmond. "We can give you a lift there if you like but you'll have to walk back."

This didn't seem too bad to John so he agreed there and then, a lift one way to the city was more than welcome. They could always pick up a lift from a passing cart on the way home if they were lucky. So, two days later, Saturday arrived and the pleasant day planned now beckoned the young couple.

"Are you ready?" called Will to his elder brother, who was still eating a piece of toast for his breakfast having already washed and dressed for the day.

"I'd put on some gloves and a scarf if I was you, it's freezing out there, I wouldn't be surprised if we had some snow today."

"I hope not," said John "We've got to walk home afterwards."

The two brothers and Edmond climbed onto the cart. Will and Edmond sat in the back to allow room for their guest who would be joining them on the way. The cart set off for Norwich and was on the main road at the Metcalf's residence in less than five minutes. John climbed out and knocked on the back door of their cottage to be greeted by Billy Metcalf.

"Morning John. It's a cold one today, you'd better try and keep sheltered as much as you can cos it looks like it might snow."

"We should be inside for most of the time," said John. "I've got to see a tailor to be measured for a jacket and breeches, then we're going to the market square to look around the shops. After, we're going to eat at an inn close to a warm fireplace I hope. I'll look after her, she'll be safe."

"I've no doubt about that," replied Billy. "Have a nice time the pair of yer."

Amelia exited the door and bid her parents goodbye before she climbed onto the cart on to the front bench beside the driver, who in this case was John, just as far as the Bishopgate Bridge that is. Both John and Amelia were dressed in their Sunday best as this was a special day out for them both, however, their Sunday best outfits were both partially hidden by a long coat and scarf in John's case, and a thick knitted woollen shawl and bonnet in Amelia's case. The journey was a short one, about fifteen to twenty minutes on route through Mousehold Heath before John finally pulled the cart up at the bridge on the riverside road.

"Have a nice day, you two," said Edmond, who climbed over onto the front bench of the driver's seat now vacated by John.

"We will" said Amelia, and with that, the couple crossed the Bishopgate Bridge and headed towards Whitefriars whilst the cart continued its journey up the riverside road towards the timber yard.

"How far away is this tailors? It's cold, and I just want to get indoors and into the warm," said Amelia.

"His shop is at Palace Street, just a few doors down from the Horse Shoes Pub, not far."

It was indeed not far, for just minutes later the pair arrived at J. Walpole's the tailors.

"This man is the best value for money suit maker in the city," said John as they opened the front door and entered the shop.

"Good morning, what can I do for you?" said a voice emanating from a room at the back of the shop.

John and Amelia looked to where the voice had come from and saw, silhouetted from a back window, the figure of a man rise up from a chair holding a half made garment in his right hand. He was a thin wiry man with a short-cropped grey beard that matched his equally grey hair. Though of ageing appearance, the man was smartly dressed. He wore a suit of black breeches with a matching waistcoat that was worn over an equally smart white under-shirt.

"I need to be measured up for a Sunday best suit," said John.

"Any particular style or colour?" asked the man.

"Just a plain black suit," replied John. "With a waistcoat please, but nothing fancy."

John had seen the man's smart waistcoat and had decided there and then to have one of his own to go with his new outfit. This would seem like quite an extravagance for a working man to afford in such times when working men could ill afford the plain clothes on their backs, yet alone smart suits. John, however, was an employee of the parish church of Sprowston, and the church expected their employees to be neat and tidy in appearance. So the Reverend Henry Banfather had set aside the price of a new outfit for John within the church accounts, which was gratefully received by John of course.

A brief spell of measuring and ordering was followed by promises of time allowed for the construction of the garment, which in this case was a week and a half. In the meantime, Amelia sat warming herself at the fireplace whilst the men conducted their business, of which was concluded in just forty minutes.

"Thank you very much, Mr Walpole," said John. "I'll be back to collect the suit a week on Wednesday."

Walpole agreed the time, and bid his fond farewells to John and Amelia as they left the shop before returning to his own duties at hand.

It was on the walk from Walpole's to the market square when the first flakes of snow began to fall. Just a few odd ones at first that John had noticed and he had asked Amelia if it was just his imagination or not that he had seen a flake or two.

"No I saw a snow flake too," Amelia replied, and moments later those few occasional snowflakes were joined by others until light snow flakes began to blow all around in the cold north wind.

"I hope we don't get too much of this while we're in the market," said John.

"I hope not too," said Amelia. "It's cold enough out here without us getting wet through too."

Soon after, the couple had reached the market square, and began to stroll around the market generally taking in the sights and checking out any potential purchases. Sometimes, they would buy an item but mostly, they would just enjoy looking at what was for sale in each of the stalls. In the meantime, the light snow continued, leaving a light dusting all over the city streets. Very soon John and Amelia decided that an open-air market was no place to be on a cold snowy day. The decision was made to look around the shops in the surrounding square and maybe take shelter in an inn if the snow was to get heavier. Amelia spotted a shop selling knitted items, namely scarves, gloves and bonnets. Mittens seemed like a good idea at that very moment and the shop was selling them at tuppence a pair. This seemed like a fair price to them so they quickly entered the shop to purchase the mittens and take brief shelter.

The snow continued and became harder with no sign of any let up from it. It was now just gone midday, and the decision was made to stop at an inn to enjoy a warm drink and a meal. The couple chose to go to an old coaching inn called the Angel, which was famed for its cock fighting events which were usually held on Friday and Saturday nights. They entered the inn, and made straight for the old wooden serving bar where a large balding man was serving ales and food.

"Yes sir, what can I get you and your lady?" the barman asked.

"We'd like some hot food and a hot drink please," replied John.

"We've got stew and dumplings and warmed dark ale," said the barman.

The pair both agreed that the food offered seemed fine for the both of them, so the barman called through to the kitchen for two more bowls of stew and two hot ales. Soon after, a girl brought out the food and ales into the bar whereupon John paid the two and halfpenny due. They found seats and a table within close proximity of a large lighted fire which was at the far end of the bar room. They quickly sat down knowing that the warmer end of the room would be the most desired as more people came in from the cold.

"Pity the old King's Head isn't here anymore," said John. "My father and grandfather both worked there. I would have liked to have seen what the place was like."

Twelve years earlier in 1812, the King's Head was pulled down to make way for a paved alleyway that linked the market square to the castle ditches. All this was done at the personal expense of Alderman Davey, a dignitary of the city's local authority. He was said to have joked at the time that he intended to put a hole through the King's Head. However, and unfortunately for him, some citizens of the city took the comment seriously and mistakenly thought that he intended to kill King George III. A guard was said to have been placed at Davey's house after he had received death threats over the comment. The alleyway that he created still remains and is called Davey Place.

Relief from the coldness of the winter's day was had by the couple as they enjoyed their hot food and ales within the warmth of the open log fire. It was nearly an hour later when the barman came over to clear up the bowls and tankards from their consumed meal.

"Thas a helluva snow we're avin out there," said the barman. "Are yer far from home?" he asked.

"Not too far, Sprowston," replied John. "Why? It's not that bad out there is it?"

"As bin snowing heavy for a while now and it's settling quick. Are yer walking home?"

"Yes we are," said Amelia.

"Well you'll either ave to sit it out or risk the walk home now. Glad I'm not out in it."

Both John and Amelia immediately made for the door to see just how hard the snow was coming down. It was heavy and it had obviously been settling for some time, clearly no weather to be walking home in.

"What'll we do?" Amelia asked with a slight hint of panic in her voice.

"I don't know," replied John. "Sit it out I think."

"We've got rooms for rent here if yer get stuck and ave to stay the night," said the barman. "We've got a cheap one you can rent for a penny an hour or sixpence a night. A lot a young couples like you use it," he continued, with a wry smile upon his face.

"No we're fine thank you," said John.

"Well, if you're staying ere in the bar, I'll warn yer now there's cock fighting in ere later and it'll be busy for the rest of the night."

John looked at Amelia. He didn't like the idea of her being in a bar at a cockfight that was full of drunken gambling men.

"Can we have the room?" said Amelia. "I'd rather be with you than in this bar when the fighting starts. Besides, if it doesn't stop, we might need somewhere to stay for the night."

John thought for a minute and then came to his decision.

"We'll rent the room for a couple of hours and see how bad it gets out there. If it gets worse, then we'll stay the night here, though God forbid what your father's gonna think and say when we get back home."

The barman smiled as he took John's money. He had taken many a tuppence of a young courting couple in the past, even if these two didn't seem quite as keen as all the others. He led them upstairs to a small attic room with sloping ceilings which had just enough room to sit a wooden double bed between the pitch of the roof and two small bedside tables either side. Within one of the sloping ceilings of the room, there was a small window housed within a roof dormer that overlooked a rear courtyard within sight of the castle and the castle mound. The barman left to return to the bar and leave the young couple alone. John stood at the window gazing outside deep in thought of possible trouble that may lie ahead should the weather not improve. It was still snowing outside but Amelia wasn't the least bit as anxious as John was at that time. She relished having a moment alone with the man she loved, as they were all too rare with the busy working and social life that he lived. John, however, was more focussed on how they were to get home and avoid the wrath of Billy Metcalf and his wife, should he and Amelia have to stay the night at the inn.

Amelia sat down upon the bed. She looked to John who was still standing at the small window and peering out at the falling snow.

"It's cold in here, please come over and sit with me and keep me warm."

John did as requested, he came over and sat beside her, putting his arms around her and tightly pulling her towards him. She looked up at John, her eyes looking directly into his, and without neither thought nor hesitation, the pair kissed intensely, their grip upon one another becoming tighter and tighter. They fell back upon the bed and John slightly raised Amelia's dress to allow his right leg to settle between her legs. They kissed and they writhed and they rubbed together stirring a feeling of absolute pleasure overcoming them as they became more intense in their passion, a passion that was to be briefly broken by John as he faced Amelia.

"Do you want to go through with this?"

"Of course I do, don't stop," Amelia replied, and the pair continued kissing and writhing until breaking away to remove their clothing. As they undressed, John couldn't but help staring at his lover as she slowly undressed stage by stage from the bulky dress clothes to the beautiful naked form that was before him. This was the first time he had seen a beautiful fully naked woman in the flesh in his life. She climbed inside the bed to join John who had already climbed in trying to hide the obvious sight of his excitement, though unknowing to him she was just as aroused as he at the thought of what lie ahead. The lovers kissed again and again, their embrace had become tighter and tighter as before. John rolled onto Amelia who had positioned herself ready to take him. John tried to enter Amelia with only partial success which had to be remedied with Amelia's guiding hand. She instructed John when to be gentle and when to try harder whilst John also had to suppress his own eagerness. Like so many on their first time, it was all so much a clumsy affair trying to be gentle and cause little pain but together they achieved their task of their first full sexual experience and virginity lost. Amelia bore her discomfort and pain of her first time bravely whilst John, like so many young men on their first time, didn't take long or know much of what he was supposed to do without instruction. Amelia didn't mind though, with her discomfort was the relief that her first time had been achieved and that barriers had been crossed. After, they lay together deep in thought of the event that had just come to pass.

"I didn't mean for that to happen," said John.

"Don't be sorry, I wanted it to happen," she replied.

This took John by surprise. It hadn't occurred to him that Amelia would have had the same desires as he did. He thought that like him, she would have to behave in the correct way and that any carnal desires would have to be suppressed until marriage. Unknown to him, he was loved by a young woman with more passion and a more adventurous nature within her than he had himself. She seemed to him now even more loving and more affectionate than she had ever been as she lay across him, her head resting upon his chest gently caressing his shoulder with her fingers. Now and then she would kiss his chest where she lay. Then the words "I love you," were uttered from John's lips. Amelia rose up and gazed into her lover's eyes. It was the first time that she had ever really heard him talk from the heart. She smiled and gently kissed him on the lips. To John, she was the most perfect vision of anyone or anything that he had ever seen, and that moment was the realisation that this beautiful girl was to be the love of his life, and he to her.

Soon after, John climbed out of bed to fetch his pipe from his coat pocket, he peered out of the window to check on the weather.

"It's not snowing quite so heavy now, we might be able to walk home after all."

"I hope you're getting back in here with me again before we go," said Amelia.

John smiled and immediately re-joined her in the bed becoming aroused at once at her invitation, and once again the couple made love, enjoying the moment as if the pleasure would never again come back into their lives.

The snowfall all but disappeared, leaving settled snow upon the rooftops, pavements and roads, to be broken up by the wondering pedestrians and horse traffic of the streets, leaving a slushy mess behind.

"We'd better go, the two hours are nearly up for the room," said John.

They both climbed out of bed and quickly dressed ready for their walk back to Sprowston and home. Before leaving the room, John left an extra penny at the bedside table for the cost of cleaning the bed sheets. With that, John and Amelia made a hasty but discreet exit from the Angel Inn. No one at the inn even noticed them leave, they were far too busy preparing for the evening's entertainment of cock-fighting to be bothered of another courting couple who had paid the hourly rate for the use of the attic room.

At last, they were back out in the cold air and the slushy streets of the busy city making their way back home. Luckily, as they neared the old city wall where the old Magdalen gate had once stood, they managed to catch a ride on the back of a passing cart as the cart driver was heading through Sprowston on the way to Wroxham. Soon the cart had reached the Metcalf's cottage and John thanked the carter kindly for the ride home. Walking hand in hand, the couple strolled to the back door of the cottage. John kissed Amelia on the cheek, and she squeezed his hand and returned a smile to her lover, but before anything was said, the door opened and Elizabeth Metcalf opened the door.

"I began to get worried when it snowed. I wondered how you were going to get home."

"We took shelter at the Angel Inn and had a meal there, we sat in front of the fire till it cleared up," Amelia replied.

"Good job it did clear up, you could have been stuck there all night. At least you got her home safely, John, I knew she would be safe with you."

Amelia followed her mother inside, turned and looked towards John. She smiled with a look of mischief in her eyes and winked to her lover. A smile and a wink was returned back.

"I'll call for you tomorrow if yer like," he said.

"I'll see you then," she replied, and with that, she closed the door and John left for home. Thoughts of the day, that had just been, stayed in the minds of the lovers for the rest of the evening and the following day. The couple were reunited the following evening when John called at the Metcalf's cottage, whereupon an evening pretending that the trip to Norwich had been an uneventful one was broken when the couple managed to steal a moment alone. They agreed that sometime in the future they would make a journey to Norwich again and rent the attic room at the Angel for another two hours. This they did from time to time.

Chapter Thirty-Two

The coldness of that very winter finally faded away into the warmth of spring, bringing with it the feeling of better times ahead and lifting the spirits of everyone. Once every four weeks or so, John and Amelia would go on their trips to Norwich to look around the shops and enjoy some discreet time at the Angel Inn. The pair were now together at nearly all the parish events, and consequently, many wondered just when they would be making an announcement as to their future together. To them however, they were not going to be rushed into anything by any third party and were quite happy to leave things be for the moment.

It was early May and there were plans to be made for the forthcoming Magdalen Fair to be held once again on Robert Welton's meadow. The Reverend Henry Banfather had taken it upon himself to call off a meeting of tithe collections from the landowners from within the parish. Instead he would call a meeting of all the major parishioners to serve both purposes of collecting the annual tithes and discussing the forthcoming event. He had some proposals of his own that he wanted to bring to light in such company of distinguished parishioners. To his surprise, John was asked to attend and record the minutes of the meeting. This was not a duty he had ever been asked to perform before, previous Magdalen Fairs had always been a casual affair. Occasionally some parishioners would come to the organisers with ideas, but no meeting had ever been called in the past.

"I just wanted to kill two birds with one stone and discuss the event while everyone is assembled at the vicarage," the parson explained.

Nonetheless, it was still a first for John, but he reasoned that Henry Banfather just wanted to take more interest into the social events of the parish. The meeting was to be held on the following Saturday. Banfather knew that ale was always served to the tithe payers and that generally a lot of ale was consumed by the end of the meeting. It was kind of a traditional social event of its own to all the landowners; and who were they to break from tradition? Henry Banfather's way of thinking was that Saturday would be the ideal day so as to allow time on the following day of rest to recover from any hangovers.

Then the day came, and the invited landowners and farmers all arrived one by one at the rectory totalling around fifteen all in all. Everyone was seated in the main dining room around the large dining table that seated ten. The rest sat on any surrounding chairs or stools within the room of which some had been brought in conveniently for the event. Amongst the fifteen most prominent members of the parish present were Thomas Woodruff Smyth, owner and resident of Sprowston Manor. It was sheer luck that he happened to be present for the meeting as most of his business interests were far away in Surrey where he originally resided. Sprowston Manor was purchased as a mere country retreat, and so the running of the estate was left to his personal solicitor, Samuel Le Neve. Le Neve also resided at the manor and was also present at the meeting on request from his employer.

There was William Cannell, the owner of Cannell's brickyard on Barker's Lane. He was the employer of Billy and Simon Metcalf. He was a gruff looking man of middle years with greying hair and thick bushy sideburns. He wore well-tailored clothes black and green in colour, though still seemed un-kept within them due to his portly physique.

The most elegant of the party was John Stracey, owner of Sprowston Lodge. This was a manor house in its own right and was part of the estate of neighbouring Rackheath Hall. Rackheath was the next village down the main turnpike road situated between Sprowston and Wroxham. Stracey's father was Sir Henry Stracey, baronet of Rackheath, and he had given his son Sprowston Lodge as a wedding present. The lodge, though part of the Rackheath Hall estate, was in fact within the boundaries of Sprowston parish and was therefore subject to its tithe payments. John Stracey himself was a young man still in his twenties who had a young wife called Constance and two infant children. Unknown to all present, he was later to have ambitions of expanding his land ownership which would affect many seated within the room.

Also at the meeting were John Lowne and Jeremiah Cozens Hardy who were also landowning gentlemen of inherited wealth. George Denmark was the son of a wealthy farmer who had been educated to become a doctor at the Norfolk and Norwich hospital. There was another solicitor present, that of Everett Bardwell. He owned a pair of cottages and a meadow on the main road through the village next to the meadow that was used for the village events. The farmer and owner of that field was present too. Robert Welton was a small-hold farmer of Blue Boar Farm. He owned just a couple of fields and rented the meadow field owned by Everett Bardwell. Welton was a livestock farmer who kept mainly sheep and pigs. He also made a living by brewing ale and selling it to locals and the village pub up the road, which was owned by another of those present at the meeting. Henry Cappendell of the Blue Boar Inn was a big burly man who was used to keeping order within his own pub. Though present, he did not really want to be there as he was suffering from a hangover after sampling too much of his own stock the previous night. One member of the group was from a family well respected within the parish, that of Nathaniel Micklethwaite. He was a gentleman landowner who rented his land and properties to tenant farmers unable to buy land of their own. He was directly descended from Lady Wilhelmina Micklethwaite whose monument at the church was so admired by Billy Metcalf and his family. He lived at the Norwich end of the village which was now becoming more built up. A man of thirty or so years, quite tall in stature and with dark hair, he was also of elegant appearance. Like John Stracey, who was a personal friend of his, he also had a young wife and two young children, though another child was on the way. The family were now less wealthy than they had been in past years having sold much of their land to developers from the city, but they were still respected none the less.

Two other small farmers were present, Gregory Wright of Stonehouse Farm which was also on the main road through the village and close to Billy Metcalf's cottage. David Poll was there, he was the owner of White House Farm which was on Blue Boar Lane.

For most, it was a day of bill paying to the church with a little ale added to sweeten the day. The tithe was a legal requirement of all landowners of the parish. They paid their dues to the church to cover the cost of the upkeep of the church buildings, and the wages and expenses of the clergy that the church institute had supplied. For the poorer farmers, it was just another tax upon them that was not welcome other than for moral and spiritual purposes. For the rich, it was just another fee that would ensure them a place within the kingdom of God and also raise their status within the community. The tithe was always worked out to affordability, and so the richer landowners and farmers always paid the lion's share.

With all the available tithe payers now assembled, Henry Banfather called for the attention of the respected gathering to begin the meeting. John, however, sat alone in a far corner of the room in front of a small singular table with the ledger book, paper and quills at the ready, and a cash box the parson had provided.

"Good day, gentlemen. Welcome once again to my home for the annual tithes meeting and also to address other issues that I will be bringing to everyone's attention later," said the parson.

"My wife and our maid will be in shortly with some refreshments, once we've finished with the first piece of business at hand."

"This year's tithes, if you are all in agreement, are to be based on the success of the last harvest, which I am sure you will all agree was much the same as the previous year, if not slightly less I think some of you would argue."

There was a slight stirring amongst the farming community. Some of the farmers silently nodded and some verbally agreed.

"It is therefore my opinion," continued the parson, "that there should be no increase in the tithe payments, and consequently, the same costs should be donated by you parishioners as was paid last year, despite the increase in costs to the church itself."

More stirrings were heard by those present as the group unanimously agreed with Henry Banfather's statement. There was some applause heard by the most relieved members of the parish, namely the poorer farmers.

"I have John Allen here with me and he has last year's ledger with him. It will be his job to go through the payments due from all of you individually and in confidence of course. He will collect either payment or pledges from each and every one of you, if you are all in agreement?"

"Yeah" and "Aye" and "Hmm," was the general response heard as everyone agreed, and one by one the gathering came to John's table to conduct their own private business, unheard by the others, as they collectively, were all kept busy in deep conversation with one another, using the gathering as the social event it always was. Meanwhile, Henry Banfather quickly exited the room to help his wife and their maid bring in the promised refreshments of bread, cheese and apples, and tea. It took John less than an hour to sort out the tithes of the farmers and the gentry, and even less time for Henry Banfather to return with the promised refreshments. With the first task now complete, it was time for Henry Banfather to call the next issue on the agenda.

"Gentlemen, if I may have your attention once more. Once again, we have the annual Magdalen Fair to deal with and to organise. I was wondering if anyone has anything to add to the event or equally anything to suggest for the event."

There was a silence amongst the group. No one really knew what to either do or suggest that was any different from the usual process of organisation. They didn't know why Henry Banfather was bringing the issue up, no one ever had before... After what seemed like a minute or so of silence, Robert Welton broke the uncomfortable situation.

"What is there to do thas different than usual? You'll be using my field and I expect John'll be sorting out everything else."

This caused a chuckle amongst the men, they couldn't understand exactly what Henry Banfather was expecting from them. That was until Henry Banfather explained his motives.

"Exactly!" he said. "John will be sorting out everything else."

A look of confusion was written over the faces of some of the farmers, but not so much upon the more educated men.

"John Allen sorts out everything for the Magdalen Fair, the Guy Fawkes celebrations, the barn dances, and weddings and funerals. He seems to be involved with just about everything this parish does."

John sat tucked away in the corner in complete confusion among the ledgers, papers and pens he had been using on the previous agenda. All the revered members of the village were in the room and they were all staring at him. He didn't know if Henry was annoyed with his involvement of so many village affairs, or what.

"I'm sorry, Reverend, but I don't know exactly what it is you're getting at," said John.

"Well John," he replied. "What I'm getting at is that I would like to forward a motion to this gathering of respected members of this parish. My point being that this parish is ever growing. In 1811 it had a population of just over three hundred, and now just thirteen years later, the population has grown to over eight hundred as the city expands. I think that we need a representative of this community for issues of a social nature. Anyone who has a community problem could go to the representative who in turn could consult the major members of this parish, such as your good selves, for a solution to that problem. Events and social gatherings could all go through this person to organise as well. What I am proposing is that the best man for that job, should you all agree, is John Allen. I now forward a motion to you all that John Allen be appointed Parish clerk."

"Just a minute," said John. "Look, I knew nothing of any of this, I haven't asked for anything. This is a complete surprise to me."

"I know you didn't ask or know anything," said the parson. "This is my idea. What I am proposing is that you be made an official clerk of this parish and that you are paid a salary fitting for that appointment. The appointment is to be paid for at a cost of an extra pound per annum to each one of you respected gentlemen of the parish, starting the extra cost at next years' tithe. John, you will be on a salary of fifteen pounds a year for these duties. That is if none of you respected gentlemen have no objection and are in full agreement."

The men gathered all looked to each other waiting for one of them to be the first to speak up. None did until the silence was broken by Henry Banfather once again.

"If there are any of you gentlemen who feel that John is not the right man for the post, or if indeed some of you well educated gentlemen feel that you could fill the roll even better, then please speak now. However, I know that you are all busy professional men and would have to set aside much of your precious time to achieve these duties, whilst John here is already doing that very job without any reward. I would like to add that any major decisions regarding the parish would still have to go through with the approval of all you land owning gentlemen, just handled by the appointed parish clerk who would keep you all officially informed. May I now have your opinion on my proposal?"

Thomas Woodruff Smyth was the first to voice his opinion.

"I, for one, agree with your proposal and so does my employee and manager of my estate Mr Le Neve. We don't have time to run village affairs and it is a good thing in my opinion that this village does have a representative for the community for any issues to be raised or events to be organised."

"I agree with the proposal too," said Everett Bardwell, the other solicitor in the group. "I am far too busy at the chambers in the city to offer my services, other than legal ones that is."

"John would be the right man for the job," said Nathaniel Micklethwaite. "We all know him, he has been at the centre of the Magdalen Fair and Guy Fawkes events as well as the church sexton. Why change a good thing? I agree with the proposal too."

George Denmark, the doctor, also agreed, and so did the two gentlemen of leisure, John Lowne and Jeremiah Cozens Hardy. William Cannell and John Stracey were in complete compliance with the decision but there was a little discontentment from the poorer farmers amongst the group. David Poll of White House Farm argued that it was, "just another expense on us poorer farmers," and Gregory Wright of Stonehouse Farm agreed with him. However, Robert Welton and William Yallop both agreed with the majority that a parish clerk was now needed as the parish had expanded.

"Well, gentlemen, with only two against the motion I declare the motion to be carried, and therefore, I am happy to announce that John Allen is now duly declared parish clerk. And you can write that in the recording of this meeting John."

There was a cheer and a laugh from the men seated in the room, and a "Thank you all I hereby accept the position," from John. Shortly after, the meeting was adjourned, and the farmers and gentry focussed on the usual merriments of the annual gathering, that of the consumption of the ale kindly supplied by Henry Cappendell of the Blue Boar inn. Leaving the respected gentlemen to their annual tithe drink and chat John felt it was time to take his leave. He was shown to the door by Henry Banfather himself which gave John the opportunity to shake the parson's hand personally.

"I would like to thank you greatly for what you did for me today. I really didn't expect any of this, but what really made me happy was that nearly everyone voted in my favour."

"Good deeds should be rewarded, both in and out of the kingdom of heaven," said the parson. "Everyone can see what you do for the community so it is right that it should be recognised for the good that it is. My warmest congratulations to you John, this is what you deserve."

"It would still not have happened had it not been for you, and for that I'm grateful," said John.

He shook the parson's hand once more and left the rectory to head straight to his mother's cottage to tell her the news which was received in the expected delight and pleasure.

The Magdalen Fair took place just a few weeks later as planned. John had taken a trip to Norwich, accompanied by Amelia, to find more entertainment for the event and a short two-hour stop at the Angel Inn while they happened to be there. Unfortunately there were no acrobats or jugglers available like the previous year, but a Scottish piper was booked. He was a retired soldier of a highland regiment who was making a living the only way he knew how. As usual, the Burlingham dance troop performed their dances again, and Harold Stringer and his dog Tilly showed up to do the same tricks. John had found this year particularly hard to find new acts for the event as many of the performers were already booked to do rival fairs and carnivals which were now springing up at different parishes in increasing numbers. Consequently, it was noticed that numbers were down from previous years. However, John did organise two barn dances at Stonehouse Farm later that summer which were much more successful and were enjoyed greatly by the locals.

Later that year, John had the easier task of building a large bonfire and a stuffed Guy as the November 5th celebrations had come once again. As usual large numbers of locals turned up for the celebration which again had the usual attractions of hot roasted potatoes and chestnuts, hot tea, beer and coloured lanterns. All of John's family were there, his two brothers of the Allen name and all of his half siblings had come with his mother and Thomas. John would join them later when he had made his speech and had lit the bonfire. Will and Ed came over to greet their mother too but after the pleasantries chose to stay around the stall serving hot beer. Then the time for lighting the bonfire finally arrived. John had made a long lighting torch from a wooden branch, its end wrapped in cloth soaked in lamp oil which he lit from one of the coloured lanterns carried by a child of the village. He held the now lighted torch aloft beside the bonfire and began his speech.

"Remember, remember, the fifth of November,
gunpowder treason and plot.
I see no reason why gunpowder treason,
should ever be forgot."

"We now light the flames and give thanks that the king and the government were not blown up on that night and that the catholic plot was thwarted. Let us not forget that Guy Fawkes was just one of a number of plotters and the one who had volunteered to light the fuse. He was the man used to do the dirty work. Let us now light our own fire with our own Guy Fawkes sitting on top as a celebration of that famous night."

John lit the fire to the applause of the crowd, who slowly became more visible, illuminated by the light of the fire as the flames grew higher. Then he left the fire, and the effigy of Guy Fawkes, to burn in full view of the crowd while he joined his mother and family. They were also joined by the Metcalf family.

"Evening John, nice speech yer made when yer lit the fire," said Billy Metcalf.

John thanked him for the kind remark. Together the families of John and Amelia stood silently watching the flames of the fire, almost mesmerised by the fire's hypnotic effect. That was until the silence was broken by Sarah who again reminisced of times gone by, as she always did on that night. John and Amelia quietly stood hand in hand in the firelight.

"You know, this night more than any reminds me of that night when you were born John." said Sarah.

"You always say that on this night, Mother," John laughed.

"Why, what happened that night?" Amelia asked.

"We were all together right here in this field on this very night of November 5th. Me and John's father, my first husband, Jacob, my own mother and father, my brothers and sisters. My waters broke and I had to be rushed back to the cottage. In the early hours of the following morning, John came into our lives. We were so proud of him, our first-born child. That's a feeling that everyone should know. I hope that one day you'll go through the same experience. Oh and by the way, happy birthday for tomorrow."

"Yes, happy birthday John!" said his younger siblings.

John smiled and tightened his grip to Amelia's hand but said nothing in reply. The mood returned to that of tranquillity as the families continued to watch the fire slowly burn. After a short while of fire watching in silence, John turned to Amelia and looked into her eyes, and he held both her hands.

"Will you marry me?" he asked.

A smile beamed from her face, which was half illuminated in the firelight, and she flung her arms around him, pressing her face to his, cheek to cheek.

"Of course I will," she replied, and together the lovers kissed, as they shared the tender moment that would be with them for the rest of their lives.

"Can I tell my family?" Amelia asked.

John nodded, and Amelia immediately rushed over to her mother and her sister to tell them the news, which was met with a shriek of delight from her mother. This in turn alerted John's family. Thomas Walker approached Billy Metcalf.

"What's appened then? Is it what I think it is?" asked Thomas

"It is," Billy replied. "They're getting married at last."

"Bout time too," said Thomas.

Billy came over to John and shook his hand.

"Well done son, couldn't be more pleased."

Behind Billy were Thomas and Sarah. Sarah immediately hugged her son. "I'm so proud," she said, and immediately left to talk to her future daughter in law. Thomas congratulated John with a handshake and the rest of John's half siblings all crowded around their elder brother just as eager to share in the joy of the good news. The rest of the evening was spent much the same way as word spread around the event, even reaching the hot ale stall where Will and Eddie were spending their evening. They came over immediately to find out if the rumours were true or not. To most, however, it was no surprise, just destiny taking its course to a couple who were meant to be.

Chapter Thirty-Three

There were preparations to be made for the forthcoming wedding, of which the couple had planned for Christmas Eve. But before the big day, there was the task of finding accommodation to live in, and to John's knowledge, nothing was available within the immediate vicinity. He did, however, put the word out around the village that he was looking for a place in the hope that somebody may know of a place currently vacant or soon to be. He would if necessary have to try the more heavily populated area of New Sprowston which was nearer to the city but was further away from his place of work. It was agreed, however, that if unsuccessful, the couple would stay at the Metcalf's cottage until a place became available, as Amelia's sister Beth had married her intended man, David Locke, earlier that year and was now living with him in the city. This left Amelia with a room all to herself which would be adequate as their first marital bedroom. Neither John nor Amelia was keen on that idea, like so many young couples the privacy of their own home seemed the more desirable option.

Time passed to early December, and it seemed more likely to John and Amelia that they would have to take Billy and Elizabeth's kind offer of accommodation at their home as nothing had as yet come available within the village. John's working life at the forge and the church had left him with very little time to go house hunting. The winter time leading up to Christmas was always a busy time for John as the coldness and the harsh living conditions brought its usual higher mortality. Likewise, Amelia was allowed no time away from her job at the manor to find a dwelling. It all seemed out of their hands and the couple began to accept what the outcome was likely to be. That was until one dull cold and dreary Wednesday morning early in that same month of December. John was working at the forge as usual with his two brothers and Edmond, and Edmond's son Johnny, when the sound of a horse was heard approaching the yard. This was the sound that farriers and smiths always picked up on as potential business.

"Sounds like a customer for a new shoe," said Eddie.

Edmond went outside to see who the customer was whilst the rest continued with their work of wheel making in the workshop and nail making in the forge. Voices could then be heard from outside as Edmond dealt with the customer but little attention was paid as to what was actually being said. It was more likely that Will would shoe the horse as he had the least pressing work to do, and it was likely that he would be helped by Edmond's son young Johnny who was still learning his trade. Then Edmond came to the door and looked towards John.

"John, can you come out here, there's a man ere to see yer."

John put down his tools, confused at who would want to see him this early in the morning. There outside stood a smartly dressed man holding his saddled brown mare by its bridle. John recognised the man immediately as being Everett Bardwell, the solicitor who had sat at the meeting when John was nominated and elected parish clerk.

"Good morning Mr Bardwell, what can I do for you?" John asked.

"Good morning John. It's more of what I can do for you really," he replied.

Everett Bardwell was one of those dandy young gentlemen, smartly dressed and charmingly dignified. He wore a tall black hat which covered his dark brown wavy hair and his smart black attire was obviously his work clothes at the chambers of his majesty's magistrate's courts, of which he was then on his way. However, this pressing business he was about to conduct meant a slight detour to the Fox smithy.

"Word has just recently come to me that you are to be married soon, and by the way, congratulations. It has also come to my attention that you are seeking either lodgings or full accommodation within this area for your new life as a married man. Is that so?"

"Yes it is so," replied John.

"Well," said Bardwell. "It just so happens that I have a cottage next to my own on the main road that could do with some tenants to fill it. I have been using it to store a few things but the coldness and the emptiness of the place is damaging my stored furniture and not doing the building any good either. What the place needs is the warmth of a fire and occupation to dry out the damp. Would you be interested in renting the property?"

John smiled. "I would be very interested in renting your property," he replied.

"I thought you would," said Everett. "I don't have much time to discuss the details right now but if you come to my house tonight at around six, I should be at home, we can discuss the details then. You can see the property for yourself, but only in candlelight I'm afraid."

"That would be fine by me nonetheless," said John. "May I bring Amelia with me?"

"Of course you may. I'll see you both at six then."

With that, Everett Bardwell took his leave and mounted his horse to begin his journey to the courthouse in Norwich at the Shire Hall.

This was great news, and John was beside himself with joy. He knew the very cottage that adjoined Everett Bardwell's, it was situated virtually at the end of Church Lane on the main road and next to Robert Welton's field where all the functions were held. He knew it had a large rear garden and that a small field was situated behind the garden which also belonged to Bardwell. The field was used by Robert Welton for grazing livestock for some of the year and later in the summer months used as a hay meadow. He was sure that Amelia would fall in love with the place, it being on the same road as her parents and closer to the manor where she worked. He would fetch her to view the place just before the appointed time.

It was five thirty when John knocked on the Metcalf's door, to be answered by Amelia herself.

"What brings you here at this time of the evening?" she asked. "You're here earlier than usual."

"I've come to fetch you. We're to meet a man this evening, he's got a cottage to rent not too far from here."

Amelia took a deep breath, but before she could say anything, John spoke first. "Quick, get yer shawl and bonnet on, we're to meet him at six."

She rushed inside and John followed to say hello to his future in laws. They greeted him with the usual politeness they always did, but with surprise and joy once they had heard exactly why he was there to see Amelia at that time of the evening. The family wished them well, and with Amelia sufficiently wrapped up warm against the chill of the winter air, the pair set off in the direction of the cottages to make their appointment. Soon after, they knocked on the cottage door which was immediately answered by Everett Bardwell.

"Ah, John, come in… and this must be your intended young lady. I've seen you helping John at church on Sundays."

"This is Amelia Metcalf, and Amelia, this is Mr Everett Bardwell who I told you about earlier," said John.

"Pleased to make your acquaintance, Miss Metcalf."

"Likewise," replied Amelia.

"Well, let's get down to the business at hand," said Everett.

Carrying a candle lamp, he led the young couple through his own small and neat cottage to the back door and out into the darkness of his back garden. There was no boundary between the two properties, but why should there be? Both properties belonged to the same man who lived alone with just his work as a solicitor to keep himself amused. He led them into the next-door cottage for its viewing.

"Here we are then," said Everett.

John and Amelia looked all around… it was basic and it was cold and dark but it had everything they needed to become a home. The kitchen had a large fireplace ideal for cooking and there was a nice sized parlour with another fireplace and hearth. Beside this was a set of stairs leading to the bedrooms. There were items of furniture within the parlour which were covered in sheets. It was obvious to John and Amelia that underneath the sheets were a wooden dresser and what looked like a sideboard and two armchairs. Everett then led them upstairs to view the bedrooms.

"There are two bedrooms both small I'm afraid, but ideal should you have children in the future."

This remark raised a smile to both John and Amelia.

"All in good time," said Amelia.

At the top of the stairs and within a small landing area, there was a very small fireplace that obviously shared the same stack as the downstairs fires but this one had clearly seldom or never been lit before. They entered the bedroom to find that it was plane square in shape and larger than they had expected at about ten feet square and had one small window.

"This is it," said Everett, "and as you can see the other bedroom is just off this one."

A smaller room of about ten feet by seven adjoined the main room separated by a straight wall and doorway. John could see that the layout was almost exactly the same as Thomas and Sarah's cottage on Church Lane.

"It's perfect," said Amelia.

"I agree," said John.

"Until now I didn't want to let this cottage out," said Everett. "One never knows who you could be living next to. But when I heard that you were looking for a place, it struck me that you could be a very good tenant. You're not likely to cause any trouble as I know that you have a sensible head upon your shoulders and would always pay the rent on time. All I ask is that you respect my fondness for my privacy and tranquillity and we should all be able to live here as neighbours in peace."

"We will respect your lifestyle at all times Mr Bardwell," said Amelia.

"The rent will be a shilling a week, if it is to your satisfaction?"

John agreed the price.

"Then it's settled then," said Everett.

"Not quite," said John. "You still have furniture in here. Is it to stay or do we bring in our own?"

"The furniture stays for you to use. It's only old stuff from my past life but you'll need a few more things, and a bed of course."

John and Amelia agreed, and with the deed done, they thanked Everett Bardwell for his kindness as he had only rented the place to them out of the respect that he seemed to hold for John. The couple set off eager to tell the good news to their families. Days later, the couple cleaned the cottage and its furniture, and began to move in their own belongings and newly acquired furniture kindly donated by various friends and family members from all around. It was not long before the cottage was ready for John and Amelia to begin their new life together as a married couple.

Finally, the big day came, the day that everyone had been waiting for. On a snowy Christmas Eve in the year of 1824, the families of Allen, Walker, Fox and Metcalf all assembled at the church to witness the joining in matrimony of the couple. Aside from the families, there were also present a large number of friends and parishioners, such was the popularity of the couple. For the clergy, Henry Banfather, this was a ceremony dear to his own heart, being a respected friend and work colleague. Sarah Walker shed a tear to see her first-born son find a wife of his own and Elizabeth Metcalf shed a tear for the loss of another daughter. After the ceremony, the families joined together for a brief celebration at the Fox cottage and smithy for food and beer. After a couple of hours, the young couple then left to begin their new life together at their own cottage to find on arrival the cottage had been made ready for them. Lanterns had been lit and fires were alight in the kitchen and parlour. Just an hour earlier, Will and Eddie had entered their cottage to prepare specially for John and Amelia's arrival. The newly married couple entered the cottage and were not seen again until the following morning on Christmas day when they went to church. The beginning of their new life together had begun. Who knew what would befall the newly-weds? Happiness and bliss? Or sadness and pain? Everyone knew that life was a lottery. One could only do and live in the way one thought was right, and for John and Amelia, their trials were all to come.

Chapter Thirty-Four

A happy time of new-found freedom had come to the newly-weds. They had spent a quiet week away from the usual chores of employment to enjoy a honeymoon period all to themselves, which finally came to an end at the new year of 1825. Life returned to the harsh reality of hard work in the bitter cold of winter, then to return to the warmth of home and a loving spouse. Like all married and working young couples, life settled into a routine, albeit a happy and contented one. Time passed until crocuses and snowdrops emerged again to be followed by the daffodils of spring. The bitter cold weather was eventually replaced by April showers and broken sunshine. On one Saturday morning in the middle of that very month, John had spent three busy hours working in the workshop on wheels and in the forge replacing two shoes on a large shire horse brought in by Gregory Wright from Stonehouse Farm. With the work done, he then kept an appointment he had made earlier to go to the church and see Samuel Horne. He was a local builder who also doubled up as the village undertaker. Arrangements had to be made with a family named Garrod whose elderly mother had passed away. Between John, Samuel Horne, Henry Banfather and the Garrod family, a time and day had to be agreed by all parties as to when the funeral would take place. Another hour passed until all the arrangements had been agreed, then John left the church and paid his mother a visit whilst he was in close proximity. It had seemed to him that since he was now living as a married man, he didn't see Sarah nearly as much as he would like. He knew that she would be pleased to see him and he knew that the visit would take just enough time till Amelia returned home from working at the manor. She had been asked to come in this weekend as Thomas Woodruff Smyth was entertaining a large party of business guests to his country retreat.

Sarah was indeed pleased to see her son but would have liked to see Amelia too. She enjoyed Amelia's company and had warmed to her almost instantly from their first time of meeting. John stayed at his mother's for another hour while he enjoyed not only Sarah's company but the company of his half siblings too. Then, knowing that Amelia should be returning home from work, it was time to take his leave.

"I'd better be going, Mother, Amelia will be home soon."

"It's been lovely to see you, send my love to Amelia won't you."

"I will," he replied. "Next time I'll bring her with me."

With that, he bid his farewells and left his mother's cottage for the short journey just up the road to his own home. On arrival, he found that Amelia had already arrived and was sitting in front of the fire in the kitchen.

"Oh you're home," said John. "I wondered if you would get home before me."

"I've been home an hour, I left early because I didn't feel very well. Mr Marler said it would be alright."

"Are you alright? What's wrong?"

He could see that Amelia looked a little paler than she usually did. She was a girl who always had colour in her cheeks.

"I felt sick. In fact, I was sick, I had to run outside of the washroom and I chucked up out in the yard."

"Oh, do you think that it's something you've eaten that didn't agree with you or do you think that you're coming down with something? We've got some rhubarb preserve, maybe that'll help settle your stomach."

Amelia laughed. "That won't help me, you fool, I think I'm pregnant, that's why I'm feeling sick."

John didn't know how to reply, he was speechless. He just looked at Amelia but the words just wouldn't come out. Amelia laughed again. "Well say something!" she said.

"How do you know? Are you sure?"

"A girl knows," said Amelia. "I've been suspecting it for a couple of weeks, and now I'm getting morning sickness, I'm sure of it. I was feeling a little sick yesterday morning but it wore off. Now I've had it again, I know I am."

John immediately grabbed his wife, and kissed her and held her in a tight embrace.

"Oh my darling, that's wonderful, I do so hope that it's true."

"It is," said Amelia. "I know it is. If my sums are right and everything goes well, the baby should be here around the end of the year or into the New Year coming. Who knows? It might even be a Christmas baby."

"Have you told anyone aside of me?" John asked.

"I haven't told anyone, just you and I know. I don't want to tell anyone for a few weeks when it's definite and nothing's happened to the baby. You know, just in case there's a miscarriage. It often happens to mothers on their first pregnancy."

John agreed and then he kissed Amelia again.

"You're a clever thing, you are. We're going to be parents."

Amelia smiled and kissed John back on his lips.

"You're going to be a father," she said.

It was nearly a month before the expectant parents finally released the news to the surrounding families. The morning sickness continued for a short while but finally wore off and no miscarriage had occurred, so it was thought that the time was right to break the news. Both had fought the urge to tell of the news but when the time did come, it was greeted in the overwhelming joy expected especially from the grandparents to be.

The remainder of that year seemed to pass by quickly for the couple as they eagerly waited for the time of the baby's arrival. John as usual continued with his busy workload for both parish and smithy but still set enough time aside to make in the workshop a beautiful cradle made of oak. Late September of that year heralded the news that the very first passenger steam railway had opened a service from Stockton to Darlington. It was just the beginning of what was to become a revolution in travel and make the whole of Britain seem a much smaller place.

Amelia's now visible pregnancy rekindled the old memories once again for Sarah at the November 5th celebrations, then the busy time of the Christmas celebrations came along to pass all too quickly in its usual way. The New Year celebrations came with the dawning the year of 1826. Many an ale was consumed by the men and many a hangover was nursed for the return of normal working life, which had only been briefly interrupted. Just three days into the year, on a Tuesday morning, John was as usual working in the Fox smithy when his mother in law, Elizabeth Metcalf, came calling. He instinctively knew why she was here, he had been waiting for this day and had thought it should have come a week or two earlier than it actually did.

"John, you'd better come home, the baby's on its way."

He immediately put down his tools and grabbed his coat to be at his wife's side.

"Good luck John, hope it goes well," said Edmond.

"Be strong brother," said Will. Eddie said nothing, he just shook John's hand. Will had already said what needed to be said for him.

John quickly headed back to his home, while his mother in law, Elizabeth, dropped into Sarah's cottage to alert her to the situation. Sarah had already agreed earlier to help with the birth in any way she could, to accompany Elizabeth Metcalf and the village midwife, Dorothea Woodhouse. Dorothea had already been alerted by Elizabeth Metcalf who had called in on her way to the smithy. She would soon be on her way to John and Amelia's home to deliver yet another baby into the village. John arrived home in double quick time to find Amelia on her feet and pacing up and down the parlour and breathing heavily. She was clearly in the early stages of labour, and on seeing John, she wrapped her arms around him and cried on his shoulder.

"It's coming and I'm scared," she said.

"It's alright, you're in safe hands now. Both our mothers know what they're doing and so does Mrs Woodhouse. She'll be here any time now."

No sooner had the words come out of John's mouth then there was a knock on the door from the mid-wife.

"There you are, what did I tell yer!" he said in a jovial manner.

This caused Amelia to laugh despite her time of obvious distress. Dorothea Woodhouse entered the cottage to find Amelia laughing despite her pain. She smiled back.

"Well, there's a good sign, it's nice to see an expectant mother in such good spirits," she said.

This made Amelia laugh even more, though only briefly.

Dorothea Woodhouse was an unattractive woman of thirty-three years of age. Her hair was already greying and lines and creases were already engrained into her face prematurely for her age. She had been married and widowed to a local farm labourer who had died of dropsy after just eighteen months into the marriage. With no children and no means of support, she took to midwifery through the experience of helping her four sisters with childbirth years earlier. She had also sought and gained some limited medical knowledge from the local parish doctor George Denmark who could see the benefits of her learning some emergency procedures. Consequently, the high birth rate kept her with a busy living.

Soon after, Sarah Walker and Elizabeth Metcalf arrived, and Amelia was taken upstairs to the bedroom whereupon the three women prepared for the task of Amelia's first childbirth. John sat below in the living room waiting and listening, as this was the usual tradition for fathers at the time.

Four hours passed, and this time it was John's turn to be the one to be pacing up and down the parlour. He could hear the noises from up above of Amelia's obvious distress. Loud noises were followed by breaks of rest and encouragement and instructions were made from the three women helping. Then the time finally came that all had been waiting for, as the sounds of Amelia's screams were followed by the cries of a new-born baby. Shortly after, Sarah came down the stairs to tell John that he could go up to see his wife and their new beautiful son. John, without hesitation, ran up the stairs to be greeted by his mother in law and Dorothea Woodhouse. He looked behind them to see Amelia lying in bed and looking exhausted, but cradling her new-born son. She was looking down at him hardly able to take her eyes off him, staring at his tiny face as he looked around trying to make sense of his first sights of this world around him. She then looked to John and handed their new son to his father who gazed down at him with tears welling in his eyes.

"What are you going to call him?" Dorothea asked.

"Alfred," said Amelia. "He's called Alfred John Allen."

***

It was two weeks later on Sunday that all the families joined to witness Alfred's baptism. The baby was feeding well and seemed in good health. He had downy fair hair and his eyes were still the dark blue of a new-born. All in all, Alfred was a healthy baby with a solid family base around him, his future looked good. The nights of course were broken for John and Amelia, and like all new parents' times were hard for them. John would go to work greatly fatigued as his son had been crying in the night for his mother's breast or to be changed. This was a completely new experience of having a human being so greatly dependent upon one's self and took some getting used to for a young couple. Alfred had been put into the oak cradle John had made for him. Amelia would reach over in the dead of night and gently rock baby Alfred back to sleep when he stirred. However, it was more likely that he cried to be fed and would prefer the comfort of his mother's arms than to be alone in his cradle.

It was just four months almost to the day since Alfred's birth on a night in early May. Alfred had been put in his cradle as usual whilst his parents settled down in their bed beside him. Amelia had made sure that he was wrapped up warm and was comfortable just as she always had before. He stirred in the darkness at eleven and his mother saw to him by putting him to her breast and checking that he was still dry. The next whimper came less than an hour later. Amelia changed his linen nappy, patted some wind from him and settled him down to sleep once more. Amelia was exhausted and drifted into a deep sleep straight after.

A faint light of dawn broke through the gaps in the curtain at the window. This always woke John after years of a working life. He yawned and rubbed his eyes as he began to stir ready for another day's work. The movement woke Amelia whose thoughts instinctively were towards her baby son, and she rose quickly to check that he was fine.

He lay still as if asleep, but something didn't look right. There was a still and expressionless look upon him and his eyelids were slightly opened but didn't look as they usually did when he slumbered. Amelia quickly put the back of her hand to his cheek and then under his nose to feel for breath… there was none… and his cheeks were cold. Alfred didn't move.

"John! John! There's something wrong!"

John immediately jumped up.

"I think he's dead!" she screamed.

John did as Amelia and checked for any signs of life from his son. No breath came from his nose or his mouth and his tiny chest showed no movement. He picked Alfred up and gently shook him… nothing… then John patted him on the back like Amelia did to release any wind after his feed… there was still no movement. He could feel that Alfred was cold and lifeless… he was gone.

Amelia cried hysterically and cradled her dead baby in her arms, and she kissed his lifeless little head. John sat on the side of the bed, his face buried in his hands sobbing for the loss of his son. Gone was the little being whose skin seemed so soft and whose downy hair felt so comforting to the touch. Gone were the little bright eyes that would stare up at his mother and father of who had found instant love upon his very being. Gone was the wonder and speculation of who the person that the tiny infant was to

195

become. Gone was the fun and games of play between parents and child longed to be enjoyed in the future. All was gone, just pain and heartache was left in its place.

It was late morning before John could gather himself enough to go out and inform the family as to what had just occurred. Firstly, he travelled up the road to Billy Metcalf's cottage to tell Elizabeth Metcalf who he knew would be at home. The news delivered was greeted as expected with great shock and floods of tears, but Elizabeth gathered herself together ready to be the strength and support that Amelia needed at this time. John then walked to his mother's cottage to tell Sarah of the loss of her first grandchild, and again the news was greeted in much the same way. He finally visited the Fox smithy to tell Edmond, Will and Eddie. As dreadful as it was, sadly, the news was not so uncommon. Alfred had succumbed to who knows what? Could it have been a disease or cold or malnourishment? No one would ever know. The sad fact was that Alfred had just died in the night in much the same way as so many young infants did. No one could ever deny that the high infant mortality could only be attributed to the harsh living of the times. Three days later, Alfred John Allen was laid to rest within the burial site of his grandfather Jacob, just off the path leading to the doors of the church itself. The family's thoughts were that the spirit of his grandfather would watch over him and care for him.

Chapter Thirty-Five

The week after Alfred's funeral was a subdued time for John who had quickly returned to both his work at the smithy and his duties at the church and parish. The forthcoming Magdalen Fair approached, and it was decided amongst the community that the event was to be cancelled partly due to the bereavement of the event's main organiser, but also the poor turnout of the previous year played a part.

Elizabeth Metcalf had brought it upon herself to stay in the company of her daughter as much as possible, to not only console her but to give support and strength whilst John was away. Amelia was grateful for the company especially at the weekends when her sister Beth came over from Norwich to visit. Beth had not yet conceived any children from her still as yet short marriage but was hoping for a family of her own in the future. Seeing Amelia lose a baby had cut deep, knowing the desire to have a baby to cradle and to love for herself.

On a Saturday, two weeks after Alfred's burial, Beth came to Sprowston to see Amelia, but first stopped at her mother's cottage up the road. Elizabeth was at home and so was her brother Simon, but Billy Metcalf was out working at the brickyard as he always did on Saturdays. Tea was by now a less expensive commodity as it once was, and Beth stayed for a quick brew and a chat before paying a much-needed visit to her poor sister.

"How is Amelia coping?" Beth asked as she poured the tea.

"She's quiet as you'd expect," said Elizabeth. "I told her to go to church and see parson Banfather. I thought that maybe he could say the right words to her, but she didn't seem keen on that idea."

"That's because she needs her family close to her rather than strangers," said Simon, who was sitting at the fireside armchair.

"She needs another baby to replace Alfred as soon as possible so she'll have that to keep her mind busy," said Beth. "And John? How is he coping?"

"He's quiet, but he's keeping busy," said Elizabeth. "Working seems to be his way of dealing with the situation. I don't know how they are together when they're alone in the house though, but he'll be glad that you're here today to be with her."

"She needs women around her who understands the kind of thing that she's going through, and has an idea of the way that she's thinking. I'm afraid that men don't have any idea about these things, they just think that their job is to show strength and talk about the problem as little as possible," said Beth.

"That's not always bad," said Simon. "If you don't have strength and support at these times, you just go to pieces and are unable to carry on."

"Hmm maybe," said Beth.

"We'd better get down the road to see her," said Elizabeth. "She'll be on her own right now. John's working at the smithy this morning and at the church later."

Beth agreed, and the tea was quickly drank, allowing mother and daughter to take their leave and go visit Amelia, who was indeed at that time all alone. Shortly after,

Elizabeth knocked on Amelia's door and immediately let herself in as she always did, to find Amelia sitting in an armchair in the living room.

"How are yer girl, are you coping alright?" her mother asked.

"I'm coming to terms with it," said Amelia. "It's just moments when I find it hard, and the wondering why it all happened."

"We'll never know why," said Beth. "It just happened that's all. I'll put the kettle on, you look as if you need a cup of tea."

Beth went into the kitchen and filled the kettle from a pail of water kept on the kitchen floor. She then hung the kettle over the kitchen fire from an iron rod that had been built into the fireplace for the purpose of cooking and boiling. As she prepared the teapot and cups, she could hear her mother talking to Amelia in the adjoining room.

"How's John? Is he coping?"

"He is coping, but he is a lot quieter than normal. I know he cries when he's alone, I sometimes hear him if I'm upstairs and he's down below. I think he's finding strength in his work. If he's so busy, it takes his mind off what has just happened."

"How do you cope? What do you do to try and keep your mind off things?" asked Beth.

"I read and go out for walks sometimes to see John at the forge or sometimes to see his mother down the road. Then there's always you two to keep me company of course."

Elizabeth smiled. "That's what we're here for," she said.

"Do you and John talk things over? Has he been a shoulder to cry on?" asked Beth.

"He doesn't say much about Alfred, he seems to keep it bottled up, but he has been a shoulder for me to cry on. If I start weeping, he's always there to give me a hug or a cuddle and he seems to understand."

Beth rose up hearing that the kettle had boiled and returned into the kitchen, coming back into the living room moments later with a wooden tray of three cups and a filled steaming teapot.

"It's just the nothing to do to fill the gap." said Amelia.

A tear began to roll down her face. "Alfred took all of my time. My thoughts were completely on him, listening for any cry or noise. When will he want changing? When will he want feeding? What clothes do I have for him? Now there's nothing, and no one to care for other than John. All I keep doing is staring at the cradle. John took it out of our room and put it in the spare room, but I can't help it, I just keep going in there and staring at it."

Amelia began to cry and her mother and sister immediately jumped up to her aid to console her in her state of distress.

"There, there," said Elizabeth. "It'll be alright in the end."

A brief spell of tears was had but soon settled down as Amelia composed herself, and Beth returned to pouring the tea.

"We were saying before we came here," said Beth. "We were saying that what you need is another baby as soon as possible. Nothing will take the place of Alfred but what you need is to be a mother again and spend your time looking after another baby."

"Well, that's easily done," said Amelia. "'Cos I'm pregnant already."

"You're what?" shouted her mother.

Amelia smiled amidst the tears she had just cried.

"I'm pregnant already... I suspected that I was just before we lost Alfred, but with all that's happened, I haven't been paying any mind to it. The last few days I thought of it again and I'm still not bleeding. I was sick to the stomach at the time we lost Alfred

198

and was for a short time after, and still am some mornings. John just thought it was through grief, but I know it isn't."

Elizabeth hugged Amelia. "Oh, my girl!"

Beth chuckled with tears streaming down her face. "That's what we want some joy back into this house again. Have you told John yet?"

"I haven't told him anything. I wasn't sure at first, but now I know I am. I don't know how to tell him after what's happened."

"Just find strength my girl, and you'll see that it's just what he needs to hear."

Meanwhile, John was working at the smithy in deep thought of the events that had prevailed within the last few weeks. He worked quietly shaving spokes for wheels and cutting out mortises into the felloes and hubs of the wheels. Ed, Will and Edmond were fully aware of the pain that was deep within John's mind. Knowing him as they did, not being a man of an aggressive or fiery nature, they still chose not to bring the subject up of his loss. He would deal with it in his own way, was their opinion, and unless he wanted to talk it over they would always be there for him.

It was approximately ten in the morning when the group of smithy workers finally stopped for a bite to eat and a drink. This morning, they had their break in the kitchen of the Fox cottage as sometimes Molly would prepare bread with cheese and table beer for the group. It seemed awfully quiet at the table these days. Everyone seemed to be treading on eggshells as not to say anything that may upset John.

"Me and Eddie'll start making the rims in the forge for them wheels you're doing this afternoon while Edmond's making them felloes for Stracey's wheels. Thas if no one comes for any shoeing that is," said Will.

"You can finish the wheels I'm doing if you like," said John. "They only need knocking together then you can make the rims. I've got to meet someone at the church with Samuel Horne, the undertaker, to organise a burial."

"Would that be George King and his wife by any chance?" asked Edmond.

"It would be, and how do you know?"

"Because it's common knowledge around here that their baby son died two days ago the same as what happened to you. Do you think thas a good idea to go when Henry Banfather is quite capable of sorting it out himself?"

"It's my job to sort this out, I've done it many times before. Why should this be any different?" said John

"Because it's only two weeks since you buried your own child, that's why. Why can't parson Banfather sort it out?"

"Didn't ask him. I'm just doing the job I always do."

"Oh John, maybe you need to give it a little time first," said Molly, who was busy passing out the cups of beer. "Whatever you do, don't mention it to Amelia."

"I'm not stupid I wouldn't do that."

"John, I'm sorry, I didn't mean to imply you were," said Molly.

"How is she? How is Amelia dealing with this?" asked Edmond. "We've all felt it a bit awkward to ask in case you get upset."

"She's as you'd expect," said John. "She cries in my arms at night. I can see the hurt she feels in her face. I wish that we'd have had another child, that would have kept her mind busy and not on what has just happened. I put the cradle away so as not to remind her."

"Is she alone much during the day?" asked Molly. "I noticed she comes here from time to time, but what about the rest of the time?"

"Her mother comes over to be with her a lot, and her sister comes at the weekends. She should be there today, and I thank them both for that."

"Well, at least she has family with her," said Will.

"You know, this is the first time that we've been able to talk to you properly about this," said Edmond. "We've all been half scared to."

"I'm sorry, I didn't mean for this to affect you lot," said John.

"Well of course it's gonna affect all of us, cos we all care for you and Amelia," said Edmond. "If anything is on your mind thas troubling you, then you should be able to talk to us cos we'll listen. Which goes back to the first issue of do you think it's a good idea to deal with the burial of George King's little-un?"

"I'll be fine," said John. "I still have strength to carry on, and sooner or later Amelia will too."

"If you say so, we'll respect your decision then, but don't shut us all out cos you've got a family here that cares for yer."

John agreed, and the rest of the break suddenly seemed less awkward and strained as if a great weight had been lifted. They knew now that John was strong enough to carry on just by his words and by his manner despite their concerns. Soon after, he left to make his appointment at the church and he met George King and his family, along with the undertaker and Henry Banfather just as he had said. Together, a date and time was set for the funeral service of the poor lost infant child. After, John left to go home and be with his wife once more, and on arrival was pleased to see that Amelia wasn't alone, she was in the company of her mother and sister as he had expected.

"Had a busy day?" Amelia asked.

"The usual stuff, wheel making and church business to sort out. How are you feeling today?"

Amelia smiled. "I'm fine too."

Then John noticed that both his mother in law and his sister in law happened to be smiling too for some unexplained reason. All three of the women were smiling.

"What's happened? Is there anything I should know?" he asked.

"Yes there is, just sit down for a minute, I've something to say."

John did as Amelia said and sat down among his in laws.

"Now what is it?"

"I'm pregnant again."

John immediately leapt up and kissed his wife.

"Oh my darling that's great news, that's just what we need. I'm so pleased you couldn't imagine. How long have you known?"

"I suspected I was before we lost Alfred, but I wasn't completely sure, but now I know I am. If I am right, then the baby should come in January."

John hugged Amelia again and tears began to well in the eyes of everyone within the room, including Beth and Elizabeth Metcalf as the emotions of the moment began to sink in to all.

"How do you feel?" John asked. "Are you scared because of what happened?"

"I'll never get over the loss of Alfred but this is the only way forward and I miss having a baby to care for."

John kissed Amelia again.

"Come on, we're going to tell everyone," said John. "Good news is just what everyone needs right now."

Amelia smiled and fetched her shawl, and together John, Amelia, Beth and her mother Elizabeth visited Thomas and Sarah at their cottage at Church Lane, then to the smithy to tell Edmond and Molly, John's brothers and of course, Anne Fox of news of the coming of a great grandchild for her. The news was greeted with great joy and relief for the couple. Never was there a baby more needed to ease the pain for John and

Amelia. However, the tragedy that had occurred had taken away some of the euphoria and replaced it with cautious congratulations which in turn was detected by the couple. The news did lift a weight of the minds of the family almost at an instant though.

Once again the busy lives of the couple and the surrounding family seemed to make the wait for the new arrival a short one. In late January of 1827, Amelia gave birth to a baby boy in the same bed and within the same cottage. He was named Frederick John Allen, and he resembled his lost brother. He slept in his brother's cradle which was brought out of the spare room and put back in its original place beside the bed of his proud parents. Grieving for Alfred's loss had lessened for John and Amelia as they now worked hard to care for their new-born son who had taken his place.

Chapter Thirty-Six

John and Amelia watched their son grow with a hidden unease, fearing he could suffer the same fate of his brother Alfred, lost less than a year before his arrival. Often they would check that their infant child was still breathing as he slept at night. But Freddie had so far survived and was now two years old and showing no signs of sickness or weakness. Consequently, his mother and father doted on him, and he returned the love back to his parents in the way that only a two-year-old knows how. Early into this new year of 1829, more joy was brought into the house of John and Amelia when it was announced that Amelia was expecting another baby, due in mid to late September, everyone was thrilled of course.

One Saturday afternoon in mid-February, after John had finished a morning's work followed by church duties, he returned home to spend some quiet time with his wife and son when there was a knock at the door. Both John and Amelia expected the door to open immediately thinking that it was most likely to be Billy and Elizabeth Metcalf or maybe even Beth, as they often came to visit at the weekend. The delay that followed the initial knock made it apparent that the caller at the door was not a familiar family member so John answered the door. At the door, to his surprise, was none other than his neighbour and landlord Everett Bardwell.

"Hello John," said Everett. "I was wondering if I may have a quiet word with you and your dear wife."

"Of course Mr Bardwell, please come in. We don't owe you anymore rent money, do we?"

"Good Lord no," said Everett. "No this is about something else that may greatly concern you both."

"Please sit down," said Amelia, slightly confused at whatever could have brought Everett Bardwell knocking at the door.

"Now, what can we do for you?" asked John.

"As you know John, I am employed as a legal solicitor in Norwich based primarily at the city courthouse. I mostly represent clients for private litigations and financial claims, and I work for a firm based around the area of the courtrooms, that's where our offices are situated. My employers, that of Willerby and Spencer, have decided to expand their business to the area of the courts of Bow Street in London. They have offered me a new position in their London office, that of partner to their new branch. This offer is too good to turn down so I have decided to accept the position. However, there is one thing… I will be leaving Norwich to live in London, and therefore, I will have to sell the cottages and the meadow. It will release the capital enough for me to purchase a property more local to my new place of work."

John looked towards Amelia before returning his focus on Everett Bardwell.

"So what does that mean? Do we have to leave and if so when?" asked John.

"No, no, of course you don't have to leave, not if I can help it you don't," replied Everett. "I was just making you aware that you could soon have a new landlord. I'll be selling the properties as a concern with the tenants included. That is unless you would consider purchasing the properties yourself? I would much rather sell the place to someone who is local and who already appreciates the property and its surroundings."

"Oh I don't know," said John. "I don't think I have nearly enough to buy all that. How much are we talking about?"

"I was thinking of about three hundred pounds as an asking price, but I'm sure that I could reduce that figure to you by fifty pounds to two fifty. It's a fair price."

"It's a very fair price but I'm afraid that it's far more than I've got. In fact, I don't think I even have the fifty yet alone the two hundred. I can't afford it I'm afraid."

"That is a shame," said Everett. "Because I can't think of anyone I would rather have sold the property to than you and your lady wife. Never mind, I will endeavour to ensure that the properties go to a new owner who will respect the position and agreement of your tenancy."

"That's very kind of you," said Amelia, who still had kind respect for Everett Bardwell nonetheless. After all, it was he who had offered them the cottage to rent just in time for their wedding, and now he was kind enough to offer them first refusal to buy the place. Albeit for more than they could possibly afford, but at a knock down price none the less.

"Well, I had better bid my farewells, and of course, I will keep you informed of the progress of the sale when it arises."

John and Amelia thanked Everett and politely showed him to the door. They talked briefly of the conversation that had just transpired but both agreed that there was nothing that either of them could do about the situation and just accept that Everett would be leaving, and a new landlord would be taking over their home. If the new landlord should decide to give them notice, then they would deal with the situation then. Till then, they would carry on as usual.

The following morning was Sunday service at the church and of course, John was to play his usual roll at the event. He set off with his family and arrived as usual half an hour before he would toll the bell to summon the worshippers of the parish for the beginning of the service. Henry Banfather would also arrive early to discuss the service to come and to prepare for the baptism. John would always fetch the water and fill the font for the occasion.

"Good morning John. Good morning Amelia," said Parson Banfather, who was also accompanied by his own wife Mary Anne and their two sons Henry and Edward, aged ten and eleven respectively.

"Good morning Reverend," replied John.

Mary Anne Banfather and her boys came over to see little Freddie and his mother, they always had a soft spot for tiny tots. John and the Parson headed into the vestry to bring out the hymn and prayer books ready for distribution. The record book was brought out ready for two public baptisms that were to be held that morning.

"Refresh my memory would you John. Who are the baptisms for this morning?" asked Henry Banfather.

"John and Catherine Land, they have a baby girl they're calling Mary, and Richard and Florence Barber are naming their son Richard after his father."

Henry took note of the names so as not to put him in the embarrassing position of forgetting in the middle of the service.

"So, everything fine with you? I see Amelia's positively blooming in her pregnancy," said the parson.

"Amelia's doing well and so is Freddie, but we had a bit of a surprise yesterday afternoon when our landlord Everett Bardwell came knocking at the door. He told us that he would soon be selling his cottages."

203

"Why is he selling them?" Henry asked.

"He's been offered a new position as a partner in his firm, but at an office in London near the Bow Street courts."

Henry Banfather raised his eyebrows. "I take it that he is selling his properties with you as sitting tenants?"

"He is, in fact he offered the properties to me at a bargain price, but obviously I can't afford them."

"How much was he asking?"

"His asking price is three hundred pounds for the two cottages and the meadow at the back. He has offered it all to me for two hundred and fifty. He wanted a quick sale, that's why they're all being sold together," said John.

"You can't afford to buy them then?" asked Henry.

"Good Lord no," said John. "I've got nearly fifty pounds saved up but I can't afford two hundred and fifty, that's far too much"

"Oh well, never mind," said Henry. "I'm sure it will all work out for the best in the end."

Then Henry pulled out his watch from his jacket pocket. "Oh my word, you had better start ringing the bell, it's time."

John did as instructed, and very soon the first of the worshippers began to arrive, to be greeted by Henry Banfather who was standing at the church doors ready to greet his flock. Amelia and Freddie took their usual seating positions in the church, and were soon joined by the local villagers who all sat in their own usual places. Another service was held and the two babies were publicly baptised. Eventually, the worshippers bid their farewells to Henry Banfather and his family and left to resume their Sunday day of rest. John began gathering up the books to put back into the vestry.

"John, before you leave, could I have a quiet word with you?" said Henry.

"Yes, of course," replied John, though not entirely sure why.

With the hymn and prayer books put back, the last book to be put away was the large church record book that Henry Banfather had entered the two new baptisms into. John then shut the vestry door behind him and walked over to Henry Banfather who was at that time talking to both his wife and Amelia whilst the children played outside in the churchyard.

"You wanted to speak to me, Reverend?" he said.

"Yes John, let's sit down over there, I just wanted a quiet word."

John and Henry Banfather moved over to a bench over at the far end of the church out of earshot from the wives who were still talking at the doorway of the church. John couldn't understand at all just why the parson could have wanted to talk to him in private.

"This cottage and land that Everett Bardwell is selling, you told me that he had offered it to you at a cut price. Is that correct?"

"Yes that is correct," replied John, slightly confused.

"Well, would you like to purchase the properties in question?"

"Why… yes, I suppose I would, but I can't."

"I have a proposal to make to you John," said the parson. "It is not uncommon for a diocese to come into a business arrangement with employees from its own parishes. Some churches, with the approval of the bishop, have been known to make loans of certain sums for the very reason of purchasing property. It's the church looking after its own. How the arrangements are done is that the diocese lends the sum required for the purchase but holds the deeds of the property until the debt is paid, plus a little extra for church profit."

"Oh I dunno about that," said John. "The word debt doesn't sound good at all. I've always tried to pay my way for everything in life."

"Yes of course, I know that John and that is why I am making this very proposal to you," said Henry. "The church doesn't lend money to just anybody you know, and I know you to be what you are, a man of substance and integrity. The Bishop would most likely agree to the loan on my say so as to your good character and reliability. Also think hard about this; the church can't lose if you default on your payments. That's because it is already holding the deeds and could automatically seize the property from you. But also think hard; what would you be better paying? A rent and ending up with nothing, or paying a loan and ending up a landowner?"

That last statement seemed to make a lot of sense to John. It wasn't often that working men of his class broke through into land ownership and very few even had the chance. His grandfather Bill Fox had run a successful business at the smithy but never actually owned the cottage and its workshops, he had rented it from the Micklethwaite family. Now this could be John's chance in life to break through.

"What would I have to pay and for how long?" John asked.

By now, Amelia had re-joined her husband and had realised the nature of the conversation.

"I would suggest that you paid your entire annual income of fifteen pounds per annum of parish earnings until the loan is paid. That should be in my estimation about fifteen years or so. You could live on the money from your wheelwright and smith work. How does that sound to you?" asked Henry.

"It sounds like a very tempting offer Reverend, but before I am to agree to such an undertaking, I would like to think it over for at least a day. Could I come and see you tomorrow evening with my decision?"

"Of course you can," said Henry. "That's a wise thing to do. You know I'm always here at the rectory, come and see me when you like."

"Then I'll see you tomorrow evening, and you'll know one way or another," said John. With that, John, Amelia and little Freddie bid their farewells and left the church for home. Amelia raised the issue with John on the walk home but it was decided that they would discuss it properly at home once Freddie was settled down and asleep. Freddie was blissfully unaware that a great deal was now on the minds of both his parents.

It was after lunch when Freddie did finally settle down for an afternoon nap, and which finally enabled his parents to sit down at the table and talk over the issue that lay before them.

"It's an awfully big debt," said Amelia. "What'll we do if we can't pay?"

"Well, it's like the parson said, they can't lose because they will be holding the deeds to the place until it's paid. They would just take the cottages and the land from us and end up owning more property and land. It's true what Henry Banfather said, paying a rent or paying a loan, you still have to pay anyway."

"I'm just scared that's all," said Amelia. "It's a lot of money."

"No one gets a chance like this," said John. "We could be landowners and make something of ourselves."

"I'll leave it to you, you're the man of the house and you should know if you're able to do this."

"I'll have given it enough thought by tomorrow night," said John. "I'll know by then what I'm to do."

That evening, John and Amelia did indeed give enough thought needed to make the decision. Not much sleep was had that night what with the thought of taking on the church loan and little Freddie crying at various times. However, resilience is had when parenting young children and it is often found that a capability to do with less sleep often develops when necessary. The result being that the following morning, John and Amelia, though slightly fatigued, were ready for the day ahead. To John's surprise, he was greeted by Amelia's opinion on the subject as she had made her decision in the night.

"I was thinking," she said, while serving breakfast at the table. "Maybe this is our only chance to make it good in life. Rent or loan, we still have to pay to live here so why not pay to own the place ourselves."

John took heed to Amelia's opinion but didn't commit himself to make his decision there and then. He said that he would still give it more thought during the day and would make his decision when he was sure. However, his thoughts did lean towards the same as Amelia's. At work, he didn't mention the offer to his brothers or to Edmond. He didn't want to be influenced by others who were not to be immediately affected by the decision. So, after his day's work and with the thought of the loan still on his mind, John set off in the direction of the rectory to see Henry Banfather.

The knock on the rectory door was greeted by the housemaid, Caroline Lewis, a young local girl of plain appearance who had been working as maid for the Banfather's for just over a year. She showed John into the drawing room and soon after, Henry entered the room to greet his guest.

"Good day John. I presume that you have made your decision?"

"I have Reverend, and I have decided that you are right, it is better to pay a loan than to pay rent, so I have decided to accept your kind offer subject to the agreement of the bishop."

"Well done, I knew that you would have the good sense to accept. I will write to the bishop immediately and await his answer, which I know he will agree to. The church does tend to let each diocese run its own affairs, but this is a necessary procedure none the less."

"One thing, Reverend. There's a little thing that I would like to add to this agreement. I have just a little short of fifty pounds to my own name. I would like to use forty of it towards the purchase, just so I know that I have paid some of it myself. It would just give me some peace of mind."

"Whatever you think is best John," replied Henry. "As soon as I get official approval, I'll let you know and we'll make all the arrangements then. A transaction such as this usually needs a solicitor, so hopefully Everett Bardwell will do us all a favour and deal with this himself. He is an honest man and this would be to his own benefit to do this quickly. I'm sure you could do well to ask him."

"I will," replied John, and with a handshake, the business at hand was concluded.

John bid his farewells to leave for home and to tell Amelia of the transaction that had just occurred. She was pleased despite the fear of the unknown and the large sums of money that she was not used to having associated in her life, but the thought of owning the very house that she was to live in waylaid her fears a bit less. Later, John knocked on the door of Everett Bardwell to inform him that he would indeed accept his kind offer of the properties now that he had found a financial backer. Everett was more than pleased that John was able to buy the place and readily agreed to deal with all the legalities at no more cost than a pound to cover the land registry at the courts. The Bishop did agree to the loan just as Henry Banfather had said he would. The whole deal was done and Everett Bardwell had moved to London within six weeks. John's loan of two hundred and ten pounds plus loan fee was to be paid over fifteen years just as Henry Banfather had suggested and with that John Allen was the new owner of two cottages and a three-acre meadow at the rear of the buildings. Just weeks later in late September Amelia gave birth to a baby girl who they named after her mother Amelia. To save confusion, they affectionately called little Amelia, 'Millie'. These were good times for the family again.

Chapter Thirty-Seven

A chill sat in the air which had felt like a continuation of a long late winter, but was in reality the early spring of 1831. The previous year had seen the passing of the unpopular king George IV who was succeeded by his brother, William Duke of Clarence, to become King William IV. The new king had promised an end to royal extravagances so enjoyed by his predecessor and therefore, has become a much more popular monarch within his realm. To the general population, there is hope that the changing of the monarchy could herald in a new brighter future.

In the Fox smithy, these events so far away from their own lives seem to hardly touch them, life and work is business as usual. Two horses from passing traffic had come in to be shod and were quickly dealt with by Will and Eddie whilst Edmond and John were busily fitting iron rims to four wheels from two carts of local farms in the village. Edmond's son Johnny was busy in the workshop cutting out mortices on wheel felloes, so it was slightly later than usual that the workers finally managed to stop for a food break of hot milk, bread and cheese, brought out as usual by Edmond's wife Molly. As it was Friday, there was talk amongst the men of the coming weekend.

John's younger brother Will was a young man who up until now had managed to distance himself from the trappings of married life, and so still enjoyed many of the vices that a kindly genteel wife would find most distasteful from a husband. Aside from visiting the odd hanging at the castle gates, he was a regular at cockfights and bare-knuckle fights within the city. Unknown to his family, the ladies of the night all knew him too as an occasional visitor. Usually, he was found in the local pubs, the Blue Boar Inn and the newly built Royal Oak pub situated near the boundary with the neighbouring village of Catton. A quiet life didn't at all seem appealing to him like his two brothers, of whom he resembled only in looks. Everyone, however, accepted Will to be the way that he was and some even envied his carefree ways.

"I won't be in tomorrow morning," said Will. "I'm going to the castle to see the hanging."

"Who's being hung this time?" asked Edmond.

"Richard Nockholds, the one all those people were calling for mercy for outside the Guildhall."

"Weren't he the one who set fire to all those haystacks around the county?" asked Eddie.

"He did much more than that," said Will. "He was one of the leaders of those riots in the city last year when those weavers complained about their wages being cut. Shortly after the riots were crushed by them troops, he waited for one of the factory owners and threw vitriol into his face. It was later that he set fire to the haystacks over a dispute over some farm machinery I think. Don't know exactly what all that was about."

"It's been a while since you last went to a hanging. Wasn't the last one that dumpling poisoner?" asked Edmond.

"That it was," replied Will. "Must have been about two years ago they hung John Stratford. He put some arsenic into some flour meant for his lover's husband who was ill and dying in the workhouse. Someone used the flour meant for the husband to make dumplings for their family. Some man who worked in the workhouse I think. Anyway, the man and his family were all sick and the man died. They knew that it was Stratford who had put the arsenic into the flour cos he wrote a note onto the paper that the flour was wrapped in and they matched his handwriting. Turned out he had got his lover pregnant and she bore his child. He tried to do away with her husband so his own wife would never find out. He was hung outside the new city prison, not at the castle."

"Anyway," said Will, looking towards his brother Eddie. "I suppose that you'll be seeing that young maiden again, Mary Howard isn't it?"

Ed coloured up, he was far more like his elder brother John in personality, a more modest young man though not so community minded as John. Ed preferred to keep his life as private as he could, but he lived in a village, and like all villages it hardly goes unnoticed if one forms a relationship with a local girl.

"Might be," he replied.

"Pay no attention to that piss taker," said Edmond. "It's good that you've found a gal and I hope that you end up married to er."

"Here, here!" said John.

"Well now that you've mentioned it, we are getting married," said Ed.

Everyone looked at each other in complete shock at what Eddie had just said, but they didn't have time to make any comments on the subject because Ed spoke first.

"I was going to tell you all on Sunday when we're all with Mother at lunchtime after church. But you might as well know now, it makes no difference to me."

There was a reaction of euphoria amongst the gathering as the unexpected news sank in. "Oh my word! Well done and congratulations," resonated within the workshop.

"So how long have you kept this news from us?" asked John.

"Saw her father last night and asked his permission, but we decided to marry two nights before."

"Well done boy" said Edmond. "When are yer gonna marry her?"

"Don't know yet. We've got to find a place to live first and then book a date at the church, which I hope you'll sort out for us please John."

"I can do better than that," said John. "I can rent you our cottage next door. I've been meaning to rent it out for a while now to bring in a little extra income. We've just been keeping old furniture and stuff in it since we moved into our place."

John and Amelia had moved into Everett Bardwell's old cottage upon purchase as it was slightly larger than the one that they had been renting from him due to an extension built upon it several years earlier by a previous owner.

"Thank you," said Eddie. "It had already crossed my mind to ask you if the place was available, now you've saved me the job. Mary will be pleased when I tell her. Me and hers going to Norwich tomorrow to buy some ribbon and stuff for her wedding dress. I think she's buying a new bonnet. We're spending the day there and we'll have a meal somewhere at some inn I expect."

"You ought to try the Angel, they'll look after you there," said John.

"That's where I thought we might go," said Eddie.

There was a wry smile momentarily on John's face as he recalled the time when he and Amelia had gone there one snowy day and hired the attic room for a couple of hours. He wondered if Eddie had heard of the attic room for himself, where so many a young courting couple would go to be alone together.

Mary Howard was a local girl who was known to most of the family. She was the daughter of Jack Howard, a farm labourer from Manor Farm who worked with Thomas Walker. She had grown up just a stone's throw away from where Thomas and Sarah lived and where John, Will and Eddie had been raised. She was from the other block of farm cottages closer to the church and which had also been drawn into the manor farm estate. Mary was a pleasant girl who was plain looking, not a beauty in any means but not ugly either. She had red hair and pale skin and was physically well proportioned though not very tall at about five feet. The family had known her since she was a small child and John knew that his mother Sarah would welcome her into the family with great enthusiasm. She was known to have a sensible head upon her shoulders and would undoubtedly make a good wife for Eddie. Little did they know of the important role she was to play within the family in times to come.

"Well," said John. "Since this seems the time to make announcements, I suppose I'd better make one more of my own. Amelia's pregnant again and she's expecting our baby in October."

"Congratulations!" and "Well done!" were once again called out by the men.

"I can't wait to see Mother's face when she gets all this good news," said Will.

The following day, Will and some of his friends from the village did indeed travel to Norwich to watch Richard Nockholds execution at the castle gates. A large crowd had gathered for the event, some calling for mercy, some were selling souvenirs, but most just wanted to see the man hang as a curiosity and entertainment. Meanwhile Eddie and his new intended Mary Howard visited the shops and stalls around the market square. Mary purchased her ribbon and a new bonnet for her big day and the couple stopped for lunch at the Angel inn. They came out of the inn three hours later hand in hand.

Sunday came and the good news from both couples was delivered to their mother Sarah on the morning journey to church. Sarah and Thomas and indeed all the family were overjoyed. Seldom had two happy events been announced at the same time and equally the news was well received by friends and colleagues at the church, especially Henry Banfather who always regarded John as a close friend. Eddie and Mary had decided that there was no reason to delay their marriage now that they had found a place to live. Consequently, as soon as the banns had been read in church three times over three months, the family all gathered to witness their joining in early June. John and Amelia now had new neighbours and a small income generated from the rent of the next-door cottage.

***

Just weeks after Ed and Mary's wedding and on one summers evening after a hard day's work at the smithy, both Eddie and John sat out in the rear garden, ending their day by enjoying a smoke and a small beer as the sun lowered from behind them. They watched the sky slowly turn golden in colour behind the treetops in the distance across the rear meadow. Amelia was busy inside putting the children to bed with the help of Mary who had by now befriended Amelia, and had quickly fitted in as a new member of the family.

"You know, I was looking at this garden the other day and I was thinking that it's quite big enough to have a workshop and forge built on it," said John.

"Why would you want to do that?" asked Ed. "Our smithy on Church Lane's good enough isn't it?"

"Yes it is. But should anything happen, say Edmond died or the landlord Micklethwaite decided to evict or something, you know, anything. We'd need somewhere to go to carry on working and keep the competitors away."

"What's the point you're making?" asked Ed.

"The point is that I just feel that I could build a smithy here bit by bit, one that I could call my own."

Ed looked at John in surprise. "Why?" he asked.

"We're still working for Edmond in name, and though I know we're all equal in his eyes and that's good, if anything happened we would need somewhere to work. Sprowston is getting bigger and so is the workload, if we had another smithy, we'd be able to cope, and that would stop anyone trying to muscle in on our patch. The wheelwright business could be at Church Lane and the farrier work could be done here. I think that having another smithy could be to all our advantages."

"How do you think that you'll build these new sheds with only a little money?"

"Bit by bit," said John. "That's what they are, just sheds. If I could build them in timber as I could afford 'em, then within two or three years I should have three or four sheds, enough for a smithy and stable. We could build them ourselves, we're good enough carpenters."

"What about the forge and the bases for these sheds?" asked Ed. "Thas brickwork and tiles. You'll need the materials and a bricklayer. How are you gonna pay for that?"

"I've been thinking about that too," said John. "Robert Welton is paying me for the hay he cuts from my meadow and he's also asked me if he can rent the field to graze his sheep during winter. I should get a small income from that, maybe even enough to save up for the materials and the cost of a bricklayer. There's the rent I get from you too remember, the two rents should give me enough to at least save up for each shed as I can afford it. I should be able to get a good deal on the bricks from Cannell's brickyard, I've got family who work there remember. They also know all the local bricklayers who come to the yard and follow the carts in search of work as they deliver the bricks to all the sites. Come to think of it, what about Uncle Billy? He's a builder, I'm sure he would do us a good deal."

"Hmm," said Eddie. "How do you think Edmond will react to all this?"

"I'll put it to him as I did to you. I think we need to expand the business to two forges."

"Hmm, good luck," replied Ed.

"There's plenty of time, I've got to build the sheds first, and by the time they're built, he might spot the need for them by himself."

Ed wasn't convinced, he sensed a family feud could be in the making and felt that maybe John should be cautious where Edmond was concerned. The sun lowered as the evening drew in, and the trees in the distance seemed to fade away as the light faded from the golden dusk. Quietness came as birds began to roost for the night leaving just the last song of a blackbird to resonate around the countryside before the darkness of the night finally set in.

At work the following morning, nothing was said of John's plans for the future, but John did make a point to visit Simon Metcalf at Cannell's brickyard where he was able to buy five hundred Norfolk red bricks and two hundred and fifty red pemmant floor tiles, at cost price through his family connections. When John returned, he told Edmond that he had purchased the materials for a base for a new store shed that he was planning to build. Edmond saw no malice, and in fact, thought that it was a good idea of John. The eventual construction of the shed started a month later and took just over another month to build with the help of Edmond's elder brother, William, or Uncle Billy as he was better known to John. Uncle Billy laid the foundations and base at a cheap rate for family whilst John did all the timber construction including tiling the roof in red pantiles that Billy had sold to him, again at cost price.

Time wore on, and John continued to squirrel away the rents both from Eddie and his new wife and from Robert Welton on his field at the back. By October he had saved enough for more bricks and floor tiles to build a base for the second fifteen by fifteen feet square shed. However, later that very month, the thought of any building work was quickly postponed as the day finally came when he was once again summoned home by his mother in law whilst at work in the forge. Amelia had gone into labour to give birth to their third child. As was the routine, the local midwife Dorothea Woodhouse was called and so was Sarah to lend her help and support alongside Elizabeth Metcalf. The birth seemed to come much faster and easier than the previous two, almost as a routine but no less painful. By five in the afternoon on the 20th October, 1831, a slap of a hand to the rear end of a new baby brought the wails of its first breaths. A baby boy was born to John and Amelia who they were to name Henry Edward Allen. Once again the family was re-united in the joy of yet another new arrival.

The coming of winter saw John postpone the construction of the next shed and instead continued to save as much money as he could to fund its construction, which he resumed in the following spring. The construction took just over six weeks with the help of John's uncle Billy who built the foundations and base as before, while John constructed the main structure in timber. The next venture planned was the construction of the forge, but this project was to be in the distant future due to the cost. This building was to be constructed entirely in brick with a forge fire and chimney construction within. In the meantime, John had decided that now maybe was the time to tell Edmond of his plans to create another smithy on his own property.

"Why do you want to do that?" Edmond asked.

"I think we're able to expand the business to two smithies, one for horse shoeing and ironworks and the other for wheel making," replied John. "Sprowston is getting bigger as Norwich expands and draws closer to its boundaries. The population is increasing and the through traffic is increasing, and so is the demand for our work. I think that we should move with the times and meet with the demand for what we do, before someone else does."

"So you're not going it alone and starting a rival smithy?" Edmond asked, with a slight look of anxiety upon his face.

"No I'm not starting as a rival, but I would like to be made a full partner of this business. This business is yours by name left to you by your own father, but I am now able to create new workshops, a forge and maybe a stable later in the future. I think that should allow me to come in as I've always worked with you like a partner in all but name. Also consider this, if anything should happen to you, what would we all do? Young Johnny's still got a little way to go before he's ready to take on the business for himself, and what if the Micklethwaite family should decide to sell the cottage and forge to someone who wants it for themselves? We need another forge and workshops as a backup, but mostly we need to expand."

"I'll need some time to think about this before I come to any decision, but firstly I need to know if you are planning on leaving our smithy."

"No I am not, I would never just leave you like that. All I am asking is that we become two smithies as equal partners."

"I'll come to my decision tomorrow," said Edmond.

Thought of little else were on the minds of both John and Edmond that night. John was worried that he may have hurt Edmond with his plans. He had never wanted that but he had felt that now was finally the time to have his name upon the business too. Why not? He had always equally sorted out the orders and organised the stock materials as well as the work itself, surely Edmond could see that. The following morning at the smithy, Edmond summoned John over for a quiet word.

"John, I've thought hard about what you are proposing and this is the way that I see it. You are right, Sprowston is getting bigger. Soon, the boundary between the city and here will be virtually on our doorstep. I think that we should expand to two forges because if we don't, then someone else will. But as for you being an equal partner, this is how I see it. I think that this new smithy should belong to you in name as it is on your property and you've paid for its construction. The smithy here is the Fox smithy which was in my father's name and that I will eventually leave to my boy when I'm gone. I think that you are right that I should do mainly wheel making here and that you should do horse shoeing at your place. If we're too busy here, then we'll send the custom to you and the same applies the other way too if you're too busy. Equally, if there's little to no work at wheel making, then we'll lend a hand at horse shoeing and blacksmithing and the other way too. That way the family is looking after each other and we've both got our own businesses. Should suit everyone, if you agree that is?"

"Sounds good to me, but it'll be a while," said John. "I've only got two sheds to my name and no forge or stable. I reckon it'll be two years before I can afford to build the last two sheds and a forge fire."

"I'm sure you'll get them built before then," said Edmond. "Until then, we'll carry on as usual, but what I'd like to know is are you working alone or are Will and Ed gonna join yer?"

"Don't know yet, we'll worry about that when the time comes but till then we'll carry on the same till I've built 'em."

Edmond's prediction proved to be correct, John did indeed manage to construct, with the help of his uncle Billy, a fully functional forge by the beginning of August in the following year of 1832. Jobs began at the new forge within a month, though John still had to construct a stable and wood store in the future just like the Fox workshop had. This would have to be put off until there were enough funds saved to finance the venture. He did exactly as what was agreed nearly a year earlier than planned or expected and made his living solely on horse shoeing for the local farms and passing traffic. It was agreed that it was more convenient for Eddie to work at John's forge alongside his brother, he was living there and all. This also pleased the wives of the brothers as it was always useful to have the husbands close by. The arrangement seemed to suit Edmond well as he had found that with fewer men now at the yard, all the focus was now on wheel making without the distractions of the farrier trade. This was much more to his liking. Equally, John had found that he had more time for other duties at the church and parish and he enjoyed having his wife and children around. John and Eddie even had enough time for digging and laying the foundations for the forthcoming stable and wood store. The winter set in, and John continued to juggle the work between church, parish and farrier. The November 5th celebrations came and then Christmas and the new year of 1833, which led to another announcement from John and Amelia in mid-February, another baby was expected.

Chapter Thirty-Eight

The May Day celebrations had taken over as the main event on Robert Welton's meadow, replacing the old Magdalen Fair due to rival fairs and events tempting both revellers and traders to go elsewhere. John, of course, was the organiser of this event, and aside of the Maypole and the organising of local children to dance around it, he also performed much the same duties as the old Magdalen Fair and see to the entertainment and the stalls.

At home, John and Amelia have eagerly awaited the arrival of another baby and have taken it upon themselves to teach young Freddie and Millie to read and write. This is a tradition that has served John's family well in the past and would do in the future. In this period of time, more people of working life are trying to break away from the shackles of illiteracy than in times past. The children, like so many so young, preferred play out in the garden than study, but of this time, children have learned through discipline to obey their parents and consequently, have learned well.

By late August the last of the sheds and out buildings are built to be used as a stable and a wood store. John's yard is now complete and has as many out buildings as the Fox smithy. Together, the two businesses are able to turn over enough work, sometimes even sharing jobs. Edmond's son Johnny has now virtually completed his apprenticeship as a wheelwright and is working with his father, knowing that someday it will be his turn to take over the running of the Fox Yard. Will shares his time working at both smithies, whichever workshop is the busiest at the time. Sometimes Edmond finds himself having to put wheel-making work to the Allen yard. As predicted, there is plenty of work for both workshops from all local farmers and passing traffic.

On Tuesday the 15th October, John was woken up in the middle of the night and told to go to Dorothea Woodhouse's cottage and fetch her as the baby was now on its way. It was hoped that the baby would come on the 2nd birthday of its older brother Henry, but as always, was just wishful thinking from all concerned. Dorothea was there within the hour; she was quite used to being called up in the middle of the night such was the nature of her job. It was decided however, that there was no need to call either Sarah Walker or Elizabeth Metcalf for this birth, instead, Ed's wife Mary, would come from next door to help Amelia in any way she could. Knowing that Amelia had been through this ordeal on more than one occasion, she had expected that there would be little to do other than support Amelia in her hour of need and just do as Dorothea should instruct her. Meanwhile, John carried the children downstairs while they slumbered and laid them upon some makeshift bedding of cushions and blankets. It was to be another long night and better that the children were away from earshot of their mother in her distress. Only Freddie woke as he was carried, he was the last to be brought down while Millie and Henry had stayed asleep none the wiser.

"Is Ma gonna be alright?" Freddie asked.

"Shh! You'll wake up your brother and sister. She'll be fine just go back to sleep," whispered John.

John covered Freddie with a blanket and he soon drifted back off to sleep alongside his two siblings. An hour passed and then two. Not much noise was heard from down below where the children lay just the muffled sounds of women's voices and footsteps upon the wooden floor as Amelia paced up and down the room in the discomfort of her labour. In time, the sounds increased to that of screams and strains. John sat listening quietly down below in his favourite armchair smoking his pipe while he watched over his sleeping children. Amelia's cries finally came to an end to be replaced by the cries of a new-born baby. John smiled knowing that it was all over and yet another child was here to bring more joy within his household. Ten minutes passed and Mary came downstairs smiling. "It's a girl, a beautiful little girl."

Emotion was clearly visible all over Mary's face, she had only witnessed one birth before in her life, that of her younger brother, and then she was just a child. She had found it all a frightening experience then, but this one seemed to her to be beautiful, with the end result this beautiful baby girl cradled by Amelia.

"Can I go up?" John asked.

"Not yet. Dorothea is cleaning up, but it won't be long."

Mary returned upstairs where once again more shuffling and footsteps were heard as the women above cleaned up, and made the room and the mother and child more clean and comfortable. Soon after, Dorothea Woodhouse came down carrying two buckets, one contained all the waste of the birth and the other water from the cleaning up. Both were to be emptied into a hole dug out in the rear meadow.

"You can go up and see Amelia now," she said. "Mother and baby are just fine."

John climbed the stairs and entered the bedroom to be greeted by the sight of Amelia cradling her new-born baby girl, who in turn was being doted upon by Mary who had found the whole experience overwhelming. Amelia handed the baby over to John who smiled and kissed his new beautiful daughter.

"What are you gonna call her?" Mary asked.

"We thought that we would call her Adelaide after the queen and Charlotte after the old queen. Adelaide Charlotte Allen," said John.

"Little Millie will be pleased that she's got a little sister to play with, she always said that's what she wanted," said Amelia.

Just an hour later, the children began to stir having slept through the whole ordeal none the wiser. Little Henry was the first to rise but was far too young to understand what was going on around him, he just searched for his mother. Then Freddie woke and straight away asked if he had a new baby brother or sister yet. Millie was the last to wake, and the three children were taken upstairs to see their new baby sister for the first time. As expected, the children were pleased and full of questions as all small children do at such a happy event. But eventually, the novelty of the new arrival soon wore off as they were to find that small babies don't laugh and play with the rest of the gang, they just cry, feed and smell a bit at times. But they were still glad to have her all the same. Two weeks later, the rest of the family shared in the joy of her arrival as together they witnessed her public baptism on Sunday church service. It was noticed how closely she resembled her sister Millie as a new born. For some unknown reason, everyone called her by her middle name Charlotte instead of Adelaide, her first name. The children were the first to do so and soon the habit took hold by the adults. Consequently, it was decided that she was to be known as Charlotte from then on.

Charlotte seemed to be thriving well, but these were days when sickness and disease could strike at any time and claim many a life of one so young. Everyone was fully aware of this not least John and Amelia who had already experienced the pain of losing a child with the tragic loss of their first born, Alfred John. It was just a week after the family had gathered to witness Charlotte's baptism, Amelia noticed that her baby seemed to have caught a slight cold. As all mothers know, these are not easy times with an infant so small and so young, so full attention was given to her. John was made aware that Charlotte was slightly under the weather and Amelia did as all mothers would do, kept her infant warm and fed and made sure that her airways were clear of any fluids or obstructions. Experience had told her to expect about a week of unpleasant times until the cold finally cleared up. Needless to say, Charlotte found the whole experience unpleasant and cried constantly for the comfort of her mother.

Five nights of crying and nursing her child took its toll on Amelia, who found the role of caring for a sick baby on top of running a house full of small children exhausting. Little Charlotte's body temperature was beginning to get irregular, often turning from sweating and over-heating to shivering with cold. Amelia did all that she could do by wrapping her baby up warm when needed and loosening the wrappings accordingly. However, there was still no improvement and soon, it became apparent that Charlotte was not keeping down her milk. Water was given to her using a spoon to keep her hydrated. With the lack of nourishment Charlotte was taking in, she became weaker, and by the end of the week John and Amelia both knew what the outcome was likely to be. Charlotte was just two days short of a full calendar month old when the inevitable outcome finally came. She was cradled in Amelia's arms on a cold November morning whilst the children slept. John had stayed awake all night beside Amelia waiting for the end to come. When the end came, Amelia just buried her face into the belly of her dead child and sobbed. John embraced both his wife and daughter trying to show strength for his wife as men try to do at these moments, but tears ran down his cheeks none the less. They had lost their second child, and worse, they would have to tell Charlotte's siblings the news when they awoke. They woke two hours later and could immediately sense that something was wrong.

"Children, sit down, I've something to tell you all," said John.

Amelia left the room and returned upstairs where the lifeless body of Charlotte lay in her cradle, put there earlier by her parents. The children sat down as instructed, but Henry, being one so young at only two years old just sat beside his playmates playing with his sister's rag doll, made for her by her grandmother Sarah. Millie and Freddie sat silently waiting for their father to speak.

"Your little sister has died and gone to heaven. She's happy now and is being looked after by God."

The children just sat there, they didn't cry. To their advantage, they had young age, innocence and their lack of full understanding to fully comprehend the tragedy that had just befallen their family. Freddie was the only one to break the silence and ask a question.

"She's gone to heaven?" he asked.

John nodded, though his heart weighed heavy knowing that he would have to choke out any answers asked by ones so innocent.

"Will she be happy?" Freddie asked.

"Yes she's happy now." John replied.

"Is she playing with angels?"

John nodded but quickly left so as not to let the children see how upset he was feeling and see the tear rolling down the side of his face. No more was said to the children on the subject after that and John left soon after to tell his family of the tragic news and to organise a burial at the church with Henry Banfather and the local undertaker Samuel Horne, both of which conveyed their deepest sympathies. At his mother's cottage, Sarah was alone, but she immediately knew that things were not well on seeing her son as he entered.

"What's happened?" she asked.

"The baby's died," he replied, shaking and eyes glistening once more. Sarah rushed over and immediately embraced John, and there she wept upon the shoulder of her eldest son. Sarah had already been told days earlier that Charlotte was not well and knew that there was always a chance that the baby wouldn't survive. But the pain of seeing her son so brutally hurt for a second time was more than she could bear.

"I'm so sorry my boy, I don't know what to say to you," she said after she had composed herself from her own initial grief.

"How is Amelia and how did the children take it?"

"Amelia's as you would expect her to be," John replied. "She's devastated but she's carrying on for the sake of the little-uns. They're too small to take it all in, thank God. Freddie just asked if she was playing with angels and Millie just sat quiet. Henry... well, Henry's just two and doesn't know any of it. I know he'll ask one day and even about Alfred when he's older, I'm just glad that they're all still young so's it don't hurt 'em."

Sarah squeezed John's hand. "I remember when we lost your brother, Vincent, he couldn't have been any older than Charlotte, we just found him lying there in the morning. I know what you're both feeling and it's horrible, but you will get over it in time. The joy of your other little-uns will see to that."

"I know," said John. "It's just hard that's all. You know I slightly remember when we lost Vincent. I was very small then too, barely older than Freddie. You've got a nice big family now to keep you happy."

"I couldn't be happier than I am with all my children. You three from Jacob, my four from Thomas, and of course Tom and Keziah, my stepchildren. I'm happy with you all and so shall you be with your children and your lovely wife."

John managed a slight smile in response. "Tell the family what's happened, she's to be buried on Saturday at ten."

"I will," said Sarah, and she embraced her son once more before he left to tell the Metcalf's, then to return back to support his wife and family. The following Saturday, the whole family of Allen's, Fox, Walker's and Metcalf's all attended St Mary and Margaret's church to see the laying to rest of little Charlotte, who joined her brother Alfred and grandfather Jacob in the churchyard. John and Amelia drew strength and support from their family to carry on.

Chapter Thirty-Nine

Amelia's face wore a troubled look when she returned home from a visit to her mother's cottage. It is now three months since Charlotte's loss and until now a feeling of normality has returned within John and Amelia's lives, albeit for the well-being of their surviving children. However, John could see that something was troubling Amelia on her arrival.

"What's happened?" he asked.

"As if we don't have enough tragedies in this family," said Amelia.

"What's happened?" repeated John.

"David Lock has died suddenly. They think that he was poisoned by something at work. My sister's a widow."

"Oh my God!" said John. "I thought that we'd had enough death in this family lately without another tragedy. You say he was poisoned?"

Amelia nodded.

"Him being a dyer, that doesn't surprise me, he must work with all sorts of poisonous stuff. What will Beth do now?" said John.

"She's coming back here to Sprowston to live with my parents. She's no children to support and no means to support herself. She'll have to find employment somewhere cos father can't be expected to do it all. David's funeral is on Friday at St Mary's, ten o clock, we'll have to go."

John agreed, it was only right to pay respects to a lost family member even though he had barely met David Lock more than half a dozen times in his life. Within the week, John and Amelia joined the Metcalf family to pay their respects of the passing of Beth's husband David, and then to help her pack her belongings at her city home to bring them back to her parent's at Sprowston. John had borrowed the horse and cart from Edmond especially for the day to serve both purposes of transport and haulage. Less than a month later, Beth had found local employment at Manor Farm. She was working as a milkmaid and butter maker within the dairy. Despite seeing her sister suffer such a loss in her life, Amelia was glad to have Beth around again. She had missed her company and now within months of both sisters suffering painful losses in their lives, they could draw strength from one another, consequently, Amelia became a more frequent visitor at her parent's cottage. Her brother Simon, had left his parents cottage just a few years earlier and had married a local girl, Jane Kittle. This had allowed Billy and Elizabeth Metcalf to have more than enough room for their daughter to return home. Simon was still living locally within Sprowston just a short walk away from his place of work at the brickyard. He and his wife Jane, now had a daughter of their own, Elizabeth, named after her grandmother but called Lizzie to avoid confusion. Simon still had great concern for the welfare of both his sisters and increased his visits back to his parent's cottage to keep in touch with them both.

Meanwhile, John continued his busy workload in both parish and smithy. Henry Banfather had found him to be almost his right hand man in both church and parish duties, and both men had great mutual respect for one another. The Allen forge did well being in its convenient position at the side of the main road from Norwich, pulling in a regular horseshoe trade. Orders for wheels would sometimes come in from local farmers who knew John personally, but the orders were usually passed on to the Fox forge as was agreed by John and Edmond. However, it was on one such occasion in mid-May 1834 that John paid a visit to Edmond at the Fox smithy with an order of four wheels to fit onto two carts from a farm in nearby Rackheath.

"I've got a fair workload already," said Edmond. "You'll have to do these ones yourself. You can have Will if you like, he could make 'em and shoe some horses too. Me and the boy ere have got three double wheel orders came in just yesterday, and thas without the orders we already had. We've got a load of ironmongery for the builders working on expanding Cannell's yard too. The horse trade is keeping you flat out busy so Will should be a help to you on that and do the wheels too. That should be about right for both of us to manage, don't you think?"

"Well if you don't mind losing Will for a while, you can ave im back as soon as things quiet down" said John

"Not likely, you can ave im for good," Edmond laughed.

"Now, now thas enough of that!" said Will, who was in the back of the workshop working with young Johnny and listening to every word said.

The following Monday, Will began to work with his brothers once again, but this time, at the Allen smithy, and there he continued to work for longer than initially thought. Two months passed and both smithy's found it more convenient to keep Will where he was, neither one seeing the need for him to return to the Fox smithy. Indeed, Edmond had found downsizing his concern more to his liking, keeping just himself and his son with a constant living. As work and funds came in, John found enough money to purchase a working horse and an old cart he was able to fix up good as new. Everything was now in place to take on a larger workload as the demand dictated.

***

The children had been put to bed an hour earlier when John came into the house having cleared up the forge and put the horse in the stable for the night with some feed. He washed his face and hands in the kitchen as Amelia had put out a bowl of water and cotton flannel for him. It had been a warm summer's day and there was a late sun set, so John and Amelia settled on chairs placed outside to see the remainder of the day pleasantly staring across the fields as the sun lowered from behind the cottage, each with a cup of ale in their hands.

"I've been waiting to get some time with you alone today," said Amelia.

This aroused John's curiosity, either she had something pressing to say or his luck was in and she was feeling either passionate or broody.

"Any particular reason?" he asked.

"You're gonna be a father again," said Amelia.

John smiled and took his wife's hand and kissed it tenderly.

"When's this one coming?" he asked.

"Sometime in March I think."

"That's wonderful," he replied.

John raised his cup and tapped it to Amelia's.

"To our new arrival," he said.

"Our new arrival," said Amelia.

"We've got to think of another name now, anything in particular you like?" asked John.

"I have," said Amelia. "I'd like to give this one the name of one of our lost babies should it be boy or girl. Alfred if it's a boy and Charlotte if a girl. It would be a fitting tribute to them."

"I agree with that," said John. "We both liked those names in the first place. What about middle names? Have you thought anything about that? I quite like the name Mathias if it's a boy, Alfred Mathias, that sounds good."

"I like that, it sounds good to me too," said Amelia. "Alfred Mathias, it's agreed then. I thought that we could use Adelaide again only for a middle name. She could have the same name only the other way around. Charlotte Adelaide, I liked both those names and it would be a nice tribute to Charlotte."

John agreed, and with that, the name of the forthcoming baby was settled there and then. Neither John nor Amelia could ever remember finding it quite so easy or quick to choose a name for their babies. But both were proud to be honouring their lost ones in such a way.

The remainder of the year was spent much the same as always in a rural village, the pace of life was slower but the work was harder. John's workload increased during the harvest, horses needed shoeing, carts needed repairing and wheels needed making. Nails and metal bracing straps were made for the local builders, and when the winter came there were the November 5th celebrations to organise. The increased workload from the church returned as the death rate rose in the cold winter months. Amelia continued to work hard as a mother and wife whilst carrying a growing child within her. Christmas came and passed and the new year of 1835 came in to being. Finally, the cold and harsh times looked like drawing to an end as crocuses and snowdrops flowered around the woodlands to be followed by daffodils and the emergence of the warmness of spring.

"John, you'd better fetch Mrs Woodhouse, I think it's started," said Amelia, early on a cloudy mid-March morning. "And get my mother, I'd like her to be here with me."

John quickly dressed and made straight to Dorothea Woodhouse's cottage. Soon after, and with the midwife alerted, John made towards Billy Metcalf's to tell Elizabeth's mother of the news. The knock on the door was answered by Billy who was holding a piece of toast, enjoying his breakfast with his wife and daughter Beth.

"Morning John. Are you here for what I think you're here for?" he asked.

John smiled. "She asked me to fetch her mother after I'd been to the midwife's. The baby's on its way."

"I'll be there in a moment!" called Elizabeth, who could hear everything said from inside. She quickly grabbed her shawl and put on her boots.

"Can I come?" asked Beth. "I'd like to be there with her."

"If you like" said John, "but we thought that you were working today, that's why Amelia didn't ask you, she thought you couldn't come."

"Oh poo to work," said Beth. "It's not every day that you're there to see your sister have a baby. I'll tell 'em the truth tomorrow, won't be the first time a girls taken a day off to help her sister with childbirth."

"She'll be glad to have you there with her," said John.

Soon after, the three hastily made the short journey up the road to John and Amelia's cottage where Dorothea Woodhouse had already arrived and was already being helped by Mary who had heard goings on from next door. Today was to be a house full of women, John had thought to himself with a quiet chuckle.

The women set about preparing the birthing bed and laying out dry towels and warmed water for cleaning. Mary saw to the children by both seeing to their needs and playing with them both inside the house and in the garden. John let the women have full run of the house and decided that there was nothing that he could do to help as everything was already being seen to. It was better that he should carry on working at the forge alongside his brothers.

"Call me when its time," he told the women, and all agreed it was better to be dealt with in this manner. Besides, they had been through this many times before, this was nothing new to John.

The hours of the day continued to pass as John continued to work fully aware and half expecting to be called in at any time. The call finally came from Elizabeth Metcalf just after twelve noon and John immediately put down his tools and headed for the cottage.

"Good luck," said Will.

"Well done," said Eddie. "Everything will be alright."

John entered his cottage and could instantly hear the unmistakable sounds of Amelia's screams of child delivery from upstairs. Mary had taken the children next door thinking it a better place to be at such a moment and less crowded. Moments later, the familiar sound of screaming followed by the wails of a baby signalled to John that it was all over and another baby was brought into his household. The usual time of cleaning up was had before John was allowed to go up and see his wife and new baby.

"We have a boy," said Amelia, who was cradling her new infant son in her arms. John sat down beside her on the bed to take a look at his new son for the first time. He smiled at first sight.

"He looks like the other Alfred too," he said.

Amelia smiled. "They all look alike as new-borns. They would do, they're all brothers and sisters."

Elizabeth Metcalf and Beth came into the room to have another look at the new arrival.

"I'll go and get Mary next door and bring the children to see their new brother," said John.

Amelia agreed, it was time that Alfred was introduced to his brothers and sister. Meanwhile, Elizabeth was given her new grandson to hold and together with Beth, the two women stood doting at the new-born. Shortly after, the children came up with Mary and their father. Alfred was of course greeted warmly by his siblings and questions were asked like all curious children. "Where did he come from and was he a gift from God?"

Amelia answered. "He is a gift from God and he looks like you all did when you were babies."

Life began to return back to normal except for the sleepless nights usually experienced, and the fatigue that accompanies it. Amelia seemed to cope well at first, she was an experienced mother after all and this was her sixth born child. But a week passed and she began to feel more fatigued and unwell. At first, she began to run a slight fever and had stomach cramps. John thought it wise to fetch the local doctor George Denmark to look at her. He checked her over and diagnosed influenza, giving her a tonic to take and advised complete rest. Mary helped with the children while Amelia was unwell, only bringing Alfred to his mother for feeds. But as time wore on, Amelia's condition worsened. She was given hot milk to keep up her strength which she found hard to keep down and she found little desire to get out of bed. John became anxious and sensed that there was more to Amelia's condition than influenza. Mary continued to care for the children and could see the worry written all over John's face. Days later, the doctor was fetched once again, this time he took more time to examine her. He returned downstairs to speak to John.

221

"She says that she hasn't had a sore throat or running nose just a fever and feeling of sickness and fatigue?" the doctor asked.

"That's correct, she gets stomach pains and sleeps a lot," said John.

The doctor paused for a moment.

"I fear it could be more than influenza. It could be that she has blood poisoning or infection caused by the childbirth."

John's heart sank, knowing the danger that his wife could now be in.

"Can you do anything for her?" he asked. "Is there anything you can give her?"

"I can give her a tonic for now, but if she gets worse and is in pain then I can give her some laudanum, but that is only if she is in pain. I'm afraid that things are not well, it could go either way. She could recover with her own strength of body and mind or I'm afraid we could lose her. It's in God's hands now, I'm sorry I can't do more."

John thanked the doctor for all he had done and paid him for his time and medicine before showing him out of the house. After informing Mary, quietly out of earshot of the children, John returned upstairs to be with his wife. He held her hand for an hour as she slept, though said nothing at all. Leaving the children in the care of Mary, he left his house and headed for the church, whereupon he prayed for his wife's survival. Another hour had passed till John returned home and together with Ed and Mary, he fed the children and saw them tucked away for a night's sleep, finally sitting down at the table to talk things over properly with his brother and sister in law.

"What'll I do if I lose her?"

"Just pray John and maybe you won't lose her," said Eddie. "Though God forbid if the worst does happen, you've got us to help. Talk to Amelia and tell her to find the strength to live, for the sake of the children."

"I can't lose her, I just can't!" said John, burying his face in his hands.

Mary and Eddie stayed for as long as they could to support John but as the night drew in, they eventually had to leave for the bed of their own home. John spent the night awake in a chair beside his wife as she slept, contemplating of the possible events to come. The baby cried in the night, briefly disturbing Amelia who was always there to feed her infant. In the morning, the children came in to see their mother who woke on hearing their voices.

"Do you feel well now, Ma?" asked little Millie.

Amelia smiled. "All the better for seeing you my love," she answered.

Millie laid her head on her mother's lap. Little Henry climbed onto the bed and cuddled his mother whilst Freddie held Amelia's hand. She kissed all of them one by one but said nothing, knowing herself how ill she was but not wanting to cause neither worry or alarm to her children. Alfred woke from within his cradle and Amelia fed her baby whilst the children returned downstairs to John who had prepared the children a breakfast of warmed milk and toast. After seeing to the children's needs, John brought up some breakfast to Amelia who tried to eat but felt much too poorly to manage much.

"Please try," said John. "You've got to keep your strength up."

Amelia took John's hand.

"If anything should happen to me, please promise me you'll care for the children. Marry again, and quickly if you have to, for the children will need a mother."

A tear began to roll down John's face.

"Please live, I can't live without you. I love you, please live."

He kissed her hand, her face and her lips as his tears moistened the cheeks upon her face. She tried again to eat and drank some of the milk before settling down to sleep again. From then on Amelia seldom woke, and when Alfred cried for his mother's breast, he was given watered down cow's milk instead.

The days passed slowly, and together Mary, Elizabeth Metcalf and John cared for the children as Amelia lay in a state of delirium. There were spells of her shivering with cold, followed by sweating through over-heating. John tried to give her fluids to drink but by now Amelia was hardly aware of any events around her. Eventually, one morning, word was sent to Billy Metcalf that their daughter was now gravely ill. The Metcalf's immediately came to be by her side. By now the children had already sensed that all was not well as seldom were there so many visitors at the house at one time. Billy and Elizabeth talked to John on the seriousness of the situation while Beth played with the children outside, and Mary saw to the needs of Alfred. The day drifted into night and with help from the family, the children were once more put to bed, but this time Billy and Elizabeth stayed to be with their daughter. Beth and Simon were told to go home; their parents saw no need for their children to suffer the mental agony of watching their sibling's possible end.

It was a little after midnight that Amelia's breaths seemed to get shorter and shorter, slowly and eventually, to the dismay of all… she breathed her last. John grabbed Amelia's hand and kissed it in the same tender way that he always had in her life. Tears flooded down his face. Billy Metcalf stood motionless in the back of the room while his wife Elizabeth, sobbed on the lap of her dead daughter. It was nearly an hour before the three were able to find the strength and courage to cover the bed sheet over Amelia's lifeless face and return downstairs into the parlour.

"I've got to tell the children in the morning," said John. "They'll want to see her one more time before she's taken away."

"We'll stay here with you. You'll need some support for that. Can't leave you to face that one alone," said Billy. "I'm just going home to tell Beth, but I'll be straight back," he added.

Billy just needed to be alone for a moment, and the walk back to his cottage was all the time he needed. He cried all the way there.

Dawn broke, and John went next door to tell Eddie and Mary of Amelia's loss. After the initial tears and condolences wished, he returned back home knowing that the children would rise at any time. In the meantime, Elizabeth fed Alfred some milk upon his cries for his mother. John was thankful that Alfred was too young to know just what was going on around him, but soon after, the children rose, having heard their little brother's cries and the voices of the adults from down below in the living room.

By now Mary had come into the house to lend any support she could. She warmed up some milk and toasted some bread for the children before their father would sit them down and inform them of their mother's loss. Freddie and Millie already sensed something had happened, they could see the redness in their father's eyes from the tears that had flowed. Only little Henry seemed unaware of the grief within the room and would only have hazy memories of this day for the rest of his life.

"What's the matter, Daddy?" Millie asked.

John sat the children down together at the table.

"Now children, I need you all to be very strong," said John. "A terrible, terrible thing has happened and we've all got to show enough strength to get through this… Your mother has died and gone to heaven, but we've still got each other. I'm sorry I don't know how else to tell you."

Their eyes glistened and tears flowed. At first, tears came from the elder two children, followed by Henry who almost needed prompting into tears as the confusion of the loss took time to sink in, but his tears did come.

Then, tears welled up in the eyes of the adults as their hearts were broken by the sight of the children crying for their lost mother. Billy and Elizabeth Metcalf, Eddie and Mary Allen and of course, John, who would never want to witness such an event ever again in their lives. Shortly after, the children were taken up to see Amelia for the last time. They sobbed at the sight of her, and Henry grabbed her hand.

"She's cold, Daddy" he said.

John guided the children back out of the room and covered Amelia's face once more to await the visit from the undertaker, who he would have to see later that day. News of Amelia's loss soon spread around Sprowston and visits from friends and wishes of condolence were made for the rest of that day.

Chapter Forty

Never was there to be a harder task in John's life than having to escort his children to the church service of their mother's laying to rest. It was only with the strength and support of the family around him that he found the ability to get through the whole torrid affair. Henry Banfather had commented on how John and the children had been dealt a cruel blow and that God had chosen to take Amelia for reasons unknown to mortal man, but for perfectly logical reasons known to him. To Henry Banfather, this was God working in mysterious ways and there was no reason to question his motives. There were, however, some amongst the mourners who quietly, did indeed question the motives of a so-called loving God.

After the service and the internment, a few close family members returned back to John's cottage for a family gathering in an attempt to support John and the children in any way they could. Billy and Elizabeth Metcalf had, along with their surviving offspring Simon and Beth, decided to join John's family, Thomas and Sarah Walker, his brothers, Will and Eddie and his wife, Mary. Edmond also came along with Molly to pay their respects, and try to give comfort to John and the children. The women saw to the needs of gathered family by preparing food and drink, and caring for the children, who at this time in their lives would always have the memory of this day etched deep in their minds.

How many times can a person give deepest sympathy to a bereaved loved one? "If there's anything we can do to help in any way, you just have to ask," was said to John more times than he could count that day. His reply to his friends and family's kindness and obvious concern was that he wanted to keep the children close by him while he worked, and that Mary would be there to help with the children, especially with Alfred. In the days that followed, however, he would sit alone in the house at night after the children had been put to bed, milling within his mind just how he would now cope without Amelia. Many of the family now thought it best to just leave John alone to work out for himself where his life would go and not ask of his plans for the future. It was best for a time of healing and all issues could wait until the time was right. Sarah, however, wasn't going to let her troubled son get through this on his own, she had every intention to talk to John but would just bide her time until she knew when it was right to approach him.

John did exactly as he had said he would do and kept the children with him at all times. While he was working at the forge, the children would play out in the yard or on the meadow, with playtime briefly broken when they would be called in and fed by Mary, who was always there for them. On the occasions that John would perform his parish duties, he would always bring the children along to the church. Henry Banfather was always pleased to see them and took it upon himself to volunteer his services and time to continue with their education. Three hours a week were spent at the vicarage teaching the children reading and writing. Something John thought most important and that Amelia would have done had she been there. Henry could see the need and the desire by John to continue his children's education and was more than happy to help John in the only way he could.

One Saturday afternoon, John was required at the church to help Henry Banfather with a wedding service for a local couple, that of Robert Neave and his sweetheart, Imelda Lockwood. He had brought the children along with him as was now his routine, though baby Alfred was left at home with Mary. The wedding service was a usual affair consisting of a church full of family and friends joyously celebrating the joining of the couple, then to be followed by a few ales served at the Blue Boar Inn. Soon after, with the service performed and the wedding guests making their way to the inn, Henry Banfather bid his goodbyes to John and the children and returned home to the vicarage. The prayer and hymn books were cleared and the church was swept while the children played out in the churchyard. With the work done, John closed the church doors behind him and beckoned the children to join him for their short journey back home. In the distance, the sounds of men shouting and dogs barking could be heard getting ever closer. John looked towards the direction of the sounds to see two men heading towards them on a neighbouring ploughed field following two lurcher dogs. They were in hot pursuit of a hare, which at that point was twenty or so yards ahead of the encroaching hounds. By now, the children had joined their father watching the excitement from the next-door field as it drew closer and closer to them, and in their very direction. The terrified hare finally reached a gorse bush that separated the field from the churchyard, briefly taking shelter for a second or so until the dogs reached the bush and frantically tried to force themselves in to make a grab at the animal. Panicked into exiting the bush from the other side, the hare then broke through and ran into the churchyard directly past John and the children, and directly towards the church building itself. With nowhere else to go to escape from the pursuing dogs which had by now found a gap and were trying to force their larger bodies through the gorse and into the churchyard, the hare saw a dark hole on the side of the main church building at ground level and made straight for it to shelter from the savage animals. The hare bolted into the hole, which was in fact, a broken cast iron air vent that vented the crypt situated directly under the church floor. Unknown to the watching children, the hare had entered the dark crypt with little chance of escape. The vent it had entered though at ground level outside was in fact, six feet higher than the floor of the crypt, so consequently, there was unlikely to be an exit for the poor animal. The children were, however, pleased that the hare had escaped from the dogs which were busy barking at the vents entrance. They didn't know of the hare's dilemma from within. John was fully aware but was not going to tell them so as not to upset them. The event seemed to etch itself firmly on the memory of young Freddie. Unknown to him, the very memory of that event in his childhood would one day resurface again in his adult life.

The following Monday, John returned to his work in the workshop with his brothers, while the children played out in the yard. Will, as usual dealt with the horse trade while Eddie and John constructed a full set of cartwheels for Ben Walker who had just taken to renting the smallholding of Mousehold Farm. Mary, as usual, looked after baby Alfred and housework in both of the adjoining cottages. Soon after, the brother's mid-morning break John heard voices coming from outside in the yard but paid little attention knowing that the children were out there playing. But then, his attention focused on the sounds as he heard the unmistakable voice of his mother Sarah as she acknowledged the children's greetings.

"Father! Granny's here!" shouted Freddie.

Sarah entered the workshop to find her three eldest sons all hard at work, all of whom greeted her warmly.

"Hello, Mother, come for a visit?" said John.

"I have," she replied. "Just a mother's worry for her children, can't get out of old habits. I'll keep coming till I know that you and the children are coping alright."

"Let's go into the cottage," said John. "I'll make some tea."

John led Sarah into the cottage and the children followed, they were always pleased to see Granny.

"Now, I hope you children are all being good for your father, and to Mary and Eddie," said Sarah. "Times are hard right now so you've all got to be good for each other."

"We are," said Millie.

Little Henry silently nodded, not fully understanding his grandmother's meaning.

"Where's your baby brother?"

"He's next door with Aunt Mary," replied Freddie.

Meanwhile, John hung the cast iron kettle over the fire which he had stoked, just saving it from dying out and prepared a pot of tea to be filled when the kettle boiled.

"Now, John, I've come to check on you because I'm worried about you and the children. I need to know that you'll all be alright."

"We're all fine," said Millie.

This caused a smile from John, which pleased Sarah. John had hardly smiled at all since Amelia's passing.

"I'm glad to hear it my dear," Sarah replied.

"We're coping," said John. "Mary looks after the little-uns during the day and Amelia's mother comes here regularly to see 'em. The parson's teaching 'em to read like Amelia did and I teach 'em sometimes in the evenings when I've got time, just now and then mind."

John returned into the kitchen to see to the kettle which was now boiling. Young Henry was now getting restless, all he wanted to do was return to his game outside in the yard. So Freddie and Millie took him back out to return to playing. It was lovely to see their grandmother but nothing beats a good game out in the yard. Sarah was quietly relieved though, because she could now speak to her son alone as she had planned to all along. He returned into the parlour moments later with two cups of hot tea.

"Right John, now the little-uns are out of the way I need to talk to you, and you must listen hard to what I have to say… Those children need a mother and you need to find another wife, and quick at that."

John paused for a moment as he took in what his mother had just said, and why she had said it…

"That's what Amelia said I should do just before the end," he replied.

Sarah nodded. "That girl always saw sense, she had a good head on her shoulders she did. So, what are you gonna do then?"

"I don't know yet," said John. "But I do know that I need someone for the sake of the children. Amelia was right about that, but no woman is gonna marry me just like that and take on four children, it's too much to ask."

"What about Beth?"

John raised his eyebrows in surprise. "Beth?"

"Yes, Beth. She's just lost her husband and she has no children of her own. She would see the sense in caring for her sister's children. She would be perfect."

"Don't get too hasty," said John. "She might not want to get married again yet alone take on four children. It would be a huge thing for her to have to do and I wouldn't want to put such a burden upon her. No, I'll just let things be till the right

227

woman turns up who needs a husband, and who would be willing to marry me. We're still coping and that's all that matters."

"I think that she is the right woman and I think that you should think hard at what I just said, it would be good for all of you."

"Just let it be, Mum," said John. "I can't ask Amelia's sister."

"I don't see why not, and there's no time to let it be," said Sarah.

Coincidently and unknown to both Sarah and John, the very subject of a union between Beth and John had already been talked of just the evening before. In a cottage just up the very same road which housed the Metcalf family. The very subject had been on the lips of both Billy and Elizabeth Metcalf whilst sitting at the dinner table, and in the presence of Beth.

"I fear for John and the children," said Elizabeth. "He can't manage to look after the little-uns, and work at the forge and the church. It's too much for any man."

"Assa woman's job to look after little-uns. You can't expect a man to do it, his job is to work and provide," said Billy.

Then there was a brief silence as both Billy and Elizabeth looked at Beth in a very funny way. A way she had never seen them look at her before.

"What?" said Beth. "What are you looking at me like that for?"

"You... you would be the right one," said Elizabeth. "John needs a wife and quickly at that. The children... Amelia's children... they need a mother."

"Yeah, and you need a husband," said Billy.

"You two have been talking, making plans, haven't you?"

"We may have had a quiet word," said Billy.

"Well you shouldn't have," said Beth. "Me needing a husband or John needing a wife doesn't mean we should get together. He's Amelia's husband and you two should put that idea out of your heads. He's been coping fine up to now."

"Coping's not living!" replied Elizabeth, who always liked to have the last word in an argument.

Though the idea had now been suggested by both parents and shrugged off by them both, the thought had now been implanted in the heads of both John and Beth. Neither one had thought deep affection of the other previously but they both mourned Amelia and felt great pain at her loss. However, the idea had now been suggested by both families and despite how uncomfortable they both felt, there did seem to be a kind of logic behind the idea.

It was at least a week before Beth felt comfortable enough to go and visit John and the children after what had been suggested by her parents. John had also felt uneasy as what had been suggested by his mother despite the logic of its content. But Beth still felt that polite visits were still necessary, they were her sister's family after all and she was still concerned for their well-being none the less. So, just after Sunday service at church, Beth told John that she would pay them all a visit accompanied by her parents and possibly with Simon, should he happen to turn up. She kept her promise and paid John a visit in the early afternoon, in the company of her mother. Billy Metcalf would have come too had he not have fallen asleep in his favourite armchair after his Sunday lunch. Simon failed to turn up too, like father like son, he too was asleep.

On arrival, the children were as usual playing out in the yard and adjoining meadow whilst John sat inside caring for baby Alfred. It was only fitting that his sister in law, Mary, should have some time off from childcare at least one day a week. John immediately got up and made some tea for his guests while the two women stood over the cradle watching Alfred as he lay peacefully sleeping. The sight of a baby at peace always brings a smile to a woman's face, especially of the family who is maternal by nature.

"How are things, John?" asked Beth.

"We're coping. We have a routine that we all live with and we're surviving."

"Have you thought about the future?" asked Elizabeth.

"How do you mean?"

"Are you gonna find another wife? These children are gonna need a mother to care for 'em while you're working."

"Mother, be quiet," snapped Beth.

"No, it has to be said, we've got the little-uns to think about," said Elizabeth. "John needs a wife and quickly."

"You sound just like my mother," said John.

"Then she can see sense too. What are you gonna do?" she asked.

"Keep surviving until a woman turns up who would want to take on another's children and it would have to be one that I would want to marry too."

"What about Beth?"

"Mother, shut up!" snarled Beth.

"Well, it has to be said!" shouted Elizabeth.

"You *have* been talking to my mother, haven't you? She said that very thing herself the other day!" said John, clearly taken aback by Elizabeth's remarks.

"No, I haven't seen Sarah, but it sounds like you two are the only ones who can't see the sense in it."

"Mother, that's enough!" shouted Beth. "I'm sorry John, this is her doing, and my father too. I have said nothing and I have nothing to do with any of this."

"It's alright, I know you haven't done this," replied John. "They're all trying to play match-maker that's all."

"We've only got you and the little-uns interests at heart," said Elizabeth. "We're all worried about yer. This is not the time to get sentimental or lovesick, it's time to think hard about the little-uns and their survival. John, you've lost your wife and the mother of your children, and Beth, you've lost your husband and your home and you've no children. It makes sense what you both have to do. Think about it, look at each other and think hard. Could you live with each other as man and wife? If you're not in love now, you could learn to love each other in time. The fact is a man has his role in life and a woman has hers. Beth, you could have a place to live and a man to support you as well as being a mother and part of something good. John, you could have a wife and a mother to your children again and Beth even looks like Amelia a bit.

The last comment of Elizabeth's speech caused a slight smile from both John and Beth despite its serious intent.

"Right!" said Elizabeth. "Neither of you is gonna listen to me or Sarah, so the best thing to do is leave you both alone to talk this over without an old-un like me interfering. But both of you think hard about the facts before you dismiss all what I have just said."

And with that, Elizabeth drank up her tea, rose and left the cottage to leave John and Beth inside with only Alfred to keep them company, and he was asleep.

"I'm sorry this had to happen," said John, "but I can see that their intentions are good."

"So can I, but I don't need pushing into anything," replied Beth.

"I have to say the thought had only crossed my mind for a short moment before, but when my mother came and spoke to me of it I thought more of it."

"I didn't think of it until my mother and father said of it, but now it's stuck in my head" said Beth.

Then both she and John began to laugh.

As the pair talked, John seemed to look at Beth in a completely different way than he had before. He began to notice her mannerisms and studied her physical form more than he had done previously. He noticed the way she talked had slight similarities to Amelia's ways as well as her resemblance as a sister which was always apparent. Unknown to him, Beth was looking at him differently too.

"Tell me, why didn't you and David have children? You must have tried."

Beth sighed. "David was not a passionate man. We did have man and woman relations at first, but without any children coming along. It wasn't long before he seemed to lose interest. He would come home from work tired sometimes but more often he would go out after work and then come home worse for the ales. In time, I found that I wasn't all that interested in him in that way so it didn't seem to matter anymore."

"You didn't want to leave him?"

"No, why should I? He wasn't a bad man, he didn't hit me or anything, we had a home and there was food on the table. I was married to him so that was my life. I'm sure that if he had wanted children badly enough, he would have tried harder."

"Did you want children?"

"Yes, I would have loved a child of my own, but you can't always get what you wish for. I had chosen David as my husband and so I had to live with the consequences of that decision."

"Would you like to have a husband and a family still?"

"Yes."

"Do you think you could care for Amelia's children?" asked John.

"Yes," replied Beth.

"Then could you marry me?"

"Yes, I think that I could for everyone's sake," replied Beth.

"In that case, I'm asking you now, will you marry me?"

Beth paused…"Yes… I will."

John took Beth's hand and kissed it in the same tender way that he always had with Amelia. Then the pair embraced and kissed, though the feeling was a strange one for them both. Neither had courted or fallen in love, they had just made the decision to pair, out of necessity. These were two lonely people who had just suffered great loss in their lives and saw a necessity and urgency to join together, as well as their need of companionship. But though strange the feeling was of their first kiss, there was still a feeling of warmth and tenderness none the less. Maybe this was the right thing to do after all.

John called the children in from the garden and told them of the news of how Beth was to become their new mother. Their response was muted at first as it was hard for ones so young to know exactly how to react, but eventually, there were small smiles of acceptance. Then Eddie and Mary were told, as was Will. All were somewhat relieved, this seemed an answer to everyone's wishes in these hard and emotionally strained times. Beth then returned with John to Billy and Elizabeth Metcalf's cottage to inform them of the news.

The following day, John visited Henry Banfather at the rectory to book a date for the forthcoming wedding which was to be held as soon as possible. Henry and his wife were delighted, they too had real concern for the plight of John and his family. Maybe at last, this was the end of tragic times for the family. Before returning back home and to continue an afternoon's work at the smithy, John paid a visit to his mother's cottage. Sarah was delighted, maybe now her son could have contentment back in his life.

On the 12th July 1835, just three months after his proposal, John married Beth at the church after Sunday service, friends and family all attended. Henry Banfather could scarcely recollect a marriage that had brought so much delight and relief as the one he had just performed. He was equally pleased himself to see his friend and colleague recover from his time of tragedy.

Chapter Forty-One

Being thrown into the role of mother-hood is a daunting experience for any woman, but being thrown into the role of mother for four children, including a four-month old baby, must be beyond comprehension. Beth, however, through sheer necessity, rolled her sleeves up and got on with it. If no one had respected her before, they were sure to now, as she was a credit to both herself and her lost sister Amelia. She became a more familiar face to the children once her betrothal had been announced and soon began sharing the role of caring for Alfred with Mary whenever she had spare time to herself. She had never thought for one minute that things were going to be easy so she worked hard at the role at every time spent with John and the children. Once married, she had prepared herself for a life of toil but with the stability of a home life, she never had expected any more than that. What she got in return was all of the above and more, as a time of self-discovery, cherished moments, love and tragedy were all to engulf her life.

***

"Can Beth tell us a story?" asked Millie, as she lay in bed alongside her siblings at dusk on a summers evening.

John looked at Beth. "Amelia used to tell them the story of the hunter in the forest who came across a giant bear with a thorn in its foot," said John.

"I know that one," said Beth. "Mother used to tell it to me, Amelia and Simon when we were children. Did she ever tell the one about the pretty girl who had left her village to take a basket of apples and bread to her grandmother who lived in the next village on the other side of the woods?"

The children shook their heads.

"She followed the path through the woods which led to her grandmother's village, whereupon half way through she found lying at the side of the path a leather purse dropped by some earlier traveller. She picked up the purse and looked inside. To her great surprise, she found that the purse contained five gold coins and a gold ring. She looked to see if anyone was around looking for the valuable purse that had obviously been lost. There was no one there, so she put the purse in her basket and continued her journey, eventually reaching her grandmother's house to give her the apples and bread which was a gift from her mother.

"Thank you, my dear," said her grandmother. "You are the second visitor I have had today. A young man who looked like a rich lord came by earlier in great distress having lost a purse containing gold coins and a ring which once belonged to his dearly departed mother."

"Where did the man go?" asked the pretty girl. "For I have found such a purse on the side of the path leading through the woods."

"He said that he would return on his white horse within the hour. His great hall was but two miles away," replied her grandmother.

The girl waited for an hour but the man didn't show.

"Grandma," said the girl. "If the man should return, tell him I travel through the woods and I have found his lost purse."

Her grandmother gave her a farewell kiss and the pretty girl set off on her journey home. Halfway through the woods, at nearly the spot where she had found the purse, she heard the sound of a horse trotting behind her. She looked back and there was a dashing, handsome young man in fine clothes, riding upon a white stallion.

"Hey!" shouted the young man. "Are you the girl who has found a lost purse and has a grandmother who lives on the other side of the wood?"

"That I would," replied the girl, who was quite taken aback at just how fine and handsome the young man was. "Is this your missing purse?" she asked.

The man smiled. "Yes that's the one," and took the purse from the girl. He opened the purse, and found the five gold coins and the gold ring.

"My mother always said that her ring would one day bring me happiness and contentment, because she wished it so. She told me to find and marry an honest girl so her wish would come true. All of my life, I have searched for a girl to be my wife and wear the ring of my lost mother. You are an honest and pretty girl who has returned my mother's lost ring, so now I ask you, would you be my wife?"

The pretty girl agreed and the man put his mother's ring onto her finger, it was a perfect fit. Together, the handsome young man and the pretty girl lived happily from that day on, just as his mother had said so."

The children smiled, this was a new bedtime story they had never heard.

"I can't remember Amelia ever telling that story to them," said John.

"She wouldn't have," said Beth. "I just made it up."

"Did you?" asked the children.

Beth just smiled. "Good night, you lot, sleep tight," and she left the room hand in hand with John. Soon after, the children were all fast asleep. An hour later, John and Beth retired to bed as well. Baby Alfred was already sound asleep in his cradle and so could not hear the sounds of John and Beth making love in the bed beside him. To John, this was a pleasure to make love to a new wife who so resembled his last and who he found that he was drawing closer and closer to. To Beth, this was love making as she had never known before and had never had the passion for before. To both, it was felt as if it was meant to be despite the memory of Amelia, who was now gone but never out of their thoughts. John kissed her on her lips and then down to her neck. She tingled with pleasure as he worked down to her breasts which in turn stiffened and gave goosebumps all over her body. She parted her legs to allow John to rub his leg upon her most sensitive areas. He was now fully aroused and soon entered her. The pair made love and writhed in a way that Beth had never experienced before. Shortly after, the pair let go both having experienced complete fulfilment. They lay together exhausted, though nothing was said. For a while they just lay hand in hand staring at the soft illumination of the candlelight. Soon, John found it hard to keep his eyes open and like so many men after lovemaking, he was spent. Fatigue soon set in sending him drifting off into a deep sleep. Beth, however, lay awake, her mind in deep contemplation as the realisation had come to her, a feeling of belonging and pleasure as she had never known before. A feeling to need someone and to be needed. Her first husband, David Lock, had never made love to her in that way before and she had never had the desire to make love to him that way, it was all just a duty. For John, it was different, he already had the experience of a happily married man, and he knew how to make love and pleasure a woman. He and Amelia had always enjoyed a healthy sex life ever since their first time at the Angel inn on that snowy day. There was a realisation in Beth that despite the hard work with the children, they needed and cared for her. John also cared and needed her and she needed him, now that she had finally realised that she loved him. This new life was for her and she had no desire to be anywhere else. What both Elizabeth Metcalf and Sarah Walker had predicted had happened. In the course of time, John and Beth had grown to love one another as man and wife, and not out of necessity.

***

Beth continued to enjoy her new role in life and the children grew to accept her as their new mother. There is closeness between Beth and Millie who seemed to have eased into the role of mother and daughter almost without trying. Beth sees Amelia in Millie's eyes and recalls the similar ways in Millie's manor of Amelia when she was a young girl.

The cycle of another year passes and John puts together another harvest festival celebration to be followed by the celebrations of November 5th, Christmas and the new year of 1836. John's life is back to its usual busy routine of parish and business duties to perform, and life seems to have returned almost as it was before. Just three days before the Good Friday celebrations, baby Alfred took his first steps to everyone's great pleasure. Now in the warmth of spring, he could play out in the garden and the meadow with his elder siblings under the watchful eye of Beth, and Mary, of course. John played his usual part at church in the Easter Sunday celebrations of which all the family and most of the village attended and enjoyed as a very special day. The day ended more special than John had ever known an Easter Sunday to be before, for as John and Beth finally retired to bed at the end of the day, Beth uttered the words, "I'm pregnant," to John's obvious delight. To her great joy, she was expecting her first baby and, together with John, was eager to tell everyone the great news, especially the children. The following morning, the news was broken to them and they were indeed overjoyed, especially Millie. With a new child on the way, Beth could now feel a real part of the family and not just a new addition.

It was just two months after the announcement in early June. The days had become long again and the weather fine once more. John and Beth would spend the early evenings sitting out in the garden as the sun lowered and the children played their last hours of the day, before being put to bed as the dusk settled to a golden illumination once more behind the distant trees. The calmness of these days was eventually broken when baby Alfred developed a summer cold. It is a very uncomfortable time when any child takes ill but with a one-year-old infant, this is particularly difficult especially at night. The memory of how Alfred's lost sister Charlotte had succumbed to a chill four years earlier had made everyone fully aware of the dangers. The beginning of his illness saw a tired and grizzly little man which was followed by a sneezy and snuffly little fellow. Then, at what is usually the final stage of a cold, was the irritating cough. Alfred's cradle was in its usual place beside John and Beth's bed. Beth constantly saw to Alfred, both at night and day by trying to reposition him, sitting him upright to ease the irritation and by giving him warmed milk and water to keep him hydrated. However, like a curse that always seemed destined to befall upon John, their worst fears came to pass. Alfred's cough developed into a whooping cough. The sound of Alfred's distress resonated all around the house keeping his parents awake with worry and fatigued with stress by day.

"Will he be alright?" asked his young siblings, who shared their parents concern on hearing the distressing sounds of the whooping cough. Neither John nor Beth could give any assurances as to Alfred's well-being, fearing that the worst may happen. On the third night of Alfred's suffering, John and Beth's worst fears proved to be justified when Alfred slumped in Beth's arms, having suffered another bout of coughing from which he never recovered. He died within four minutes of losing consciousness. The sound of howls and cries of his distraught family filled the house. Another beautiful child was lost, and to add to the tragedy, the very same child who had lost his mother at birth only a year earlier. Only the five-year-old Henry was oblivious to the tragedy when it happened. He had slept through the whole thing and only cried in the morning once he had been told of the tragedy. Once again, John had to see Henry Banfather to arrange a time for a funeral. The parson could hardly believe yet another tragedy had befallen his friend.

Two days later, close family assembled at the church to see Henry Banfather conduct yet another funeral service. They witnessed a little casket containing Alfred Mathias Allen be laid to rest within the same resting place as his grandfather, Jacob, sister, Charlotte and brother, Alfred John, and next to his mother, Amelia. John held steady trying to support his inconsolable wife Beth whilst his mother Sarah kept the children with her. She quietly wondered if her son really did have a curse upon him and what more could possibly happen?

Chapter Forty-Two

The harvest festival arrives again and is celebrated in its usual way within the church walls. However, away from the church, there is a change from the usual celebrations, instead of each individual farm holding a small get together as was tradition, this year, the parish clerk organises an event on his own meadow. This celebration is much the same format as the small individual farm parties, of which food and ale is supplied, but this year it has become a much larger village event. John has organised a local fiddle player and singer for entertainment. It is funded by the landowners and farmers who find this larger communal event much more to their liking as their individual costs are lower. Comparisons are made to the old Magdalen Fair that had been annually held within the village and was organised by John, but sadly, was no more. Food was laid on, and as tradition, the children were given priority at the food tables which was dealt with by their mothers and other women of the village. The local men, of all farm related trades and the farmworkers themselves, enjoy their time at the ale stall which was laid on as usual by the landlord of the Blue Boar Inn, Thomas Olyott. He had taken over the pub some six years earlier from Henry Cappendell. At the stall, Thomas Walker and his work colleagues from Manor Farm enjoy the ales while his wife, Sarah, is kept busy helping the rest of the women see that the children were fed. Of course, Sarah makes time to spend with John and his children and his expectant wife. Overall the day goes well and everyone leaves in a happy mood. Many reminisced with John of the good old days of the Magdalen Fair, but most agree that this new local celebration feels more enjoyable in its community spirit, as it was less open to outsiders.

It seemed that no sooner one celebration was over than another came to pass. Autumn had set in and very soon after, the November 5th event arrived. This time John organised the event to be at its usual place on Robert Welton's field. Thomas and Sarah Walker made their annual appearance as Sarah would seldom miss an event organised by her son. She stayed with Beth and helped to look after the children while John performed his civic duties running the whole event. Again, Sarah thought of times gone by, as she always did on that very night, when she, as a young woman, had gone into labour to give birth to John early the following morning. She thought back to the time when Amelia was still alive and was also expecting her first child on the November 5th celebrations, though sadly the outcome of their first-born was to be short lived. Now, once again, another baby was on its way during the same celebrations. To Sarah this always seemed to be a special night of reflections of happy times gone by and happy ones to come, despite the tragedies that seemed to have fallen upon John in recent years.

Christmas came, and then the new year of 1837 came to being. This was a year that John and Beth hoped would be a time of happiness and new beginnings. However, by now, the baby was overdue and a concern began to edge into John's mind, a feeling that something bad could possibly happen if it didn't hurry up and arrive. It was a week into the New Year on a Sunday morning when John rose to begin his usual duties at the church. Beth rose to prepare breakfast of warmed milk and toast. All seemed well enough, though Beth was quieter than normal. John wondered if anything was wrong but said nothing. Together they all left for church, though it was earlier than usual for Beth and the children who would usually join John at the church later. With Beth so heavily pregnant, it was thought best that the family should all remain together in case of emergencies. John tolled the bell to summon the local worshippers who arrived not long after, and Henry Banfather conducted his usual Sunday service, though no babies were christened on this particular service. The usual greetings were had for John and the family from Thomas, Sarah, and Edmond and his family. After the social gathering, everyone returned home for lunch and a restful Sunday afternoon.

Beth had prepared a lunch of stew and dumplings, which everyone enjoyed, though John still noticed how quiet Beth still seemed. Everyone stayed indoors, close to the warm fire as it was a cold January day outside. John read a book and Beth repaired worn clothing with needle and thread. The children played games and drew pictures in chalk upon slate boards. The evening drew in early as was the time of year and by seven the children were put to the warmth of their beds. At last, with the children tucked away upstairs, John was finally alone with Beth and was finally able to ask her what was troubling her.

"What's wrong?" he asked. "You've not been yourself, you've been quiet and distant all day."

"I'm worried," replied Beth. "I haven't felt the baby move all day, in fact I haven't felt it move since last night."

John looked at Beth and a feeling of gloom came over him, but he tried to keep his feelings hidden, it was his job to reassure his wife and try to keep her from her worrying.

"I'm sure the baby's going to be alright," he replied. "I remember Amelia sometimes worried if her babies had a quiet day but they all eventually moved in the end. I expect this one's having a rest before it makes its long awaited appearance."

Beth tried to smile but nodded instead. She hoped John was right, but until the baby moved again she would continue to worry for its well-being. This baby was due at any time which increased her concern. John, however, tried to hide his anxiety for Beth's sake, after all the ill fortune that had befallen him he knew all too well that the worst could happen at any time.

Monday came, and then Tuesday, and still there was no movement from the baby so the decision was made to call on Dorothea Woodhouse for her opinion. She arrived promptly upon John's fetching and was led upstairs to Beth who was waiting in the bedroom. Straight away she put her ear to Beth's swelled maternal bump. She felt around the bump, prodding and feeling the baby's position with her palms. There was silence as she examined, then she lifted her head and looked to John, there was a serious expression upon her face.

"I'm sorry I can't find any movement and I can't hear anything. I fear your baby could be gone."

Beth began to cry, she had known all along that things weren't right. John held her tight to him and she wept upon his shoulder.

"I'll let you two be on your own for a minute or two but I have to talk to you after," said Dorothea.

John nodded, still trying to console his wife. Dorothea left the room and came downstairs into the parlour where Mary was sitting with the children. Mary instinctively knew all was not well by the expression on Dorothea's face. Freddie and Millie also sensed that something was amiss. Mary looked to Dorothea but asked nothing, Dorothea just shook her head in a silent answer. Mary knew not to press Dorothea for any more information, not in front of the children.

"Come on you three," said Mary. "We're going next door to my house while your mother and father talk to Mrs Woodhouse."

"I don't want to go," said little Henry, but Millie grabbed his hand and led him out of the cottage with Mary and Freddie. A few moments later, John and Beth came down into the parlour to talk to Dorothea as to what to do next.

"Are you alright my dear?" Dorothea asked. "I'm sorry to have to give you that kind of news."

Beth nodded but was too overcome with grief to be able to reply.

"You say that you've felt no movement since Saturday evening?"

Again, Beth nodded but said nothing.

"Well if the baby is lost and has been since Saturday night or Sunday morning, I would have expected it to come by now. What we'll have to do is wait I'm afraid. We'll wait another day and if still nothing happens, then we'll call the doctor and see what he says."

John and Beth agreed, still hanging on to a glimmer of hope that their baby was still alive and was not detected by Dorothea Woodhouse on her examination. After Dorothea had left, John and Beth made the decision not to tell the children what was happening, they had seen enough tragedy in their all too short lives and there was no harm for this news to be kept from them.

Another twenty-four hours passed and there was still no sign of childbirth, though Beth was feeling very uncomfortable, more through stress and anxiety she thought. The doctor was called in and an immediate examination was held. Once again Beth had her maternal bump prodded and felt and a cylindrical stethoscope made of wood was used. The doctor listened and put his stethoscope down.

"I'm afraid I can't hear anything; I think your baby's lost."

Beth's eyes glistened as tears formed but this time she tried to keep composed.

"What do we do now?" asked John.

"Wait," said Dr George Denmark. "It's been known for a woman to hold on to a dead baby for up to ten days from the death to when she finally passes it. If we wait a few more days, I'm sure it will pass. If it doesn't, then maybe it will be as well if you come with me to the hospital to help encourage it out. I'm sure that won't happen though."

John and Beth reluctantly agreed, and with that, the doctor took his leave and was bid farewell by the couple. The doctor's prediction proved to be right, for it was the following Saturday when Beth finally felt some kind of movement from within which indicated that something was going on. John was out in the workshop working with Eddie on some wheels, while Will was absent, he was in the city to witness another hanging from the castle gates. They were about to have their mid-morning lunch when Beth raised the alarm.

"Eddie, can you and Mary have the little-uns? I don't want them to be in the house if anything bad should happen," said John.

Eddie agreed and put down his tools to go and talk to his wife. Meanwhile, John made haste to Dorothea Woodhouse's little cottage up the road whereupon he returned with Dorothea in somewhat of a hurry. Both knew fully well the seriousness of the situation that was ahead.

"It's alright my dear, I'm here now," said Dorothea on her arrival. "Now, nature has a way of doing things on its own, so what I want you to do is pace up and down the room and try and let gravity do half the job for you. If you feel uncomfortable, then bend over and crouch for a while. What we want to do is try to move the baby into the right position to pass through. Sooner or later you'll get it right and things will start moving."

Meanwhile, John made haste to alert Beth's mother Elizabeth to the situation at hand. On hearing the news, she immediately returned back with John to be at her daughter's side. Billy Metcalf wasn't home, he was out visiting an old work mate and enjoying an ale at the Black Boy's pub in Colgate, Norwich.

Dorothea was confident in her commands and Beth obeyed without any hesitation. However, deep in Dorothea's thoughts was a concern that she had kept hidden from both John and Beth. The fear that the baby would not go into the correct position, or maybe get stuck while passing through. An hour passed and then two, Beth paced up and down the bedroom as instructed between periods of rest. She crouched and bent down as Dorothea had suggested but still the baby didn't come. She could feel the pains inside her as her body tried to expel the foreign body that was within her. Her mother sat anxiously watching and giving encouragement whenever necessary and John stayed in the room also to give her much needed support. He would hold her hand as she rested before getting up and pacing the room once more.

Another hour passed until finally Beth called out. "Something's happening!"

This was time for John to leave the room and let the women do their job. He returned downstairs into the parlour where he could hear Beth's screams while Elizabeth and Dorothea gave encouragement as Beth finally gave birth to their child. Then her screams of childbirth finally ended and there was silence where usually there were the joyous cries and wails of a new-born baby. Nearly another hour had passed when finally Dorothea came downstairs carrying a pail containing the expelled placenta and cleaned up fluids in one hand and in the other, she carried a rolled blanket containing the lifeless body of their still-born child.

"Can I see the baby?" John asked.

Dorothea placed the pail on the floor and handed over the blanket containing the dead infant to John. As he held it in his arms, Dorothea then opened the blanket to reveal its contents… John stared down to see the lifeless cold body of his dead baby son. He had been dead in the womb for a while so there was no light pink complexion of a new-born baby, instead his colour was reddish purple and his lips were dark. However, John could still make out his features and the shape of his little head and he felt sure that he would have resembled his mother Beth… a tear began to roll down John's face.

"What are you gonna do with him?" he asked.

"Whatever you want me to do with him," Dorothea replied.

She often had to deal with still-born babies if their parents couldn't cope with disposing of the remains. Sometimes they would be put on a bonfire in her garden or buried deep within the garden of the parents with the birth waste. Often, the parents of the dead infant would enter the churchyard at night and bury their dead child themselves in a secluded corner somewhere, without the blessing of the local clergy. It was an unofficial way of laying to rest a dead child not christened into the house of God. Tolerated but seldom talked about.

"I'll bury him at the church myself," said John.

Dorothea nodded and left the dead infant with its father. She picked up the pail and took it outside. John followed.

"Leave the pail beside the workshop and I'll bury it in the corner of the meadow."

Dorothea put the pail down and returned into the cottage to see to Beth one more time before she was to leave to return back to her own home, her work done. John carried his dead son into the empty workshop and laid the wrapped body onto the workbench. Leaving the workshop, he locked the door behind him to prevent the children from entering. He returned to the house and climbed the stairs to the bedroom to be with his wife. On entering, Elizabeth Metcalf left the room to let John be alone with his wife. Beth lay waiting for him, she looked shattered from her ordeal. John sat upon the bed and embraced her tightly, and again she sobbed on his shoulder.

"Oh John, we had a son," she cried.

"There, there, come on my love, we'll get through this, I know we will," said John, as Beth sobbed more and more.

But John knew not what else to do or to say. How on earth do you console a mother who has lost a baby? Just try to be a shoulder to cry on and let the tears flow until they are all cried out.

Slowly she regained her composure and eventually felt able to talk to John once more.

"Where is he?" she asked.

"He's wrapped up in a blanket and locked away so the children don't find him. I'm going to make a casket for burial myself and bury him within the church grounds."

"Can I see him?"

"I don't think that would be a good idea," said John. "He's been dead for a while and didn't look good. I think it would be upsetting for you to see him like that. Best you just get well again and get your strength back. There'll be another baby to come one day, I know there will."

Beth kissed John and she rested her head upon his shoulder again and lay quietly deep in thought. Together they sat and said nothing, their minds just milling over the events that had just come into being. For a while, they sat together in deep embrace until eventually John finally let go.

"I'll make some tea, it might make you feel better," he said.

He left the room and beckoned her mother to be with her while he made the tea. She immediately re-joined her daughter and sat down beside her and held her hand. John returned ten minutes later with three cups of hot tea.

"Do you want Mary to be with you too?" John asked.

Beth nodded.

He quickly drank his tea, got up and quickly left to fetch Mary from next door. Mary came out in an instant and made straight upstairs to be with Beth. John stayed below as he thought that it was better that Beth had female companionship to help her through her ordeal. However, it was time for him to tell the children what had just happened. Next door, Freddie, Millie and young Henry were all there in the care of Eddie. They sat quietly together while John explained to them what had just happened, and that their little brother was no longer to be. There was little reaction and no tears, for young children often find it hard to shed tears for those they never knew, but there was disappointment that there was to be no new brother or sister. These were children who had endured tragedy before, to the point that they had almost grown to expect it. They just nodded their heads to what their father had to say and sat silently.

With the terrible event now explained to the children, it was decided that it would be best for them to spend the night at Eddie and Mary's cottage. After all that Beth had been through, she would need a quiet night. John returned back home to be with her once more, but no sooner had he re-entered the house, he was greeted surprisingly by Mary who had ran down the stairs in great haste.

"John! Go quickly and get Mrs Woodhouse or the doctor!" she shouted.

"Why what's happened?"

"She's bleeding, heavily. It's just started. We noticed blood appearing on the top sheets. Go quick! The doctor will be the best one to see!"

Without hesitation, John ran up the road. He would fetch Dorothea Woodhouse first as her cottage was the nearer, but Doctor Denmark lived at the other end of Sprowston nearer the city. Within a few minutes John arrived at Dorothea's cottage which was just a few doors away from the Metcalf's cottage. He banged on the door, and within a moment Dorothea answered.

"Could you come back quickly please? Beth's bleeding heavily, she needs help."

"Oh my word, I'll be there straight away," she replied. "You'd best get the doctor."

"That's where I'm now going," he replied.

Dorothea put on her shawl and made straight for John's cottage, while John headed in the opposite direction towards the doctor's house at the far end of the village. He arrived within ten minutes, and again he banged on the front door. The door was promptly opened by the doctor's wife.

"I need the doctor quickly, my wife's bleeding after childbirth!"

"He's not here, he's at the hospital. He always works there on Fridays and Saturdays."

"What'll I do?" asked John, in a state of high anxiety.

"You could try Mrs Woodhouse the midwife. I'm sure she would know what to do when this happens."

John didn't reply he just ran back in the direction of his home. As he ran, a sinking feeling was felt in the pit of his stomach. *'I can't lose her, I can't',* he thought as he ran. *'Why is this happening? What have I done? I've tried to be good. Why is this happening?'*

Soon, he was back home. Mary was downstairs while Elizabeth Metcalf was upstairs with Dorothea Woodhouse and Beth.

"How is she?" he asked.

"Still the same. Mrs Woodhouse is with her."

"I couldn't get the doctor. He's in Norwich at the hospital, his wife just told me to get Mrs Woodhouse instead… I'd better go up."

Mary nodded and John climbed the stairs. In the bedroom, Beth laid silently in bed as her mother held her hand. Dorothea was trying to clean up using a cloth and a pail of water.

"The doctor's in Norwich at the hospital, he can't come. Can you help her?" asked John.

"We can only hope the bleeding stops, it often does. That's all the doctor would do too. Just stay with her and keep her comfortable."

John sat on the bed beside his wife. Beth lay with her husband on one side and her mother on the other, both held each hand. She said nothing but she was shivering; her hands felt cold and clammy to the touch, she was in shock. More and more Dorothea mopped and cleaned the blood that was flowing from Beth, and tighter and tighter became the grip on her hands by John and Elizabeth Metcalf either side of her. She became colder and colder, and in time, seemed to drift off to sleep. Still the blood flowed, and Beth could be seen to get visibly paler in her face. Her breaths became lighter and lighter…eventually, she stopped breathing… she was gone.

Elizabeth Metcalf buried her head onto the chest of her lost daughter and sobbed. John buried his face into his hands and tears dripped through his fingers. Another wife was lost, another who he had loved. Another tragedy had befallen him. Where was it all to end?

Chapter Forty-Three

On a snowy winter's day in early February, the family gathered to the church for the laying to rest of Beth Allen and her baby son. Their final resting place was to be within the same burial plot as Amelia. At the service, conducted by Henry Banfather, it was decided that the baby would be formally named John after his father. The whole affair was a turbulent event as tears were shed as much for John and the children as they were for poor Beth and her baby.

"What more could befall poor John and his family?" was asked amongst the congregation, though no one except Sarah actually said the words directly to John. Her worry for her son was far more intense and only she could talk directly to him without any misgivings of his reaction. John stayed silent throughout the service, he just gazed as Beth and their baby were lowered into the grave above Amelia's own casket, buried less than two years earlier. After, John and the children returned home with Eddie and Mary, Sarah came also to lend her support to John. Not much was said there either, there was a distinctly subdued atmosphere within the cottage. Most sat warming themselves in front of the two lighted fires in the kitchen and parlour. Mary had prepared food and had fed the children and she had also made hot tea and toast for the adults who quietly ate and drank without knowing what to say to John at such an awful time. Just Sarah would talk, to try and raise spirits by raising a short conversation with whoever was closest. But any conversations raised would soon die down to yet another period of uncomfortable silence. That was until, to everyone's surprise, John broke the silence as he turned and looked to his eldest son.

"Freddie, I need to have a word."

Freddie immediately looked up in surprise, wondering what his father could possibly want from him at such a time.

"You'll be starting your apprenticeship as from tomorrow and not in six months like we spoke about earlier."

Everyone looked up, bemused why John had suddenly come to a decision like this on a completely unrelated subject, and on such a day.

"Is everything alright, John?" asked Eddie. "Why is he starting tomorrow?"

"I just think that an early start will be in his best interests, that's all."

"I thought you said another six months after his tenth birthday, so he will have some extra time to learn his reading and writing," said Mary.

"I know what I said, but have you seen how well he reads and writes? He doesn't need any more lessons; he needs to learn a trade. With all the tragedies that seem to land on this family, I want him to be able to support himself as soon as he can in his life."

Sarah watched and listened but said nothing. She knew what John was talking about. If anything should happen to him, there would be only a few able to care for his children in his absence. Freddie learning a trade and a living could only be a good thing in an emergency. However, Mary and Eddie's thoughts differed. They could see John's point but couldn't help thinking that he was acting more out of emotions than logic.

What harm could another six months make in a boy's life? These were to be the end of his childhood days and now they were to be cut short because of tragic circumstances. Freddie, however, was not in the least bit upset by the announcement. Like all children, he longed for the day when he would become a full-grown adult, and to him this was just the first step. He had always admired the way that his father had made his living and he longed to emulate him, now was finally his chance to learn. So, the following morning, John brought Freddie into the workshop to begin his apprenticeship as a wheelwright and farrier, though his first jobs were more menial tasks of passing tools and sweeping up the yard and workshop.

"I'm going to Norwich to pick up some supplies," said John, later that morning to Will and Eddie, who both looked at each other in confusion. John hitched up the horse to the cart and disappeared for the city, and did not return for another three hours. Neither Will nor Eddie had any idea why John had so hastily left and wondered just what supplies were needed. That was until on his return, they saw on the back of the cart a new wooden bed with a new wool filled mattress. They watched from the workshop door as John could be heard banging and sawing from his upstairs bedroom only to emerge from his back door with the remains of his old marital bed completely broken and sawn in pieces. John carried pieces of the old bed to the end of the garden and onto his meadow. He stacked up the pieces and then dragged the old blood stained mattress, which had already been removed from the house, and threw it onto the pile of wood that had once been his bed. He then returned back to the workshop and gathered a pile of wood shavings that young Freddie had swept into a pile. Carefully placing the shavings around the bottom of the stack, he returned to the forge fire and lit a lamp from the flames. Using the lamp, he then lit the shavings to the stack which slowly spread into a full bonfire. As the flames grew higher, crackled and smoked, John just stood beside, silently staring into it as if in a trance.

"What's he doing?" asked Will.

"Let him be," said Eddie. "He's burning the old bed, and the memories that went with it. Who can blame him? He's just witnessed enough horrors for any man. Two wives, four children all lost. Watching Beth bleed to death just hours after holding his dead son in his arms. Leave him be... let him burn the pain away and try to begin again."

The fire rose sending a plume of smoke high up to be driven by an easterly wind across Robert Welton's neighbouring field, then, in time, the flames eventually died down into glowing embers until just ashes were all that was left. John stood silently throughout, watching the fire burn until all was gone and there was nothing more.

***

A young apprentice in the Allen forge is now beginning his trade. He has watched his father at work in the past during his childhood years and has always lived around John's working environment. Now Freddie is working with John for the first time on a full time basis and is enjoying his new way of life. Many years earlier at the Fox smithy, it was noticed by Bill Fox and his son Edmond, that John, as a boy was hard working, and he was a natural at forge work. Freddie was a chip of the old block and like his father has fitted well into working life at the Allen smithy, he is a natural when learning his trade. With no mother to go to in times of distress, Freddie has drawn closer to his father, who also seems to have changed since the last tragedy. John has become a much quieter man than he had been, instead of always being first to greet a friend or acquaintance with hello or good day, he would now only reply a greeting and would seldom get drawn into long conversations, unless it was work or parish related. He seemed different visually too, he seldom smiled. Many said it was like all the happiness had been taken from him. All colour seemed to have drained from his face and his eyes seemed to have a yellowy tinge around the whites. He still has time for his children though, these were the loves in his life that luckily hadn't been taken from him yet.

Freddie begins to take an interest in his Father's role at the church and accompanies him whenever he can. He helps him with maintenance work both within the church building and out in the churchyard. Sometimes, John would let Freddie toll the bell on Sundays to summon the worshippers as he was now big enough and he would even let Freddie help dig a grave ready for a funeral service if it didn't interfere with his apprenticeship work. Overall, John is pleased in his son's interest and commitment and is happy to have him tag along. Freddie's interest in the church work has not gone unnoticed by Henry Banfather who was always impressed by Freddie from the time he was a scholar with him at the rectory along with his siblings.

More sad news came to the family just after the Easter celebrations that year when Anne Fox finally passed away having reached the long age of ninety years old. Everyone had been expecting her end to come for some time but, as all times of family loss, was still painful when the end finally came. She was buried with her husband Bill, in the churchyard within sight of the plots of where Jacob and the children, Amelia and Beth lay, just off the path leading to the church doors. Then, another major event came into being weeks later on Tuesday 20th June. Everyone was busy clearing up after a day's work in the forge and the workshop. Eddie was covering the forge fire, Freddie was sweeping the yard and Will and John were putting the tools away and sweeping the workshop when John was suddenly alerted to a sound in the distance.

"Can you hear that?" said John.

"Hear what?" replied Will.

"The church bell, someone's ringing the bell… kids I reckon."

Everyone looked at each other in confusion.

"I'd better go and see what's going on, maybe I'll catch the little buggers," said John.

He immediately set off for the church ready to confront the culprit who had the nerve to ring the church bell in his absence. As he walked, he was joined by two more local men, farm workers on their way home who had also heard the ringing. They were old enough to remember the old days of the wars against the French when the bells were rung to spread news of major events, but they also wondered who could be ringing the bell at that time of the day and on that day of the week. The bell was still ringing when they arrived. On entering the church, and to John's surprise, he found the mysterious bell ringer to be none other than the parson, Henry Banfather.

"Hello Henry," said John. "Is all well? I heard the bell ringing and thought it was young-uns messing around."

By now, a small crowd of up to ten parishioners had followed and gathered into the church on hearing what they thought was an alarm. Henry stopped ringing the bell and turned to address the small crowd. He pulled from his jacket pocket a note of paper which he opened up to read. It was clearly visible that it was something official as it had a red seal at the head and had been printed and not hand written.

"I've just received a message direct from the bishop of Norwich at the Cathedral," said Henry. "This same message is being sent to all the parishes in this county. The message reads, that early this morning the King passed away peacefully in his sleep."

The crowd gasped at the news, but Henry continued his reading.

"The ring of accession was placed upon the finger of the young Princess Victoria who is now our queen and sovereign. May King William now rest in peace as he is received into the hands of God, and may God save our new Queen, Victoria."

Everyone looked at each other not knowing quite what to do or to say until Henry then asked if the small gathering would like to say a small prayer for the departed king and for the new young queen. The congregation obliged and soon after, left the church having also received instructions from Henry Banfather to spread the news around the village. John took it upon himself to do as Henry had said and he and many of the others from the group covered a wide area all over Sprowston shouting "The king is dead! God save the new Queen Victoria!" Everyone was under no illusion of the great importance of the news of the changing of the monarchy, to the first queen in over a hundred years to reign over them. However, none of them knew that the event was to mark a new era in British history, the end of what was known as the Regency period to the new Victorian age.

"So what do you think this new Queen will be like?" said Eddie, the following morning while everyone was sitting out in the yard on their mid-morning break.

"Don't suppose anything's gonna be any different to us," said Will. "She's just a slip of a girl who has got great riches and power handed to her. All the changes are likely to be in London and the palaces. Nothing's gonna change around here I shouldn't think."

"I think there are great changes ahead," said John.

"How'd you mean?"

"There's more and more of those steam machines everywhere. Boats and ships, steam carriages and machines in factories. The new queen's just begun when times are moving faster. I think a lot of changes are coming"

"Hmm, maybe you're right," said Will, who was not altogether convinced at what John had said. From his point of view, he had only seen life from a slow moving rural setting of which he only ventured into the city to drink, witness hangings and occasionally use a street girl. He never thought to look hard at his surroundings and notice the growing population and the urban life that was encroaching, with its factories and industry, and his village expanding with it. Freddie sat quietly listening to the conversation and felt that his father was right, but then he was always going to be bias towards John's opinion. But initially, Will was right, there were no visible changes within the village and the novelty of having a new queen soon passed, and people continued with their own struggles of life in the same way they always had.

The long warm summer days continued with the hard work that accompanied it. The harvest came as late summer merged into September bringing the whole community together once more as crops and produce were brought in. Apples and nuts were falling in late September and early October, and so diets became less mundane than in harder times. Livestock would be slaughtered giving some much-needed protein to the locals who were eager to buy cuts from the slaughtered animals, if they could afford it that was. Soon after, the cold winds from the north and the east came, blown over from Scandinavia and northern Europe to signal late autumn and early winter. Another November 5th celebration was held on Robert Welton's field and once again, John was kept busy with its organisation. This year, there was quiet talk amongst the locals how there were visible changes in John's appearance since the loss of his two wives. There was paleness in the colour of his face, there were shadows beneath his eyes, and a sad look that had never left him since Beth's loss.

***

Sarah Walker is accompanied by her husband Thomas at church on Sunday service. Also with her are her youngest two children, David and Elizabeth Walker, who are now grown up but unmarried and still living with their parents. From the back of the church, she watches her eldest son, John and his eldest son Freddie, who are busy passing out prayer and hymn books. The sight of John causes her quiet concern, a concern that she has had since not long after Beth's sad demise. He is still not looking well at all, many have said that losing his two wives and four children has taken its toll on him, and that he seems to have almost given up. Sarah, however, knows her son better than that and knows that with three surviving children to care for giving up would never have been an option for him. No, this was something else. Call it a mother's intuition, but Sarah knew that something more underlying was at hand. She surmised that the only way to find out what was wrong with John was to go and talk to him alone. So, on the following Tuesday on a cold February morning, she came to the forge on the pretext to pay a visit to her three sons and her grandchildren, but in reality, to see John alone if possible.

"Hello, Mother," said her three sons, who were all labouring away in the workshop and in the forge. Eddie and John were showing Freddie how to shave wheel spokes while Will was outside seeing to a shire horse that needed re-shoeing, brought in by Ben Walker, a small-hold farmer who ran Mousehold Farm on the Salhouse Road.

"What brings you here?" asked Will.

"Just thought I'd pay you all a visit," Sarah replied. "Hello Freddie, where's your brother and sister?"

"Next door with Aunt Mary doing their reading and writing," Fred replied.

"I'd better leave them be then," said Sarah. "Can't interrupt an education, that's far too important."

"Come into the cottage and get beside the fire, Ma, I'll warm some milk," said John.

Together, mother and son headed straight into the cottage where the fire was still just alight from being lit in the morning before work. John was completely unaware that this was exactly what Sarah had wanted all along, to be alone with him. He immediately stoked up the fire, added another log and filled a cooking pot with milk and hung it over the fire.

"It's not like you to visit on a cold day like this. We usually see you on Sunday's after church."

"That's because I wanted to see you alone John. I've been watching you closely since Beth died last year and I'm worried sick about you."

John looked in surprise at his mother.

"Yes, I'm worried about you. You don't look well and I've come to see if there's anything wrong or if there's anything I should know. You know what I mean, your state of health."

"I'm alright Ma, there's nothing for you to worry about. It's nothing that I can't get through."

"There is something wrong, isn't there? Is it about you losing Beth and Amelia or is it an illness?"

"It's probably a bit of all those things," said John. "Yes, I have been feeling a bit under the weather lately but it's nothing serious, I'm just a bit sick and run down thas all. It hit me hard losing Beth and it's made me a little ill, but I'm sure it will pass. I've got the little-uns to look after so I can't afford to be ill."

"Do you think that maybe you need to see a doctor?"

"No, I don't think it's as serious as that. A lot has happened to me in my life lately and it's taken its toll on me I expect, but I'm sure it will pass."

"If you feel any worse, promise me you'll see a doctor, we're all worried about you."

"I will, Ma, I promise I will," said John.

Sarah stayed a little while longer to have her warmed milk and she even managed to see her grandchildren for a moment, but she left with no more peace of mind than when she had arrived. She could see that John wasn't well and she wasn't convinced that he was going to do anything about it. She hoped that he was right and that his ill health was just stress related as he had said. Hopefully it would pass and he would be back to his old self, if not for the children's sake.

Just weeks after Sarah's visit, the topic of conversation around the village was the latest news that two paddle steamers had become the first ships to cross the Atlantic without the aid of sails. On 22nd April 1838, the SS. Sirius arrived at New York having set sail from Britain on the earlier date of 4th April. The following day on 23rd April, the Great Western, the biggest steel ship in the world arrived after a quicker journey having set sail four days after the Sirius on 8th April. Built by Brunel, the ship begins a new transatlantic service and heralds a new age of steam travel. The news begins to convince Will that maybe John's earlier prediction of changes ahead were not so far-fetched after all.

John's health saw no improvement in the months that followed, if anything, he seemed even more fatigued and still he had a gaunt look upon his face. Ed and Will saw the change day by day at the work place. His appetite seemed to lesson and consequently, he lost weight. Still there was a yellowy tinge in his skin and around the whites of his eyes that never seemed to go away. One morning, Eddie finally spoke to John, as both he and Will had quietly talked on the subject to their mother, and all agreed on their concern for his health and the need for him to see a doctor. He waited until Freddie was back in the cottage and out of earshot.

"John, me and Will are worried about yer and think you need to see a doctor. You're not getting any better. We can all see it and you know it too."

"You've been talking to Mother, haven't you?" John replied.

"Yes we have, and she's worried about you, we all are. Your skins starting to go jaundice like a new-born baby. Something's wrong I know it is. Please, for mother's sake and the little-uns, go and see a doctor."

John hesitated before he answered, he knew Ed was right but he had been putting off going to the doctor for the fear of anymore bad news that may come into his life. However, he could now see that the family's concern meant that he could no longer postpone the inevitable.

"For Mother's sake, I'll call at Dr Denmark's place tomorrow if he'll see me," he replied.

So the following day, John made the trip to the far end of Sprowston to a detached cottage on the main road where resided Dr George Denmark and his family. His knock on the front door was promptly answered by the doctor's wife, Caroline Denmark.

"Hello John," she answered with a smile. Caroline Denmark was a very pleasant woman by nature and knew John socially through her husband at parish events.

"Would it be possible to see your husband at any time, Mrs Denmark?" John asked.

"I think it would," she replied. "He's got a couple of hours free at the moment before he goes to the hospital. Would it be of a medical, parish or social nature that he is needed?"

"It would be of a medical nature and it would be me that he would need to examine."

"Come in, I think that he can see you right away."

Caroline showed John into the hall entrance and left to fetch her husband. Within just a moment, George Denmark came into the hall to greet John.

"Hello John, I hear you need to see me on a medical issue. Come this way I'll see you now."

The doctor led John into a room at the rear of the cottage that had been converted into an office and surgery. There was, however, no couch, just a wooden chair on the other side of his wooden desk. George Denmark was a man in his late thirties, close to the age of John himself. He was of average height with early greying dark hair. He was neat in appearance, his clothes showed little wear and were well laundered. He was well spoken as he was a man from a wealthy middle class family who had paid for him to be educated in a top school of the day. He looked at John and immediately he could see things weren't right with him upon appearance of his face.

"Hmm, I can see the discolouration of your skin and in your eyes that things aren't at all well. How are you feeling yourself physically?"

"I've been losing my appetite for a while now doctor, when I eat I soon feel full and often feel sick."

"Tired? Are you tired at all?"

"All the time," said John. "It's as if all my strength seems to have gone."

"Open your shirt, I need to have a listen inside," said the doctor.

John did as he asked and the doctor produced his wooden cylindrical stethoscope and put it to John's chest and then his stomach. Putting his ear to it, he listened but said nothing. When he was finished listening, he then prodded John's stomach and around his back with his fingers.

"A slight swelling of your belly?" he asked.

John nodded.

"Any pain?" he asked.

"An aching feeling deep inside around my back."

"You can put your shirt back on now John," he said.

John did as instructed.

"Tell me, do you drink heavily?"

"No not heavily," John replied. "I have a few ales like all men but I seldom go to the Blue Boar. I just have a tankard of ale with my evening meal and sometimes at lunchtime."

The doctor sat down at his desk face to face with John and he paused for a moment before finally delivering his diagnosis.

"I think that you have all the symptoms of a diseased liver. You say that you don't drink all that much... that's strange because liver disease is often seen with much heavier drinkers, alcoholics, in fact. I can't understand why you should have a diseased liver, you don't fit the category, but I'm sure that's what you have none the less."

"Can you cure it? Is there anything that can be done?" asked John, who was by now obviously concerned.

A gloomy look came over the face of the doctor who proceeded to shake his head.

"I'm afraid there's nothing that I can do to cure you but I can give you some laudanum if things get too uncomfortable."

"Am I going to die?" asked John.

The doctor sighed, and then nodded. "Yes, in time I think you will," he replied. "I'm sorry I can't tell you any different."

"How long do I have?"

"It's hard to say. Weeks, months, maybe even a year or so, everyone is different. They last in their own time and they go when they're ready. I'm sorry John, that I can't be more specific than that. After all that has happened to you and your family, I can't believe that you're now going to have to go through yet another ordeal, all I can say is that you've had to endure more than most men."

John sat for a moment staring at the doctor with an almost blank expression on his face.

"Sometimes I wonder if God has abandoned me for whatever reason he has... He must have a very good reason for this."

The doctor didn't know how to reply to John's comment, he just looked down to the ground and shook his head.

"I'd best be going," said John, and he rose up from his chair to leave. The doctor stood up too.

"All I can say to you John, is make preparations. Prepare for this for your children's sake, to make sure they're looked after when you're gone."

John nodded and shook the doctor's hand. The doctor saw no need to ask for payment for his consultation, this was a diagnosis he wished he didn't have to make. John left from the front door but couldn't remember leaving the doctor's house, he just found himself walking home and wondering how he was going to break the news to his family, and what he must do to ensure that his children would be cared for. He arrived back at the smithy within fifteen minutes, though he could hardly remember any of the journey. He was spotted walking up the drive by Eddie who thought it best to go out and talk to John well out of earshot of young Freddie who was busy shaving spokes in the workshop. The pair walked to the end of the drive out of earshot of everybody.

"What did the doctor say? Is it anything serious?" Eddie asked.

John nodded. "It is serious and there's nothing that he can do. I'll have to talk to you, Mary and Will later, and well away from the children. I don't want to worry 'em."

"Oh God, John, what is it?"

"He says my liver is diseased and there's nothing that he can do. He says he doesn't know how much time I have but to make preparations for when the time comes."

Ed gasped at the news and his heart sank. He put his arm around his brother and he struggled to speak as he fought to hold back tears that were beginning to well up.

"If there's anything I can do, just say," he said.

"We'll have to get together and talk. Plans will have to be made for the children," said John.

Ed nodded. "I'll talk to Will and Mary when I get them alone, maybe Sunday afternoon would be a good time. The children could go to mum's cottage for an hour or two. Tell Freddie that he's needed to look after the younger ones."

John agreed. "We'd better get back to work. Try and be as if nothing is wrong, I don't want anybody worrying, especially the children."

Eddie agreed, and did as John had asked and returned to his day's work, although he was hardly focused on his job at hand. Later that day, Ed did indeed manage to get both Mary and Will alone long enough to tell them the terrible news that had befallen them all. Both were shocked and devastated as one would expect, but they saw the need to keep their composure in front of the children.

Sunday morning came, and once again John rose early to give the children their breakfast before making his usual journey to the church to prepare for Sunday service. The children would normally get dressed directly after breakfast and since Beth's demise they would accompany him to the church early before the parishioners arrived. However, on this morning, John made an announcement as he served up their warmed milk and toast.

"You three will be coming to church later with Aunt Mary and Uncle Eddie."

Freddie looked up in surprise. "That means I can't ring the bell this morning."

"That's right," said John. "I need to speak to the parson on important business and I can't be looking after little-uns while I do so. So when you're dressed, you'll be going next door and I'll see you at the church later."

There were no arguments from the children, they accepted the situation and obeyed their father. Soon after, John left for the church, leaving the children with Ed and Mary. On arrival, after the short walk to the church, he made a point of knocking on the door of the nearby rectory to ask Henry Banfather if he wouldn't mind coming to the church slightly earlier as he wished to speak to him alone on a private matter. Sensing that all was not well, Henry promptly followed to see John as he had requested.

"What can I do for you John?" he asked on arrival.

"Thank you for seeing me Henry, I'll get straight to the point. I'm afraid that all is not well with us at the moment. I have just had some tragic news come to me."

"It's your health, isn't it?" said the parson.

John nodded.

"I've been to see the doctor and it isn't good news. He says that I have a diseased liver and that there's nothing he can do for me, it's just a matter of time. I needed to tell you so as you know that you'll have to find someone else to look after the church for you when I'm too ill to do it."

Henry Banfather's eyes closed as he gasped upon the news that he had just heard from his friend.

"Oh John, I am so sorry. I could see that you were ill but I had no idea that you were as ill as that. I just don't know what to say to you."

"My worry is the children, what's going to happen to them?"

"Do they know yet?" asked Henry.

"No, and they're not to know anything's wrong until nearer the time. This afternoon, they're going to visit my mother. I've told Freddie to take care of the younger two while they're there. I'll be talking to Eddie and Mary and Will to discuss what happens next and to make plans. Until I know the outcome of that meeting and what to do, I still have the problem of paying back the loan from the church to deal with, so I'll have to speak to you later once I know exactly what it is I have to do to solve the problem."

"John, don't worry about the loan, just do exactly as you're doing and think of the children first. I'm sure that we can come up with a solution to the loan that will be to everyone's benefit. If there is anything that I can do to help you and your family in any way I will do it, rest assured."

"Thank you, Henry, you've been a good friend and a great help to me and my family over the years. No one could be more grateful than I am to you."

John shook the hand of his dear friend and colleague Henry Banfather who had always looked out for him and treated him as a very special parishioner indeed.

"I'd better ring the bell now," said John. "Soon be time for Sunday service."

Henry nodded.

John rang the bell to summon those who would worship at his church that day. He did his duties in his usual way passing out the books on the arrival of the local worshippers. Prayers were said, hymns were sung and sermons were read. A baby girl named Hannah Ingram was publicly baptised before the locals left for home and their day of rest.

After lunch, John sent the children off to visit their grandmother Sarah for the afternoon. Freddie was instructed to care for his younger siblings, and this he did as obedient as ever. As arranged, Eddie and Mary joined Will at John's cottage to make plans for the events to come. John made a pot of tea for everyone who was seated at the table and then the meeting began.

"Well, you all know why you're here," said John. "I need to lay out a plan for what's going to happen when I'm gone."

Everyone stayed silent, not knowing exactly what to say to John on such a sensitive subject. It was better to let John do the talking and raise any issues that needed to be resolved in due course.

"Obviously, the children are my first concern. Eddie and Mary, I have to ask you now if you will take over the role as parents for me. They can't end up in an orphanage or the workhouse and Mother's too old to have 'em."

"Yes, we'll take care of that," Eddie replied. "Me and Mary have already talked this over and of course, there was never really any doubt that they would be with us."

"Thank you both for that. That was the most important thing and they'll be happy with you two. We'll talk about the finer details of their care later. All I needed to know is that they have a secure home to live in and be raised by a stable family."

John turned to Will.

"I need you, Will and Ed, to make sure the boys learn their trade. Teach 'em wheel making and cart repairing and horse shoeing so's they can make a decent living in life."

Will nodded. There was never any question on that issue. Then Will spoke up.

"John, if you don't mind me asking, what are you going to do with your property? You've got a loan with the church which will have to be paid back. How will you get it paid?"

"That's where I need you all to help, you'll have to run the business and pay the loan off for me. Ed, you and Mary could move into this cottage with the children so they can stay in their own home, and you Will can move out of Edmond and Molly's place and come and live next door with no rent to pay. You'll have the whole cottage to yourself, but you'll have to keep paying the loan for me rather than paying a rent. That is until it's all paid up."

"How long is the loan for?" Will asked.

"There should be about another six or seven years left to pay. The loan was my complete earnings from my church and parish duties which are about fifteen pounds per annum. You should be able to cover it with the money you save on your rents and the rest could come from the business."

"Who will hold ownership of the properties?" asked Mary.

"Well, that's the thing," said John. "At the moment, the church is holding the deeds to both cottages and the meadow until the debt is paid. Ed, I'll have to will the properties to you as you and Mary are going to be the children's guardians. I have to ask for you to give me your solemn promise that you will sign the property to my eldest surviving son when you feel the time is right or will the property to him upon your deaths. Either way, this property should go to my offspring. Do you agree?"

Everyone nodded.

"Of course your property will go to them, you have my solemn word upon it. This property belongs to them and me and Mary will just care for it for them until the time is right," said Ed. "Will, you've just witnessed my solemn word haven't you?"

Will nodded.

"Thank you," said John. "All of you. You've taken a great load off my mind. I don't know how I can repay your kindness but I knew that I could count on all of you. I'll tell the parson tomorrow what's been arranged."

"It's what families are for," said Will. "Just one thing though, when are you gonna tell Mother what's happening?"

Chapter Forty-Four

The unmistakable sight and sounds of swallows, swifts and martins flying high in the sunny skies hailed the arrival of the summertime. Some knew that they had migrated from various parts of Africa but none knew of the journey they had undertaken to be there. Their long journey over the plains and jungles, across the Sahara Desert to North Africa, crossing the Mediterranean at Gibraltar, across mainland Europe and the North Sea and English Channel to their breeding grounds in the British Isles. All the people of Norfolk knew was that their arrival brought with them the warmth of the sunshine and longer days and pleasant summer evenings. Even despite John's situation, he was pleased to see the coming of summer, which always gave him a feeling of more pleasant times, when children played out in the sun, crops grew quickly ready for the harvest, and people had more colour in their faces. Secretly, he had hoped that if he was going to die, it would be at his favourite time of the year, of when he would be happiest in mind. However, despite the pleasantness of the summer, he continued to decline in health. What Dr George Denmark had diagnosed was only half right. John did indeed have a diseased liver but unknown to the doctor, he did in fact have a cancerous tumour attacking his liver which was now beginning to spread to other vital organs. His time was running out and he knew it, so the decision was finally made to tell his mother, Sarah. Though he surmised that she would have already guessed that something was seriously wrong. He knew she would be alone in her cottage while Thomas worked so chose the moment to break the news.

She greeted him with the usual joy and open arms she always did, until the realisation that bad news was to come when John told her to sit down as he had something to tell her. John broke the news to her in as gentle way as he could, but her reaction to the news was as expected from a mother who was to lose her son, she sobbed uncontrollably upon his shoulder. John cried also, but in time composure regained itself and they were able to talk rationally of what lay ahead and how to deal with it.

"So, who knows?" Sarah asked.

"Ed, Mary and Will," John replied. "I also told the parson because he'll need a new sexton for the church and a parish clerk for the village."

"What about the children?"

John shook his head. "I haven't told them, how can I?"

"Do you think that Freddie should be made aware? He is the oldest and is very close to you at the moment. If he was prepared, then maybe he could help support his brother and sister, because they'll need that."

"Perhaps you're right," said John.

"Speak to him, either alone or you can bring him here, and I'll be here with you, but speak to him soon or it may be too late."

John agreed. "I'll bring him here tomorrow at ten. There'll be no one here, will there?

"Shouldn't be, everyone's busy in the fields."

"Then I'll see you then, with Freddie."

Sarah embraced John again as he rose up to leave for his return back to the smithy. She wept upon his shoulder once again but kept more composed than she had on the first initial shock, but she cried again after he had left.

The following morning, John called to Freddie from the cottage, he was busy sweeping the yard outside the workshop.

"Freddie, you'll be coming with me, we're going to your grandmother's."

This surprised Freddie. It wasn't often that his father would interrupt work to go on a social call. He had a feeling that all was not as straight forward as his father was telling him, but decided not to question John and did as instructed. The journey was short and quick and very little was spoken on the way, which made Freddie even more curious. He embraced his grandmother on his arrival before being told to sit down as his father had something important to tell him. With that, he knew instinctively that something was wrong.

"What is it?" he asked, fearful of the reply.

"Freddie, this is a hard thing that I now have to tell you," said John. "As hard a thing as I have ever had to tell you in the past. Even as hard as when I had to tell you about your mother, God rest her."

"It's you, isn't it? You're not well, are you?"

"The doctor says that I'm dying. He doesn't know how long I have. I need you to be strong about this for the sake of your brother and sister."

Freddie's eyes reddened but he tried to stay strong as his father had asked. He began to shake despite trying as hard as he could to keep his composure, but eventually, a tear ran down the side of his face. Seeing her grandson trying to fight his obvious distress, Sarah rushed over and embraced Freddie to try and ease his pain. He began to cry on her shoulder but only for a short moment, as still he tried and tried to keep composed. This sight caused equal upset to John, and of course Sarah, who also fought back her tears.

"What's wrong with you?" Freddie asked.

"He says that I have a diseased liver and there's nothing that he can do for me."

Freddie rose from his chair and made straight for his father. He wrapped his arms around John and began to cry.

"Oh, Father!" he sobbed.

Tears ran down John's face as the full impact of the distress he had just caused his son began to sink in. Sarah just buried her face in her hands and cried; her heart was being broken at the sight she was now witnessing.

"There, there," said John. "You'll be alright in a moment."

There was a short moment when time was needed for his son to cry out his tears and compose himself to allow John to continue to talk once more.

"Are you all cried out now son?"

Freddie nodded, and wiped his nose on his sleeve.

"Right," said John. "Now we can talk... I will need you to have to grow up very quickly for me, son. Do you understand what I'm saying?"

Freddie nodded.

"You will have to help your brother and sister to get through this, and you'll have to be there to protect 'em. I'll need you to look out for 'em at all times when you're with 'em, and also I want you to learn your trade as a wheelwright and smith so you'll be able to support yourself and if necessary, your brother and sister if you have to. Is that understood?"

Freddie nodded again.

"From this day on, you have got to try and look at yourself as being grown up but still with lots to learn. Uncle Eddie and Aunt Mary will care for all of you, that's who you'll be living with when I'm gone. They'll be moving into our house to care for you till you're all fully grown. I want you to be good to them and be with them as you were to me and your mother. Eddie and Will are to teach you and Henry your trades, and I want you to listen hard to what they have to tell you, is that understood?"

Freddie nodded again.

"Will you promise me that you will do all that I just asked of you?"

Freddie nodded. "I promise."

"Thank you," said John. "That's good enough for me. Now, I know that this is all terrible news and a great shock for you but I must tell you now I don't want Millie and little Henry knowing about this until it's nearer the time, is that understood?"

Freddie nodded again.

"He's a good boy," said Sarah. "I know that he'll make you proud."

"I think you're right Mother, he already makes me proud," said John. "Do you think you're ready to go back to the smithy now?"

Freddie nodded again.

"Alright then, we've got this sorted out and we both understand what we've to do. I know that you won't let me down son, I've no doubt about that. Now, we had better return back to work."

Both father and son kissed Sarah goodbye and made off to return back to work, again very little was said on their journey but much was on Freddie's mind. On arrival at the smithy, Freddie said nothing, he just returned to a task he had been given the previous day, shaving a large batch of wheel spokes. As he shaved the spokes, Eddie and Will both looked to John to beckon an answer to their silent question. John just nodded his silent reply.

***

The following Sunday, Freddie took it upon himself to accompany his father to church for Sunday service whilst his brother and sister remained home to join them at church later with Eddie and Mary. Henry Banfather was having his breakfast, and spied John and Freddie from his window at the rectory as they passed on their way to the church building just a short distance away. His concern for John prompted him to quickly finish up his breakfast and go see him to privately inquire as to his health and situation.

"Good morning John," he said on arrival. "How are you feeling?"

"As well as I can be."

"You know, if this is getting all too much for you, you will tell me, won't you?"

John nodded. "I will Henry, when the time is right. For now, I've got Freddie to help me, he's been a good young man."

The parson nodded and watched as Freddie went about helping his father to prepare for the service. He helped give the church a quick sweep and tidy and fetched the hymn and prayer books ready to be passed out to the worshippers of the day.

"Do you want me to ring the bell Father?" Freddie asked.

"No, I'll do it in a moment," John replied.

"I'll go just outside if it's alright?" said Freddie.

His father nodded, knowing why his son went out. Freddie would often go out to pay a visit to Amelia's resting place, now shared with Beth. He would pick daisies and buttercups and lay them upon it. He still missed his mother terribly.

"That boy of yours must be making you very proud," said Henry.

John nodded. "I told him the other day what was happening. He was upset at the time but now he's trying to be as grown up as he can be, to help me and be strong for his brother and sister. You can't ask any more than that from a son, can you?"

Henry agreed, then, momentarily, a thought came into his head. An idea hatched that would have to wait for the moment until the pressing business of Sunday service was done and more thought was put into that very idea.

The service was held in the usual way, of sermons, prayers and hymns, and the public baptism of a baby girl called Henrietta Richards. Finally, Henry Banfather bid his parishioners farewell in his usual way from the church doors then returned inside the building to see Freddie gathering up the books and returning them to their rightful places as his father sat resting due to his illness. Henry watched quietly but said nothing, he just thought more upon the idea that had come into his head just an hour or so earlier. Soon after, Freddie and John joined their family who were waiting outside in the churchyard, to return home for a restful afternoon. The parson returned with his family back to the rectory where lunch was being prepared by the cook. He called his wife Mary Anne into the drawing room for a private conversation before lunch was to be served.

"Yes, what is it?" Mary Anne asked.

"I need your advice and your opinion on an idea that I have."

Like many men, Henry liked to be the head of his family but always knew who to go when he was unsure of what to do. His wife was always there for him to lend her support.

"Go on," said his wife.

"Tell me if you think this is a silly idea and that I must be a mad man, or tell me if you think this could be the answer to a large problem involving John," said Henry.

Mary Anne looked in confusion, but listened to what her husband had to say.

It was mid-morning the following day when John noticed, to his surprise, Henry Banfather walking up the driveway towards his yard and workshops. John was not in the workshop at the time, he was not feeling well enough to work. Instead, he had placed a chair outside the back door of his cottage and was trying to reap the benefits of some fresh air, as advised by his brother Ed.

"Good morning Henry," said John. "I wasn't expecting to see you here this morning, is all well?"

Henry smiled. "Good morning John. I was wondering if I may have a quiet word with you, if you're well enough that is. I can see you don't look well."

"I'm not too well this morning, but I am strong enough to listen to what a man has got to say," John replied. "Grab yourself a chair from inside, we can talk out here."

Henry duly responded and took a wooden chair from around the dining room table and placed it outside facing John.

"Yesterday, I was watching young Freddie going about preparing for Sunday service and trying to help you while you're in ill health. He's a strong willed boy who seems to need no real moral guidance. He instinctively knows right from wrong, good from bad, and he always seems to go in the direction of right and good like a true Christian should."

John nodded but didn't really understand where all this was leading to.

Henry continued. "For a few years now, I have watched him come and help you with your church and parish duties, and I have noticed how he has always shown an uncommon interest in all of it. I know how well he can read and write from the times he and his brother and sister were educated by me at the rectory, just after Amelia's sad loss. This John, has convinced me more, that maybe he's the right person for the job."

John was confused. "I'm sorry Henry, but what job?"

"Your job," said Henry.

John looked in confusion.

"Yes, your job John, parish clerk and sexton of the church. He would be the perfect replacement for you."

John sat silent for a moment. He had to comprehend Henry Banfather's shocking idea...

"Henry... he's only eleven years old, how on earth can you expect him to become clerk and sexton of this parish?"

"Well," said Henry. "I was thinking that after you have gone, he could be taken on, more in the line of apprentice clerk with a view to become full clerk and sexton in the passing of time."

"He can't be expected to organise village events or maintain the church, he's too young."

"I've seen him helping you to dig graves. He already knows everything there is to know at the church services, and as for village events, I could organise them with his help. Soon he'll be old enough to do it all on his own. You were just a boy when you got involved in parish work, I do believe?"

A smile began to appear upon John's face as he thought back to his earlier life. "I think I was just fourteen or fifteen," he said.

"Well, there you are then," said Henry. "The thing is John, all of the educated men in this parish are all busy professional men, or lazy men of inherited wealth. The doctors and solicitors and landowners are all far too busy and they have no desire for this job. I know that Freddie has the desire and I would wager that if you brought him here right now and asked him he would agree instantly. He holds you in great esteem and is always trying to emulate you. Also, there is the church loan to consider. If he continued your duties under the same arrangement, then the loan would still be paid off at the same schedule as before. Your property would remain untouched for whoever would inherit it."

The statement of the church loan suddenly made John sit and think hard to what Henry had said. Maybe the parson was right and this would solve all the problems after his death.

"I was going to leave the property to my eldest surviving son as tradition requires, so it would be fitting that he would carry on the loan. I have told Eddie and Mary and my brother Will to repay the loan instead of paying rent to me, I could always change that arrangement... Just a minute, what am I doing? I should call Freddie over and see if he would agree to all this first."

Henry agreed, and Freddie was immediately called over from the workshop by his father.

"Fred, Parson Banfather here has got a big thing to ask of you, if you would agree to it, but don't feel under pressure to. He was wondering if you would like to take over my duties at the church and at the parish after I am gone."

There was a look of complete astonishment upon Freddie's face.

"Now don't worry about this, because I can tell you that you wouldn't just be made to do this job. There would be a time of training for this great responsibility, and if you should find this all too much, then the parson here would be only too happy to help. He would deal with the problems that only an adult would be able to deal with."

"I don't know," said Freddie. "I wasn't expecting this."

"Freddie, I have been watching you for some time now helping your father whenever you can," said Henry Banfather. "This job is no different to what you have already been doing. You are the only one in this village who would know exactly what duties there are to do to look after the church. As for parish duties, I will be organising the parish events with help from you if you so desire, so you could learn about the process and what's required of it. I am personally in no doubt that you are able to do this as your father has been all these years."

"Son, there's another thing that you need to know," said John. "The house we live in and the cottage next door, the smithy and the meadow will all be yours one day when you are of a responsible adult age. Till then, it will be in the charge of Eddie and Mary to hand over to you at the correct time."

Freddie stayed motionless, still trying to comprehend all that was being told to him. John continued talking.

"My duties at the church and the parish were all to pay a loan of money that the church had kindly lent me to buy those properties. I would need you to carry on my duties and pay that very loan for the home that we live in, as I would do if I were still to be here. Would you agree to carry on those responsibilities where I have left off?"

Freddie stayed silent for a moment as he pondered over his decision, but eventually his answer did come.

"I already know that I can look after the church like you do," he said. "I have always helped you at the church for as long as I can remember. If I have to do this so we can all stay living here in this house and things stay the same, then I will agree to do the job, that is if Parson Banfather will teach me to do these duties as he said he would."

"I will, my boy, I will," said Henry.

"I agree then," said Freddie.

John was filled with pride. "You'll begin your training right away and you'll be made parish clerk and sexton after I am gone."

Freddie nodded in agreement, and with the meeting now adjourned, Henry shook both John and Freddie's hands, and returned back to the rectory with a proud feeling inside that he had achieved an absolute good. Freddie returned back to his work in the workshop also with a sense of pride that he had been wanted for a great responsibility, and a knowing from within that he was doing as his father had earlier instructed. He was growing up earlier and before his time. For the first time in a long while, John was seen to be in very good spirits despite his bad health.

**

The mornings were becoming colder and fresher, indicating that the autumn was not far in the distance. It had been a warm September up to now after what had seemed a long summer. Crops had been brought in as most of the village, young and old, once again, came together to help with the harvest. Mary had taken the children with her to help on the fields, including Freddie, as at this time labour could always be spared to help at the farms, as the harvest was always a priority.

Eddie and Will continued to work the smithy while their elder brother lay dying in his own cottage. He was now virtually bed ridden, only occasionally finding strength to come downstairs to sit outside in a chair and enjoy the warmth and beauty of the late summer sunshine. His illness was by now even more visible, his skin was clearly yellow and his stomach had swelled. His youngest children, Millie and Henry, had by now realised that something clearly was wrong.

"Will father be alright?" they would ask, and Eddie and Mary would try to reassure them and tell them that maybe, if they pray for their father, it may make him feel better. Soon, however, it became more difficult, and the day came when Millie finally asked the question, "Is father going to die?" She had asked the question to Mary one evening while Eddie was outside seeing to the horse. Young Henry was also present and was also of the same mind as his sister, though Freddie looked on wondering what to do or say next. Mary said nothing, but it was Freddie who once again said to pray for their father's recovery. Meanwhile, Mary decided to go upstairs to see John as he lay ill in his bed, to tell him of what the small children had said. He was awake and had heard the question his daughter had asked in the room below.

"I heard what she asked" he said. "Bring them both up, it's time they were told."

Millie and Henry were brought up to see their father, and Freddie came up to support his younger siblings under the request of Mary. John sat up to face his children who were all standing side by side.

"Now then, I heard that you asked if I was going to die," he said. "Well, what you all need to know is that everyone is going to die one day, it's just a matter of when. It will soon be time for me to go just like one day it will be your turn."

A tear began to run down Millie's cheek, but Henry, who was now seven and fully understood, stayed motionless.

"Please Millie, don't cry. I want you realise that you won't be alone, I will be watching you with your mother and with Beth. Uncle Eddie and Aunt Mary will care for you after I'm gone and I want you to promise that you'll all be good for them. Do you promise?"

The children nodded.

"I want you younger two to listen to your brother Fred. He has promised me that he'll watch over you and protect you both when he can. Most of all, I want you to be strong and keep yourselves well and alive. That's all I want, you to live full and happy lives. Will you do that for me?"

Millie didn't answer she just lunged forward and wrapped her arms around John and sobbed on his shoulder. Henry didn't cry but he did take hold of his father's hand. Freddie kept composed and tried to stay strong as his father had instructed, though if you had looked hard enough, you could have seen that his eyes had glistened slightly while still trying to keep his emotions to himself. Millie's tears proved too much for John and tears soon ran down his own face as he embraced his children. Henry still looked on; this was the first time in his memory that he saw tears upon his father's face. The image would be etched upon his memory for the rest of his life.

**

The deterioration of John continued in the week, he came to depend more upon the laudanum that the doctor had given him and consequently was in a deep slumber, free from pain and discomfort for much of the time. But the final day did come in the early hours of Thursday 20th September. No one was with him in his room when the end came. His lifeless body was discovered in the morning by Mary who had come in just after waking the children for breakfast.

John was gone, maybe to join Amelia and Beth as he had said, or maybe not. We will never know till our own time comes, but behind were left three orphans, the last survivors of a family almost cursed with the tragic consequences of living in the times they did. Little did they know that theirs was just one of many other tragic stories of families who were to move into the cities and live in the crowded urban squalor of industrial Britain, to live life as a battle for mere existence. This, however, was still a tragic tale nonetheless for a rural family such as this. On the last warm sunny day of September, John's surrounding family all gathered to see him laid to rest. Sarah quietly wondered why her son could be so cruelly punished by a so-called loving God, though she said nothing. He was laid next to his two wives, Amelia and Beth, and close to his father and his lost children. Henry Banfather conducted the service of his dear friend and colleague. Secretly, he too questioned the motives of the God he had worshipped all his life.

The following Sunday after John's funeral, Freddie came to the vicarage to await his instructions from Henry Banfather before the usual Sunday service.

"Good morning Freddie. Are you ready to begin your training?"

Freddie nodded.

"Good, now you know what to do on Sunday service don't you?"

Freddie nodded again.

"Well, I'll show you what's to be done to book weddings, funerals and communions, after this service. Don't worry, we'll go through this one step at a time, before long you'll be just as good and able as your father."

Freddie continued his training on the parish duties he was to inherit from his father. On his twelfth birthday in late January, he was officially appointed to the post of Parish clerk and Sexton of the church of Sprowston, with the help and support from Henry Banfather who had appointed him. He astonished everyone and managed the position like an adult.

Here now the story ends of this family tree, discovered by Martin Allen generations later in the early twenty first century. John and Amelia's three surviving children, did all survive into adult life as John had so wished. Frederick John Allen grew up to inherit his father's properties and business. He continued his duties within the parish right up until his death at the age of eighty. He had become the longest serving parish clerk and sexton of his age. In 1849, he married Mary Anne Riches and she bore him twins, a boy and a girl who they named John and Amelia.

Millie married Thomas Hurry in the same year as Fred's marriage in 1849. Thomas was from London and was working in Sprowston at Manor Farm. Together, they moved back to London where little was known of their outcome until Martin discovered their story on completion of his family tree, generations later. But it was Henry who Martin had descended from. His story was a more colourful one which bore a close resemblance to that of his ancestors Edward Allen and Elizabeth Lutkin. As a young man, Henry had become friends with a local girl, Emily Walker. She was the daughter of a local farmer who had a smallholding on the outer fringes of the village. A scandal was caused when Emily fell pregnant after a time of passion between the young couple, and a marriage was held outside the village in Norwich away from gossiping locals. Together they raised seven children and ran a smithy business and a pub near the centre of Norwich.

The orphans of the tree were to endure hardships and suffering as well as the joys that life can give. The eventual outcome being that Martin Allen was to discover their stories many generations later, but theirs, however, is another story.